The Amazon Code

Turtleshell Press (www.turtleshellpress.com)

Copyright © 2016 by Turtleshell Press and Nick Thacker

Printed in the United States of America

First Printing, 2016

ISBN 978-1533394637

Nick Thacker

Colorado Springs, CO

www.NickThacker.com

THE
AMAZON CODE

A BRIEF NOTE...

This book marks not only the fifth year of writing for me but also marks an accomplishment that's much closer to my heart: since I picked up a copy of James Rollins' *Amazonia*, I've longed to write a book set in the Amazon. But not just any book would do. It had to be worthy of the "thriller" name, and by extension James Rollins' name: action, adventure, sweeping plots invoking a broad spectrum of human emotion... and lots of guns. I wanted a book that the armchair traveler and the closet historian could equally be comfortable with.

I used to call the type of books I write (and what Rollins writes) "airport books," because they're the type of fast-paced fiction that one might read on an extended plane ride. The typical definition of "airport book" adds that these books are often discarded afterward, forgotten and doomed to collect dust in a suitcase or enjoy a long life on a used-bookstore shelf.

But this genre as a whole, and most certainly James Rollins' work, has always been more than that to me. He somehow weaves threads of science, conspiracy, myth and folklore, and military subjects together into a tapestry of awesomeness in every one of his books that makes me stop and think, and then think some more long after I put the book down. He creates characters that live in my mind, make me hungry for more, and, above all, make me want to emulate in my own books.

I don't know if I'll ever get there, and I certainly don't want to put forward the idea that *this* book - *The Amazon Code* - is worthy of standing next to Rollins' *Amazonia*. But it's important to note as an author where our inspirations come from, and I don't think it's a secret anymore that he is at the top of the list.

I remember meeting James in Denver at the *Tattered Cover* bookstore, and asking him to sign a copy of his newest release. I had a copy of my own newest release with me, and I offered it to him. He only accepted mine if I would sign it at the same time he signed his book. For a young new author, that moment was more important to me than any bestseller status could have been, and to this day it's what I think of when I pick up the latest James Rollins from the bookstore shelf.

So, Jim, this one's for you!

Nick Thacker
Colorado Springs, Colorado
May 23, 2016

THE
AMAZON CODE

NICK THACKER

TURTLESHELL PRESS

CHAPTER 1

The world isn't ready for a breakthrough like this. I'm not ready for a breakthrough like this.

Dr. Amanda Meron raced through the hallways of the small center, dodging metal carts full of trays of test equipment, computers and displays flashing and blinking. She lived for these moments, had dedicated her life to these moments, and she would not let them slip through her fingers.

For Amanda, it wasn't even about the research. Sure, she was fascinated by it, but it was the sense of *living* that accompanied the moments of pure scientific breakthrough.

How they must have felt, she wondered, *Einstein, Newton, Bohr.* Her childhood heroes, whom she now considered her friendly competition.

"Dr. Meron, in here. Just in time," she heard a voice call out from a room she almost ran past.

She knew this place better than anyone and yet her excitement caused her to momentarily lose her place. She slowed, turning into the glass-walled room, and took a look around. The faces of her peers, all smiling back at her, were assembled around the large computer monitor in the center of the room.

"We're ready when you are, Dr. Meron," the voice said. Dr. Henry Wu, the transplant from Stanford, stepped lightly to the side to allow room for their boss.

Amanda caught her breath and took her place next to Wu. She nodded. The screen flickered, and colors began to swirl around a central area of bursting light.

"We've transcribed over 10,000 more locations since our last neural bridge," Dr. Wu explained. "The map is now nearing 40% relational accuracy."

40%.

She almost couldn't believe it. Almost.

For the last few years — not to mention the years of schooling before that — she had been working toward this moment. Many in her field thought it couldn't be done, but the theoretical projections she'd used as a model in her doctoral thesis were more than just *whims*.

She knew it could be done.

She knew *she* could do it. If anyone could, *she* could.

"Data is now being transferred." All eyes remained on the screen. "Subject is nearing REMS, electrical impulses from the stem are now appearing in irregular rapid succession."

Amanda watched with confident delight. *This is it.* She reached out for something to hold on to, her hand finding the cold steel of a thick desk protruding out from beneath the computer monitor.

The subject, a Mr. Ricardo Herrera, was asleep in the room next door. A 67-year-old man from the nearby village, he had volunteered for a week of testing in the state-of-the-art facility Amanda had built. He and his family would be paid handsomely for his time, and with no expected side effects besides feeling wonderfully refreshed and well-rested, it would likely be the easiest money he would ever make.

"Are we recording?" she asked.

A younger technician answered. "Yes, of course. Digital and analog." He pointed to a rectangular box sitting to the side of the computer.

A VCR.

She smiled. *Haven't seen one of those in years.*

After a scare from a computer virus a few months ago, she'd decided to "go old school," as the techs called it: use analog recording technology in addition to their digital setup. The analog devices were slower, a *lot* bulkier, and plenty annoying to use in everyday situations, but they were almost completely hacker-proof. Someone wanting to tamper with their data would need to be physically present to do so.

"Subject is entering REM sleep." A dialog box on a separate, smaller monitor flashed a small message: *REM-S POSITIVE.*

The larger monitor flashed in the center of the screen again, and the colors began swirling the opposite direction. Tiny sparks of light, like miniature shooting stars, danced around the edges of the swirling vortex.

"It looks like something from a science-fiction movie," one of the techs whispered.

"It *is* something from a sci-fi movie," another responded.

The stars began to grow, then shrink, then grow again, before they died out, replaced by blackness, then a burst of color.

"Is this a dream?" someone asked.

"No," Dr. Wu replied, "our subject has only just entered REM sleep, but is currently dreamless. He is sleeping soundly, though, and we should see something soon enough."

"How will we know?"

Dr. Wu just smiled.

They all watched for another minute, then the swirling vortex of color shifted and faded. The blank screen stared back at them for a full thirty seconds. Amanda gripped the side of the desk until her knuckles were white, then released it.

Did they lose the connection?

She thought through the possibilities, trying to remember their hypothetical timeframes for these initial tests…

And the screen exploded to life again.

Blurry forms shifted around in front of her, some recognizable as people. They moved and interacted, melting into one another and changing shape.

Oh my God.

She swallowed, trying not to blink. Trying not to miss a moment.

"We've entered a dreamstate. Subject appears to be relatively lucid, attempting to focus on one of the bodies."

Her excitement almost got the best of her. Amanda's mind didn't even need to flash back to her papers and research to know what that meant; the answer was already at the tip of her tongue. If every single person in the room around her hadn't already been trained by her, she might have even begun a mini-lecture. *Dreamstate* was their term for mid-REM sleep during a subject's dream, and *bodies* referred to any "physical" noun — a typical person, place, or thing — conjured up by the subject's subconscious during a dreamstate.

It had taken two years to get here from their first attempt at viewing a subject's dream.

And now it was working.

The subject, Mr. Herrera, was trying to focus on one of the *bodies* in the dream. It was smaller than the rest, but more sharply silhouetted against the backdrop of swirling colors.

A person.

"Subject appears to be focusing on the memory of a child-body."

The narration confirmed what Amanda was watching onscreen. The image become a bit more focused still, and she could now see more of the "setting" body of this particular memory.

Herrera was in a "room" body, or at least it appeared so, as streaming rays of light glanced down diagonally from the top-right of the video. He was also moving, working around objects that were too blurry to make out.

Amanda forced her eyes out of focus, trying to break any of the involuntary paradigmatic functions they were attempting to use to make sense of the image. Forcing her eyes to make what she was seeing "blurry," the image might make more sense.

And it did.

She could now better understand what it was Herrera was remembering. He was walking through a house; a living room, then a dining room, passed by. The colors and shadows on the walls in the background established where in the image they were, and she could tell Herrera was moving quickly.

Chasing the small shadow.

Herrera was chasing a laughing child through the house.

The child stopped and turned to Herrera, and Amanda's eyes focused again on the image. Having now established a visual "baseline," she could now interpret the smears and blurry lines of the images, and in the picture recreated in her mind, she could almost see the child's face.

It was Herrera's oldest son, now in his twenties, somewhere between the ages of three and eight in the video.

She held a hand up to her mouth. *It's really happening.*

The blurriness could be fixed, as could the awkward lighting, through the use of more specific mapping techniques and — eventually — far more electrodes on the brain. After that, image manipulation and video effects rendering could sharpen it a bit more. She immediately considered the repercussions of this discovery, and tried to project how long her team might take to deliver a finished, test-worthy product.

"I — I can't believe this," Dr. Wu said from beside her. "The image is so… vivid. I never thought…" His voice trailed off as the first-person point-of-view Herrera again began following the child into another room.

"We're… *there*. Inside his head," one of the technicians said. "And we can improve the image quality by increasing the output of each of the electrodes, as well quadrupling the number of —"

"Go back!"

Amanda looked over to Dr. Wu, frowning.

"Sir?"

"Go back," he repeated. "This is being recorded, yes?"

"Y — yes, but —"

"I don't care about the current feed. Rewind the video back about three seconds."

"Dr. Wu," Amanda said, "we don't want to lose the —"

"I understand, Amanda, but I saw something…"

Amanda nodded, and the technician closest to the monitor reached out and fiddled with the controls on the computer below it. The screen changed to a computer desktop for a moment, then he double-clicked a folder and then a video file inside of it.

"Just changing from the live feed to the recording…" he said as he worked.

The video started over again, from the swirling vortex of colors to the blank screen. He dragged the cursor over the scrubbing track, "fast-forwarding" the file to a few seconds before the end.

"What did you see, Henry?" Amanda's voice was calm, but it hid concern. Dr. Wu was not the type of person to mess around or engage in hyperbole, especially not during a live testing period.

"I — I don't know. I'm not quite sure yet," he stammered, his eyes transfixed on the monitor display. "There! Stop it there, and go back a few frames at a time."

The memory they were watching was the same one as before:

Herrera chasing his oldest son through a house. But Wu seemed transfixed not on the object of Herrera's active memory — his son — but on the background.

The video's point-of-view swiveled to the left, trying to keep up with the child, and it seemed as though Herrera was running past a window. They watched the screen until Wu spoke again.

"Hold it. Right there, on the right, outside the window. That is a window, correct?"

Heads nodded. Amanda couldn't see what it was that had Wu's attention.

"Outside, just beyond the window.

She blurred her vision again, then released it. The image came into focus more, and she felt her throat constrict.

"What the…"

"Is that a person?"

It was indeed. Amanda was sure of it.

The image was small — difficult to see even when she leaned in to the monitor — but it was sharply focused.

Eerily focused.

It was a man, covered in what looked like gold paint.

"It looks like a statue to me."

"But the detail…"

Amanda shook her head. "This is a joke, right, Dr. Wu?"

Dr. Wu just frowned at the screen.

"The man — or statue — is *completely* in focus." The gold-covered man in the image, standing outside the fuzzy outline of the window, was defined perfectly in the frame. It was small, and therefore easy to miss, but Amanda knew without a doubt what she was staring at.

A man, perfectly focused, stared back at them.

"Dr. Wu," she started again, "did you somehow layer this into the feed? Maybe there's an artifact from a previous —"

"No, Dr. Meron," he responded, his voice soft. "I did not interfere with this recording. What we are seeing here is part of the dreamstate created by Mr. Herrera's subconscious. The man we are seeing is, in fact, part of Herrera's memory."

"But how can it be so *clear*? So perfectly in focus?"

Wu shook his head. "I don't know yet. But let's see what happens if we jump a few frames at a time, forward and backward."

The technician nearest the monitor and computer assembly nodded and moved some controls. The frame jumped, skipping forward. Herrera's memory moved to the left, turning away from the window as he searched for the child.

All eyes were on the gold-covered man in the bottom-right corner of the screen.

The technician pushed forward another frame, then another.

"There!" someone shouted.

Amanda jumped, startled by the sound of the person's voice.

Or startled by what she saw.

The gold-covered man had *moved*. As Herrera's memory of the scene changed and shifted, the man in the corner, standing outside the window in the distance, turned and followed Herrera.

Amanda stared back at the man. She could see his eyes, deep black and sunken into his head, and his gold face, outlined by a shimmering light surrounding his body.

The eyes were looking directly at her.

CHAPTER 2

"But how can he be *staring* at me?"

Dr. Amanda Meron was following her coworker, Dr. Henry Wu, through the halls of the facility to the staff conference room.

"He wasn't, Dr. Meron," Wu answered. "He was staring at the camera."

"The camera?"

"Well, you know what I mean. Our subject's projected memory. In this case, the memory of chasing his young son through his house, is remembered in first person, just like any dream you or I have."

"So the man was looking at Herrera? Our subject?"

"That's what we're going to find out," Wu said. "But yes, I suppose that is the most logical conclusion — the memory of the gold man would likely not have appeared unless it was a significant, yet repressed, memory. We need to ask Mr. Herrera who the man is and why he was dreaming about him."

"But why was he in focus? Once you pointed him out, it was as clear as looking at a photograph. I thought —"

"That the projections would all be distorted, blurry, out of focus? Yes, as did I. But for some reason, this memory of the man was so strong, so *reinforced*, that the electrodes were able to recreate it almost perfectly in the transmission."

"*Almost* perfectly?" another voice asked. Amanda noticed they had been joined by the same younger technician who had helped them navigate the computer's controls a few minutes ago. "He seemed pretty perfectly composed to me."

"Right," Dr. Wu said, not slowing his upbeat clip through the hallways. "But he was completely gold. The memory wasn't firm enough in its recall to recreate the man's proper attire, coloration, etcetera. Still, I do find it quite strange at the seeming insignificance of it."

"What do you mean?"

"Well, why was that man, in particular, the only thing in focus during that memory? Sure, we do not have the capabilities as of yet to recreate perfect images, but we've hypothesized on this before. The strongest memories, or the strongest *elements* within those memories, will be the things that show up the clearest."

"So that man is the most important part of that memory?"

"That's what our research suggests, yes," Dr. Wu said.

Amanda knew that, but it was encouraging — comforting, even — to hear it from one of her closest friends, and most trusted coworker. *I'm not crazy, then,* she thought.

"But why *that* man, and not Herrera's son? Or his house?" she asked.

"That is exactly the question we need to answer, Dr. Meron."

They turned and entered the conference room. Amanda had often thought the small room would be better served as a closet, but she held her tongue and pushed between the wall and the backs of chairs to get to a seat in the corner. This was her company, after all, and she was the last among them who would want to spend money on frivolous things like space and fancy conference rooms.

One technician and two other research scientists — Johnson, Guavez, and Ortega — were already there, seated across the table from

Amanda. Dr. Wu and Nichols, the last technician, sat next to her.

She started immediately. "Team — as you know, our first neurological experiment using a fully-functioning, live human brain was a success. We will begin the project assessment and start assembling a response and hypothetical model as soon as this meeting is adjourned."

She continued through the required debriefing, not stopping to take questions until the end.

Thankfully, that was only a few minutes later.

"Okay," she said, wrapping up the session. "Any questions?"

Hands shot up around the room.

She smiled. "Let me guess — 'who do we think the gold-covered man is?' 'How was he so perfectly in focus?'"

Heads nodded in unison.

"I'm wondering those same things myself." Just then, the door opened and a small, petite woman shuffled into the few square feet of remaining space.

"Dr. Meron, the lab results," the woman said. She slid a folder across the table toward Meron.

"Thank you, Diane." She turned to the techs and scientists that had joined her around the table. "As you all know, I want this to be a fully open, honest forum. We're all part of this, so this is the first time *any* of us are seeing these results." Amanda opened the folder and began reading aloud.

"Upon waking the patient at 0900 hours, the following questions were asked. The transcript and responses to follow."

Amanda flipped a page. "1 — Were you able to engage in restful sleep? Response: 'Yes.' 2 — Do you remember dreaming during your most restful periods of sleep? Response: 'Yes.'"

She stopped for a moment and looked around the room. "I'm going to skip ahead a bit."

There were a few chuckles and nervous laughs, but she continued.

"7 — There was an object — what appeared to be a human male — in the dream. This man seemed to be covered in a gold paint. Brief pause. Who is the man? Response: 'I am sorry? I do not remember seeing a man.' 8 — This man seemed to be situated outside a window in the house. Do you remember the window? Response: 'I do. This was my house, my family's house. The window, uh, must have been the front window, looking out onto the street.' 9 — And yet you do not remember the man outside the window? Response: 'There was no man outside the window. I am sure of it.'"

Amanda swallowed, then closed the folder. Without speaking, she set the folder down on the table and placed her hands on it.

What the hell is happening?

Her first reaction was anger. *My research — my entire* company — *all of it is being sabotaged.*

She kept that feeling to herself. Unfortunately, the *second* emotion she felt — that of complete shock, of wondering what was going on, was plastered all over her face.

"Dr. Meron?" Dr. Wu's voice. "Are you okay?"

Amanda felt her head spin. *Am I shaking?* She tried to steady herself on the table. She looked over at Dr. Wu, nodding.

"Dr. Meron, I am sure there is a logical explanation for this. Perhaps Mr. Herrera had temporarily forgotten —"

"No," Dr. Wu said. "We need to run another test. Please have Diane prepare the subject for another round of REMS. He will need to expedite his regular daily schedule so we can have a test prepared for this evening."

Around the table, heads nodded. Amanda could hear the voice of Dr. Wu, but his words weren't registering. *We've been sabotaged,* she thought. *It's a joke. It's all a joke.*

Dr. Wu continued. "In the meantime, is there another subject prepared for a REMS analysis?"

Diane nodded. "Yes, Dr. Wu. Actually, we have a cousin of Mr. Herrera here as well. They signed up for the same examination week."

"That will be perfect." He turned to the technicians seated around the table. "Prepare the computer and fMRI system once more."

CHAPTER 3

Dr. Wu didn't blame Amanda. For years she'd been building this project, working toward the ultimate goal and dream they both shared: recording human dreams.

The fact that she was currently overwhelmed with the reality of the situation did not surprise him. He would take the lead until she was ready to return. Knowing her, she just needed some rest and time to clear her mind.

He had been with her since the beginning of this final phase. Their careers were similar, though Amanda was certainly the savvy and creative mind that a research project of this caliber needed, while he was the lead scientist that provided the logical and analytical functions to keep it moving forward.

They were a perfectly matched team, as well. From day one they'd hit it off, her wit and charm matched by his seriousness and love for science. In most of his professional career he'd witnessed only cutthroat types vying for publication credentials, university positions, and curriculum vitae-building projects that would only further their careers.

But not here at NARATech. Neurological Advanced Research Applications was a firm like no other — focused solely on achieving the goals set by all of them, together, around the table inside that terribly cramped conference room. Political and bureaucratic considerations were, simply, not considered.

For the first years they'd worked together, he'd assumed that she had personally bankrolled NARATech — he simply couldn't fathom any other possibility for a company such as this. But after getting to know her, he overheard a few references to 'investors' and 'capital' and things of that nature, and he started wondering where Amanda had found the hands-off investors she'd collected to get this place off the ground. He couldn't imagine anyone willing to invest such hefty sums in an unproven market, especially without the massive oversight and earmarking along the way that always came with the investment money.

But NARATech seemed to be just such an organization. Headquartered in Maraba rather than Brasilia, the federal district of Brazil, NARATech was a billion-US-dollar research station with all the perks of a Silicon Valley startup, but tucked away from the bustle of city life. Dr. Amanda Meron ran the company, and Wu operated as the executive staff member.

That was it. No more, no less. It was a simple and elegant setup that allowed them to move quickly into the research areas they needed.

For Amanda's sake, Dr. Wu hoped this next test would go more smoothly. Specifically, he hoped that whatever strange phenomenon they had experienced the first time around would not plague them this time.

He motioned for the technician to begin. Again, they all stood around the computer and monitor, minus Amanda. The technician alerted Diane in the next room to switch on the fMRI scanner that would begin activating the electrodes arrayed inside the helmet their subject was wearing.

Wu watched as again the swirling colors danced and played on the screen, followed by the starbursts and sprinkling of light. It took longer this time for their patient to enter into a dreamstate, but after about ten minutes of watching, the screen went blank.

"Confirm recording," he said.

A technician confirmed just as the screen lit up in shining light. Wu was again stunned by the beauty of it. It was difficult to comprehend what he was seeing, but eventually things began to fall into place.

This particular dreamstate had much less structure than Mr. Herrera's. Abstract lines and shapes still danced in the background, fuzzy interpretations of something Mr. Herrera's cousin remembered from long ago. In the foreground, or what Wu assumed was the foreground, larger shapes — unknown bodies — moved back and forth on the screen.

The screen itself seemed to jump up and down as the shapes moved left and right. *It's a good thing I'm not prone to seizures,* he thought.

"Where are we?" One of the technicians, Johnson, asked.

Gauvez answered. "No idea, but it does look like a fun memory."

"Looks like a dance. Or a party."

There were a few chuckles, then silence.

Wu suddenly understood the context and setting. *It is a dance,* he realized. Mr. Herrera's cousin was also remembering a happy time, a moment of joy.

People, or at least their fuzzy outlines, danced around the screen. Two of the shapes — people bodies, as they would be called — embraced one another and swirled into one blob. The blob moved, turning to the side of the screen. Their subject moved its head and followed as the blob continued to move to another location in the memory.

They watched in silence for another two minutes until the two shapes reemerged from one and separated on screen.

And there, in the center of the screen, right where the two shapes split, the gold-covered man stood.

Watching.

Waiting.

Looking directly at Dr. Henry Wu.

I

"Gaily bedight,

A gallant knight,

In sunshine and in shadow,

Had journeyed long,

Singing a song,

In search of Eldorado…"

— Edgar Allan Poe

CHAPTER 4

"What do you mean, *inconclusive?*" Amanda asked. She didn't mean for it to sound so accusatory, but the past week had been a nightmare.

"I — I'm sorry, Dr. Meron," Dr. Juan Ortega responded. He had a stack of folders and papers in front of him, and he seemed suddenly too large for the small conference room. Dr. Wu sat next to Amanda at one side of the table as they posed question after question to their employee.

"I only mean that the data we've collected is insufficient to draw any educated conclusions."

"I understand the *data*, Dr. Ortega," Amanda said. "I'm asking for your *professional opinion*. You've been in every single one of these tests, have you not?"

"I have."

"Well, I would like for you to give us your best guess on what is happening. Why is the exact same, perfectly delineated man, covered in gold, showing up in more than 6% of our subjects' memories? Why is he showing up in *any* of them? What particular insight might you have that we haven't considered?"

Dr. Ortega remained silent. Amanda knew him to be a 'speak-last' individual — a personality descriptor she used for the quiet, reserved types who often had a last-minute insight that clarified, helped along, or redirected the conversation.

In other words, a valuable asset for her and her team.

"I'm not quite sure, yet, Dr. Meron. I've considered the same issues we've already worked through. All of us have examined the equipment, looking for tampering, hacking, or just anything out of place, and we've each gone through the data…"

"Do you have any other ideas? Ideas that may not be, uh, particularly *scientific*?"

Amanda saw Dr. Wu smile. She knew this was why they liked her, and why they enjoyed working here. She cared little for perception and maintaining an image — she wanted real, tangible results.

"Well, uh, I guess we could identify some of the more granular areas of demographic similarities, like income class, education, lifestyle choices —"

"We've gone through all that already. There was a gauntlet of questions during the initial trial signup phase, and there were no statistical similarities between subjects."

"I know. I can't think of anything else, outside of a Freudian 'shared intelligence' idea."

Amanda raised her eyebrows. "Go on."

"'Shared intelligence?'" Dr. Ortega asked. "Well, Freud was the first to coin the term 'unconscious,' as you know, but it was because he believed in a particular 'shared memory' of species. This was his basis for believing in and supporting ideas related to genetic similarities, instinctual behavior, and other 'natural' behaviors."

"You think some of our subjects have ESP?" Dr. Wu asked.

"I do not. It's biologically impossible for humans to produce communication via a non-physical or non-audible means. But shared intelligence goes deeper than that. It's a common thread between humans and other mammals, as well as other members of the animal kingdom in general — where do instincts come from? How does a mother *know* how to take care of her young? How do involuntary reactions, emotions, and feelings get there in the first place?"

"All great questions, Dr. Ortega, but how do we test any of this?"

"That's what I have been trying to decipher," he responded. "Much research has already been done in the field, but none of it is helpful for our situation."

"What do you mean?"

"Well, consider the fact that of the forty-seven people we have tested, only three seem to have a memory that includes the gold-covered man. And of those three, none have any recollection of that man. They all seem confused when we bring it up."

"And they don't recognize it when we show them the recordings."

"Right," Ortega responded. "So I can't say it is an *instinct* that they are feeling, or experiencing, or whatever, but it is certainly possible there is a similar thread in their lineage. Actually, if you rule out our equipment, there *has* to be a similarity somewhere, so why not there?"

Amanda considered this. "Hmm. Lineage." She looked at Wu, unsure of whether or not she should continue. Her hypothesis at this point was almost absurd, certainly in the realm of 'quack science.'

He nodded, so she continued.

"Of course there's a similarity, though: they are all related."

Ortega seemed momentarily shocked, but quickly recovered. "Right — they are. The Herrera cousins, and the sister. All of them signed up for the same week of testing, and all had different memories featuring the same gold-covered man. But since it is not in either of their collective consciousnesses *or* subconsciousnesses, I am inclined to believe we need to dig further to understand where the memory is originating."

"What are you suggesting?"

"We need to cull our database of subjects. With your permission, let's temporarily release subjects from the test unless they are confirmed to have a similar lineage as that of our three Herrera relatives."

Dr. Wu stepped in this time. "But how will we know? If we haven't identified a DNA segment that confirms or denies their relationship to one another, we have no testable hypothesis. Plus, the time it would take to run those tests, receive results…"

"I'm not suggesting we use DNA tests," Ortega replied.

All eyes turned to him again, but Amanda wasn't surprised. *This is why he's here*, she thought.

She'd hired the man for his background in genetics and psychology, not to mention his computer skills. But it was his think-outside-the-box personality that she most respected.

"Look," he said, "I'm from this area, as is Guavez. I can tell you with certainty that lineage is an important familial bond here in Brazil. Many of us can trace our ancestors to the European conquistadors and their troops, down through the local and regional tribes."

Amanda nodded. Wu seemed slightly confused, but he let Ortega continue.

"I would bet that the Herreras could also tell us their family history, at least in general terms. Many of the tribes in Central and South America were split from larger, more prominent ones that came before them, so much of their history, while nuanced, is related."

Dr. Wu spoke again, now understanding. "Of course — if they can give us a little background, we might be able to pinpoint other subjects that share a family tie. Diane —"

Diane had already started to stand from her post as 'wallflower in charge of note-taking.' Titled as an "office assistant," Diane's role was significantly more in-depth and crucial to the day-to-day operations than anyone but Dr. Wu and Dr. Meron could understand. She had a degree in organizational administration, but her skills branched out into just about every facet of the team's operations — human resources, finance, and leading double-blind, placebo-controlled studies were among them.

"On it, Dr. Wu," she said. She picked up her yellow legal pad, three pages of neatly arranged notes spreading from top to bottom, and left the room.

"Dr. Ortega, will you assist us in determining the important links of family history for our subjects?"

The man nodded, and began to stand.

"One more thing," Amanda said. Ortega's head turned to face his boss. "We are not usually a team that worries about discretion. I prefer it this way, as I'm sure you do as well. However, with the nature of these findings, I would like you to suggest to our technicians that we refrain from uploading the weekly data stream from now on, until I can make heads or tails of this."

Dr. Wu and Dr. Ortega both frowned, so Amanda explained.

"I don't often allude to our outside investors," she said. "But you both know they exist — everyone here does. We are grateful to them for their continued support, and certainly for their hands-off style of management in this organization. But until we know *exactly* what these results mean for our organization, I would urge us to refrain from opening the doors too widely."

She hoped the warning was clear.

"Your call, boss," Ortega said. "We're with you, no matter what."

She nodded, smiling.

"Besides the first set of results that went up earlier this afternoon, we'll keep everything hush-hush until we're ready."

Amanda turned her head slightly. "First set? This afternoon?"

"Uh, yes," Dr. Ortega said. "We changed the schedule last month to twelve hours earlier — it was easier for our IT consultants, since they're on the other side of the world."

Amanda stared at him. *I remember that,* she thought. *And I totally forgot.*

"Is that going to be a problem?" Dr. Wu asked, looking concerned.

"No," she responded, shaking her head quickly. "It's just been an eventful week. I'd forgotten we'd decided to do that."

"Good deal," Ortega said. "We'll keep it offline until you give the go-ahead, and I'll see where the one receiving hit originated from, just so you're in the loop."

"*Receiving* hit? Someone's accessed the data already?"

"Well, sure — someone always does, right away. At least that's how it's always been since I've been here. Same IP address every time. Usually the same time of day, even. Might be that reclusive investor you've got." He winked.

Amanda felt her blood run cold. *If they already have the data…*

She stood. "Very good. Thank you all for your hard work. Let's get the results back from Diane after you and Gauvez take a crack at this, and we'll get going tomorrow morning."

Dr. Wu and Ortega nodded, and Amanda stood to leave the room.

Time to call an old friend.

CHAPTER 5

"Amanda Meron," Paulinho said into the phone he'd holstered into the nook of his shoulder. Riding a bicycle and talking on the phone wasn't easy, but Paulinho wasn't about to let that stop him. "Get out of the way!" he yelled in Portuguese to a taxicab that screamed past. The cab driver didn't even turn to look as he honked his horn in reply.

"Paulinho, that you?" asked the woman's voice in his ear.

"Sim; yes. How are you?"

"Doing well, Paulinho. It's good to hear from you. Can we meet?"

Paulinho checked his watch — another feat of physical coordination he was immediately proud of. "Yes, I believe so. I have another appointment in half an hour, but I am downtown now."

His afternoon bike rides were just one of the many forms of exercise Paulinho engaged in during the week. While he kept no particular schedule, he considered 'staying active' to mean everything from rock climbing, lifting weights, and playing racquetball in the gym next to the government office he worked in — and bicycling, running, and swimming when the weather was nice.

"Good, I have a meeting as well. Can you meet for a cup of coffee? I can come to you."

Paulinho confirmed, then wheeled his bike onto the sidewalk next to the road. He found a small coffee shop tucked between two retail outlets, and texted the location to his friend.

He waited ten minutes, but before he'd even captured a free table outside the street-side cafe, Amanda rushed into the gated patio.

"Paulinho!" They exchanged pleasantries, ordered drinks, and sat.

"What is it that you have rushed here to tell me?" Paulinho asked, pausing to sip the warm drink.

"Not to tell you… to *ask* you," Amanda responded. "I need a favor."

His tried to read her expression, but failed. "Is everything okay?"

"Yes, I think so. But I'm not sure. It's — it's NARATech."

"Your company?"

"I'm worried about my investors. Specifically, I'm worried about who they really *are*."

Paulinho broke the eye contact when the waiter brought their drinks. They each took a long sip, paying homage to the high quality beverages, then jumped back in to the conversation.

"We've made some progress in our research — significant progress. And we've had the luxury of a mostly silent partner in my investors, but I'd like to see if you can dig up anything on them?"

"'Dig up?'"

Amanda nodded.

"Amanda, I am not a spy. I work for the financial bureau. I'm just an accountant."

"But you're my only contact in the government. You're smart, and you might be able to find some information for me — bank accounts, linking them back to a person, or persons — anything."

Paulinho finally had a read on her. *She's desperate.* He suddenly felt sorry for her, but the feeling subsided almost immediately. Dr. Amanda Meron had a fragile personality and was the epitome of an introverted genius, but she still was not the type of person to come crawling to him for favors. They'd only met a year ago, but they'd hit it off right away. Paulinho was an extrovert and socialite, and he'd sidled up to her at a dinner party, each of them the only singles at the event, and he'd struck up a conversation.

He loved her quiet confidence, her ability to exude control over her words and naturally force anyone listening to her to pause and wait for her to gather her thoughts. It didn't hurt that she was stunningly beautiful, either.

He thought about the request for a moment before responding. "Amanda, I want to help. I really do. But I cannot imagine where I would even start."

"I have routing numbers and bank account numbers from deposits. We can start there."

"What about a name; someone at the firm?" He took another sip of his coffee, then added, "And why are you so worried?"

Amanda shook her head. "I'm not worried... No, I don't have any names, that was the agreement. Besides, it's not just one person — this is an organization, one that prides itself on discretion. They agreed to fund the project to its completion, and give us complete control, in exchange for their anonymity. They prefer to be a silent partner."

"You mean a *nonexistent* partner..."

Amanda smiled. "Nevertheless, they've let us operate without oversight thus far, and we've kept up our end of the agreement — my team uploads research every week, and someone there seems to be accessing it, but they've never responded with any questions or clarifications." She paused a moment. "Fine. to answer your second question, I guess I'm just feeling... a little overwhelmed. Our project has been moving forward more and more quickly, and I came to the realization that we have no idea who it is we're really working *for*."

Paulinho nodded. "Still, Amanda, I don't know what it is I can help you with. I will certainly look around our offices for any obvious links, but if this company had a name, or a person associated —"

"It has a name. Well, I do remember what they told me when I first heard from them."

Paulinho raised an eyebrow.

"They called themselves 'Dragonstone Corp.' I have no doubt that it's an umbrella corporation, and I'm receiving money from one of their subsidiaries, another company that goes by Drache Global."

Paulinho steeled himself. "A typical structure, to save on taxes. Any idea where they're located?"

Amanda shook her head. "None. The man I initially spoke with, seven years ago, sounded French. Maybe Canadian. I've done some research online, and haven't been able to find anything on them."

"Good. I'll see what I can find. Amanda, I hope everything is okay. Please let me know if you hear anything else."

Amanda stood to leave. "I will. And let me know what you find."

Paulinho stood to see her off, then sat back down at the outdoor patio table. He pulled his phone from his pocket again and opened a browser, looking for the number of an old friend. *I wonder if her number is online,* he thought.

He scrolled through a list of office extensions for a moment until he came to the number he was looking for. He clicked the link, opening the phone app and dialing the number. He lifted the phone to his ear and waited, hoping the number was her personal cell, and not just an office line.

Pick up, he willed into the phone.

A woman's voice answered. "Juliette Richardson."

"Julie? Hello? It's Paulinho, from University." It had been years since they'd graduated, but Paulinho and Julie were close then. They'd tried to stay in touch, but their professional ambitions had pulled them apart. Their paths had crossed again a few months ago however, when he was sent to the United States to help with the cleanup of some of the financial fallout the country suffered surrounding explosions and a virus outbreak at Yellowstone National Park.

"Paulinho! Wow, twice in one year!" the woman answered.

"Yes, and I'm sorry we haven't remained in touch, but I'm calling for something else."

Julie paused on the other end. "And what might that be?"

Paulinho sighed. "Well, I remember your... *ordeal...* back in Yellowstone."

No response.

"Julie, I know you don't want to relive any of it, but I also know how distraught you were after you and Harvey couldn't get the closure you needed."

More silence.

"Julie, I was just contacted by a friend of mine working in neurological research. She came to me asking for help looking into one of her investors. She seemed a little desperate, actually, which is somewhat out of character for her." He paused. "Listen, the point is: I'm worried for her. I'm going to look into it, but I wanted to let you know first."

Finally Julie spoke. "Why?"

"Well, the company name she gave me was Drache Global."

CHAPTER 6

"Jules, I told you — I'm not interested in sitting on my butt for three weeks while you spend most of it throwing up over the edge of a boat."

Harvey "Ben" Bennett waited for the rebuttal he knew was coming, then turned back to the book he was reading: *Plants of the Rocky Mountains.* 'Reading' was probably too strong a word, since he was mostly just flipping through pages, hoping to catch some of what his father used to call "intelligence by osmosis."

He hadn't waited long enough. Juliette Richardson stopped at the doorway to the tiny living room in the cabin they currently lived in together, and spoke. "I didn't say I was seasick, Ben. I said I *might* be. My mom was, and her sister, and —"

"And you're saying 'seasickness' is hereditary," he said, not looking up from his book.

"I'm *saying* that I don't *know* if I will be or not. But that doesn't matter. I have medicine and they have these little bracelets now that —"

"Oh, come *on*," he said, laughing. "You don't honestly think those things *work*, do you?"

Julie took a few steps closer to him and stood at the foot of his recliner — a ratty, crusted old armchair that he wouldn't let her replace. It 'sat well,' as he always told her. She didn't agree, and always chose to sit on the love seat next to it.

"Let's just take a second here and realize which one of us is being the most dramatic," she said.

"You," he answered immediately, still not looking up from the 'Key to Gooseberries and Currants (*Ribes Species*)' description in the 'Shrubs' section of the book.

Julie sighed. "Right. Me. I'm the dramatic one, for wondering whether or not I'd get seasick on a week-long cruise through the Gulf of Mexico. Not *you*, who wants to *drive there*. Ben," She paused, waiting for him to look up.

Don't do it, you fool, he thought. *She wins if you look up.*

He looked up. *Damn, she's cute.*

"Ben," she repeated. "We're in *Alaska*. You want to *drive to Galveston, Texas*. From Alaska."

He raised his eyebrows a bit. *So what?*

She sighed again, then threw her hands up in the air and left the room to see to the massive pot of chili she'd been working on all day. It was an all-time favorite recipe from her mother, and since Ben liked to call himself a 'year-round chili kind of guy,' he had no issue with eating the hearty stew multiple times a day in the dead of summer.

Julie had 'officially' lived in his cabin for a few months now, and he knew neither of them was hoping to change the arrangement anytime soon. If anything, they were getting more serious, but Ben tried as hard as possible not to seem 'in love' whenever any of his fellow park rangers saw them together. He'd been able to stave off the jibes and taunts at first, but within a week of their finding out about his relationship status he was being called 'Romeo.' He quickly discovered that his fellow rangers at Denali National Park weren't any more creative with their insults than those he'd left behind at Yellowstone.

After transferring from Yellowstone, he and Juliette were welcomed with open arms onto the full-time staff at the park, Julie beginning a new role as an IT and technical support coordinator, and acting as a part-time consultant for the CDC. Her old program, the Biological Threat Research division, had been temporarily shuttered after the suspected murder of its leader and a terrorist infiltration among its ranks. She made plenty of money doing IT for the park and contracting her services to the CDC on the side, and they allowed her to work wherever she wanted. After Ben had finalized the purchase of the land in Alaska he'd always wanted and made the arrangements, he'd taken Julie along to turn the tiny trapper's cabin that sat on it into a home.

Julie entered the room again, having swirled the chili around and deemed it safe for another five minutes. Ben never understood her cooking habits. They both loved cooking, but Julie was far more 'hands on' about it. When a recipe told her to 'wait twenty minutes,' Ben could be sure she'd be hovering over it every minute, watching, poking, and prodding it along.

When a recipe told Ben to 'wait twenty minutes,' he gave it thirty, just to be safe.

"My point is that you just don't want to fly. If you wanted to fly, we could get there in a few hours and have time to kill before we got on the boat."

Ben looked up again from the shrub he was inactively studying. "'A few hours?' Seriously? Julie, it's like *9 hours* from Anchorage, and that's not including the time it takes to drive to the airport."

"It's three days of driving time. Not including hotels and food. I'm just saying —"

"I know what you're saying, Jules. I'm not doing it." He'd meant it to sound final; to alert Julie to the seriousness with which he'd made the decision, but it came across as hesitant. If he was being honest with himself, he *did* want a vacation. While he absolutely loved the cool Alaskan summers, he had to admit that sitting on a deck, bathing in sunlight while drinking a Cuba Libre sounded decent.

Not to mention Julie's attire during the week.

He knew she'd been ordering swimsuits online, expecting the conversation they were having now to go her way.

And it would. Ben knew he just needed to hold out a bit longer to make sure she knew that she didn't have him around her little finger. By putting up just a bit of a fight, she'd be that much more excited when he agreed to it.

She left the room to stir the chili once more, then returned. "I've been ordering swimsuits online, and the first one came to the office today — want me to model it for you?"

Julie flicked him the single raised-eyebrow look she used when she was trying to look sexy, which only made her look goofy.

Which makes her look sexy.

"Fine. I guess I'll put the book down," Ben said, grinning.

Julie ran off into the bedroom of the cabin, situated next to the kitchen and behind the larger living room area, and Ben closed the guidebook and placed it on the end table next to the chair.

He heard her cell phone ring, a piercing screech that she wouldn't change or turn down. She carried the thing with her everywhere, afraid that at any moment she'd be called in to handle an emergency email password change or an office computer freezing.

After another minute, Julie walked back in the room — still wearing the clothes she'd had on before.

"Everything okay?" he asked.

She shook her head. He focused on her eyes. Where there had been playfulness and joy in them a moment ago, she was now all business.

"Jules, what's up?" he stood up from the large chair and pushed the recliner in, then walked toward her.

"We need to go to Brazil."

Ben wasn't sure how to respond. "Excuse me? Brazil? The country?"

"That was a friend of mine from college. He told me Drache Global had surfaced down there, and that he thinks they're planning something again."

Ben felt his blood run cold. *Drache Global.* After he'd spent two months trying to research what the company actually did — and more importantly, who was behind it — he'd all but lost hope. The government, if they knew anything at all, wasn't offering any help, and Julie's position at the CDC hadn't been quite high enough for her to negotiate anything useful.

All he knew was that they were one of the subsidiaries of the *real* organization behind the attacks at Yellowstone National Park months earlier, and they'd mostly gotten away with the act of terror. No one but Ben and Julie knew how close the nation had come to total destruction, and he made a vow to himself that he'd never stop looking for them. They had a few different names of other subsidiaries that might be involved, including Dragonstone and Drage Medisinsk, but searches for those companies only turned up public information on their dealings in whichever countries they operated. Nothing illegal, nothing that might link them to the attacks, and nothing for Ben to follow. He'd already spent too many waking hours trying to find and follow a thread, and he'd nearly thrown in the towel.

Now, someone was handing them a lead, beckoning.

He'd be damned if he let the opportunity slip through his fingers.

CHAPTER 7

Juliette Richardson stared out the small oval window of the 737 as it flew south over the Caribbean Sea. She longed to be down there, cruising around in the bright blue waters between Mexico and Jamaica. The cruise she'd chosen would have taken them to three ports in Cozumel, Grand Cayman, and Port Royal, and they'd have spent a luxurious seven days aboard a gigantic floating 5-star hotel.

Instead, they were flying over the open waters and onward toward Belo Horizonte, Brazil, where they would have a plane change and then fly north again to a smaller municipality in Central Brazil called Marabá, where they would land in the stifling heat and overwhelming humidity to spend God-knows-how-long tracking down an organization they weren't sure really existed. They would meet up with Dr. Meron, Paulinho's acquaintance, at her research firm, NARATech, and try to piece together tidbits of information that might — or might not — point back to Drache Global.

She turned to Ben, who was sitting in the seat next to her. "You think we'll find them?" she asked.

He opened his eyes. "Hm?"

"Sorry, I thought you couldn't sleep on planes," she said.

He rubbed his eyes and sat up straighter in the seat. "I wasn't asleep. Just couldn't hear you…"

She watched him pop a piece of gum into his mouth and waited for him to respond. It took another ten seconds.

"Yeah, I think we'll find something," he said.

She raised her eyebrows, hoping to get the message across. *We could have been on a cruise right now, but you're dragging me halfway around the hemisphere because you* think *we'll find* something?

He got the hint.

"Fine," he said. "Yeah, I think we'll find them. It's a company, or an organization, or whatever. But it deals in currency, just like the rest of us. They've got to have their fingerprints there somewhere."

She nodded.

"And you said that this 'Paul' — Paulinho — guy had some information that tied Drache Global to his friend's company?"

She nodded. "Yes. He told me she thought they were connected somehow; that maybe they were funding her, but trying to keep themselves out of the spotlight."

Ben was silent for a moment. "What does her company do, exactly?"

"From what I gather online, they're a neurological research company. Neurological Advanced Research Applications, I believe. NARATech. Paulinho said they're currently working on an application to map dreamstates."

"Dreamstates?"

"Dreams. They're using fMRI technology, applied directly to the skull, to image and record human dreams."

"That's a trip. Does it work?"

"I guess," she said. "There's nothing about it on their website, but I pried Paulinho for whatever he knew about it. It's not much, but he told me they've had 'mostly positive results.'"

"Wonder what 'negative results' looks like," Ben said.

"Whatever it is, if Drache Global is actually behind it, it's probably important to something they're planning."

"Did he say anything about what this 'research' actually looks like?"

"No, except that they've had some sort of anomaly crop up. He didn't know what it was, but he said it made Amanda seem 'fidgety' when they spoke."

"'Fidgety?'"

"That's what he said."

Ben didn't respond, but instead went back to 'sleep' with his head resting gently against the rock-hard cushion of the airplane seat. His legs, far too long to be comfortable, were smashed against the seat in front of him, not helped by the passenger's decision to recline the seat as far back as it would go.

Watching Ben sit there like a crash-test dummy who had been smashed against the front of its vehicle after a failed test, Julie felt even more uncomfortable.

"Now I know why you don't like flying," she said.

Ben opened his eyes and grinned, shifting in his seat to try to find a more comfortable position. "You think *this* is why I hate flying?" he asked.

She smiled back. "Surely it's not the kind, caring staff of in-flight personnel."

He glared at her. "I know you're joking, but it still hurts to remember."

She laughed. They'd flown together only once before, when they were both invited to the White House to meet the President after the events at Yellowstone National Park. The United States government, ostensibly intending to honor them at the nation's capitol, didn't seem to think it necessary to honor them *until* they arrived — they wouldn't spring for anything more expensive than coach tickets. They spent the hours-long flight smashed together in the back row, neither seat able to recline to offer even a little respite from the miserable journey.

To top it off, the plane had run out of alcoholic beverages, leaving Ben and Julie to subsist on peanuts and half-cans of Diet Coke delivered by a flight attendant that was clearly and vocally unsatisfied with his career. The attendant made a snide comment every time they'd asked for something, and he eventually told Ben to "get up and get it yourself" when Ben asked for another beverage.

And yet, If there was anything they both took away from the experience, it was the memory of laughing at the ridiculousness of it all; an inside joke between them. Julie knew Ben hated flying for a number of reasons, but even Ben admitted he was in much higher spirits when they traveled together.

She wondered if he'd ever get over his fear of flying. It was a control issue — namely, that he knew he *had* no control — but she liked to remind him that fears could be overcome.

He always argued back, as was his custom, but Julie secretly loved to see him squirm in his seat as the plane took off and then again as it landed. She thought it made him look cute.

"You're still thinking three days, right?" she asked.

"Three days for what?"

She shot him a look. "Three days to find whatever we can about Drache Global, then the rest of the time we're on vacation. *Not* looking."

"I thought we said a week — "

"*You* said a week. We're spending *two weeks* there, and I'm not wasting half of it tracking out a mysterious organization." Julie didn't push any further; she knew Ben was much more adamant about chasing the nebulous organization that had almost cost them their lives. She wanted to know who they were as much as he did, but she was more than happy to leave the detective work to actual detectives.

Ben didn't respond at first, but when she didn't stop staring at him, he finally nodded. "Yeah, right, I know. Three days. But if we find —"

"No, Ben. Three days. That's it." She wanted to sound decisive, firm, but the words sounded tired. She *was* tired — Yellowstone and the debriefing sessions with the government and media in the following months had taken their toll, and she was ready to be done with it. Like her mother always said, "sometimes you don't get closure, you just move on."

Ben, however, was not the type of person who could simply "move on." He was far too stubborn and driven to move on. It was probably the most frustrating thing about the man. Julie loved that she could count on him to finish a project, no matter how large, but she had to balance that with the reality that he tended to focus on nothing else until the project was finished.

She was always afraid that he would eventually find some lead, a small thread of information that might pique his interest in the case once again. She'd even considered not telling him about Paulinho's call, but she knew he was too smart for that. He'd ask who had called, and he'd know it was something serious, and she would eventually tell him.

So it was with great reluctance that she told Ben about the possible lead in Brazil, put their vacation on hold, and agreed to fly to Brazil with him to dig around for a few days. If everything went as planned, they'd spend a few days with Paulinho and his friend Amanda Meron, checking through her company's investment documents and funding details, and possibly examining some of the research, then they'd spend another ten days lazing on the beautiful white sand beaches and drinking with the locals.

If everything went as planned.

CHAPTER 8

Ben massaged his hands, working out the stiffness from white-knuckling the airplane seat's armrests during their landing a couple of hours ago. He listened as the group shared welcomes and pleasantries, all of them waiting for their drink orders to be delivered. They sat around a circular table at a picturesque Brazilian cafe, an umbrella that stood over them blocking out the most egregious of the sunlight that bathed the city streets. Streams of shoppers and businesspeople moved around them on the walkway, navigating between the cafe's street-side table.

The man who'd introduced everyone, Paulinho, still stood in front of his chair, a full-width smile on his face. He'd shaken Ben's hand with a grip that seemed to want to impress, but not quite strong enough to feel useful. Ben couldn't tell if he liked him or not, but as was his usual custom, he decided that he did not, but would allow the man to change Ben's mind. The man's skin was dark, deeply tanned from the Brazilian sun, and as he drew his hand away Ben noticed a small, circular tattoo on the inside of his wrist. He didn't recognize the design, and couldn't get a long enough look at it to decipher it further.

To his left sat Julie, who blushed when Paulinho kissed her on each cheek. Ben couldn't remember if that was supposed to be a European greeting or something the entire world did, but he still thought it was strange to see it in Brazil. Across from Julie, to Ben's right, sat Dr. Amanda Meron, a young woman who seemed, in Ben's opinion, better fit for a beach volleyball team than a science laboratory. Her skin was light, but bronzed with a natural glow that only summertime in a place like Brazil could provide. Her hair was short and blond, but long enough to be pulled back in a loose ponytail that rested gently on the back of her neck. She was apparently American or European by birth, and she stood out from the Brazilian natives around them.

Ben tried not to dwell on the fact that she was absolutely gorgeous. When Julie told him about her company, he'd assumed she would be a shriveled old lady, her back hunched from years of sitting over a microscope. Glasses, probably held onto her white lab coat by a long dangling chain she would clip onto her front pocket. He pictured his late grandmother, a wide, tiny woman who had the fierceness of a bull and the shoulders to match. He thought about every other "science-y"-type person he could think of — Bill Nye, Bill Gates, some white lab coat-wearing men and women in stock photographs — all of them nerds, according to Ben.

He realized when he met Amanda Meron that he knew nothing about science.

Stealing another glance, he saw that Dr. Meron sat with her elbows on the table, back straight, her eyes gazing upward at Paulinho. *Relaxed, yet on edge.* Julie looked over at Ben, and he quickly coughed and nodded once, then looked up at Paulinho.

Julie grinned, her eyes twinkling with a laughter she kept to herself.

Ben wondered if he was blushing.

"Ben, tell me — what is it you do for a living, if I may ask?" Paulinho said, somehow talking with impeccably spaced English while keeping the huge smile plastered on his face.

"Uh, sure," Ben said. "I'm a park ranger, up in Alaska."

"Oh? Quite interesting! Is that something you do year-round?"

Ben frowned, trying to interpret the question. If it was anyone else, it would have been a comment related to weather: *'Isn't it too cold to work in Alaska in the wintertime?'* But he still wasn't sure about Paulinho. *'Is that something that pays the bills for you and your girlfriend, or doesn't she need a better man? Someone like me, perhaps...?*

"Ben?"

Ben snapped his head up, and Julie — and Paulinho and Amanda — were staring at him.

"Right, oh, sorry," he said. "Yeah, it's full-time. Pays the bills, you know..."

Paulinho's smile, miraculously, got even larger. "Wonderful! Well I'm glad we could all be here. Thank you for coming on such short notice. I assume Dr. Meron has filled you in on the details of her company's endeavors?"

Julie nodded. "Yes, thank you. And you have been looking for anything related to Drache Global?"

The waiter returned with their drinks. Two light, springy, sparkling juices for Paulinho and Amanda, a Diet Coke for Julie, and a water for Ben.

Paulinho nodded in response to Julie's question, finally sitting down. "Yes, but it has so far been fruitless. The company seems to want to keep themselves well-hidden."

"Which means they're doing something wrong," Amanda said.

"Not necessarily. Businesses often prefer to operate at arms-length from their local and national governments. Taxes are a hefty burden these days, not to mention the constant threat of lawsuits and bad publicity."

Everyone around the table nodded, accepting the answer.

"But *if* they were doing something wrong, you would find it?" Ben asked.

"Well, let's not get ahead of ourselves. I work in an office that has access to otherwise private records that businesses must file every year — that doesn't mean I will be able to find anything, if it's there. I'm doing this as a favor to Dr. Meron, and, of course, to you two as well. I've also reached out to a friend of mine who's interested in history. He's somewhat of an eccentric, but you'll like him."

Julie reached over and patted Paulinho's hand with a concerned look on her face, as if he'd just rescued her nephew's puppy. Ben took a deep, long sip of his water, trying to ignore the odd way his girlfriend was acting around the strapping, dark-skinned Paulinho. Paulinho just sat, smiling, soaking it all in.

The man's got swagger, Ben thought. He had to hand it to him. Living in Brazil, educated, wealthy, and good-looking, Ben knew the man wasn't wanting for attention from the opposite sex. He held himself confidently, his permanent smile lighting up the already sun-bleached day.

"So," Ben asked. "What's the next step?"

Amanda shook her head, forming the words. "I'm not sure what's going on, or why, but I'm glad you're here — both of you. You need to check into your hotel, and get some rest. We can chat tomorrow. And if there's anything you can tell me about this organization, I'm all ears."

Ben stood up, preparing to leave with Julie. "We're in the dark on this one, but I can tell you this: Drache Global, if they're really who's behind this, is not a company you want to mess around with."

CHAPTER 9

Juan Ortega pulled up to the tiny house at the end of the block and parked his sedan on the driveway. He made enough money to buy a better vehicle, a larger house, and live just about anywhere in Brazil, but for him it was never about wanting more.

He'd been raised Catholic, by a farmer and a schoolteacher, and frugality had always been a strong master in their home. Juan's father taught the children — nine total, including Juan — how to garden and grow food, fend for themselves, and take care of a family. His mother taught them the value of a proper education, and instilled in all of them the desire to learn.

As he collected his bag and hung his NARATech ID badge over the rearview mirror, an image of his parents came to mind. His father, smiling with the knowledge that his oldest son was carrying on the family name in a proud, world-benefiting way, and his mother, smug with the look only a satisfied mother can have when watching their grown children. They had both passed away five years ago, within six months of one another, and Juan did his best to remember them well. They had set up a small shrine in the entryway of the house, just inside the front door. He walked toward it, opened the screen door and turned the handle on the larger door behind it, and entered the house.

He passed the shrine, seeing the row of candles and framed image of his parents smiling back at him. He paused for just a moment, hoping to take a minute to honor their memory in silence, but his five-year-old daughter was already rounding the corner.

"Papa!" she yelled, bounding up toward him and jumping into his arms.

"Caroline," he said, kissing her cheek, "what are you doing home?" Caroline was supposed to have dance class after school today, so he was surprised to see her in the house.

"Mama said I could skip so we could make cookies tonight."

He smiled. 'Making cookies' meant the entire kitchen would be turned upside-down for the remainder of the night, but soon after there would be *hundreds* of cookies of all shapes, sizes, textures, and flavors to choose from. It was a family tradition his wife and their three daughters — nine, seven, and five years old — all took part in. Juan's role was 'official taster.'

"And why are you not helping her now?" he said, tickling her.

She screamed in laughter, then ran out of the room as soon as he put her down. His wife welcomed him in Portuguese, too busy to leave her post in the kitchen, and he responded and walked into the family area adjoined to the kitchen.

Before he could put the briefcase down, his oldest daughter, Gloria, came into the room holding a game. She already had the pouty eyes of a begging child, hoping to get something from her father.

"What, you too are not helping your mother?"

"I am, but we are waiting to be done with this batch," she responded. "Please?" She held up the small, rectangular box toward Juan.

"I guess," he said, "if it's okay with your mother."

She gave a quick nod, then added, "But if you're late to the next batch of dough you won't be allowed to eat any of them."

The girls laughed, and Gloria dumped out the box onto the rug in the family room. *Pega-vereta* was a children's game they'd gotten from his wife's brother a few weeks ago. The set of colored sticks fell out haphazardly on top of one another, and the game was to try to pick them up without moving any other stick. Each color of stick was worth a different point value. It was a simple game, but Juan enjoyed roleplaying for the girls when they played. Tonight, he would be a crazed surgeon, attempting to fix a patient without causing more damage. He immediately went into character, yelling at the sticks on the floor in an American accent to "clear the room!"

The girls all laughed, and Gloria picked up her first stick.

They played for a few minutes, back-and-forth, until there were only ten sticks left. All of the remaining sticks had fallen on the floor in a similar fashion, their ends overlapping closer to one side of each stick than the other, forming a point at which all of the sticks converged.

Juan tilted his head to one side as he looked at them.

"Papa, it's your turn," Gloria said.

He responded in character. "Yes, yes, I am concentrating."

But as he looked at the remaining sticks, all crossing each other at a single point, he had a realization.

I have to get to the office...

He had to test the theory.

He stood up, apologizing to Gloria. Walking into the kitchen, he grabbed his wife's hand. "I need to go to the office."

"The office?" she asked, surprised. "You just came from there."

"Yes, I apologize. It's — it's something urgent."

"Is everything okay?"

"It is, yes. But I need to get something to Dr. Meron before this evening. Something I forgot at the office."

She nodded, still confused, but said nothing more. He hated hiding the truth from her, but all of this could still be a ridiculous coincidence. He didn't want to overhype something and get everyone worked up.

But if I'm right…

He needed to get the data points from the NARATech offices and plot them on a map, then send whatever he found — *if* he found anything — to Amanda Meron. She hadn't been herself lately, and he knew it had something to do with this project. He wasn't sure what sort of pressure she and Dr. Wu were under, and it wasn't his business to know. But he cared about them; they were his team, his family. If they were feeling any sort of pressure to figure out what this project meant, and the possible ramifications of it, he was going to help in whatever way he could.

It was probably nothing. Probably just another strange recognition that wouldn't lead anywhere in particular. He would analyze the data — his specialty — and find nothing out of the ordinary. Nothing that would bring them closer to finding out why there was an anomaly in their system.

But as he turned onto the main highway that would take him north to the office complex, he had an odd feeling.

What if I'm right? What then?

CHAPTER 10

Ben's head hadn't even hit the pillow before Julie came to his side of the bed and started tapping him on the shoulder.

"Ben. Wake up," she said, her 'whisper' louder than her normal speaking voice.

He rubbed his eyes, then sat up, pushing the hotel pillow up against the headboard to support his back. They'd checked in only an hour ago, Julie insistent that they drive around and 'see the city' before settling down for the night. They'd done a loop around the small downtown district, then she'd made him pull over at a local soccer stadium to take pictures. She told him she'd always been a fan of the sport, and even though she'd never heard of the small club team she was ecstatic to see a 'real' stadium. It was getting dark when they'd left the stadium's parking lot, and Ben knew he'd only get grouchier as the long day wore on, so he made the executive decision — with her permission, of course — to head to the hotel Amanda had told them to stay in.

Julie's and Ben's approaches to staying in a hotel could not have been more different. Ben was practical, utilitarian, about it — he wanted nothing more than a clean bed, a dark room, and solid, lockable interior-facing door. Bonus points if the hotel had a bar, and even better if it had a decent happy hour. He didn't travel a lot, but when he did he enjoyed a quick glass of whiskey in whatever flavor the locals preferred.

Julie, on the other hand, could not care less about the room itself, as long as it was clean. She wanted a hot tub, workout center, and grandiose continental breakfast. Ben loved to remind her that she always forgot her swimsuit, she never used the hotel facilities, and she didn't eat breakfast, but the few times they'd stayed in a hotel somewhere together, Julie always made sure it had her "preferred" amenities.

When they'd entered the room, Julie immediately tossed her suitcase onto the second bed — another "feature" she preferred in rooms — and let her clothes spill out everywhere. She hadn't even finished desecrating the second bed before she decided to start in on the bathroom. By the time Ben got in there, a mere two minutes into their stay, the countertop was covered with hygiene products, makeup, and other accoutrements foreign to Ben.

"What is it?" he said. "I wasn't asleep. Not sure how I was supposed to fall asleep with you pacing around like that. You're stressing me out."

"There's a lot of reason to be stressed out, Ben," she said. "I was on my phone, texting Paulinho."

Ben harrumphed quietly, but loud enough for her to hear.

"Cool it — you're not the jealous type," she responded.

"Yeah, but I'm not the bronzed, soccer-playing Brazilian type, either," he said. "What's up?"

Julie slid her phone in front of Ben's face. "He sent a video. Something Amanda got on her phone. He said it's an update from one of her employees. Then it says, 'URGENT' in all caps."

Ben saw the word, and the video below it. "You haven't watched it?"

She shook her head. "No, it's… overwhelming, I think. I wanted to watch it with you."

As she spoke, Ben saw another text message coming in. He read it aloud. "'Just watched video. Please meet in lobby — on our way to you now.'"

"He didn't even watch it before he sent it? How well did you know him?"

Julie gave him a look that said, *forget about it*, then shoved her finger down on the "play" button on the phone's screen.

She pulled her head in close to Ben's, and he turned the phone slightly so they could both see.

Onscreen, a man wearing a white Oxford shirt, the top two buttons undone, glasses, and the beginning of a line of stubble on his chin, spoke into a computer-mounted camera.

"Dr. Meron, if you're listening to this, it's too —" the screen flickered as a blinding flash of light covered the view momentarily. "... We can't keep them... the facility. Dr. —" He turned to look over his shoulder, then he ducked. Another flash of light, and it looked like the man was struggling to stay seated on the chair. "Dr. Meron, please find their secret."

The video jumped again, and smoke filled the tiny screen. A loud *popping* noise emanated from the device, and even in the relative quietness of it, it was clear the noise would have been *loud* in the actual room. Julie jumped, and then the smoke cleared enough to show the employee's face. He frantically reached up for the camera, pulled it toward his face, and leaned down toward the computer. A shadow loomed behind him, shifting and turning as the man started to speak.

"...No time — please — *pega-palito*..." he repeated the words again, slower, then quickly tried repeating them a last time. "*Pega...* —" the last word was cut off just as another *pop* pushed the level of the phone's speakers, and the man on screen went wide-eyed, then started to slump.

Julie screamed, covering her mouth, and the man fell onto the table. The camera stayed gripped in his hand, filming nothing but the dark, cold look of the dying man right next to it. It attempted to focus on the close-up image, but couldn't. The man's face went blurry, came into focus slightly, then went blurry again.

Even Ben found himself repulsed. The shot continued for a few more seconds, then he saw the screen change. The man was pushed violently to the side, and a larger, black-clad figure silhouetted against the light from the doorway behind them came into view. He turned his head, trying to decipher what was on the screen. Ben leaned in, trying to capture every moment of the action. He focused intently on the man's eyes.

Eyes can tell you everything, his father once told him on a hunting trip.

The man's eyes widened, ever so slightly, then narrowed. *He found something. Something that surprised him.* Ben felt a chill run down his spine and he sat up straighter. *And he wants to keep the information to himself.*

He tried to burn the image of the man's eyes into his mind. The face was masked with black cloth, but the eyes were clear: brownish-green, almost gold-hued in the light from the computer, and sharp.

Deadly sharp.

Ben knew he'd remember them, and he vowed to himself he'd find the man that owned them.

He didn't know the employee — the scientist — that had just been murdered in front of him, but he knew he'd do what he could to figure out what had just happened.

CHAPTER 11

"Okay, okay, slow down," Ben said. "Just explain to us what happened first."

Dr. Amanda Meron had tears streaking down her face, causing the small amount of makeup she was wearing to run and stain lines down her cheeks. She clenched her teeth, then looked up at the three of them. "You *saw* what happened, Harvey. Dr. Ortega is *dead* because of... of whoever *that* was, and you don't want me to call the police?"

Paulinho grabbed her arm. "We will call the police, once we have had a bit more time to understand what exactly is going on. But I have also asked an old friend for help, and he should be here soon. We —"

"Every minute we wait it gets worse! We have to call the police *now!*" she said. She sat down in the large, plush lobby chair just inside the doors of the hotel Juliette and Ben were staying in. After Julie called Paulinho, they made plans to meet up in the hotel, then decide from there what they would do. Julie, at the request of Ben, told both of them to keep the police out of it, at least for now.

Ben shook his head. "No, Dr. Meron, that's just not true. If we call them, we might be detained for questioning, or worse. Drache Global — if that's who is behind this, after all — won't be waiting around. They're going to keep moving." Ben looked over at Paulinho. "Who's this 'old friend' of yours?"

"He runs a survival camp and shooting range here. Ex-Army, a sniper, I believe. Good guy to have next to you in a fight," Paulinho said.

"Well, let's hope we don't need him, then," Ben replied. *But, considering NARATech's headquarters right now…* he knew having someone with some military experience they could at least have nearby was a good move. He gave Paulinho a quick nod.

Amanda Meron sniffed. "So what do you think they're after?"

"We can't be sure, but the little we've been able to dig up about them suggests that they're interested in knowledge."

Julie's face flushed with anger. "*Knowledge?* Ben, these guys —"

"I know what they did, Jules," he said. "But remember, they didn't really *care* about the damage they did, and they certainly weren't afraid to kill anyone who got in their way. But, regardless of our feeling towards them, we have to admit they had an extremely scientific process, and they were absolutely bent on finding out just how far they go with this weapon they built."

Julie shook her head.

"Trust me," Ben continued, "I want them wiped off the face of the planet every bit as much as you do. But we know they're still around, and we know they're working on something. They're smart, they're quick, and they know what they're doing." He turned back to Amanda and Paulinho. "I think they're trying to steal your company's research. They're interested in what you're doing here — we know that because they invested. But they're interested in it for something *bigger* — something larger than just knowledge for the sake of it."

"What are you suggesting?" Paulinho asked.

"I don't know yet, but that's part of the reason we came here. To find out. If I had to guess, they're working on something, and they need what NARATech can provide. More importantly, judging by that video, they don't want any of us getting in their way."

Amanda stood up and started pacing around the sitting area. Her shoes, casual brown flats sequined with sparkling gold circles that could also function as comfortable office-appropriate footwear, clacked against the tiled floor. Ben was tired, and the repetitive clicking sound seemed only to make him want to sleep more. He watched the shoes, zoning out, and then let his eyes travel up the woman's legs, poking out from the bottom of the business skirt she was wearing. Long, skinny, perfect physique —

"Ben."

He whipped around and saw Julie staring at him. He raised an eyebrow.

She repeated the question. "Paulinho thought we should get to the lab, to see what Dr. Ortega was working on when…" her voice trailed off.

"No." Amanda and Ben said simultaneously. They looked at one another, and Amanda came back over to the chairs.

"No," Ben said again. The police — and probably more than that — will already be there, so there's no way we're getting in."

Amanda chimed in. "Dr. Ortega was using the Mac in the back conference room, which means he was probably trying to do more than just leave a message for us."

"What do you mean?" Julie asked.

"That's the computer we use to record our conference sessions. It's encrypted, which they'll no doubt be able to break into eventually, but it's not the computer we use for lab work. All of that is on personal laptops, and —"

"He wanted us to find something on the computer, and that's the only one that would work."

She nodded. "It's the easiest, anyway. There's a screen capture feature, as well as a screen-sharing program. We use it to record and remotely stream our meetings in case any of us are off-site. There's a special cloud-based storage drive we send everything to, as a redundant backup."

"You think he was trying to tell us something else? Something besides *pega-veretas?*" Ben asked.

Again, she nodded. "If he was in the conference room, I'm positive of that. Even if the computer was damaged, whatever he was doing would have been uploaded and stored."

Paulinho looked at Julie, and she stood up. "I'm going to get my laptop."

Amanda smiled, the makeup still smeared on her cheeks. "Thank you — both of you, thank you. I would have brought mine, but I wasn't thinking straight. This is all — I can't…"

"Please," Ben said. "Don't apologize. I know how you're feeling right now."

He offered the two of them coffee as Julie left to retrieve her laptop from their room, three floors above them. There was a percolator machine across the lobby, at one end of the great room. He sauntered over, realizing again how exhausted he was. They'd left Alaska almost two days ago, and aside from a brief wink of sleep on the plane, he'd not seen the inside of his eyelids at all. They'd driven to Anchorage, flown to Seattle, Los Angeles, Panama City, Belo Horizonte, and finally to Marabá. The driving, layovers, and an in-air time of almost thirty hours, made the total trip about thirty-five hours long. He hated flying, and he'd now done more of it in two days than he had in his entire life.

But it was worth it. He had to tell himself that, if not for him than for Julie — he loved the girl, and he didn't want her to be caught up in all of this. But he knew her well, too, and he knew she wouldn't allow herself to be left behind. She'd want to be right in the action, right next to him.

It helped that with her previous full-time role and her current consultant status job at the CDC, she had a line to the higher-ups in DC. If things went belly-up in Brazil, Ben knew she could at least alert the authorities as to their location, and let them know what events had transpired. It was too early in the game to be causing anyone any trouble, and they certainly didn't want to call undue attention to themselves, but Ben was satisfied to know the option was there.

He came up next to the first of the tall, silver machines and reached for a styrofoam cup. He pressed the lip of the cup to the spigot beneath the machine.

And the glass behind him exploded.

CHAPTER 12

Ben felt the air rush around him, and then felt the weightlessness of being lifted completely off the ground. The sensation didn't last long — he was thrown forward and over the coffee table, into the hard drywall of the lobby's south wall.

The sound of it all caught up to him. A blast from the grenade nearly burst his eardrums, and glass shards rained down around him. He fell from the wall, his frontside nearly crushed flat as he crumpled onto the table and then down to the floor. The tall coffee warmers were rolling around the tile, mostly unharmed. He rolled to the side, forcing his exhausted, now-bruised body to cooperate.

Get to Julie.

The thought crossed his mind as if it was on autopilot. All he wanted to do was find a hole somewhere, a place to crawl into and go to sleep; to pretend this was all a sick nightmare.

But they were under attack. The gunfire started next, rattling the rest of the glass sheets that protected the hotel lobby from the outdoors. He heard the unmistakable sound of automatic rifles, seemingly spraying bullets from every possible direction, and he continued the roll. He finally sat up and began crawling, aiming for the doorway-sized gap between the wall and the information and check-in counter.

There had been no one else in the lobby before, just the four of them, and Ben was grateful for that. He reached the counter and pulled himself up to a crouching position, leaning back against the wall to catch his breath. He was out of sight to the front of the building, but he could see — and hear — the bullets landing on the wall over and around the location of the coffee table. The table itself was shredded, the three coffee containers all now leaking and spraying their hot contents into the air.

Smoke and dust from the grenade's blast and crumpling drywall confused the air in front of him, but Ben forced himself to keep his eyes open, to try and see if Paulinho and Amanda were still in the lobby.

Paulinho looked athletic enough, and Ben hoped he fit the description. He couldn't see anyone across the hall from him, and he chose to believe the pair had fled into the smaller hallway behind the lobby after the explosion. The gunfire stopped for a moment, and he saw a pair of soldiers creep into the lobby. They turned from one side to the other, both looking for targets.

We're the targets, Ben realized. He wasn't sure how it was all connected, but he knew these soldiers were the exact same ones that had destroyed Amanda's company and murdered her employee. He felt a surge of anger, then adrenaline, but had the resolve to pause and remember that he wasn't armed. Even if he had been, there would be nothing he could do against their guns and training.

He was a sitting duck, and they were in between him and Julie.

He forced himself to breathe, sliding over a few feet to his left, fully hiding now behind the check-in counter. It wouldn't do much good, but it bought him a few precious seconds.

They're trained well. They're not going to just leave here without searching thoroughly. They'll find me, and then —

He was cut off by the sound of more gunfire, this time farther away.

Jules.

He started breathing faster, now unable to control his excitement. *If they found her...*

He forced the thought out of his mind, knowing it wouldn't lead to anything productive. *You need a plan, Harvey.* He looked around. There wasn't even a fire extinguisher hanging on a wall. The three computers at the check-in station all had keyboards and separate monitors, but if he threw them at the attackers it wouldn't do much more than call attention to himself.

I have to get to Julie. He dared himself to stand up, peering out over the counter.

The soldiers were gone.

The lobby was empty, save for the dust and remnants of smoke still billowing around the ceiling.

He stood up a bit more, now able to see the entire lobby area. Paulinho and Amanda were nowhere to be seen, and neither were the soldiers.

What the hell?

He heard a shout from outside the building, then another stream of gunfire. His eyes caught the far-off flicker of a three-round burst of gunfire from an assault rifle, and he instinctively ducked behind the computer in front of him. The shots never landed, and he rose back up to see the exchange.

Another flash of light — only one this time, and he heard a sickening thud and a scream as the bullet apparently found its mark. Another yell, unintelligible, rang out, followed by more shots.

He watched the exchange for a few more seconds until a huge spotlight lit the parking lot in front of the hotel. The blinding brightness of the yellow glow stung his eyes, but as they adjusted he saw an empty parking lot, full of glistening dew and a thin haze of smoke in the air.

Nothing else moved. He waited a full minute, then another. He thought about reaching for his cell phone to call Julie, but then remembered they hadn't even set up their international service yet.

Another minute passed, and Ben stared at the parking lot until a shadow moved. It grew, the shape of a man emerging from it, silhouetted in the glow. He walked toward the hotel, taking a long, circuitous route through cars and between pillars, obviously attempting to remain behind cover.

He got close to the first of the broken glass walls, and stepped through. He was now in the lobby.

"Paulinho!" he shouted. He raised his weapon, a short, stubby pistol, in front of him. A longer rifle was mounted on his back, diagonally between his shoulder blades.

Ben watched and waited.

"Paulinho? If you're alive, now's a good time to prove it to me, buddy."

Ben held his breath.

Paulinho stepped out from behind the wall separating the lobby from the hallway. Ben winced, waiting for another gunshot or explosion, but none came.

"Well, look at that! You survived!" the man yelled toward an obviously shaken Paulinho.

"Reggie!" Paulinho said. "Are — are you sure it's safe out there?"

Reggie crunched over broken glass strewn about the lobby floor and came to embrace Paulinho.

"It's safe, for now," Reggie said. "They'll be back for their flood wash, though." Reggie motioned toward the massive light array that was pointing at them from the parking lot. "I set up staged-detonation rounds, mostly for effect. Made it seem like a whole squad was up on the hill. They never saw me — decided to get away with what they had, probably to regroup and come back later."

They stood together a moment, then Reggie urged Paulinho toward the wall at the back of the lobby. "Still," he said, "probably smart to get out of the light. Anyone with an aim half as good as mine could hit you from out there."

Paulinho turned to face Ben as he stood from behind the booth.

Ben brushed off his sleeves and jeans, wiping away the dust and fragments of drywall that had collected there. He lifted a hand, still unsteady from the explosions, and waved.

"Harvey!" Paulinho shouted. "Please, join us. Julie is here, too."

Ben felt a wave of relief pass over him. He glanced out toward the parking lot as he started walking through the lobby, but couldn't see anything other than the brilliant light of the flood lamp. He reached the other side, joining Paulinho and Reggie just as they had turned the corner into the hallway.

Julie rushed forward and grabbed Ben, embracing him. Her laptop bag bounced on her shoulder, swinging along behind her as she ran toward him. Amanda stood behind her, terror in her eyes. Ben thought about saying something, but nothing seemed appropriate. The woman had lost her company, her employees had been murdered, and now it was clear she was being hunted. Nothing Ben could say would do anything to calm her.

He looked again at Julie. "Are you okay?"

"I — I heard everything, and then I looked out, and… I rushed downstairs when it all started."

He squeezed her, then let go. "I'm fine. Glad you're okay. Did you see anyone else in the halls?"

"There were a couple of families, and a few other people. We all ducked into our rooms when it started, but I think the hotel's mostly empty."

Paulinho introduced Reggie to the group. "This is Reggie, our history expert. He's also an ex-Army sniper."

Reggie bowed with a practiced flourish, and grinned. "*American* Army, in case you were wondering. Glad to meet you. Sorry it's got to be under these *less-than desirable* circumstances."

Ben immediately felt turned off by the man and his cockiness. He was about the same age as Ben, mid-forties by the looks of it, but he hadn't lost an ounce of his Army-days physique. Chiseled jawline, hardened brow, and the ability to smile with his mouth, yet keep his eyes cold and calculating.

Ben stuck out a hand, preparing for the man's death grip. It came, and Ben forced himself to keep his expression muted as he felt his fingers and palm being crushed together in the vice grip.

"We owe you a thanks," Ben said. "I'm not sure we'd be alive without you."

The man waved off the thanks. "It's nothing. Just glad Paulinho had the sense to give me a ring before it all went to hell here. I like history, but I *really* like a good fight." He turned and looked behind them at the devastation in the lobby. Pieces of ceiling tile and lighting fixtures littered the floor, and dust and chunks of wall continued to fall as they became fully dislodged from the structure. Ben could hear police and ambulance sirens ringing out from the distance, closing in.

"Like I said, though, we should be clearing out. They'll be back, and I'm guessing they'll be a little better prepared."

"Where are we going to go?" Amanda suddenly asked. It was clear what her question really meant: *Can we really hide from them?*

Reggie considered it a moment. "You're the girl they're after, right?"

She nodded. "Amanda Meron," she said.

"*Dr.* Amanda Meron," Paulinho added.

Reggie raised an eyebrow. "Then we just need to hide *you*. They don't want anything to do with the rest of us."

Amanda looked confused. "Excuse me?"

Reggie burst out a laugh. "I'm kidding!" He smiled, surprised for some reason that no one else shared his affection for mildly off-color humor. Ben watched him closely, still not trusting the man that had saved their lives. In an instant, his facial expression changed. His eyes and brow receded back to its prior state of cold nothingness, and the smile was replaced with the look of someone who'd been through enough in life to deserve a serious outlook on it. "Here's the plan: I'm in charge, at least until we're clear of these bozos. When I say we're safe, *then* — and *only* then — do we try to figure out what they want with you, Doc."

Everyone but Ben nodded, and Reggie continued. "However, we do need a destination, so we might as well get somewhere safe that might also help us along. Any ideas? A library? An office?"

Amanda shook her head. "No, just somewhere with a good internet connection. Julie — the laptop?"

Julie's face brightened a bit. "Right! I forgot all about that." She swung the laptop bag around and unzipped the top, showing off the silver machine tucked inside. "Here it is."

Amanda explained to Reggie. "Let's move out. Anywhere but here. We think Dr. Ortega — one of my employees — was trying to tell us something. I'll need to access our shared folder from the secure cloud backup site."

Reggie was already moving down the hallway, but he nodded and motioned for them to follow. "Right on. Sounds good; let's take the side exit, see if we can't get out and around the building. I parked over the hill in the parking lot next door, and we can all fit there."

"What about their stuff?" Paulinho asked.

"Right, and our rental car?" Julie added. Ben and Julie had a rental, but Paulinho and Amanda had driven over in Amanda's hatchback.

"You won't need it anymore," Reggie said, still talking over his shoulder. "Besides, you ever see those movies with the cars that blow up when you turn the key?"

Julie shot a glance at Ben, but he didn't say anything. *This guy's sick,* Ben thought. *But he seems to be confident enough to get us through this.* And if Ben knew anything about these situations, it was that confidence — if nothing else — just might be enough to carry them through.

CHAPTER 13

They drove for what seemed like hours, toward Reggie's self-described "compound." He wouldn't give more detail until they'd arrived, but only said that it was where he lived and worked when he wasn't in the city. When Ben awoke again and looked at the dash clock, he was surprised to see that they had, in fact, driven for nearly two hours. Straight north, almost reaching into the lower basin of the world-famous jungle territory. Most of the drive was pitch black, and Julie and Ben had used the time to catch up on their sleep.

Amanda and Paulinho were on Julie's laptop, using Reggie's ad-hoc wireless network from his cellphone to connect the computer to the internet and download the information Dr. Ortega had left for them.

Julie had been right — Dr. Ortega had indeed been trying to tell them something, without the information getting into the wrong hands. He'd meticulously organized the images in the folders into numbered files, then uploaded an explanatory video he'd titled *pega-veretas*. The video was large, and since the phone had an almost-unusable download speed, they'd been waiting the entire drive to discover what the video and files were all about.

Ben heard a gentle *ding* as the download finished, and he nudged Julie. She wiped a trickle of drool from the side of her mouth, then looked up at the computer on Amanda's lap in the front seat.

"It's done," Amanda said. Paulinho stretch up in the seat behind

Amanda's, next to Ben, and looked over her shoulder at the screen. "Ready?"

She pressed play before anyone could respond.

"Dr. Meron, if you're watching this, there is a good chance I am dead. I…" the man in the video, Dr. Juan Ortega, swallowed hard, then clenched his teeth and began again. *"I — I'm sorry. Please tell my family that I love them, and…"* He couldn't finish the statement. *"Yes. You know. Well, at approximately 8:55pm, the NARATech facilities were breached and entered by what appears to be a military operation. They immediately shot and killed our two guards on duty, and raced toward the main laboratory section, where I was testing a theory. I was able to move to the conference room and begin uploading this video, along with some of the research that I believe proves my theory."*

The man was analytical, and Ben could tell he was trying to outline the events in as clear and concise way as possible. To him, it must have seemed surreal, but his education and training took over and he tried to keep his voice steady for the camera, providing as much detail as possible that might be useful in the inevitable police investigation that would follow.

"I will try to send a quick update directly to your phone, but it will no doubt be low quality. Since you are watching this video, you've obviously seen that video, and the message therein. Here is the entire message: I have a theory about the golden man we have seen in the dreams of the subjects. 'Pega-veretas' is a game I play with my daughters. I saw the sticks, and how some of them seemed to point in a certain direction."

The man paused once more, gathering his thoughts, then continued.

"There is not time to fully describe my thought process, so unfortunately the scientific method will have to wait." He smiled. *"I'm sure you can understand the results I've collected in these folders."*

The video ended, abruptly, and Ben wondered if there was supposed to be more to it. He almost asked, but Amanda and Paulinho seemed more concerned with the files tucked away in each of the folders.

"What's the 'golden man?'" Julie asked.

Paulinho seemed stumped as well, so they all waited for Amanda to respond. When she did, she turned to her left to address all of the small SUV's occupants.

"It's exactly what it sounds like. A man, completely gold-colored, that we've been observing."

"Like *watching*?" Paulinho asked.

"Yes, but in our subjects' dream-states. They have dreams, we observe the dreams and record what video we can, and then discuss the results when they wake up. But in some of our subjects we're seeing this golden man. He's always looking directly at us."

"How is he looking at you?"

"Well, technically it's an impression from the subject's subconscious imaging. Their mind is preparing the image of the golden man, and they are preparing it in a way that the man is always looking directly at the subject — what we have been calling the 'camera.'"

Ben shuddered. The research they were doing at NARATech was even creepier than he'd initially thought. Recording dreams? 'Watching' peoples' memories?

"This golden man has been the subject of much debate in my company for the past month. We couldn't figure out why he shows up in only some of our patients' memories, and why the patients themselves have no idea who he is."

Ben leaned forward in the chair. "Wait a second — the patients don't *know* about the golden man?"

Amanda shook her head. "No. They're completely clueless, and sometimes even argumentative when we show them the playback of the recording. They're adamant they've never seen the man before."

They sat in silence for a moment, taking it all in. They turned left onto a long, dirt road, and Amanda spoke again. "What's more, our technology isn't strong enough to clearly transpose all of the electrical signals output by the brain. We generally get close, and we can tell, for example, that a subject is walking down a street, or driving, or at a party, but we can't see faces clearly, and most objects are blurry shades of light."

Ben waited for her to say, '*but.*'

"But," she said, "the golden man — when he shows up — is *always* perfectly in focus. Every time, without fail. No matter where in the images he appears, he's perfectly outlined, and we can even see his facial features."

Ben had almost forgotten that Reggie was in the front seat, driving, until he spoke up.

"Sounds like you've stumbled on something worth killing for. I'd say you're in over your head, but I'm no expert."

CHAPTER 14

Julie was shaken, but did her best to keep her fears hidden. If Ben had taught her anything, it was that no good could come from broadcasting your fears and insecurities to the world. She wasn't sure she completely believed him, but she had to admit that forcing herself to calm down, breathe, and exude confidence instead of weariness was at least helping her keep cool in the situation.

So far, they'd been shot at, nearly blown up, threatened, and chased, and there was no sign that it would stop anytime soon. Julie wanted to go home, to go back to their quaint, beautiful, and simple cabin in the woods deep in the heart of Alaska, but she knew she couldn't.

As Ben said, there were problems you ran from, and problems you didn't. She wasn't entirely sure what it meant, but it always seemed to make sense in the situation. So far they'd only experienced the type of problem you weren't supposed to run from, and this "problem," she knew, was also that type of problem.

Ben was probably the most stubborn person she'd ever met, save for her father and grandfather, but Ben was definitely the closest to her. He'd made it his mission to find Drache Global, Drage Medisinsk, or Dragonstone, whomever they might be, and bring them to justice. It was a long shot, and it was likely going to get him killed, but there was nothing she could do to convince him of that.

She'd even tried leaving, but she couldn't do it. Hours of arguing and slamming doors had taught her that there was *nothing* that could force them apart, except, ironically, death. It was an interesting game, fighting about something that might lead to death, but being unable to win the game without actually dying.

She thought about that now, as the SUV pulled onto the fourth and final dirt road, this one a long driveway that led to a run-down shack sitting in the middle of nowhere. It was unbelievably small, no more than ten feet wide, and Julie had to do a double-take when she realized it was the only real building in the area.

Surely we're not going there?

A large hill rose up from behind the house, casting it in an even deeper shadow than the night was able to provide. Set a good distance away from the house, Julie could see a lone light, affixed to a tall pole, gently illuminating a tiny four-walled structure, in a pale yellow glow. This building, too small to be anything more than a simple storage shed, sat next to a long, covered area lined with picnic tables, plastic chairs, and chest-high wooden benches.

"The shooting range is to the left, and the survival course's main camp is directly behind the house, going up and over the hill." The man driving, the former Army sniper Paulinho had introduced as Reggie, motioned with his head as he described each station. "We use the range year-round, but I'm only running a winter course right now. Better weather for it, I guess, so people were only signing up then." He chuckled, then grinned. "Kind of seems pointless to me, to only prepare for the worst during the best time of year."

He pulled up to the shack, and Julie could see that it was completely dark inside. The only light in the entire area, actually, was the light pole near the shooting range. Reggie put the car in park, then turned to address the occupants inside with him. "Stay here a sec, while I disable the defense system. Shouldn't be any trouble, but it's outdated, and I can't afford an upgrade right now."

While he said it, he pulled out his phone and opened an app. "Also," he added, flicking around on the screen of his phone with an outstretched index finger, "let there be light."

With a dramatic flourish, he poked at the screen and the entire compound was brilliantly lit up in daylight-bright white light.

Julie involuntarily brought her arm up, shielding her eyes, while Amanda and Paulinho gasped audibly.

Reggie laughed again. "Impressive, no? One of the best home defenses you can invest in is great lighting. Anyone sneaking onto my property in the middle of the night will have to be invisible if they don't want to be seen."

He tilted his head to the side. "Actually, I take that back. They'd still be seen. They just wouldn't know it until the *other* defenses kicked in."

No one in the SUV asked what the 'other defenses' were, and Julie was partly glad they didn't. She hadn't been able to decide if she trusted Reggie or not, though he had been the one who'd saved them from the terrible onslaught at the hotel. Part of her wanted to trust the man, but another part of her seemed to sense the hesitation in Ben, and borrow it from him.

After a minute of playing with his phone, Reggie finally looked up and unlocked the car doors. "Great. I think that's most of them. Home sweet home." He pulled the handle and exited the vehicle. Paulinho did as well, followed by Amanda, then Ben and Julie. It felt good to stretch her legs, but she could also feel the fatigue of adrenaline and lack of sleep finally setting in. Whatever the plan was, she hoped it involved sleeping — safely — for a few hours at least.

"Let's get you all inside, then figure out this 'golden man' stuff," Reggie said. He led the way into the miniature home, the four others trailing behind, still skeptical. He paused at the front door, turning around. "What are you waiting for? Let's go!" Reggie poked out a sequence of numbers on a tiny numerical lock control mounted above the door handle, and the door clicked and swung open.

Julie reached the door next, followed by Ben and the others, and she stopped at the threshold. Reggie had disappeared.

She stepped a foot into the building and then saw a staircase to her left, strategically hidden from view from outside the house. Reggie popped his head up the stairs. "Come on," he said. "Ain't got all night." The man's head disappeared again from view, and Julie followed.

The stairs turned once, then opened up a flight below the floor into a strikingly different setting. A basement room, easily three times the size of the main building above her, awaited. A couch, two armchairs, and a well-appointed bar faced her, spaced out nicely against the backdrop of a beautiful, early nineteenth-century English decor. Wallpaper, crisply glued and in perfect condition, covered the three walls she could see, and an arched entryway led further into the dwelling.

"My ex-wife put most of the furnishings in here. I'm a stickler for order and cleanliness, so I probably would have made it look like a hospital room if it were up to me." Reggie was already behind the bar, pouring himself a glass of bourbon. He swished it around in the glass as the others joined Julie downstairs, and he held it up to them. "You'd actually be surprised at the quality in beverage choices here," he said. "Good enough to make any American proud."

He held up the glass, a signal of offering to the rest of the group, but only Ben obliged. He stepped up to the front of the bar, pulled out a gorgeous solid wood barstool and sat on it. Reggie seemed more than pleased to pour the man a drink, and Ben held it up, inspecting the color.

Julie thought the two of them might completely disregard the rest of the team, consumed by their love for fine spirits, so she cleared her throat.

Amanda walked closer to the bar. "Mr., uh — Reggie…" Reggie looked up but didn't offer his last name to the woman. "Sorry… I mean, thanks. Thank you for what you did back there."

He nodded, scrunching his face slightly to exaggerate the expression.

"But, we, uh…" her voice trailed off.

"I know," he said, interrupting the awkward silence. "You need to find out who wants to kill you."

Her eyes widened slightly, probably surprised at the man's bluntness, but then she nodded.

"Yep, working on it."

Julie watched the man pour himself another glass, then refill Ben's. He carefully placed the bottle back on the rack it came from, the unlabeled decanter facing perfectly out toward the room. He turned back to Ben. "That's a 1970, and it goes down about as well as anything twice the price. I know the guy who makes it — local, actually."

Julie watched as Ben closed his eyes and took a long sip.

Unbelievable.

Ben was the type of man who could so focus on one thing she often thought there was something wrong with him. She often told him he'd die one day pushing himself too hard, unable to quit when he needed a break. The only two things she'd ever known to be able to break him from his focus was herself, offering something he couldn't provide on his own, and a good glass of whiskey.

And this glass of whiskey must have been particularly good. He'd essentially blocked out everything else around him, taking in the aroma, then the taste, then the feel of the liquor.

He looked at her, and she raised her eyebrows. *Done?*

He snapped out of it. "Sorry, just… it's good."

She wanted to smack him. "I'll get a bottle of it for you before we leave."

"No, can't do that," Reggie said, unaware of the unspoken fight going on between Ben and Julie. "It's local, but it's not actually for sale. Sorry. I might be able to —"

"Listen, Reggie Whoever You Are. We're really thankful that you're here and all, and that you've taken us in to your underground safe house, but we *really* need to figure out who's behind all of this. And I —"

Reggie held up his pointer finger, giving Julie the immediate urge to smack him as well. "We're already working on it."

This time, Paulinho, Amanda, *and* Ben seemed surprised.

CHAPTER 15

"I forwarded the file from Amanda's phone to my own online storage system when you were sleeping." He reached below the bar and pulled out a shiny silver remote control. Pressing buttons on it, Julie watched as a huge projector screen rolled down from the ceiling and onto the wall nearest Ben, opposite the couch. "Wasn't any trouble, since it wasn't encrypted anyway. Still wouldn't have been, since I've got…"

Reggie realized the others were staring at him.

"Look, I'm not a hacker. It was easy enough. The point is that I wanted to have it ready to queue up here in the house, so we wouldn't have to wait around any longer. Grab a seat, let's figure this out."

He grabbed his glass and headed over to one of the armchairs. Ben and Julie followed, and soon they were all seated facing the giant screen. True to his word, Reggie had gotten the video and other files downloaded onto whatever computer he had hidden in the house, and the main video was loaded up and ready to go.

"We don't need to see this again, correct?" he asked to no one in particular. When no one answered, he hit a button and went back to a directory listing of the other files. Clicking the first one, he sat back in the chair, relaxing into the comfortable plush of the upholstered furniture piece.

Julie watched the screen as a map appeared. It was a map of the

Amazon Basin in the center, but zoomed out enough to show nearly the entire continent of South America. Rio de Janeiro was at the bottom-right of the map, labeled in handwritten text that had been painted on the digital image.

He pressed forward and watched as the screen changed. The same map was displayed onscreen, but another handwritten label appeared. *'Cristo Redentor,' #1,* was written above a line that stretched from Rio to the edge of the top-left of the map, cutting through the Amazon basin.

"Christ the Redeemer," Paulinho said, translating from Portuguese. Julie immediately recalled the image of the large statue of Christ in her mind, sitting with arms outstretched atop a Brazilian mountain.

They stared at the image a moment, then Reggie progressed to the next image. This image was the same map, but the line changed almost imperceptibly, and the label as well: *'Cristo Redentor,' #2.*

A third image came up; still the same map, but another line, and another label: *'Teatro Municipal.'*

There were only three images in the folder, so Reggie scrolled through the directory and went to the second of the folders, one labeled *'Florianopolis.'*

The first image appeared, the map shifting slightly and yet another line appearing. The label read, *'Hercilio Luz.'*

Paulinho explained. "Hercilio Luz is a well-known bridge in Florianoplis, Brazil."

Reggie scrolled through five more images, each with a perfectly straight line drawn on it in a slightly different location, and each with a unique label. Julie was amazed at the clarity of the writing, and the lines, no doubt traced with a ruler by Dr. Ortega moments before his death.

They scrolled through a few more folders, mostly labeled after locations and in Brazil, but there were a few from around the world. One was as far away as Paris, France, and showed the location of the Eiffel Tower, the diagonal line superimposed on the map connecting the two locations.

"What do the locations have to do with your research, Dr. Meron?" Julie asked. Amanda hadn't spoken since they'd arrived, and Julie wasn't sure what the woman was thinking.

"I don't know yet," she said. "I'm not sure why Dr. Ortega went through all this trouble. It seems like he's just drawing lines from the location of the subjects we studied to… something else."

"Locations of what, though?" Paulinho asked. "Where the subjects were born? Or where they were last known to be living?"

"I don't think so. The labels are of tourist attractions, and I remember some of these tests. The dreams we recorded sometimes had very recognizable scenery in them. The Christ the Redeemer statue was particularly striking in some of them, and I'm sure the Eiffel Tower would have been, as well."

"So these people — subjects — visited these locations," Ben said. "Then Ortega drew lines from the locations to… something else. So what?"

"Dr. Ortega wouldn't have gone through the trouble if he didn't —" Amanda's voice stopped mid-sentence.

"What is it?" Paulinho asked.

"Pega-veretas," Amanda said. "What does it mean?"

"It's a game, just like he said," Paulinho answered. He paused a moment, trying to think of the best translation from Portuguese. "Rods, or sticks — '*pick-up the sticks*,' I believe it's called."

CHAPTER 16

Ben had seen this game before. Sticks, or rods, laying on each other on the floor, and two players attempted to pick them up one at a time without disturbing the other sticks. He'd never played it, but he'd seen it in toy stores as a kid. Amanda stood and walked to the map, pointing at the line. "He's drawing the 'sticks' on the maps," she said. She was getting excited, and Paulinho and Reggie stood to join her near the map. "Reggie, go back. What other folders are there?"

Reggie followed her instruction, showing them the list of folders within the directory. Amanda read the list, then pointed. "There! *'Zoomed images.'* Pull that one up."

Reggie did, and the first of the images appeared onscreen. The label was one they'd seen before: *'Cristo Redentor, #2.'* The line also appeared, drawn to extend past the edge of the image toward the top-left of the screen. But the map itself was zoomed in much closer to the Christ the Redeemer statue. They could see the outline of the mountain's topography, dotted nearby with the unmistakable shape of houses and buildings. What was most evident, however, was the word *'subject,'* scrawled in Portuguese near the base of the mountain.

There was a tiny 'x' near the word, and the line began and extended from it.

The next image was similar, but with a different 'x' and a different line.

"All the lines are diagonal, from top-left to bottom-right," Julie said. "Or vise-versa."

The next image, however, changed that theory. It was another 'x,' another 'subject,' and yet another line, but this one was sharply descending from the top-right of the screen to the bottom-left. The title of the image was "Estátua da Liberdade."

"The Statue of Liberty," Paulinho immediately translated.

"It seems like the lines are all pointing at the same spot, right?" Julie asked.

As soon as she said it, Ben spoke up. "Is there a folder with all of the lines added to one map?" he asked.

Reggie flicked through the folders again and found one labeled *'Convergence'* in Portuguese. He clicked on the first image, and everyone in the room gasped. Ben stood up and walked toward the screen.

"They're all converging on the *exact same point,*" she whispered. "It's... just like he said. 'Pick-up sticks,' but the sticks are these lines. They all cross each other, at some point in..." her voice trailed off.

Amanda picked up the rest of the sentence. "...In the Amazon rainforest. Reggie, can you print these?"

Reggie nodded. "Of course." He navigated around the menu system on the computer.

Ben squinted at the top-left of the map, mostly centered on the upper half of the South American continent, and saw the words *'Floresta Amazônica'* written in the same clear, delineated handwriting. There was a circle hastily drawn around the convergence point of the lines, and they all took a moment to examine the map.

"But where is he getting the directionality of the lines?" Reggie asked. He navigated back to the list of folders, searching for anything that might be helpful. Paulinho told him to stop at one of the last folders.

"Positioning Screenshots, or Placement Screenshots," he said as

Reggie entered the folder. Ben examined the first image. It was nothing more than a splash of color, shades of lighter and darker colors, all blended together, with a grid carefully drawn on top of the entire image. Lighter blues and yellows appeared near the top, and darker shades toward the bottom. On the bottom-right of the screen, against a background that was a similar golden shade, he saw a man staring straight at him. As Dr. Meron had explained, the man was perfectly in focus. It was too small an image to see the man's facial features, but Ben could tell the man was standing in front of something large. He forced his eyes out of focus, and an image seemed to appear around the golden man.

"Christ the Redeemer," Julie said aloud. He saw it too. A fuzzy triangle dominated the image, dead-center, with a much smaller triangle of a bluish tone sitting on top of it. There was sky around the "statue," and Ben knew it was a view looking up at the statue, the mountain itself covering most of the picture. The golden man was placed in the image, standing still and, as always, looking straight at the subject.

"Well, if that ain't the creepiest thing I've ever seen," Reggie said.

Ben had to agree. He'd never seen anything like it, and it wasn't even a faked image. "You mean this is a screenshot of a *recording* of someone's dream?" he asked.

Dr. Meron nodded. "We're getting better every month at rendering the images. More and more sensors, designed to pick up the exact locations of neurons firing in the brain, allow the computers to project certain lights, colors, and pictures onto a screen. It's just creating a visual representation of what's happening electronically in the brain."

"This is amazing," Julie said. "How do you even do something like this?"

Amanda nodded again. "Thank you. It's been a long process, but the basic technology and techniques have been in place for years. We started with an eight-by-eight grid of lights placed on a piece of board in front of our subjects, and when we'd light one of the lights, a certain area in the brain would light up as well. The same place would light up the same way every time, and by tracking that information thousands of times with hundreds of subjects, we were eventually able to create a 'map' of the brain. That map could then be used in reverse: we told the subjects to think of one of the lights lighting up. To actually picture it in their mind.

When they did, the same areas of the brain would light up the same way, as if they were physically seeing the lightbulb turn on and off. Eventually, that research allowed us to know what type of image, for the most part, their brain was conjuring up."

Reggie smiled. "Fascinating. Then, naturally, you took it a step further, and started recording their dreams?"

"Dreaming and how dreams are produced is one of the most understudied fields in neuroscience, because it has been impossible to 'see' someone else's dream. We've had to work from descriptions, and as you all know, remembering a dream that happened the night before can sometimes be a challenge."

Ben agreed, but he still wasn't sure what this all meant, and what Drache Global wanted to do with it.

"So, again, how is Dr. Ortega determining directionality?" Ben asked.

They all turned back to the image onscreen. "It seems like he's calculated approximately where the golden man is standing, in relation to the subject and the recognizable scenery in the image. In this case, the statue of Christ the Redeemer."

Paulinho pointed at the two elements in the image, the golden man and the statue. "He drew a grid over the image, probably to help determine distance. I guess you could theoretically calculate distance by measuring the size of the statue, and where the subject is in relation to it, since we easily know that information. Then you could triangulate the location of the man, and in what direction he's facing."

"Yes," Dr. Meron said. "Yes, you could. It seems to me that the man in the image is placed so a line could be drawn from the subject, to the golden man."

"The same 'lines' we've been seeing on the other maps."

"I wouldn't be surprised," she responded.

They played around with the images in the folders, guessing and estimating, and tracing the lines on the large projector screen. Each of the images in the 'Placement Screenshots' folder showed a similar image: an out-of-focus view of an easily recognizable tourist attraction or major location, and a golden man standing somewhere in the image. Every time they imagined a line segment connecting the subject to the man, then extended the line segment beyond the golden man, they realized there was a corresponding map of that exact scene, viewed from above. Dr. Ortega had drawn in all of the lines, extending them off each of the maps.

Reggie pulled up the convergence map once more. "I'd have to say Dr. Ortega has done some fine work here. I'm no map expert, but I've done my fair share of planimetric and topographic navigation. Everything seems to check out."

No one disagreed, but Ben asked the question that had been on his mind since they'd seen the convergence point. "So, we've got a golden man showing up in people's dreams, and this little man is trying to point us somewhere. We know it's somewhere in the rainforest, but the question I'm wondering is: what *exactly* is he pointing us to?"

No one answered.

Finally, Amanda spoke up. "I don't know. I have no idea what this is, and we couldn't figure out what any of this 'golden man' stuff meant a month ago. But Dr. Ortega died trying to tell us, and I want to go find out what it is."

Reggie raised his eyebrows. "You're being chased by a group of military-trained killers, and you want to go traipsing out in the jungle? If they don't kill you first, the jungle surely will."

"I think what we've discovered here has something to do with why they're trying to kill me," Amanda said.

"I don't doubt it, girly, but that doesn't mean it's a smart idea to just run into the most deadly environment on Earth, chasing a creepy dream-dude."

"Reggie," Paulinho said. "You're a skilled survivalist, and you teach camps for people —"

"I *teach*, I don't run into the jungle with an army trying to kill me."

"But you could help us get there?"

Ben watched the man's jaw clench and unclench a few times, trying to decide what to do.

"We'd have an advantage out there for a little while at least, that's for sure. I doubt they're expecting a deep-jungle campaign, and I know they're not as prepared for it as I would be. I can keep us alive, I think, as long we stay ahead of them. But if they catch up…"

Ben walked over to Reggie and clapped him on the shoulder. "I'm going into the jungle, Reggie. You've already helped us more than we could ever repay, but I have to ask for your help once more. You're not obligated to come with us, but I'm going."

Reggie looked Ben up and down. "'Bout as stubborn as I'd suspected." He walked back over to the bar and poured himself another drink, this time a much taller one.

"Fine," Reggie said. "Let's do it. Let's go find this little golden man's secret."

CHAPTER 17

Reggie left the group in the living room of his underground bunker and walked into the rear rooms of his home. It was a relatively small layout, less than 2,000 square feet, but it was more than enough for him. The main living room and bar was the showpiece, where he entertained his wealthier clients and sold his high-end survival camp packages to corporate executives. They always wanted the 'best of the best,' even though they had no idea what that meant. It was a cycle of men trying to impress other men, and weekend-long survival camps were the new golf courses of Brazilian business networking.

He'd originally designed his packages for people like him — well-trained military types who wanted to keep their edge after their active-duty deployments. He had a few clients who paid him for range use, but most of the people who frequented his camps were nothing more than enviro-tourists, generally clueless about the world at large, but interested in 'saving the whales' or whatever else they decided they were into that month.

After a few bad reviews and numerous complaints about the extreme difficulty level of his 'best of the best' courses from the executives and enviro-tourists who couldn't take it, he crafted a much more appealing survival camp: one that mixed semi-primitive camping with a few classes on fire starting and basic survival techniques, spread out over the course of a weekend. Clients drove in on Friday evenings and could be back in their lumbar-supporting office chairs early Monday morning. He taught them nothing they couldn't learn in a Boy

Scout handbook, but took out any of the details that required them to actually do anything physically demanding.

In order to maintain his *own* edge — and sanity — he created a few more courses for the clients who were *actually* interested in wilderness survival techniques. He had a shelter-building course, a mini-course on fire building, and a long-term Expedition Training Course that was his pride and joy. The course took twelve students on a two-week-long adventure into the rainforest, carrying nothing but a single backpack that held worst-case scenario gear like navigation equipment and fire-starter materials, a first aid kit, and MRE rations. He carried the pack himself, and slept near it, to ensure that none of the students snuck anything out of it in the middle of the night.

Reggie prided himself on the fact that none of his students had ever needed to use the backpack.

Still, he kept a few of the backpacks stocked and ready to go, in case he ever needed to "bug out" of his bunker.

It was these backpacks he was looking for. The hallway connecting the living room and bar area of his bunker to the two back bedrooms and kitchen had a centralized bathroom on side, and a large, walk-in closet on the other. In the closet he kept a gun safe for his personal collection, some overstock products he sold at the range and for the classes, and the backpacks.

They were customized Kelty Falcon 4000 packs, each slightly reconfigured to match his body type. He preferred these models that had a smaller main compartment and extra additional pockets attached to the pack's frame. Each of the three packs were stocked similarly, but one had an additional Stingray tent inside for traveling with a larger party. One of these packs was enough for one person to survive up to a month; with rationing, three people could survive for a few weeks, assuming they couldn't find their own fresh water and food.

Since he would be traveling with the group, they wouldn't even need a pack — he was more than capable of keeping them alive for some time, barring injuries. But Reggie had considered the circumstances and decided that taking the packs would offer extra protection, security, and support for whatever journey might lie ahead. Not knowing their exact destination already placed them at a disadvantage, and they were about to journey into one of the most dangerous types of wilderness climates. He didn't want to doom them to failure before they even left the house.

He grabbed one of the packs and unzipped the top flap. He added the folded printouts of the image of the convergence of lines over the rainforest, the best version of a 'map' they'd get, and checked the rest of the contents and did a quick inventory. Deeming it ready for use, he repeated the process with other packs and walked over to the gun safe. Unlocking it using a fingerprint from his left index finger, he swung open the great door and selected some of the pieces inside.

Three Sig Sauer P226 9mm handguns and a rifle, a Henry-Arms AR-7. He was a fan of the rifle's footprint — broken down it could fit inside his pack, and was a mere 3.5 pounds. The .22-caliber ammunition was a bit small for the 'stopping power posse,' the group of weapon-heads and survivalists who believed that larger ammunition — more 'stopping power' — was always better, but he'd used the AR-7 as a go-to weapon without a problem. He placed the pistols in the main compartment of the backpack and began lashing the rifle to the outside.

As he did, he felt a gentle rumbling beneath the bunker's floor. The floor was nothing more than smoothed concrete, two feet thick, but he hadn't placed anything over the bare surface in the closet. He looked down, waiting for the rumbling sound to end. It lasted a few seconds, drifting off into nothingness, then started again.

He felt a surge of adrenaline even before he fully understood what the sound meant. Slamming the gun safe's door closed and waiting for the nearly inaudible *click* of the lock, he left the pack where it lay on the floor and ran back into the living room.

"We're going to be attacked. Those are shells, and I need everyone here to remain calm and start heading up the stairs."

The others around the room — his friend Paulinho, Dr. Amanda Meron, and Ben and Julie — still discussing the images on the projector screen, looked at him as if he was insane.

"Sorry," he said. "Can't really explain now, but there was a shaking sound. I recognized it, but you just need to trust me. Amanda, they found us. Somehow."

At that, Amanda stood and stared at him, wide-eyed.

"It's fine," he said, hoping to reassure her. "They're not here yet, but they know I've got an underground bunker. I built this place to be a home, not a fortress, so they'll eventually get in. We need to be out of here well before that."

She nodded, and Ben walked toward him. "What do you need me to do?"

Reggie paused a moment, taking in the large, well-built man in front of him. *He's starting to trust me. Good.* "Thanks, Ben," he said. "Grab the two backpacks in that closet, the ones up against the wall. I'll get the one next to the gun safe, and then we're out."

He turned to the rest of the group as Ben slid by him and into the hallway. "Head up the stairs, but wait at the top until Ben and I are there. There's a back door on the shack that'll lead us out and over that hill. I expect to be well-hidden and almost into the trees by the time they start shelling the house."

He didn't wait for the rest to follow instructions. He turned and followed Ben into the closet to get the rest of the gear, only taking a moment to assess the group his fate was now tied with.

In all his years training and preparing survivalists, he knew only one characteristic that separated the 'executives' and 'tourists' from the real-deal, hardcore survivors.

Mindset.

He hoped that the group now following him into the most excruciating climate he'd ever known had the mindset of staying alive.

CHAPTER 18

The shells were working their way closer to the bunker. Ben saw dust and small rocks falling from the crevices between the slabs of concrete that made up the walls, and he winced every time one of them landed.

"They're getting closer," Ben said to Reggie as he swung the two packs over his shoulders.

"They're not aiming for the shack. Not yet, anyway. They're aiming for where they think the other bunkers are."

"*Other* bunkers?"

Reggie grinned. "Come on, let's get upstairs. Yeah, I submitted plans to the county when I had this place built. They're pretty particular about excavating and digging around here, so close to the forest. The plans showed thirteen smaller bunkers, all spread around my land. Couple hundred acres."

Ben had to laugh. "So you just submitted plans that would be in the public record, showing that you had a bunch of random bunkers around here."

Reggie nodded once. "Yep. Nothing like fake plans for an extra layer of defense."

Ben followed Reggie up the stairs, where the others were waiting.

He noticed now, seeing the shack from the inside, that the walls were also concrete, the outside of the building obviously built with a facade.

Yet another layer of defense.

"Reggie, it seems like you've spent quite a bit of money protecting yourself down here," Ben said. "Why all the security?"

Reggie just shrugged. "Seemed like a good idea at the time." He didn't elaborate, instead changing the subject back to the situation at hand. "Come on, out the back door when I say 'go.' Run straight ahead, over that hill, and don't stop running until you're well into the woods. Ben, you take the lead. I'll follow behind."

Ben nodded, and stood by the closed door.

"Oh," Reggie said, turning once again to face Ben. "Here, take this." He handed Ben a handgun, pewter-colored and heavy. "Sig Sauer P226 9mm."

Ben turned the weapon over in his hands a few times. He wasn't a pro, but he'd handled a fair share of firearms as a park ranger and growing up hunting with his father and brother. He felt the gun's weight, checked the magazine, and nodded at Reggie.

"Good deal," Reggie said. "Oh, and do not let the Brazilian authorities catch you with that. They're not too fond of locals or tourists carrying them around, and even if they don't arrest you on the spot they'll detain you longer than TSA when they find some tweezers."

A shell landed right next to the shack, and Ben felt his insides vibrate with the explosion. The shack itself stood strong, but pieces of rock and ceiling material rained down around them. Amanda covered her ears.

"Go!" Reggie yelled. He pulled the door open and shoved Ben out. Ben started running, heading straight for the tall hill that stood behind the house. He pushed his legs as hard as he could, hoping the others would be able to catch up.

He rounded the top of the hill and continued down the other side, suddenly realizing he was about to walk into the densest forest he'd ever seen. Whereas the woods he was comfortable with back home were mostly large pines, spread evenly with branches that didn't start until halfway up their trunks, the trees and bushes here were tangled together, gripping each other like twisted fingers, forming a tight web of foliage that seemed to be impenetrable.

He ran toward it. As he drew nearer, he saw a few spots wide enough to run into. He aimed for the closest of these, a break in the foliage he hoped would allow him to break through the wall of forest life he was heading towards.

He could hear the footsteps of the others close behind him now, the shells no longer drowning everything out. They were still attacking, but he hadn't heard anything other than the steady barrage of explosions hitting the ground since they'd started running. He hoped they wouldn't be able to see them out in the open. Even in the forest, he knew they'd be no match for the heavy artillery raining down hell on Reggie's land behind them.

After he'd been running for another minute, dodging trees and bushes, and jumping over fallen logs and pieces of broken rock, he heard Reggie yell out from behind. He slowed, then stopped and turned around.

Julie was there, panting but otherwise doing well. Paulinho and Reggie showed no signs of exertion, but Dr. Amanda Meron had her hands on her knees, heaving gasps of air. Reggie came over and placed his hand on her back, then said something Ben couldn't hear. She nodded, and Reggie walked up to Ben and the others.

"We need to keep moving forward," he said. "They'll get bored eventually, or they'll find my bunker empty. Either way, they're going to figure out where we're headed soon enough."

"Where *are* we headed?" Julie asked.

Reggie gave her one of his typical, cocky grins. "Straight through this stand is a stream. That stream picks up and heads west a bit more, then a mile later empties into a larger pond. I've got a buddy who lives there. Small cabin, usually only him and his wife."

"Why are we going there?" Paulinho asked. Reggie was now in front of Ben, walking deeper into the trees behind the hill. They followed closely, none of them wanting to fall too far behind in the dense, shadow-laden forest.

"He owns a plane, and maintains an airstrip he uses for regional flying. Supply drops, tourism, search and rescue, that type of stuff. He can fly us as far as Manaus, which should be just over five hours. Give us some shut-eye, which I know I'll need."

They walked along in silence until they came to the stream. Ben was still carrying the backpacks, but Paulinho walked over and offered to take one. They each strapped one to their backs while the others waited. When they finished, and Reggie approved, he turned and started following the stream without speaking a word.

Ben had long since stopped hearing the shells, and he wondered if they had already found the bunker, or if they were just out of range. He hoped it was the latter, and that whoever was trying to kill Amanda — and now them, as well — had decided to call off the search.

Julie walked up to Ben and found his hand. She grabbed it, interlocking her fingers with his. The stream they were following provided a narrow walkway next to it, and it was just wide enough to fit Julie and Ben side-by-side. The jungle was silent, likely due to the artillery shells scaring away any wildlife from the area. Ben enjoyed the quiet, and with the trickling light from the rising sun finding its way through the cracks of the forest canopy, the scene around them was growing more and more beautiful by the minute.

He squeezed her hand, and she looked over at him. *It's going to be fine*, he thought. They didn't speak, opting instead for the unusual silence of the jungle.

They reached a clearing, and Reggie held up a hand. He crouched down right at the edge, then slowly stood and stepped forward. Ben could see the pond in front of him, on their right, collecting the stream's water and providing a natural lake for the animals and plants around them. The cabin Reggie had mentioned was straight ahead, marking the opposite edge of the clearing. A dirt road led away from the cabin and into the forest nearby, twisting around the larger trees. It was a picturesque scene, a greener and denser version of his own cabin at home.

"What's wrong?" Ben asked, stepping closer to Reggie. Reggie had stopped again, still examining the cabin from a distance. Ben could see a car, a mid-sized SUV similar to Reggie's own vehicle, parked outside the cabin. He assumed Reggie was being cautious, not wanting to scare whoever might be inside.

"Look at the window," he replied, his eyes still glued straight ahead.

Ben squinted, not able to see at first what Reggie was referring to. Then, as his eyes adjusted to the growing morning light, he saw it.

The window was broken, a large round hole cracked away from the glass. The lower pane on that window had two smaller holes in it, barely visible from this distance. *Bullet holes.* The idea that whoever was following had beaten them here was more terrifying than the thought that they'd already killed whoever was inside the cabin.

Ben hoped to God the husband and wife — Reggie's friends — hadn't been inside when they'd come.

But he knew these people wouldn't have wasted bullets just to shoot through windows. Something had happened here, and it had no doubt ended in bloodshed.

Reggie started walking toward the cabin, holding a pistol. Ben hadn't seen him draw the gun, but it had appeared in the man's hand somehow. Ben started forward, but Reggie turned and held up a hand.

"Stay there. All of you," he said. "Let me check it out first."

Ben stopped, and felt Julie's hand grab the inside of his arm. He wanted to follow, wanted to see what had happened inside, and he wanted more than anything to help. *If something happens to Reggie...*

He didn't allow himself to finish the thought.

Reggie reached the cabin and crouched below the window. He lifted the gun up, holding it near his face, and peered over the windowsill and into the house. Time stood still as Ben watched the man. Reggie didn't move, holding steady at the window, taking it all in.

In a moment, everything changed.

CHAPTER 19

The window cracked, shattering outward in a tiny explosion, and Ben heard the sound of gunfire from inside the cabin. Reggie yelled something, stood up again and aimed his gun into the single-room cabin.

Ben couldn't take it any longer. He started running forward. He had a weapon but it felt useless now in his hands, nothing but dead weight. He hadn't fired a gun nearly enough times in his life for the action to be natural, but he ran anyway. The man who'd saved their lives multiple times in less than a day was in danger, and he reacted the only way he knew how.

But before he could reach the window Reggie was still standing in front of, Reggie turned to Ben. "False alarm," he said. "It's a kid. Might need help. Says he fired at a shadow — must've seen me coming."

Ben wasn't convinced they were safe, but he followed Reggie to the front door of the cabin. Reggie turned the knob, swung the door open, and called out. "You in there?"

A muffled 'yes' reached Ben's ears.

"Okay, kid," Reggie replied, "we're coming in. Don't shoot, okay?"

Another muffled response, then Ben saw a gun slide across the wooden floor toward the threshold. Reggie stopped it with his foot and picked it up. He handed it to Ben, who held it gingerly with his fingers, as if it were police evidence he was afraid to tamper with.

"I'm sorry..." he heard a voice say. "I — I freaked out, and shot. I thought they came back."

Reggie stepped inside and rushed over to the couch. Ben followed behind him, at once taking in the scene around him.

The cabin was small, and he could see the entirety of it from the doorway. The kitchen and fireplace sat at one side, a bed at the other, and a small couch faced the window at the back of the cabin. An outdated, round-faced television sat below the window on a stand.

The furniture inside the cabin was mostly what Ben would have expected, but it was the blood that took him by surprise. On the back of the couch, smeared against the wall, and nearly covering the floor, streaks of blood were caked and drying. No surface seemed safe from it. In the kitchen, Ben could see two dirty piles of clothing, legs sticking out from them. *Bodies.* Ben nearly vomited as he stepped inside. His shoes immediately tracked blood-stained footprints below him, but he wanted to see the person on the couch.

The young man looked to be college-aged, with sandy blond hair that hung over his ears and into his scared eyes. He was tall, skinny, and seemed every bit as out of place in this corner of the world as Ben felt. The kid was shaking, holding the right side of his torso.

"You're wounded?" Reggie asked.

The kid nodded, and Reggie tried lifting the kid's hand. He yelped in pain, but Reggie comforted him. "I'll need to take a look at it, if we're going to patch you up. Where'd you get the gun, by the way?"

Reggie ignored the bodies, and Ben wondered if he'd seen them or not. *Were they his friends? The husband and wife?*

The kid spoke slowly, trying to breathe in a gentle, steady rhythm between words. "I — I grabbed it from the table right here. Bernard kept it there."

Reggie didn't seem to react to the statement, but Ben knew the man would be comparing the kid's words with what he knew of the man and woman who lived here. This statement must have checked out, as Reggie didn't respond.

There was a roll of gauze in the kid's hand, covered in blood. Reggie took the roll and ripped off the outer layer of dirtied fabric, then started dressing the wound.

"Looks like a knife wound," Reggie said. "Ragged hole, definitely not cut with a bullet."

The kid nodded again, still struggling in pain, but let Reggie work on the wound.

"The good news is that it's relatively small. Should heal up on its own, pretty quickly actually. You'll be able to walk, but it's going to hurt like hell, though." The kid seemed to struggle a bit with this information, but to his credit he clenched his jaw and nodded. Reggie continued dressing the wound.

Finally, Reggie looked up. Ben could see something in his eyes. *Anger?* The man's voice was calm, gentle even, but his eyes held a fury that terrified Ben more than the blood, the dead bodies, *and* their attackers. Reggie didn't say anything to Ben, but instead turned and addressed the kid.

"What's your name?"

"Rh — Rhett," he stuttered.

"Rhett, what happened here? Who killed the man and woman?"

"Bernard? And that's his wife, Emelia. They were shot, the same guys that stabbed me."

Reggie flashed a glance to Ben. *They beat us here.* "They stabbed you, but shot them?"

"They — they were trying to enter the house quietly, I think. I was at the door. Opened it, then… we couldn't get to the gun in time."

Reggie nodded. "Okay, just relax. I'll get you some water."

Ben followed Reggie into the kitchen and the two of them pushed the bodies to the side, out of the way of the sink. Ben struggled with the task, still feeling uneasy from all of the bloodshed, but Reggie's calm resolve strengthened him. When they finished, Reggie turned the faucet on and grabbed a plastic cup sitting nearby. Ben heard a noise at the door and saw the three others — Amanda, Paulinho, and Julie — standing in the doorway.

Ben's eyes immediately met Julie's, and he saw the horror on her face. No one spoke, but the message had been received. *They beat us here.*

Reggie came back to the couch with the water, and raised Rhett's head to help him drink from it. When he had finished drinking, Reggie helped him sit up a bit higher on the sofa, his back supported by a pillow. "Rhett, we need to find whoever it was that hurt you, and killed the Olivars."

Rhett looked at Reggie when he said the couple's last name, but Reggie continued before the kid could ask any questions. Julie, Dr. Meron, and Paulinho stepped into the house and closed the heavy wooden door behind them.

"They were my friends, and I have a feeling that I have something to do with why they were killed; why you were targeted. Anything you can tell me about what they looked like, or what they may have said?"

Rhett thought for a moment, then said what Ben had been afraid of. "Not much, no. They were dressed in black, like some sort of military special forces group or something." He took a long, slow breath. "They didn't say anything, either. Just stabbed me, left me for dead, and raided the house."

Ben looked around. Aside from Rhett's and the couple's blood everywhere, the cabin looked to be in order. Not even a picture on the wall was hanging improperly.

"Raided the house?" he asked.

"Yeah — looking for something, I guess. Not sure what, but they only stayed in here for a few minutes. They walked around the cabin a few times, but then they left. That was about half an hour ago.

Looking for something? Ben had no idea what they would have been looking for, aside from Dr. Meron.

"Rhett, why are you here?" Reggie asked the question in his blunt, no-nonsense way, but Ben sensed no hostility toward the young man.

"I was here to help the Olivars with their deliveries. I'm out of law school for the season, and needed to get my flight hours in. I'd always wanted to visit the rainforest too, so I thought I could make a little money on the side doing it. I didn't know they were in with some bad people, but I guess..."

"They weren't," Reggie said. "Like I said, this isn't your fault. Those men are after us — you were all just in the wrong place at the wrong time." He turned and looked at the rest of the group; four scared and worried faces looked back down at him. "The good news is that you're going to be just fine. That'll start healing up and you'll be as good as new in no time."

Reggie pulled Ben aside. "They were looking for any other ways out of here," Reggie said so only Ben could hear it. "Keys to the car, any cellphones, that type of stuff. That SUV parked out front is no doubt rigged, but if we hurry we still might be able to get to the plane. The runway's through the trees that direction, and it's impossible to see from the road."

Ben took in this information. *They came here to make sure we couldn't get out of the jungle. They killed the pilot, and the wife and kid he was with. If they already found the plane...*

He waited for the inevitable.

"The bad news is," Reggie continued. "We still need to get out of here, because they're very likely making a pass through the jungle and will come back here to check for us. You need to come too, or you'll most certainly be dead."

"Okay," the kid said.

"And," Reggie added, looking back into the kitchen at the legs of his friend Bernard Olivar poking out, "we need a pilot."

CHAPTER 20

Julie hoped Rhett was more skilled than he was giving himself credit for. After Reggie told him they needed a pilot, Rhett argued for a few minutes, telling them all he wasn't capable of flying on his own yet. Reggie argued back, reassuring him that he himself had some limited flight experience, and would be an able copilot in a small bush plane like Bernard's. Julie was unconvinced that the kid would be good enough to take off on what seemed to her like a terribly short runway, but she knew there were no other options.

She hoped stab wounds didn't make it harder to fly airplanes.

They'd found the plane exactly where Reggie said they would — nearly hidden by the tall trees and dense forest canopy at the end of a narrow path about a half mile from the cabin. Bernard had liked the pseudo-secret hiding spot, according to Reggie, as it made him feel like a drug-running outlaw every time he disappeared below the canopy to land the plane. The plane itself was unregistered, another fact Bernard had been proud of. A 1983 Cessna P210N Centurion, the small plane was capable of holding five passengers and a pilot, with room for luggage or gear. Rhett explained to everyone that Bernard often took the seats out and used the extra space for hauling more equipment to drop zones on the supply routes he frequented. He'd flown with Bernard three times already, usually taking over the controls once Bernard had gotten the plane to cruising altitude.

"You're going to be fine, kid." Julie heard Reggie encouraging

Rhett near the front of the plane, while Ben and Paulinho loaded their backpacks into the storage area. "Like I said, I've held the controls once or twice, and as long as you handle the landing, we'll be all right. How's that cut?"

Rhett nodded, not looking away from the controls.

Julie tried to ignore the conversation, but couldn't. Both men seemed to consider themselves only amateur pilots. *And I'm going to fly with them willingly?* She looked at Ben.

"We're going to be fine," he said. She knew how he felt about flying, and she was amazed that he seemed to actually believe what he'd just said.

Reggie spoke again to the group. "Everyone stand over by the tree line. I'm going to get her started up."

He didn't explain why he wanted them to stand back, but Ben sidled over to Julie and whispered in her ear. "He said the SUV in front of the cabin was very likely rigged with explosives. He probably thinks the plane —"

"Stop," she said. "I don't want to know."

Ben shrugged, and Julie turned and walked toward the trees as Reggie climbed up into the cockpit of the aircraft. She heard the door slam.

A minute passed, then the airplane's engine sputtered to life, the low hum reaching her ears. She waited. Ben pressed his hand over hers, and she felt him squeeze. *He's nervous too,* she thought.

Another minute passed, and Reggie hopped out of the pilot's seat and waved over to them. "If she was going to blow, she'd have done it already."

Julie wondered how the man could seem so nonchalant, but she followed Ben and the others over to the plane. Ben helped her inside, and they all buckled their seatbelts as Rhett taxied the plane to the runway. He waited at the edge, checking and re-checking the instruments and displays in front of him. Reggie was smiling from the copilot's seat, but his eyes contradicted the rest of his face in their hard, semi-closed way. She waited.

Finally she felt the lift force as Rhett pushed the throttle down and started the plane on its takeoff sequence. The kid seemed calm, collected, and perfectly focused on the task at hand as the plane accelerated, then finally rose slightly as the lift forces pulled the plane upward. He pulled the nose up, and Julie felt the momentary weightlessness as their centers of gravity shifted and they became airborne. She'd never flown in a plane as small as this, and the jumpiness caused by the bumpy runway was immediately replaced by the smooth and gliding feeling of flying.

She looked over at Ben. His knuckles were white, his eyes fixed straight ahead, but she didn't bother him. Once they reached their cruising altitude, he would calm down a bit and be able to relax.

"What do you think we're looking for?" Paulinho suddenly asked.

Julie and Amanda looked over at him, and Ben, still starting straight ahead, raised his eyebrows slightly.

"I mean, what's the big deal? Amanda's company has been doing amazing research since they started. Why are they after you now?"

Amanda shrugged. "I don't know. It all seems so strange. One week we were working on capturing dreams, and now I'm a fugitive."

"What do you think the golden man has to do with all of it?" Julie asked.

"Again, I have no idea. That seems to be the beginning of it all, though. When one of our employees uploaded the data, I believe someone on the other side accessed it right away. After that, all of this started."

"One of the investors?"

"Probably. They were always hands-off, but their only requirement for continued funding was first access to anything we discovered."

Julie considered this. She didn't know anything about high-tech venture capitalism, but it seemed odd that an investor would seem disinterested enough in their investment to be hands-off, yet require immediate access to any new findings. It definitely didn't check out, but Julie didn't press Amanda for more.

A few minutes later the plane pushed out of its steady ascent and leveled out. Ben released his grip on the armrest and his hand immediately found Julie's. She looked over at him, trying to gauge how he was feeling without explicitly asking. His eyes seemed tired, their brows bent into an expression of worry. Or stress, she wasn't sure. He stared back at her, nodding slightly. She smiled, then turned to look out the window once more.

"We're on our bearing now," Reggie called out from the cockpit. "We'll fly into Manaus, then find a boat to take us upstream."

Paulinho tapped Reggie on the shoulder. "Where exactly are we going? Those lines crossed, but they didn't exactly tell us the destination."

Reggie smiled. "No, I suppose not. But that location is remote enough that we'll be able to narrow it down much easier when we get close. I jotted down the coordinates before we left my place." Reggie flashed up a piece of paper, on which he'd written some numbers. "It's in the middle of the Basin, between the Purus and Jaruá Rivers. Still a pretty large region, but it's a good place to start."

Julie wasn't convinced. "Pretty large region? Seems like that's quite the understatement."

"Yes, that's probably true. But we're not in Manaus yet, so there's not much we can do."

"What's in Manaus?" Paulinho asked.

"A professor. I've never met him in person, but we've exchanged emails before. He has some pretty interesting — and compelling, I might add — theories about that particular region of the jungle, so I thought of him right away when the maps came up on the screen. He's also a Jesuit priest, someone who's got access to some of the things we don't. Like records."

"Records of what? And what is a Jesuit priest going to be able to find that we can't?" Dr. Meron asked. She didn't sound excited by Reggie's suggestion, and Julie had to agree — this man, someone they'd just met, was leading them across a continent in search of something worth killing for. She wasn't sure if Reggie was being cryptic on purpose, or if it was his usual style.

"I'm with Amanda," she said, unable to stop herself. "This all seems a bit far-fetched to me, and — no offense, Reggie — we don't even know your last name."

Reggie faced forward again, then sighed. He turned back around and looked at each of them in turn. "Fine, I'm sorry, you're right. You have no reason to trust me. I've got no way to change that right now, so… you'll just have to trust me."

Julie waited for him to continue. She hadn't forgotten that he *still* hadn't told them his last name.

"Before I joined the Army, I taught history at a community college. I've always been a history buff; still am. I first reached out to Father Quinones back then when I was working on a paper, then I was deployed on and off for the better part of ten years. He teaches at the Federal University of Amazonas, in Manaus. His specialty is in religious history of this region, with a focus on the religions of the native and uncontacted tribes here. He'll be a great asset to have, especially because of his connections with the Jesuit Order."

"Who are they?" Ben asked.

"Catholics. The Society of Jesus, actually. A male order of the Catholic church."

"A fraternity?"

"Well, yes and no. He can explain it better, but it's essentially a congregation that's part of the Catholic faith. What's important here is that the history of the Spanish conquerors in this territory and the Catholic church are very closely intertwined with the mythologies and histories of the area.

"What I'm interested in is Father Quinones' knowledge of the Quito Jesuits — the order that was started back in the early 1600s, in Peru. I think there's some interesting reasons to cross-reference what we know about the region we're heading into with any information we can find on its history."

"Can you give us the nutshell version?" Ben asked.

"Bits and pieces. Mostly just typical stuff we've all heard of before. You know, El Dorado, the City of Gold, all that stuff?"

The rest of the group was silent.

"Are — are you suggesting —" Amanda's voice cut out before she could phrase the question.

"No ma'am," Reggie responded. "I'm certainly not convinced we're *looking* for the city of El Dorado, at least not yet anyway. Just that it's by far the most dominant piece of history this region has to offer, so we might as well be versed in the lore and mythology of it. It shows up time and again in historical texts, and we're about to be neck-deep in the center of the myth."

"Why is that?"

Reggie looked at all of them again, slowly. "Seriously?" He sighed. "Well, I thought we were all on the same page. My bad. That 'golden man' that's been haunting your dreams? It's a pretty obvious reference to our lost city."

Amanda's voice rose. "If you think I'm going to believe that —"

"Dr. Meron," Reggie said, holding up a hand as he twisted around further to fully face them, "El Dorado means 'the golden one,' which also originally meant 'the golden man.' I hate to break it to you, but the moment your magical computer caught a glimpse of that little gold dude, you were on the hunt for the most fabled city of all time. Whether that's an actual city of gold or something else, no one knows — but we are looking for *something* out there, right?"

"I don't believe…"

"I know, and that's okay. But if we're going to be thorough, we need to check all the boxes, dot our t's and cross all our I's, all that stuff," he said. "Father Quinones should be able to fill in any blanks we have as far as the history of this area is concerned, and with the two of us putting our heads together on it, I'd bet we can pinpoint where those lines are crossing, down to a twenty-mile radius at least."

No one spoke, everyone still staring at Reggie, shocked. Rhett sat in the pilot's seat and hadn't spoken a word since they'd taken off, but Julie thought she saw his shoulders rise and his ears perk up a bit at this last bit of information.

"I'm as skeptical as the rest of you," Reggie said, "but we have to try. We know we're heading into the heart of the rainforest, one of the most inhospitable places on the planet, and we're running out of time. Don't you think it's a little strange that the guy telling us all where to go is covered in *gold?*"

Still no one responded. Their fates had been sealed as soon as they took off, and no one argued to change their destination.

Julie and the others used the flight time to rest and try to sleep. No one spoke of the events down at the cabin and Reggie's bunker, or at the hotel, but she knew it was on all their minds. They were flying into the center of the Amazon rainforest and being chased by a group of well-trained killers.

They had hardly any gear, had no idea what they were actually looking for, and the thumb drive and Julie's laptop with a dying battery they'd left at Reggie's house was useless out here.

It was an impossible task, and once again Julie had no idea how she'd gotten involved in this mess. She was scared, feeling helpless, and mostly useless, but she knew there was no alternative. She knew she'd follow Ben to the ends of the earth, and she knew she was as stubborn as he was when it came to protecting someone else.

They would figure this out, or they would die trying.

CHAPTER 21

Paulinho was just as surprised as the others to hear Reggie start talking about the myth of the great lost city, but he was too tired to argue. The hum of the plane's engine eventually overcame the excitement and anticipation they were all feeling and the group fell into a restful silence.

He leaned back against the headrest and almost immediately slept.

Paulinho had never been very good at remembering the dreams he had during sleep, but as soon as his eyes closed he was deep into a recurring dream he'd experienced as a young boy, then a young man; one that came back every now and then.

The dream was difficult to see, as were most of the dreams he had. Swirling lights of different colors flashed in front of him, most deep hues of dark blues and greens. He'd seen pictures of the Aurora Borealis over the North Pole, and this effect was similar. It was a peaceful dream, and it always surprised him with its beauty.

The next phase of the dream was the same as it had always been: some of the dancing lights became darker shadows, still lit up in color but now faded, as if shadows of their previous shapes. These smaller lights grouped together in front of the larger, brighter lights, and become one, like the center of a kaleidoscope that was constantly twirling and mixing the colors and shapes.

These darker shapes grew together, still twisting and moving, and the lighter colors swirled even brighter around them. Paulinho took it in, knowing he was asleep but still somehow able to enjoy the show.

This particular version of the dream seemed longer, and even more vivid, than the other dreams he'd had, but he didn't care. It was beauty in its purest form, seen from inside the head. He imagined he was watching his own brain during the act of thinking, lighting up as his thoughts and emotions and cares mixed together into a spectacular light show.

He couldn't move when he watched the dream, at least not in the same way he could move around in other dreams. His body didn't exist in this dream, it wasn't the type of landscape his mind would allow him to move through, even if he tried to force it. He was stationary, given one single view of the light show and no others, forced to watch the artwork unfold as a spectator, even though it was a creation of his own mind.

The only power he had over the dream was to end it, he knew. He was aware that he was dreaming, but the simultaneous feeling of the dream combined with the sleep convinced him to stay asleep. He allowed the dream to play in his mind as long as it wanted, or until someone else woke him up.

CHAPTER 22

"Good afternoon," the older man said as the group filed into the spacious office. "My name is Archibald Quinones." Father Quinones took care to shake each of their hands, one at a time, while looking them in the eye as they introduced themselves. When he reached the last person, Reggie, he smiled warmly.

"It is fantastic to finally meet you in person, Reggie," Quinones said, gripping Reggie's hand with both of his own. "I hope you will forgive me for not reaching out and keeping in touch."

"No, no, that's my fault," Reggie said. "Things get busy…"

"…and life goes on." Quinones kept the smile and ushered them all in. "Sit," he said, pointing them toward a large leather couch and two chairs on either side of it. Two more chairs sat across from it, both framing a massive hardwood bookcase, full of books. Ben thought these types of bookshelves were a little pretentious, but he couldn't help but assume the man in front of him had read every single one.

He passed in front of one side of the bookcase and caught a glimpse of a few of the titles.

Archibald Quinones, PhD.

Okay, so he didn't read *all of these,* Ben thought. He was impressed, and he sat down in the chair. The room, Ben noticed, was perfectly appointed. The bookcases matched the deep mocha-colored leather of the chairs, and the couch, while a lighter shade of brown, was of the same make and style. A huge area rug spread from beneath the couch to the chairs, lined with large, subtle tan and gold stripes. The carpet beneath was of a similar tone, but neutral enough to provide little interest for the lingering eye.

Ben wasn't much for interior design, but he recognized comfortable luxury when he saw it. Two paintings hung on the wall across the room from him, a large rectangular landscape of a mountain range, and a smaller picture of a scene from the crucifixion of Christ. The desk at the far end of the room was large and hardwood, yet plain enough to not warrant much thought. *A practical, simple solution for a necessary workstation.* Ben loved the room, and only thought it might be improved if there was a rolling whiskey cart tucked away in a corner.

They'd reached the man's house after landing and driving another twenty minutes, and like Reggie's compound, this house was relatively unassuming from the exterior. Father Quinones lived alone, drove a small sedan, and owned a modest home. But as soon as they walked into the man's study, Ben understood that the man took great pride in the place he did most of his work, and therefore spent the money to ensure he and his guests felt comfortable in the large office space.

Quinones offered them all water and tea, and when everyone declined, he took the seat next to Ben's at the opposite end of the bookcase and began to speak.

"I would love to hear of your adventure so far," he said, jumping immediately into the topic at hand, "but I understand from Reggie's phone call you are in a hurry."

"We may be in danger," Reggie answered. "There's a… *group* after us. Not sure who they are, or what they want, but they seem pretty interested in Dr. Meron here."

Dr. Quinones' eyes sparkled as he looked over at Amanda. "Yes, Dr. Meron — what a pleasure! I've been reading of your company's work for the past half hour. *Very* intriguing research."

Amanda cleared her throat. "I'm flattered, thank you. But what's online is really only scratching the surface."

"Oh, I'm sure it is. But you are doing testing in fMRI technology, no? Studying the effects of electromagnetic pulses emanating from the brain during REM sleep?"

Amanda looked confused. "How —"

"It's all context clues, Dr. Meron. And it helps if you have an interest in scientific matters, as I do," Dr. Quinones replied. "I didn't have time to scan through all of the published papers on your company, but it does appear that you have some *very* interesting research going on back home."

Dr. Meron nodded.

"And I'm assuming since you've met up with my friend Reggie, he's been telling you all sorts of things about myths and legends, hoping you'll take the bait."

As Amanda nodded once again, Ben felt relieved to hear that the older man had none of the bravado and cockiness of the younger ex-Army man. He felt reassured that Archibald Quinones would point them in the right direction.

"Well, what types of myths and legends has he been feeding you?" Quinones asked.

Reggie himself spoke up. "Well, let's start at the beginning. They've been recording dreams," he said.

"*Recording* dreams?"

"Yes — they're actually able to record video from the subject's subconscious mind, using technology that maps certain areas of the brain."

Father Quinones sat silent for a moment, thinking. "I see. Go on," he said, finally.

"Well…" Amanda took over the explanation. "Yes, I guess that's accurate enough. But we've been seeing an anomaly as well, only in certain subjects sharing a common ancestry."

Archibald Quinones sat forward in the chair, focusing intently on Amanda Meron. "What sort of common ancestry are we talking about?"

"They're all linked together, pointing back to a local tribe. One that we believe originated in the Amazon Basin."

Father Quinones was at the edge of his seat. "And the anomaly? What was it?"

Dr. Meron explained their findings — the golden man, how it was always in focus, and how it was always looking directly at the subject. She tried to explain some of the computer modelings they had done to disprove their theories, attempting to prove to the rest of them that the anomaly was not a practical joke. She continued on, adding that their current destination was probably somewhere between two of the Amazon's largest tributaries — the Juruá and the Purus rivers — and Father Quinones finally stood up and turned to the bookcase behind him and Ben. Amanda stopped mid-sentence, waiting for the man to return to his chair. When he did, he opened the book he'd grabbed from the shelf and started flipping through its pages.

"This is a book about the earliest tribes of the Amazon, written by a Jesuit priest during the Spanish expansion into the region. Most of the firsthand encounters we have were written by the Spanish, as they were generally the first Westerners to visit the area and document their findings." Quinones flipped a few more pages. "We have to assume that the Spanish conquistadors and their explorers documented their findings well enough, but even if they were a little off in their specific descriptions, there's one particular characteristic about this book — and every other I've come across — Spanish or not — that I can't help but think about as you're telling me this."

"What's that?" Paulinho asked. He'd been silent the entire meeting, sitting next to Rhett as the group discussed their plans.

"Well, the Spanish mapped the region nearest the Amazon river — the main tributaries that fed the larger river we call the 'Amazon.' But the Amazon Basin is a much larger expanse of land. Most of it has been well-documented, and modern civilization has reached a lot of it, as evidenced by the number of small villages and cities dotting the Basin's geographical area. But there is still one section of land in the Amazon Basin that has almost no mention in the published Spanish documents, Jesuit manuscripts, and modern writings."

The group waited for the professor to continue.

"The area between the Jaruá and Purus rivers, near the western border of Brazil, is almost nonexistent in the texts."

Ben's eyes widened, but he didn't say anything to interfere with the man's train of thought.

"This area is particularly special, in my opinion," Quinones continued. "While much of the Amazon has been allotted to farming, harvesting, and study, this area — just northeast of the state of Acre — has not been interfered with. There are some tribes living there, but we have yet to designate this area as a national reservation."

Amanda and the others were silent, but Reggie spoke next. "*Very* interesting." He paused, looking around the room, then repeated himself. "Very interesting, Dr. — Father — Quinones."

"Please, call me Archie," Quinones said. "I'm assuming by your inflection that this region is the same region you're investigating?"

"Well," Reggie said, "it's pretty high up the list."

Quinones chuckled.

Reggie continued. "Yes, that's just it — there's something else we didn't tell you — something Amanda's company was working on." Ben appreciated that Reggie didn't give Quinones the full details about the deaths at NARATech. "They think they've been able to pinpoint the location of this tribe. The one their subjects have descended from. There are some details we can get to later, but the long and short of it is that we think this tribe is located somewhere between those two rivers."

Quinones raised an eyebrow — a thick, bushy, salt-and-pepper crop of hair above his eye — asking for more information.

"We — I — was hoping you'd be able to fill in the blanks; help us figure out exactly where to go next."

Ben was surprised to see that Quinones' dancing eyebrow could extend even farther up his forehead. The man seemed fully intrigued now. Fully invested.

"Yes, I believe I can," Father Quinones replied. He stood up again and began pacing. "There is an old document I came across as a young man, something I found buried in the Jesuit archives. It has held my interest for almost three decades, though I dare not write or speak publicly about it, as its mystery has long been debunked as mythology."

Archie walked to the edge of the area rug and turned around, soaking up the moment and extending his full lecturing powers as a professor. His eyes grew wide and bright, then his voice fell to a soft, near-whisper.

"The *real* location of the lost city of El Dorado," he said, with a dramatic flourish of his hands.

CHAPTER 23

Ben chuckled, and he noticed Rhett and Reggie smiling as well.

"Yes," Quinones said, "that is the reaction other people had as well." Ben stopped smiling, but Quinones didn't appear to be upset with him. "They are not wrong to be skeptical, either," he continued. "The 'lost city' idea has long been proven false."

Ben waited for the man to say *'but…'*

"But," Quinones said, "this document supposedly predates anything I've found that references our fabled city. First of all, it was written by Gaspar de Carvajal, a Spanish dominican missionary who traveled with Francisco de Orellana during the first voyage of the Amazon river. Francisco Pizarro himself ordered the expedition, and Carvajal was one of the few surviving members. He captured his account and details of the journey, and much of what we later historians know of the early Amazonian tribes is found directly between the pages of his work, *"Relacion del nuevo descubrimiento del famoso rio Grande que descubrio por muy gran ventura el capitan Francisco de Orellana,"* or *"Account of the recent discovery of the famous Grand river which was discovered by great good fortune by Captain Francisco de Orellana."* He paused, noticing the blank expressions of the group. "I agree," Quinones said, "he should have hired a publicist to help with that title.

"Anyway, there was much in the document that historians have long believed to be fabricated, such as Carvajal's mentions and detailed descriptions of large, inhabited cities with huge monumental structures, complete with agricultural areas and paved roads. It has been suggested that the rainforest basin's soil cannot handle any sort of sustainable farming, and likewise we have yet to uncover any of these 'monumental structures' or 'paved roads.' Still, the accounts of the interactions the party had with the indigenous peoples has proven to be mostly accurate.

"But in the published work, there was no mention of a 'lost city,' a 'golden man,' or anything of that nature. It was only when I came across another book in the archives that I began developing a theory. This work in question was published by a Jesuit priest who captured firsthand accounts of explorers in the region and translated them. He recorded a story told to him by a Peruvian man who told the priest he knew Gaspar de Carvajal in Lima, just before he died in 1584. The story was told to the priest in Spanish for the priest to later translate it into Latin. Most of it is just an abbreviated account of what *Relacion* already covers, but there was one particular story that stood out. It is a story about a tribe with a great chief who would be decorated in gold dust, then jump into a lake.

"What's amazing about this story is that it *almost perfectly* lines up with later accounts of the Zipa tribe of Muisca Confederation of present-day Columbia. The Zipa were known to offer gold to their goddess by covering their chief with gold dust, then throwing gold objects and jewelry into the water as the chief washed himself in it."

"The 'Golden Man,'" Reggie said.

"Or the 'Golden One,' in different legends," Quinones said. "But not the 'Golden *City*.' Lake Guatavita has since been explored, to great disappointment. Other cities in the region covering Brazil, Columbia, and Peru, have been scoured for any of these 'gold objects' that might point explorers to the legendary city of gold, but nothing of the sort has ever been found."

"So how is this story any different? And why are there so many surviving legends if the city doesn't exist?" Amanda asked.

"Well, first of all," Archie said, continuing his lecture, "there are numerous historical accounts that claim reference to a 'lost city of gold.' In 2001, actually, an Italian archaeologist discovered a missionary's report in the Jesuit archives in Rome. The archeologist, in this report, describes 'a large city rich in gold, silver and jewels, located in the middle of the tropical jungle, called Paititi by the natives.' There are conspiracy theories now that suggest the Vatican is keeping the location of this 'Paititi' a secret, but I do not believe this. Which brings me to my point, and the question you asked.

"Due to what many others may dismiss as a translation error, I believe this story doesn't reference a *city* at all. There was a specific line that caught my attention when I first read the account."

The group waited for Quinones' revelation.

"The priest wrote, 'que estaba cerca de la gran pueblo antigua que vio por primera vez el oro...'"

Amanda spoke, translating the Spanish. "I only know a little Spanish, but I think that's, 'It was near the great old city that he first saw the gold...'"

Quinones smiled, a thin, sly line on his face. "*Almost*. In Spanish, the word 'pueblo' means town, or city. But the word's roots come from the *latin* word 'populus,' which means 'people.'"

Rhett had been listening quietly, but now nodded. "This guy told the priest that he'd been told a story by Carvajal himself, about a 'great old *people*' and something about gold as well."

"Exactly. And everyone thereafter began searching for a *city* — a physical location — made of pure gold. But my hypothesis is simple: *El Dorado* refers to a *lost tribe*, not a *lost city*. That fully explains why such a secret can remain hidden for four centuries."

"How so?" Rhett asked.

"Well, you can't hide a city forever — they don't move," Quinones said. "But if *you* are the secret you're trying to keep — if *you* are the city — all it takes is a strong desire to remain hidden."

The group was nodding slowly, and Ben found himself being

swayed into belief. *It makes sense,* he thought.

"A tribe? Then how do we find them?" he asked.

Quinones smiled his cryptic smile again. "Don't you see, my friends? We do not need to — they have found *us.*"

II

"…But he grew old—

This knight so bold—

And o'er his heart a shadow—

Fell as he found

No spot of ground

That looked like Eldorado…"

— Edgar Allan Poe

CHAPTER 24

Valère felt the nervousness creeping up his spine. His old friend, the feeling of anxiety, was now omnipresent in his life, but it still shot up in pangs of crippling fear whenever he got too worked up. Where he should have been able to discern between excitement, an adrenaline rush, anger, and terror, he now only felt nervousness. More specifically, his heart began racing and he felt a wave of shakiness grip him. In turn, he gripped the edge of the desk and held on tightly, waiting for the worst of it to pass.

This particular wave was no doubt caused by the blinking light on his wall-mounted display, and what that signal represented. SARA, the Simulated Artificial Response Array semi-AI that controlled his office and communications, an internal project that was nearing the end of its alpha testing phase, also noticed the signal and immediately alerted Valère. Her voice was still metallic and somewhat hollow, as it had always been, but Valère had recently "upgraded" the computerized female voice by giving it a British accent. "She" tended to communicate in French, Valère's native tongue, but was also fluent in British and American English.

"Monsieur Valère, there is an incoming connection. Mr. Emilio Vasquez, from his estate. Shall I connect?"

Valère nodded without looking up from the blinking light. SARA saw his reaction from one of the many cameras mounted inside the walls of the office and immediately authorized the connection. Emilio

Vasquez's rounded face appeared on the screen in front of him, in full HD resolution. It was too large, in Valère's opinion, and showed his partners pockmarks, scars, and spotted skin in too much detail.

"Mr. Vasquez," Valère began. He kept his grip on the edge of the desk and didn't sit down.

"Valère, what's this I hear about the Company bombing a hotel in Brazil?"

Valère swallowed, trying to not show his weakness. He sniffed, tilting his head back slightly. "It is not the *Company's* actions to which you are referring, my dear friend, but my own. And it wasn't a *bombing*, but an *extraction*."

Vasquez's eyebrows raised. "Oh? And what exactly did you *extract*?"

"That's not of any importance at this stage. I —"

"'Not of any importance?'" Vasquez said, his voice raising. "Listen to yourself, Valère! Who are you taking orders from? And what gives you the right to cut me out of —"

"I did no such thing," Valère said. "And you know I have full authority to send Joshua's team anywhere I please. This extraction was just such an act. While we didn't attain custody of the —"

"Wait, you mean the extraction *failed?* Jesus, Valère, you were lucky they didn't leave corpses everywhere! You must think you're above —"

Valère held up a hand, interrupting Emilio. "It is not *luck* when they are the best-trained security force on the planet. They knew the hotel was nearly empty, and I told them to make an 'audible entrance,' but to be careful not to leave any collateral damage."

"Then why did they fail?"

"The fault for that is mine," Valère said. "I told Joshua he wouldn't need more than a few men, as the target was unarmed, untrained, and traveling with a small group of civilians. However, there was an unknown variable during the extraction, and Joshua was taken by surprise. I told him to track the target, regroup, and be prepared for a full engagement. He will not be taken by surprise again, that I can assure you."

"You don't need to assure me," Emilio said, "I didn't even know about this 'attack' until ten minutes ago. I'd suggest you brief the Company, for both our —"

"The Company is fully aware of the situation, and has already provided Joshua with additional men and supplies for the trip."

Again Emilio's eyebrows raised, but he didn't ask the question he was undoubtedly thinking.

"They are following the group into the Amazon rainforest, we believe. The Company has given me full authority over Joshua's team, but they will expect results. I am confident that Joshua's team will produce, but I have nevertheless taken additional precautions. I had to act quickly, so I did not alert you to my actions."

"And Joshua — you've explained to him about his father?"

"I have been communicating with him as though I am his father."

Even on the screen, Valère could see Emilio's eyes bulging. "You — you *what?* How are you doing that? If Joshua learned that we —"

"Hacking an email account is not a miraculous endeavor, Emilio," Valère said. "Especially when the Company owns the servers. Joshua is a professional — a few short emails directly from his own father, with my own email address in the cc field, and he was off to begin pursuing our target. He needn't be burdened with any news of his father's involvement with our research in Antarctica."

Emilio nodded, thinking, and Valère waited for the inevitable question.

"Who is the target?"

"Her name is Dr. Amanda Meron, and she runs the research branch of NARATech."

"NARATech? But she can't —"

"She absolutely does not know what NARATech used to be, and she never will. We've grown out of the facility in Brazil so we've allowed her to claim its usefulness for her own interests. Her company's research is focused on retrieving images from the mind using functional magnetic response imaging, and they have achieved great success."

He paused a moment, finally feeling the nervousness subside.

"However, we have data that suggests their research has taken an interesting turn, one the Company was quite interested in pursuing. We need her to cooperate until we can verify her company's claims, before they go public with the information. After that…"

"…You won't need her any longer."

"Precisely."

Emilio smiled. "Valère, I wish you would keep me in the loop about these things. You know I can be a great help to you and the Company."

"Yes, yes I do," Valère said. "You shouldn't worry yourself with these trivial matters. Your value to us is as an investor, consultant, and advisor. Please forgive my hastiness in moving forward without you."

"Not a problem, Valère," Emilio Vasquez said. "So, her company, NARATech — it's different from what we established in Brazil a few years ago?"

"It is now. SARA coordinated the move of our subjects to a proper facility that will require far less logistical organization and security, but we had an empty facility left behind. NARATech was only ever an internal facility, so there was no need to change the name and rebrand. Dr. Meron's research fit nicely with our long-term goals, so we offered to fully fund her company and remain silent partners. She owns the shares and the research outright, but the namesake belongs to us, as well as the right to first access to any of their findings."

"I see." Emilio Vasquez turned away from the screen, and Valère could see the man looking at something behind him. "Valère, I need to attend to other matters, but I appreciate your willingness to keep me abreast of changes and developments."

"And I shall. Thank you, Emilio." SARA didn't wait for Mr. Vasquez's response — she cut the connection, and the blinking light on the monitor went dark. Valère sat down at the desk, replaying the conversation in his mind. The next few days would prove quite taxing, and he needed to maintain a calm, collected preparedness if the Company was to accomplish this next phase of their goal.

He told SARA to schedule another appointment with his doctor.

CHAPTER 25

"You can stay here tonight. You need the rest." The older man, Archibald Quinones, guided the group to a bedroom at the end of the hallway. "The ladies may sleep in here, and you —" he motioned to Rhett — "stay in my bedroom. There is a restroom attached; it will be best in case you need to dress your wounds. The rest of us can find room on the floor in the office, or in the living room."

He paused at the outside of the door leading into the guest bedroom, where Amanda Meron and Juliette would be staying. "I apologize for my lack of accommodations. I usually do not host more than one or two at a time, and even then it is rare for someone to stay the night here."

Amanda smiled at Archie and grabbed his arm. "Please, Archie, do not apologize. We are more than grateful for your help so far."

Archie patted Amanda's hand and turned to Paulinho, who had extended his hand toward the man in thanks. Archie grasped his hand, then looked down at his wrist. "Interesting design," he said.

Paulinho frowned, then saw that the man was referring to the tattoo on the inside of his wrist. "Right, yes," he said. "It is a design from a necklace my grandfather had. When he passed I had it imprinted on me as a reminder of his life."

"He must have been a special man. Do you know what it means?"

"I don't," Paulinho said. He laughed. "I just always liked the necklace, and he always wore it underneath his shirt. I used to grab it when I was a boy and tug on it." The memory seemed to warm Paulinho, and he took a moment of recollection. Archie respectfully waited, then turned to the rest of the group.

"Tomorrow I will find us a guide and a boat, though we will likely have to share it with tourists. I've only ventured into the jungle a handful of times, and admittedly I was a much younger soul then. But I do think there is something to your myth, and I would like to help.

Ben's ears perked up at the man's mention of 'venturing into the jungle,' but Paulinho spoke up before Ben could.

"You don't intend to travel with us, do you?" he asked.

Quinones smiled. "It is a foolish venture, no? An old man traveling with a band of young, strapping explorers?"

Reggie looked from Paulinho to Quinones, then at Ben and back. "But seriously, Archie — you're not…"

"I am going to go with you, provided your acceptance of my desire. I believe I can be of help to you in the jungle, even if I am the slowest of the group."

He winked at Ben. "But I do not think I would be the slowest."

Ben wasn't sure if he was insulting him or just making a point, but he didn't care. He spoke up, arguing against the man's wishes. "Archie, I — it's a real pleasure to meet you and all, but… I don't think…"

Archie lifted his chin and tilted his head back slightly. Somehow, it seemed to Ben not insulting and condescending but regal and endearing. "Please," Quinones said, addressing Ben directly, "allow this old man one final indulgence. I will be an asset to your team, and I vow to not hold you up. Besides, I have some ideas about how to map the expedition, and I am no amateur when it comes to wilderness navigation."

"Archie, this isn't *just* an expedition. There are *killers* after us. This isn't your fight," Reggie said.

"Nor is it yours," Quinones responded. "It seems to me they want something from Dr. Meron, and therefore I believe she needs all the help she can get. I know of many of the tribes we may encounter, and which we'd be wise to stay away from." Quinones stopped pacing and walked to the center of the room, a physical statement of assertion. "I am going with you, and that's that. I see you've brought packs. I know you're more than capable of keeping one more person alive, Reggie, and we can leave as soon as you are all rested and ready. It will be early, so I suggest you all get some sleep."

Reggie smiled at Ben. Ben hesitated, then grinned back. Their team had grown by one.

CHAPTER 26

The dog was a labrador retriever mix, dark gray with lighter specks to match his white front paws. It was young, its feet still oversized compared to its body. But, like any young dog, it was fast.

Joshua found himself exerting more effort than he'd intended trying to keep up with the animal, who was now leading him through alleyways, across streets, and up the large sloping side of the city. He'd raced off after the runaway pet immediately after its owner lost it, but he hadn't anticipated running behind the dog for more than a block or two.

The animal continued, jumping over a pile of trash at the end of the alleyway. Joshua stretched out and leaped over the trash pile, closing the distance between himself and the mutt. The dog looked back at him as his foot splashed in a puddle, its tongue lolling around out the side of its mouth.

Joshua could have sworn the dog was smiling at him.

"Come here, you little bastard," he said, smiling right back. The dog slowed a bit as he reached the end of the alley and tried to decide which direction to turn. Joshua launched himself forward into a diving tackle and reached forward, arms outstretched.

He'd calculated the distance perfectly. The dog was about to run to the right, but Joshua spread his hands out and brought them around the animal just as he landed, his body inches from the dog's. The dog huffed a quick panting breath of defeat, then allowed himself to be wrapped up into Joshua's arms.

"You really thought you'd outrun me?" Joshua said. The dog's huge brown eyes stared up at him, the jovial twinkle of satisfaction still in its eyes. "Let's get you home, buddy."

The dog had been walking with its master in a park three blocks away as Joshua was out on a morning run. The owner had tried letting the dog off of its lead to choose a spot, but the dog had other plans. Joshua began chasing after it as soon as he caught the terrified look in the owner's eyes. He'd always had a soft spot for dogs, and he knew the feeling of losing such a loyal friend.

He walked back to the park, still carrying the dog. The owner, a young woman in her early thirties, saw him and began jogging over. When they met, Joshua allowed the woman to reattach the lead before setting the dog on the ground. The animal stretched its legs, whined once, then harrumphed and sat on the sidewalk. The woman tried to thank Joshua in Portuguese, but he just shook his head and smiled.

She tried thanking him again, this time reaching for a pocketbook.

He held out a hand. "No, please, it's fine. Happy to help."

His phone vibrated silently in his pocket, and he reached for it and pulled it out. *Perfect timing.* The woman got the hint, nodding profusely and thanking him as he turned away and answered the call.

"Joshua." He spoke the word slowly, articulating it carefully, as was his custom. The person on the other end would be using a computer to analyze his vocal performance, matching it against the library of wavelength files he'd supplied to the Company. He waited for the caller to verify his identity while he forced his breath and heart rate down to a slower, steady pace.

He looked around the small park. No more than a rusting playground in the middle of a grassless knoll, the park was the only such feature on this side of the city. The mist had only recently lifted, and the dewdrops were still sparkling on the few blades of grass they had to choose from. Besides the woman and her dog, there was no one else outside. It was a pristine scene, even considering the weary, run-down area of town his team had been assigned to.

"Very good," the voice on the other end of the phone said. "Joshua, we have an updated SITREP and possible location."

Joshua grimaced. He hated his employer's use of military jargon and acronyms. His contact at the Company, like his own father, had no military experience or training, choosing money and influence as their primary weapons of choice. The real work, the work that actually *mattered*, they left to people like Joshua.

"Go on," he said, already growing impatient. The sound of the man's voice only reminded him of his failed mission the night before.

"The plane landed in Manaus, and the group visited a home in the city. They stayed the night, and are now leaving."

"And where are they going?"

"It's impossible to know at this stage, but we believe they will be traveling by river, possibly preparing to embark up- or downstream."

Joshua took in the information, immediately parsing it against what he knew of the situation. If they took a barge or public boat, it meant they would be with other people, tourists, and they would have to go in quietly. Collateral damage was not an option on this mission. The hotel attack was only planned because the Company wanted a quick turnaround. Joshua's reconnaissance of the establishment convinced him that there would be no deaths, outside of a few of the group members too stupid to get out of the way as they came for Dr. Meron.

"And why would they choose to travel so slowly in that case?" he asked. "Why not take a plane, or drive?"

"We believe it means that they are heading into the rainforest; their destination is therefore most easily reachable via one of the feeder rivers, and there are no airstrips nearby. It's the rainy season, so the waters will be flowing higher than normal, meaning boat travel is the most sensible transportation choice."

Joshua knew this as well, but he didn't interrupt his employer.

"In addition, they may have an additional team member. A professor, the owner of the house they stayed in. We can't tell for sure until we have eyes on, but you need to be aware."

Joshua nodded, still thinking. "Mission parameters remain the same?"

"No," the voice said. Joshua's ears perked up slightly. "*If* they in fact head into the jungle, we will have no need for the stealth we've required thus far. The objective is the same — we need Dr. Meron, alive, or we need whatever it is she is looking for — but there will be no local authorities in the rainforest to wonder about any 'loose ends' you need to tie up. Once they leave the city, we're interested in speed."

This is good, Joshua thought. The sooner the mission was accomplished, the sooner he could get back home. He was usually more than happy to be in the field, but this particular mission was one he despised. His father's emails explaining the parameters and objective were strange enough — usually he'd get at least a phone call with the mission details — but his contact at the Company had also proven to be nearly insufferable to work with. The man called every day, expecting an update, offering his "advice" to Joshua about how best to control the unfolding situations, and even suggesting how he should manage his team. He'd held his tongue so far, but he wasn't sure he'd be able to refrain from comment much longer.

"I'm pleased to hear that," he said. "My team is growing restless, and given last night's —"

"Please, do not worry about last night," the man said. "We are hoping to include more data points for our next intelligence briefing, and —"

"If you would have allowed my team to do our *own* intelligence gathering, this wouldn't have been an issue... *Sir.*" Joshua said.

There was a long silence, and Joshua steeled himself for a dressing-down. The first million dollars had already been safely wired to his accounts, but he was very interested in receiving the *other* half of the money as well, upon successful delivery of Dr. Amanda Meron to the Company's headquarters. He hoped he hadn't just argued his way out of a job. He waited for the man's response.

"Unfortunately we cannot do that," the voice said. "It isn't an issue of trust, but of *data sensitivity.*"

Joshua almost asked what the difference was, but caught himself.

"We will remain cognizant of the developments, and provide you with remote support in whatever way possible. You are in charge of the ground team, as well as your particular *methods* for retrieval of the Company's interest, but we must retain control of the reconnaissance."

Figures, he thought. *Whatever.* "What is the remaining time on the beacon?"

Joshua didn't know the details, but the Company had ensured him they were tracking the target using a GPS beacon. He wasn't given the specifics, another fact that irked him, but he knew the Company operated in ways that seemed frustrating to him. He assumed the beacon was placed in a bag one of the group's members was carrying.

"The device will be charged for a total of at least two days, but starting this morning it will go into a low power mode, and will only emit a signal every hour, then every four, until it dies."

Joshua shook his head. *We shouldn't have started tracking them until we* knew *they'd go off the grid*, he thought. But he knew they would have done a lot of things differently, had he been fully in charge of the mission. He made a mental note to renegotiate his contractor status with the Company next time he was in the office.

"Fine," he said. "Then I need to get my team on the road. I'll be out of signal range, even from the satellites, once we hit the heavy jungle cover, so my updates will be sporadic."

"Understood. Thank you, Joshua."

Joshua hung up the phone and started walking back to their safe house nearby. He saw the woman and her dog rounding the corner near the edge of the park, heading back in his direction after a lap around the square. He smiled, waving as he crossed the street.

The dog whined again, its tail wagging as Joshua left them behind.

CHAPTER 27

Ben's group set out early the next morning from Archie's home. The old man had a surprising cadre of equipment, and he and Reggie had spent an hour that morning discussing what to take and what to leave behind. They finally settled on just adding some smaller survival tools and devices to the three packs they already had. Reggie was mostly unimpressed with the offerings, claiming much of the gear was "too old," "outdated," or "just for looks." The two men took turns throwing friendly insults at one another as the rest of the group worked on cooking, eating, and cleaning a massive breakfast.

Their location was within walking distance from the house, only two blocks south, so they began walking up the gentle sloping street just as the sun was inching over the horizon on their left. When they reached a small shack set off from the street a few paces, Archie stopped and pointed at the building. Ben looked above the tiny building and saw a simple, hand-painted sign written in Portuguese, with an English translation just below it: *Boat Tours.* He was surprised to see another hand-painted sign covering the only window on the shop's face: "*Closed.*"

"It's open," Archie explained. "They just don't do a lot of marketing. Helps keep the tourists out." He turned around and addressed the group. "Wait here. I'll be able to get us a pretty good rate."

Archie walked across the cracked concrete walkway that led to the shop's front door and banged on the window. Footsteps sounded from inside the building, and a heavyset, drooping old man yanked the door open. Ben watched the two older men exchange words, the shop owner exaggerating his speech with wild arm and hand motions. Finally, Archie turned back around and smiled. He walked back to the group.

"Great," he said. "We just need to find the boat down at the docks. They'll call down and tell the captain to expect us."

Without waiting for a response, Archie began walking south again, the group in tow.

Ben sped up to match Archie's pace. "Tell me again why we have to take a boat? Wouldn't it be faster to fly?"

Archie shook his head. "No, it's the end of the rainy season, so much of the lower areas are flooded. The rivers are easier to navigate, but runways are either nonexistent or in unknown condition."

"What about flying over to Peru or Bolivia first, then heading north into the area we're looking for?"

Archie chuckled. "The place we're going is as remote as any; some of the most unforgiving environment on the planet. You do not just 'hike in' from those countries — the only place to fly to in Bolivia right now is La Paz, and then you'd need to cross Las Cordilleras and the Altiplano, and of course navigate the cliffs and falls to get down to the levels of the upper basin. If we survived that, we'd then need to figure out how to get downstream the rest of the few-hundred miles we'd need to travel, since we didn't bring a boat. The forest is so dense in these parts that traveling is only possible on the river, and believe me, we will want a boat."

Ben nodded. "I'm all for using a boat, it just seems slow."

"It will not be. The river's width will make the current slower in most places, so it will not be a challenge to push the boat upstream. Besides, the boat is big, and has a motor. See?"

Ben followed the man's finger as he pointed down the street. They'd slowly rounded the top of the hill and were now descending down the other side. The stretch of docks connecting Manaus to the rest of the Amazon River were now in full view, and the sight took Ben by surprise.

Behind him, Julie and Amanda both gasped.

"Woah," Rhett said.

"Welcome to Manaus," Paulinho said, the last of the group to clear the ridge.

Ben wasn't sure what to expect when Archie had explained that they'd be traveling by boat. He supposed the boat would have been an open-top, flat-bottomed boat, pushed along by long poles of some sort. They would pile their supplies in the center of the deck, each taking turns pushing them along upstream until they reached their destination.

He could only have been more wrong if he'd guessed they would travel in a canoe. The docks in front of them stretched across his entire field of vision — boats of all shapes and sizes nearly stacked on top of one another, crammed together closer than the houses and buildings on each side of the street they were on.

But it was the size of the boats that most surprised him. The largest stood a full three stories above the water, wraparound decks on each level, like a floating civil war-era Atlanta mansion. There were three or four of these gargantuan boats, two of them already full of tourists, hanging over the railings and gawking at the passersby far down below. He was close enough to see individual faces now, and there were families, smiling and pointing as they held their phones out over the ledges and snapped selfies.

The smaller boats were still large by his standards — two- or three-stories tall, some twice as long as the largest of the tourist boats. There were freight carriers, flat-topped and powered by massive diesel engines, and other commercial-looking vessels, all bobbing along beside the others.

Even between these larger crafts Ben could see dozens of small, single-person boats, pushing against each other as they fought for dockside real estate. Some of the smallest vessels carried loads of bananas, fish, and other sacks of goods, while others sat empty, awaiting the return of their owner.

The noise was nearly deafening now, as they reached the edge of the congregation of dockworkers and tourists that gathered for the morning departures. The sound had been slowly increasing in volume, but it was only now that Ben realized how intense it had gotten. Vendors yelled for attention, tourists shouted at one another, corralling family members together, and the normal hustle and bustle of urban city life competed with all the rest of it.

The midsummer sun was still low on the horizon, but it was already nearly sweltering. Ben wiped his forehead with a wrist and smiled at Julie.

"Crazy, isn't it?" he said.

"I had no idea it was this… big."

He nodded, turning back to the living picture in front of him. The heat, the noise, and the volume of people and boats all screamed for his attention, but nothing could compare to the river, sitting silently behind the scene.

The river was absolutely marvelous. Ben could barely see the shore on the other side, and the large bridge that traversed the body of water was only visible for some distance before it too vanished. The sparkling morning light gave it a sheen that contrasted sharply with the horizon and sky above it, and painted a perfect backdrop for the thousands of travelers preparing for their journeys.

"Our boat should be one of the midsize ones," Archie explained. He pushed his way through a group of locals and veered off to the left. "The boat is called the *Adagio*," Archie said. "Means 'slow,' but don't let that fool you — speed isn't nearly as important as integrity. *Adagio* has the fuel capacity to get us to the higher basin and back twice, and our skipper isn't as opposed to traveling at night as some other captains are. He's also the only one around who didn't have a tour planned, so we will have the boat to ourselves."

"There it is!" Rhett pointed to a large, three-level boat that floated behind three smaller boats on the water. *Adagio* was stenciled in all capital letters on the bow. Aside from trails of reddish residue that had crept up the boat's side, the *Adagio* was pristine white. One man hauled in lines and curled them up on the deck of the boat, while another, undoubtedly the skipper, watched from inside a glass-enclosed front window. The boat itself was facing the city, but a gentle foam of wake had already formed behind the giant floating machine, the engines already heated up and prepared for departure.

Ben and the others picked up their pace as they descended the rest of the slight hill and approached the docks. The chaos of the masses of people bustling around the makeshift harbor was heightened from their closer perspective, and Ben was growing more and more anxious as every second ticked by.

"Are you okay?" Julie asked, grabbing for his hand. He allowed her to bring his hand in around her waist, pulling his body closer as the walked side by side.

"Yeah," he said. He knew she was only trying to help, but her question only reminded him of his own reclusive tendencies and discomfort of crowds and busy places. "Yeah, I'm fine," he repeated. "I just need to get on that boat and find a quiet corner."

"Soon enough," she responded. Juliette leaned in closer and whispered into Ben's ear. "And maybe we can find a corner big enough for *both* of us."

He smiled, starting to feel more relaxed already. Some quiet time with Julie would be more than welcome, considering how insane the last few days had been. He started daydreaming a bit, hoping the boat ride would be mostly uneventful and give them all a chance to decompress.

Rhett had been walking a few paces ahead of them, and he suddenly turned and darted back into the safety of the group. His eyes were wild, wide-eyed, and it was clear he was distressed.

"That guy, right over there," he whispered. "He's in a black t-shirt and jeans, sunglasses. He's one of the guys that attacked us at the cabin."

CHAPTER 28

Ben saw the man Rhett was describing immediately. He was standing to the side of the docks, between two smaller boats, and looking directly at their group.

"Everyone's going to stick together," Reggie whispered back. "We split up, we're toast. There's bound to be more of them patrolling."

They continued walking, listening for further instructions from Reggie. Archibald, Amanda, and Paulinho formed one smaller group in the back, while Ben, Julie, and Rhett walked directly behind Reggie.

"He's going to radio in and tell them which boat we're heading toward, so we need to plan a distraction. Ben, you have that pack?"

Ben nodded, swinging the backpack he was wearing around to the front of his body.

"Left-side pocket, second from the top," Reggie said. He didn't explain more. Ben fished around for the zipper, then grabbed the small, cylindrical device. He held it tightly in his hand, at first surprised to find such an object in their gear, but then remembered the type of paranoid survivalist they were dealing with in Reggie. "Keep it hidden, and don't throw it until I say."

Reggie turned in a full circle, then faced forward and continued walking. "They've got two more grunts posted up beneath some of the stands on each side of the road. Sunglasses, jeans, and t-shirts. Same uniform. These guys aren't trying to stay hidden — they know we know they're there."

Still doesn't make me feel good about it, Ben thought.

"Everyone listen up," Reggie said. "Take a look at the boat, and the path to it. It's a straight shot. There are three boats about the same size docked near it, and five smaller ones crammed in-between. Memorize the location of our boat, and don't forget it. Visibility's about to get very restricted."

The group visibly tensed, but no one stopped.

"Archie, you got this?"

Archie nodded, his smooth and controlled demeanor unchanged. "I will be perfectly fine, Reggie. Let's get to our boat."

Reggie smirked and addressed the group a final time. "When you hear me yell, you take off toward the boat. Don't worry about sticking together, just get to the boat. Got it? Get on, get down, and don't wait for anyone else."

Ben saw nods all around, and Reggie nudged him in the side. "Ready? Three seconds."

Ben nodded, clutching the cylinder in one hand and the Sig Sauer in the other. He felt the adrenaline starting to pump through his system, remembering the last time he'd been under so much pressure.

You're going to push through this, just like last time. You're the driver, he told himself, *you're in charge.*

"Now!" Reggie yelled. Ben reacted on instinct, tossing the grenade in front of the group about fifteen feet, half of the distance to their dock.

The grenade popped on impact, but didn't explode. Instead, thick streams of smoke poured out over the asphalt road, shielding the entire area in seconds. They ran forward, into the thickest section of smoke. Ben watched his feet, hoping each progressive step found asphalt or wood dock, and not open water.

He felt Julie bouncing at his side, her smaller body pressing into his as they ran forward in tandem. He wanted to reach out and grab her, to help her along, but he knew she was every bit as capable as he was, and he had a backpack and a gun to control.

Ben listened for any sounds of gunfire, or any indication they were being pursued, but heard none. A few people shouted cries of surprise when the smoke grenade detonated, but anyone between his group and the boat dispersed quickly enough. They didn't run into any bystanders or tourists as they reached their destination.

The *Adagio* was suddenly in front of him, and he followed along its hull until he found the gangplank. He hoped the others had been as lucky, but he followed Reggie's instructions and worried only about himself as he launched his body up the plank and into the boat. The boat's engine noise was now matched by a gentle buzzing throb as his feet fell on the boat's bottom deck. He swung the pack off his back and threw it toward the front of the vessel, then turned to wait for Archie, Rhett, Paulinho, and Dr. Meron.

They each walked up the plank without issue, and Ben helped them aboard. The four of them walked toward the front of the boat, then turned and followed Archie up a set of stairs Reggie was pointing them towards.

Reggie flew back to Ben's spot from the front of the boat. "Kick the plank out!" he yelled. "They're searching the boat behind us, and we need to *move!*"

Ben did as he was told, and without pause felt the entire boat float away from the dock. The skipper was already disembarking as the gangplank fell into the brownish waters of the Manaus Amazon. Ben fingered the weapon in his left hand, swinging it up and to the front of his body, bringing his right hand along its other side. He switched his grip, tucking his left hand under and around his right trigger finger, naturally feeling the proper hold. He waited, watching the thick cloud of smoke grow to fill the new cavity left by the large boat.

Ben kept his tense posture, squinting into the smoke, but no shots were fired through it. He couldn't hear anything but the normal noise of daily activity on the shore, knowing that their smoke-fueled getaway was only a minor attraction in the overall insanity of the busy docks and marketplace.

Their distraction had so far worked, but Ben wasn't about to lower his guard. Reggie stood next to him, also scanning the cloud for anything out of the ordinary.

"Think they're going to fall for it?" Ben asked.

"They already did, since we're still alive," Reggie said. "But that doesn't mean they're going to just walk away. They'll probably —"

He cut off his words in mid-sentence, and Ben turned to face him. Beyond Reggie, Ben saw in the distance a flurry of activity in the smokescreen. The wisps wriggled in the air, then parted. A small boat, powered by a single tiny engine driven by one of the two men onboard, broke through their visibility barrier and launched forward toward the *Adagio*. The high-pitched whine of the tiny engine sat atop the remainder of the Manaus marketplace noise, but it was all Ben could hear.

He pointed, but Reggie was still focusing straight ahead. The *Adagio* was now in open waters, but it was still gaining speed. The smoke bubble was billowing upward and receding as it lost strength, punctured by the many currents of wind and air competing against it. Reggie's eyes were fixed on the dock they'd just left, and Ben looked that direction, for a moment ignoring the single-engine craft.

A man stood at the end of the dock, the characteristic sunglasses and t-shirt, staring at the *Adagio* as it entered the Amazon's main channel. He seemed to be grinning at them, but Ben was already training his eyes on the man that stood *next* to their grinning enemy.

This man was larger — *far* larger, if the first man was a normal-sized human being. The second man was all muscle, his glistening bald head and rippling arms poking out from an unfortunate shirt that was in no way intended for appendages that large. Still, Ben cared little for the man's appearance — it was what he *carried* that held his and Reggie's attention.

The man had a long tube in his hands, and he was slowly lifting it up and onto his shoulder. It sat there for a moment, and time seemed to stand still. Ben had the handgun, but he wasn't clueless. He knew his weapon was no match for what the man was about do.

"Get down!" Reggie yelled. Ben ignored him, and instead raised the 9mm up and got into a firing stance. Surprisingly, Reggie did the same, also ignoring his own instructions. They both began firing, but it was too late.

The behemoth pulled the trigger and the RPG left the barrel of the launcher and flew straight toward them.

Ben stood still, watching his fate unfold before his eyes. A part of his mind screamed at him, trying to override his animal instinct to fight. He pushed it away, instead listening to his gut. *If we can just get close…*

Their shots, flying faster than the man's rocket, landed in the water in front of the dock and the two men. One of Ben's bullets hit the boat behind the men, lodging into the hull of the vessel. He heard the impact, even from their distance from it across the water.

The rocket landed, hitting a submerged object in front of the boat. The explosion was mostly contained under the water, but the effects of the blast were no less damaging. Ben felt his feet give way beneath him, and the terrifying realization that he was airborne hit his stomach and his mind at the same time. He reached out with a free hand for anything that might hinder his trajectory, but found nothing. The boat, thankfully, was large enough to survive the massive onslaught of water flying toward it, as well as the force of the blast's wave that pushed against it. The boat's reactive motion stopped Ben in mid-flight, aided by the hard, unforgiving surface of the wall separating the deck's walkway from the interior of the craft. He hit the wall shoulder-first, crumpling down to the deck as the boat's starboard side lifted completely from the water and into the air. He noticed, again, the unwelcome feeling of vertigo as his body became airborne.

The feeling didn't last long, however, and he hit the railing hard, landing in a heap next to Reggie.

"You okay?" Reggie yelled as the boat settled back onto the river. Reggie was already standing, reloading his own pistol from a pocket on the side of his pants. Ben pulled himself up, pushing away the nausea and throbbing pain in his shoulder, and lifted his weapon once again to fire at the men on the dock.

It was only at that moment Ben remembered the single-engine boat. The engine was sputtering, but still alive, having been throttled down as the driver pulled up alongside the tour boat and floated about twenty feet away. He peered out between the railings at their attackers. One of the two black-shirted enemies were communicating via walkie-talkie to the man farther away on the dock, but the other one, having let go of the engine's steering column, was now wielding a small automatic rifle and aiming it at Ben.

He winced, waiting for the man to start shooting. Instead, he heard the quick pops of three rounds from Reggie's gun and saw the man with the rifle flip backwards as he tripped over the edge of the boat. The second man dropped the walkie-talkie, fumbling with it as he grabbed at his own weapon. Reggie made quick work of the man, firing another two rounds at him, hitting him once in the leg and once in the chest. He disappeared into the bottom of the boat, only his backside showing as he lay dying.

Reggie looked at Ben. "It's a lot easier when they're close," he said, shrugging.

Reggie didn't wait for Ben to respond. He fired more shots at the two men on the dock, and Ben silently followed suit. They were far out of range of landing a good hit, but their ruse worked well enough to distract the larger man from loading the RPG once again. Eventually the two men lost interest and ran up the dock, ascending to the street level and into the crowds.

Ben finally started breathing normally again, his body still reeling from the shock and adrenaline. He blinked a few times, forcing the breaths in and out slowly to calm his nerves.

"They'll be back," Reggie said, grabbing Ben's forearm and pulling him away from the railing. "Time to get inside and meet our crew."

Ben nodded, not sure how they'd ended up with this man, capable of staying completely calm in these sorts of situations.

"Good job, by the way," Reggie said. He wore the same grin as always, the slight smirk betraying no sign of distress or even acknowledgement of what they'd just been through. "We'll get you shooting straight before this trip's over," he added.

The boat was moving quickly now, making progress upriver. Ben wasn't sure if they would be followed by any other boats, but he forced himself to continue looking forward. He followed Reggie toward the bow of the boat, where a small staircase rose steeply to the next level. Reggie pushed open a door at the end of the stairs, and Ben saw the bridge and small control room in front of them.

He scanned the room for Julie and found her standing at the opposite side of the room, flanked by Amanda and another man. Rhett, Archie, and someone else were kneeling on the floor. Julie, upon seeing Ben enter, ran toward him.

"I'm — I'm sorry I didn't come sooner," she said, gasping for breath. "It's Paulinho, he's hurt."

CHAPTER 29

Julie stepped away from Ben and returned to the group standing over Paulinho. "It happened when the boat rocked. We came up here to meet the captain and crewman, but then heard the explosion. Then everything went sideways.

"It was an RPG," Reggie said, walking the few paces to the center of the room where Paulinho lay on his back. "How bad is it?"

Archie Quinones turned to them. "Hard to say. He hit his side, mostly, but it could have ruptured his appendix. He can't walk, at least not yet."

Julie looked around. The captain, Juan Esquivel Garcia, had returned to the helm, steering the boat upriver and focusing his attention out the long, shallow window. His only crewman, an aging, squat Brazilian who had introduced himself as Carlo, had slowly backed away from the scene in the middle of the room and was now standing to one side, still staring wide-eyed at Paulinho. Reggie and Archie were holding Paulinho behind his shoulders, while Amanda held his feet, and all three were trying to lift the man from the floor. Ben walked over to help. Rhett, still in pain from his own injury, stood awkwardly nearby.

She wasn't sure what to do. They were being chased by mercenaries, their ship had nearly exploded and sunk, and now members of their team were being injured left and right. She wanted to pull Ben to the side, out of earshot of the rest of the group, and discuss what they were getting themselves into. She was scared, but she knew Ben was feeling the same way — they all were.

She knew what he would tell her, too. They needed to stay the course; they needed to figure out how to solve this riddle, and they needed to do it before the others caught up with them. She didn't understand why, or how they would pull it off, but she knew it was the right answer.

An idea suddenly occurred to her. "Isn't there a small medical facility somewhere close to here? On the river?"

Reggie and Archie looked over at her.

"Someone I used to work with at the CDC stayed there for a while during their residency. It was some sort of hybrid facility, shared by the Brazilian government and the regional tribes. I think they rented it out for research."

She watched as Reggie and Archie mulled it over for a moment.

Archie spoke. "Yes, there is. It is accessible from the main river, but it is difficult to spot from the water, and it's on the way. It would be a good way —"

"We can't waste any time," Reggie said, cutting him off. "It's already going to take three days at full speed, without stopping, just to get to our tributary. From there, it's a half-day's walk, at least."

"But Paulinho needs help," Julie said. "And we don't have anything here that can help him."

"They may not have anything there, either," Reggie said. "I know of the place — it's basically a field hospital, but it's really meant to be a checkpoint for researchers traveling up and down the river. A few beds, some basic medicine, and a surgeon I wouldn't trust to pop a zit. Nice guy though. Met him in town years ago; said he was taking over at this station way out in the sticks, stuck right at the edge of a huge open area just off the river a mile or so."

"It's our only hope —"

"It's not. Staying ahead of whoever's trying to kill us, and making sure we stay on track, is. Paulinho's going to be fine, he just needs rest."

Julie flashed a glance over to Ben. *Aren't you going to help me?*

Ben just shrugged. She realized the four of them were still holding Paulinho in the air. She backed away to the side, motioning for them to take the man downstairs.

"Where are you going to put him?"

"There's a tiny bedroom toward the back of the boat; the skipper usually claims it for personal use, but he's agreed to let us stash him there for a bit."

Julie looked at Captain Garcia, and he nodded once in return.

"We'll know pretty quickly whether or not there's internal bleeding," Reggie said. The four of them, carrying Paulinho, walked by her and stopped just before the stairs. "It ain't the best answer, but it's all we've got."

Julie didn't accept this. "No. Stop. He needs *help*. We aren't going to just wait around to see if he gets better or worse."

Ben and Amanda, holding Paulinho's feet, began descending down the steep steps. Reggie and Archie lifted him to shoulder height and walked slowly forward. Paulinho groaned as they jostled him around.

"I'm with you." Rhett was suddenly at her side, and she nearly jumped as the young man spoke. "He needs help. It's a good idea to stop there."

Julie waited for an answer that didn't come until the entire group had made it all the way down the stairs. They paused for a moment to readjust their hold, then continued walking across the deck toward the back of the boat. Julie and Rhett followed closely behind.

"Julie," Reggie said, "it's a good sentiment. Under normal circumstances, we would have to stop. But now? There is no help. We're it. After we leave the city, the only other living organisms out here want to kill you or eat you — or both."

Julie felt herself growing more and more frustrated. No one else offered any input. She knew she was stubborn, but she also knew she was right. "Anyone else want to weigh in?"

Amanda looked her way. "Julie, it's too —"

"Save it," Julie said. "Ben?"

Ben shrugged, then looked around, then back at Julie. "I'm fine with whatever you want to do."

Rage flashed inside Julie. *You have got to be kidding me.* "Seriously? You are *fine* with whatever I want to do?" The group had made it all the way to the tiny room, and Reggie and Archie were focused on configuring Paulinho's head and upper body to fit through the door. Julie watched on in disbelief. *He could die.*

It was as if all of the events leading up to this point were only now registering in her mind. The murder of Amanda's employee, the destruction of her building, the hotel, the incident back at Reggie's house, and now all of this — it was too much to take, but there was no other option. As much as she hated to admit it, Reggie was right. They were alone out here, just their group, the captain, and his lone crew member. There was no stopping, no going back.

She turned around and walked back toward the front of the boat. She briefly explored the remainder of the boat. A centralized set of stairs wound its way to the upper and lower deck, and she chose to go down one level. Another deck ran around the boat on this level, but the main feature of this level was the two large rooms at its center. She pushed the door open that led to the first of these rooms and found herself standing in a reasonably-sized galley and dining hall. There were two folding tables affixed to the floor at the side of the room, and two sets of folding chairs held together and fastened to wall mounts. A few waterproof bins were stacked behind the half wall separating the kitchen from the rest of the room, and she saw different labels on each one, indicating what types of foods and cooking utensils could be found in each.

Even considering the situation, Julie couldn't help but feel impressed. In the back of her mind, she was already beginning to form a travel itinerary for the next time they had the opportunity to visit the Amazon River.

Next time, she thought. *If there is a next time.*

As soon as she thought it, she pushed the feelings away. Ben was just being Ben — stubborn, boorish, and reclusive. He was in the middle of the same situation she was, fighting the same battle and handling it the only way he knew how. She forced herself to keep that in mind, even as her attitude worsened.

She had fallen in love with the man, despite his flaws. He was stubborn but strong, reclusive to a fault, but loyal to the few he trusted and allowed into his life. He could even be reckless when his stubborn side took over and he became driven to accomplish something, but he was still somehow present enough to be in control. Julie had had a few other flings, some of them more serious than others. One of the boyfriends she'd dated in college had even proposed to her, but she laughed it off and assumed he was joking. He cried, and they broke up the next day.

Even into her professional career Julie didn't see herself as attractive or desirable. She had a great sense of humor, and was mostly personable with anyone she met, but she had none of the traits and characteristics of what she thought men would want in a woman. Tall and thin with brown hair she kept "simpled" instead of "styled," as she liked to say, she was about as common as anyone else, and it didn't help that she'd chosen a career that was typically filled by the more 'cerebral' types.

So it was a surprise to her that she and Ben had ended up together, even though they had their frustrations with each other. After Yellowstone, they'd simply continued being together, neither one of them questioning their relationship. She moved into his cabin out of necessity — it was an extremely long commute — and traded in her job at the CDC in Minnesota for a more laid-back position that still fit her interests.

Julie finished her walk through the kitchen and dining hall and entered the room next door. Four sets of bunk beds were bolted to the walls on both sides of the room, and two hammocks were stretched across at the far end. She was initially shocked to realize that they would all be sleeping in the same room, then remembered where they were. There was a closet taking up some space in the far corner of the room and the door had swung open. She saw a simple toilet and sink inside, and nothing else.

How long are we going to have to live like this?

The door at the far end of the room opened. Captain Garcia walked in. He smiled and lifted a hand.

She did the same. "Who's driving the boat?"

Garcia smiled again and waved. Julie cocked her head sideways. "Do you speak English?" She realized that she had only heard him introduce himself — all of the man's discussions with his lone crew member had been in Spanish or Portuguese.

The man waved again. "Small."

"Right," Julie said. "Got it."

She stood in the room, still examining their living quarters for the next few days, and watched as the captain tossed himself up and into the first hammock, and he began to snore almost immediately.

CHAPTER 30

That night Paulinho slept in fits. He wasn't sure if it was the bed or the old, starchy sheets, or the huge bruise on his side, or just the simple fact that he was on a boat in the middle of the Amazon River fleeing dangerous mercenaries.

The group moved him to the main quarters, next to the kitchen and dining hall. Archie and Reggie had deemed him safe to move, but no one knew if his wound was going to be more of a problem if they left it alone or if it would heal up well enough. He could mostly walk on his own, aided by a simple crutch made out of a stick someone had found, but he opted to lie prone for most of the afternoon and evening.

He agreed with Juliette that he should see a doctor, but he also understood Reggie's opinion of the matter. They were a long way from home, on a mission, and time was certainly not on their side. He didn't argue one way or another — the group could determine what was best for the group, and if he was supposed to die here from a festering wound in his side, so be it.

Dinner had been served in the hall, but Paulinho was as unimpressed as the others. He'd watched Captain Garcia open one of the bins stacked in the kitchen, remove a loaf of bread, and open a can of tuna. The man retrieved a slice of bread and began to prepare his meal. He overturned the tuna onto the bread, allowing half of the juicy fish and its liquid to land on the slice of wheat bread, then held the can up for his sole crew member and watched as he repeated the process.

The skipper was done eating by the time his first mate had finished making his one-slice sandwich.

Paulinho was initially disgusted — he wasn't a fan of tuna, especially the canned variety — but as he neared the bin he was pleased to find other sandwich options available. He pulled out a jar of peanut butter and some grape jelly, and made a quick meal. Some of the group came in to join him, but the talking was reduced to simple one-word statements and answers, proving to Paulinho that everyone else was just as hungry as he was.

When he had finished, Amanda and Rhett helped him back to his bunk. Rhett's own injury was doing much better, and the kid was walking around with hardly a limp. He was quiet, choosing to sit alone rather than with the rest of the group at dinner, but Paulinho wasn't bothered by it. He assumed the kid was still getting his legs under him, and intended to give him space.

He had dressed the wound again as soon as they came on board, and Reggie had reported that it seemed to be healing nicely. Paulinho thought back to when they had begun this leg of the journey. It seemed like a year ago when they first boarded, and Paulinho was surprised to admit that they had made great progress during the day, so far unimpeded by the men who had fired on them earlier. He struggled onto the bed, but felt immediately relieved to stretch his legs out and begin to fall asleep.

Even before his eyes were closed he knew he would be dreaming again. There was something inside him, something urging him forward into sleep, that told him. It would be the same dream, the swirls and the gentle dance of the shadows in front of his eyes, part of his mind's recreation of an event he didn't remember and yet still happening in front of him, not part of him at all.

He was correct, and as soon as his eyes closed the dream began. It was stronger this time, somehow more vivid than all of the other dreams he had. The subject matter was the same — the same imagery, the same scene, but it was different. It was no longer in front of him — he was a part of it. The shapes moved around him as if he, too, was also moving. He played with the shadows, reaching out with his arms and hands and swirling their bodies around him. It was a jovial dream, one both captivating and positive as well as nostalgic. There was nothing more than colors and shapes, so it was impossible to tell where, in fact, this particular scene was taking place, but Paulinho's mind seemed to think it had been there before.

The dream lasted a mere five minutes, but to Paulinho the dream itself was an hours-long recreation of an event that he had attended before, only in his mind. The conscious part of his brain tried to make sense of the images; it tried to place the shapes and colors and events in chronological order, in some way that made sense. It was in vain, of course, as Paulinho's mind had no concept of its other half, he was merely a gracious captive of his own imagination.

The dream ended, and Paulinho entered a different phase of sleep, this one restless. His side ached, and he awoke in a cold sweat. The discomfort of the sleeping position began to cause him more pain and he sat up in bed. He swung his legs slowly over the edge and placed them on the cold surface of the boat's wooden deck. Feeling around in the dark for his staff, he collected himself and walked up to the top deck.

The clean jungle air was a welcome change from the stuffiness of the cabin, and he inhaled deeply as he leaned over the edge of the riverboat. The captain and crewman had alternating shifts during the night, and Paulinho wasn't sure which of them was currently at the helm, but the boat continued steadily upriver. Compared to the gentle hum of their engine and the water it displaced, he couldn't hear much of the jungle noise around them. He strained to listen, trying to hear anything reminiscent of what he knew the jungle should sound like at night. It seemed apprehensive, like all of them. The giant boat plowed into its home, and it retreated in silence as they passed through.

"Need some fresh air?"

Paulinho whirled around, only to wince at the severe pain the movement caused. Amanda was smiling at him from the top of the stairs.

"Sorry," she said. "I didn't mean to alarm you."

"No," he said. "It's not you, it's this…" he pointed to his side.

"At least you're up and walking around," she responded. "I'd be on my butt for a week if I even got a cut on my finger."

He smiled as she joined him on the top deck. In the darkness, they watched the deep shadows of the trees and their hidden life float by them.

"What do you think is out there?" He asked.

"Everything," she said. "Everything, and it's watching us."

He laughed. "Well, that's dramatic."

"Unfortunately I have never been in the jungle, so I get to maintain the illusion that this place is one of the most dangerous on earth, full of monsters and creepy crawlies no one's ever heard of."

Paulinho turned to her and grinned. "You have an active imagination, but that's not too far from the truth. This place *is* full of monsters and creepy crawlies, but most of them are documented and we've heard of them." Paulinho sighed. "Hey, while I have you here, I've been meaning to ask you —"

"Been having nightmares?"

Paulinho stood silent for a moment. "How'd you know?"

Amanda laughed. "Sorry, just a guess. In my line of work, friends and acquaintances usually always come to me when they're having weird dreams. You're out here on the deck, at night, and you need to ask me something. Just trying to connect the dots."

"Yes, well, I wouldn't exactly call them nightmares. It's… it's more like a really nice, pleasant recurring dream. One I've had a few times all my life."

"I can't really interpret dreams. No one can, truth be told. At least not with any reliability."

"No, it's not that," Paulinho said. "I'm not sure this one can be interpreted. I just want to know why it's getting more and more vivid."

"Are you sure it's not just because you were asleep only moments ago? You remember it in greater detail?"

"Pretty sure," he said. "It's not exactly a *vivid* dream. It's like swirls, and colors, and dancing shadows. I don't know what it is exactly, and I never will. But everything — the colors, the swirls, all of it — it's like it's happening all around me, it's more… in my face. Does that make any sense?"

Amanda thought for a moment, focusing on small rippling waves far down below as the boat cut through the water. She looked up into Paulinho's eyes. "Not at all."

They both laughed, then Amanda continued. "Seriously, though. In my profession, dreams aren't ever artistic. They are scientific exploits. Results of a strange assortment of chemicals and reactions in the brain, all melted together into one picture or video that seems to make sense to the person experiencing it. But the thing is, when you start studying it closer, you realize it doesn't make sense. None at all — the science starts to break down, and you can't re-create chemical reactions in the lab. Heck, the only way we've been able to actually study *real* dreams has been to figure out a way to *record* real dreams."

"That's what you've been doing at NARATech," Paulinho said.

"Exactly," Amanda said. "No pun intended, but it's always been my dream to figure out a way to better study dreams. I want to understand why people dream, what they dream about, and what it all means."

"It's not enough to ask people about their dreams?"

"As I'm sure you know, people often don't remember their dreams the morning after. They have a hard time piecing things back together because the human brain seeks patterns. The pattern recognition module that we are all equipped with in our heads is extremely strong and well-developed. What makes sense to our subconscious mind when we are sleeping is almost inconceivably ridiculous when we wake up."

Paulinho thought about this for a moment. He had to agree — trying to remember his own dreams was usually a fruitless endeavor. Most of the time he could recall the major events, people, and places, but the details were a mess.

"That's why in a dream you can have three mothers and a father with seven legs, and it all makes perfect sense while you're dreaming. Then, when you wake up, your conscious mind, trained over years of life and countless millennia of evolution, tries to piece things together in a streamlined way. It removes the minor details — more than one mother and more than two legs — and makes you think that you dreamt about your mom and your dad. Of course, that's not very interesting at all, so in a few hours, or a few days, we will forget about that dream entirely.

"I tell my patients to write down their dreams, as soon as they can remember them. Some of them are pretty diligent about this, and they will even keep a small notebook and pencil in bed with them and write down their dreams as soon as they wake up."

"What does that help with?" Paulinho asked.

Amanda shrugged. "You know, we're not entirely sure if there is any benefit at all to being able to more clearly remember our dreams and to be able to dictate them. Some of our patients tell us that by writing down their dreams they are more apt to fall into what is called a 'lucid dream,' a situation where the dreamer feels as if they are in complete control over the plotline of their dream."

"I've had one of those before, I think," Paulinho said.

"Most people have," Amanda said, "and most people swear it allows them to solve problems they are struggling with in their waking life, or have better relationships, or be more successful in general."

"That sounds like a stretch."

"It does, but you would be amazed at what the human brain is hiding from us." Amanda paused again, looking out over the water. "Take for instance this 'golden man' we're chasing. Our computers were not hacked, our software was not glitching, and there was no one playing a prank on us. The scientist in me keeps saying that there is no possible way an anomaly like that can happen, especially in people of a related ancestry. It's more than coincidence."

"It is a little weird."

"It's more than a little weird," Amanda said. "It's downright *creepy*. We don't even have the technology to record dreams in minute detail. The best we can do is squishy images that blend together over the course of a single dream state. But this little man that keeps showing up in all of these dreams is in perfect focus, every time. It's beyond me how that can happen, except when I remember that the human brain is a puzzle that hasn't been solved."

"And it doesn't help that someone else out there seems to want to know what the answer is as well."

Amanda visibly shook. "Our technology is patented, but it's not hard to request usage of our facilities. In fact, they weren't mine to begin with; my investors allowed me the exclusive use of the space after a few months." She sniffed, but Paulinho couldn't tell if she was crying or not. "There's no reason for people to die over this, whatever it is. This journey that we're on will hopefully give us answers, but I can't imagine it leading to something worth killing people over."

Paulinho nodded, looking straight forward. The boat turned gently, changing its bearing as the river did, winding slowly west and north over the massive expense of jungle that cut through the Amazon basin.

"Well, I think I'm going to give it a few more minutes then head inside," Amanda said. She reached over and squeezed Paulinho's hand. "You should, too. You need to rest. Please take care of yourself, okay?"

Paulinho nodded again, not responding at first. "Yes, of course. I think I will turn in now, actually. Goodnight." He turned himself slowly around, leaning heavily on the crutch and starting to walk back toward the stairs.

CHAPTER 31

"I can't believe you wouldn't back me up," Julie said.

"Jules -"

Julie cut Ben off before he could fully respond. "No, don't even start with that. You completely ignored me yesterday, and you want to try to argue with me now?"

"No," Ben said. "I don't want to argue with you. I never do. And I wasn't ignoring you yesterday."

Julie gave Ben that look that said, *this is going to be good.*

Ben sighed. "I wasn't *ignoring* you. I just *disagreed* with you."

Julie's face opened, mouth and eyes widening in unison. Ben could almost feel the impending verbal onslaught that was about to ensue. "No, wait. That's not what I meant."

"You *disagreed* with me? About what? About coming down here to look for your mysterious company you've been chasing for months? About skipping a vacation so that you could traipse into the jungle and try to get us both killed? Did you disagree about those things?"

Ben knew he had to stop the onslaught of questions before they escalated into a high-pitched maelstrom of estrogen-laden fury. He quickly said the first thing that came to mind. "Well, yeah, I disagreed with you about those things, and that's why we're here. But no — I was actually talking about, uh, specifically —"

"Are you *stupid*? Do you even listen to yourself when you talk? I can't believe I fell for this. I can't believe I fell for *you*."

Ben struggled to find the words. He stared blankly at Julie, feeling more and more like a bear caught in a trap. He'd seen more than a few bears caught in traps — idiotic hunters sometimes thought they were still a reasonable way to haul in a large catch. The bears would struggle at first, reacting and recoiling against the immense pain and shock of being ensnared in a bear trap. After a moment of struggle, they would grow quiet, as if contemplating their next move. Then, after some deliberation, the bear would inevitably react explosively, trying in vain to free itself.

As a park ranger, he'd seen a video of the entire process, recorded by some sick cameramen who had for some reason refused to help the poor creature.

"Ben? Are you even listening?"

Crap. "Uh, yeah. Sorry."

Julie shook her head. "I don't even know why I keep trying with you."

"Wait, what? What do you mean?"

"I'm not going to explain it, Ben. If you can't figure out what we're talking about, that just proves my point." Julie turned around and stomped out of the room.

Ben stood there for a second, watching the door swing shut behind her. He had obviously done something wrong, but he couldn't figure out what it was. She was mad at him for — *what?* Had he said something that had pissed her off? He shrugged, ignoring the fact that he was the only person in the room.

This was part of the reason he had focused so much attention and energy on completely ignoring the opposite sex for most of his life. His last girlfriend, if he could call it that, had been in third grade. While most of his friends had grown up to be hopeless romantics, he had merely grown up to be hopeless. His buddies at the park often tried to remind him that Julie was way out of his league, but any rebuttals he could come up with were weak — even he knew it was true.

This woman had crashed into his life almost as abruptly as the explosions and ensuing action at Yellowstone had, only months before. Their relationship was one of necessity — they were forced together.

So why did he care so much? Why was he struggling with the words to simply tell the girl how he felt? Ben knew he loved Julie, he just couldn't seem to put the three words together in the correct order out loud, and certainly not in front of her.

He walked out of the room and up to the winding staircase to the top deck. *Some fresh air would be nice,* he thought. Back home, fresh air was always in season, and it was always useful to combat whatever he was going through.

The top deck opened to him with a gust of humid, hot air. *Not the same as home, but it will do.* Ben breathed deeply and took it in, walking to the edge of the boat. They'd been traveling upriver nonstop for almost two days now, and he wondered how much longer they'd need to travel before reaching their destination.

Or how much longer we'll need to travel before they find us…

He had a sneaking suspicion "they" knew exactly where they were. Rhett, Archie, Paulinho — all of the others seemed to sense it as well. *Why would they leave us alone for a few days, after trying to stop us from leaving Manaus?*

He didn't want to think about it, but he knew the answer.

They need to know where we're going.

He sucked in another breath of jungle air. *Yes, this is good for me.* He closed his eyes and tried to let the air wash the strange thoughts and feelings out of his system. He opened his eyes, turned toward the back of the boat, and saw Amanda standing on the deck.

Or, rather, he saw the *backside* of Amanda standing near the stern of the boat.

Her legs, long for her short stature and starkly pale against the deep greenish-brown of the jungle backdrop, were the first thing he noticed. He followed the woman's form up to her back, loosely hidden behind a tank top that she had been wearing since they left the city. The shirt did its best to hide her back, but Ben immediately noticed her soft shoulder blades, perfectly shaded by the overhead sun. Her hair blew gently in the wind, each time lifting from its station and floating, then settling back down right where it needed to be.

He walked toward her.

He stepped up next to her at the end of the deck and leaned against the railing. The boat's wake cut a perfect "V" through the water, reminding Ben how quickly they were moving upstream.

"Hey Ben," Amanda said.

"Dr. Meron," he replied.

"Please, call me Amanda."

"Right, sorry." Ben wasn't sure what to say, so he did what he did best — he stood there awkwardly, pretending to be interested in a small flock of birds that were squawking at each other from opposite sides of the river. He had the sudden urge to skip a rock, or at least to chuck one as far as he could. His mind wandered back in time to when he was much younger, when his father would take him out to the lake that had freshly thawed after winter to teach him how to skip rocks.

'It all starts with the best rock,' his father would tell him. 'It's worth spending half a day looking for the perfect rock, even though you'll only get one throw from it.' Ben always wondered if there was a deeper meaning in those statements. There seemed to be multiple layers of meaning in everything his father told him growing up.

After his father died, Ben made it a point to stop trying to decipher everything anyone ever told him and just take things at face value. He assumed that people meant what they said and said what they meant, and he did his best to do the same. He was never very good with people anyway, so he used the philosophy as an excuse to grow more and more reclusive as he got older. Still in his early thirties, Ben was fit and well-built and could take on most kids a decade younger. His job as a ranger helped him stay in shape, but every now and then he felt the creeping effects of time slowly wearing him down.

"So," Amanda said, breaking the ice. Ben snapped out of the past and looked over at her. "How you doing?"

"Good, I guess. Been a while since I've been shot at."

"Yeah, I read about all that Yellowstone stuff. You're pretty much a national hero."

"Not in this nation," Ben said. He wasn't sure if that was cocky or humble. "Besides, they got the story wrong. Reporters, you know?"

"Well, Paulinho filled me in on some of the details, but I'd love to hear the story sometime." Ben couldn't be sure, but he thought Amanda inched a little bit closer to him.

"Yeah, definitely." He flicked his head back and forth, still apparently looking for a rock he knew didn't exist. "How are you doing?"

"With what? My entire business falling apart, or my employees being murdered?"

"Sorry, I —"

"No, it's fine," Amanda said. "I'm not trying to be harsh. It's just... fresh on my mind."

Ben felt embarrassed for some reason, but Amanda continued, saving him the awkward silence.

"You know, I've always been pretty independent. That's part of the reason I moved down here. I'd always wanted to start something of my own, but people thought I was naïve."

"What people?"

"Parents, mostly. My dad and mom owned a restaurant for a little while, back home. They never came out and said it, but I always knew they thought I wasn't cut out for entrepreneurship. Truth be told, I'm not. I just wanted to do research on my own terms. NARATech was a perfect fit — investors that want to turn the management burden over to someone else, a dedicated facility that was ready to go, and in a place that I've always wanted to visit."

"Well, from what I've seen, you're doing a pretty good job."

"From what *I've* seen, we are all one small mistake away from death. And it's all my fault."

"It's really not," Ben said. "No one could have predicted this, and no one could have prevented it. This 'investor' you have is the same company that I've been trying to track down for months. They're extremely powerful, very well-funded, and are able to stay well under the radar when they want to."

Ben heard Amanda clear her throat, then she wiped her eyes. "What if this doesn't lead anywhere? What if we're chasing something that doesn't exist, and we end up in the middle of nowhere with no way to call for help?"

Ben knew the questions were rhetorical, but he answered anyway. "Well, Reggie's here. He seems to have a lot of experience with, uh, this type of thing." He paused. "And, you know, we're all here, for whatever it's worth. Archie, Rhett, Paulinho. And me." He glanced at her again, and she was staring at him. He quickly looked away.

"And Julie," she said. It was more a question than a statement.

"Yeah, Julie."

"She's great, you know."

Ben nodded. "I know."

"I wish —" Amanda couldn't finish the sentence, whatever it was going to be. She sobbed, covering her face with her hands. Ben immediately felt himself leaning in toward her, unsure why he was reacting this way.

He hesitated a moment, then reached out and put his arm around her. Amanda leaned in harder, pressing her body into Ben's side before he could react. Her sobs became stuttered and she nearly forced him to hold her. She was smaller than he realized, and he had to stoop a bit to allow her head to fit in the nook under his chin. He wasn't sure what to do next, and found himself stunned into inaction.

He heard a noise, a creaking stair, and lifted his head to see Julie standing at the top of the staircase. She turned her head slightly to the side, as if trying to decipher what she was seeing. She stared for a moment, neither of them speaking.

Then, slowly and deliberately, she turned and headed back down the stairs.

CHAPTER 32

Julie ignored Ben for the remainder of the day, even choosing to eat out on the deck on her own. Ben tried approaching her a couple times, but whenever she saw him coming she darted back the other direction. The boat was large, but it was far too small to hide from him forever, and Ben made it a point to continue tracking her down whenever he could, hoping to talk. Most of his day was spent outside on the deck, waiting for Julie to pass by so that he could follow her until she walked the other way.

That evening, the boat turned again and headed down another offshoot of the river, an even smaller feeder river. The canopy of trees combined above their head and closed out the sun, causing the night to set in far earlier than anyone had expected it would. They were now far away from the cities dotting the main Amazon tributaries, and the jungle had woken up.

Both sides of the river featured life forms Ben had only dreamed of. Monkeys chattered and hollered at one another, and birds of every color screamed overhead as they searched for food. He caught a glimpse of a snake, larger than any he'd ever seen, wound around the entire trunk of a tree as it slid onto a branch. The flora and fauna seemed otherworldly to him as well. Bright greens, yellows, and blues with hints of red every now and then could be seen poking out around the large backdrop of blacks and browns. The visibility was no more than a few feet into the jungle, though Archie and Reggie had come out earlier and taken their turns trying to spot water trails used by animals.

At one point the captain himself came out to the deck and pointed at a mound of sticks and vines, piled high above the water at the edge of the river. He whispered something and Archie's eyes grew wide.

"Anaconda," he said. "They live inside those fortresses of sticks, sliding out into the water directly to stay hidden. That one is a big nest. Could be a 15-footer in there."

Ben shuddered. He hated snakes, and only dealt with them if he absolutely had to. He couldn't imagine how anyone could like the slithering, scaly creatures, especially ones that were as wide around the waist as he was.

"They're mostly harmless," Reggie said, as if that made the anacondas seem like warm, fuzzy teddy bears. "They eat mammals, but if you stay out of their way they'll focus their attention on smaller game. Plenty of other monsters around here to worry about, but honestly it's the small stuff that scares the crap out of me."

"Like what?" Ben almost kicked himself for asking the question. He knew he didn't want to know the answer. Back home the only things to really worry about were bears, wolves, careless hunters, and the cold.

Reggie turned to Ben and grinned. "Bugs, mostly. The kind that fight in packs, working together to bring down animals a thousand times their size. Species of ants you can only dream about, and specialized insects designed by the devil himself."

"Do not listen too closely to him," Archie said. "He's always had a flair for the dramatic. He's not wrong, but most of the life in the jungle is harmless to humans, as long as you are careful and watch your step. The rainforest doesn't need to be anything more mystical and magical than any other place. Sure, there is more life per square foot here than anywhere on the planet, but that's all it is — life. It wants to survive and thrive, just like you and me. Not everything wants to kill you, and even the lifeforms that can will only do so if they feel their own is threatened."

Ben listened along as they all stared out at the tree line. Both of the other men seemed to have a profound respect for the natural world, a fact he found admirable. Many people he knew had no appreciation

— no *concept,* even — that the world they were living in had existed far longer than they had, and had thrived without their meddling and help. The Amazon rainforest was no different, and in many ways more intense and more self-sufficient than any other place he had been.

The men swapped stories for a few more minutes until the sounds of the jungle took over. Ben left to take another walk around the deck, hoping Julie would pop up somewhere. He had completed an entire lap around and ended up at the same spot, only Reggie and Archie had gone down below. He was alone on the deck, and he stared silently into the trees for a minute. It seemed as if the jungle was pressing in on them, growing ever closer to the edges of the boat. He couldn't believe a boat this size could travel so far up the narrowing river, but he did remember that Archie had explained that they were traveling during the flood season, meaning the river would be wider and deeper than normal.

Still, there would come a time when the boat would no longer fit through the tunnel carved out by the jungle canopy. He didn't want to know what the plan was then, and he had not asked. He assumed, though, since there were no smaller canoes or boats of any kind on board, they would be walking the rest of the way. No one knew their final destination, which made the trip even more insane.

Ben just hoped they would find answers, wherever the clues led. He wanted — needed — to know what Drache Global was all about, and if it meant he had to travel completely up the Amazon River into an area of the world no one had seen in thousands of years, so be it.

The darkness of the jungle spooked him, and it didn't help that the animals and critters had gone silent. He could now hear the lapping of the waves against the boat's hull, but the night air, thick as it was, carried no other sounds.

He frowned. He knew enough about wildlife to know that animals became eerily quiet when they sensed danger. The jungle, over the last days, had seemed to grow comfortable with the boat's travel, so he knew it wasn't their presence that had alerted it.

He looked left and right, examining the top deck to see if someone else had entered. Seeing no one, he decided to make one final sweep of the top deck before heading back inside for the night.

He reached the second level and was about to continue down to the bottom when he heard a small noise. It was a gentle scrape, the sound amplified by the boat's hollow interior. He stepped off onto the second level and began walking toward the noise at the stern.

Night had fully reached this area of the world, and the jungle, silent as it was, was based in almost complete darkness. Ben considered going back down to see if there was a flashlight in his pack, but decided against it. *It's nothing.* He wanted to believe the noise was just something random, a squirrel or something of the sort landing on the deck and scurrying into a hole somewhere.

But his instincts were on high alert, and he began to feel the adrenaline pounding. The scraping sound, quiet as it was, was deliberate. That much he knew.

He reached the stern and turned to the right. The scraping sound came back, this time even fainter. But it sounded close.

Just below him.

He flung his upper body far over the edge of the railing, trying to get a decent look at the lowest deck of the boat. *Maybe someone was walking around for a nighttime stroll before bed.*

Ben knew it wasn't the truth, somehow. The noise was human-caused, but someone walking around would not have been in the same spot for that long. Someone was sneaking around, and he intended to catch them.

He wondered if he could jump to the bottom deck from here, or if he would miss and simply land in the water, alerting whoever it was that they had been caught and allowing them time to get away.

He stretched even farther over the railing, and saw a black boot. He could see just the sole of the shoe, thick and deeply ridged. Another instant passed and the boot disappeared.

A moment later, he heard the splash.

Whoever he had seen had just launched themselves over the edge of the boat and into the wake behind it.

"Hey!" Ben yelled, turning around and starting toward the stairs. It was a good fifty feet to the staircase, but he made the trip in just a couple of seconds. He bounded down the stairs and onto the lowest deck, and ran immediately toward the back of the boat. He squinted, trying to see in the darkness, but it was useless. Night had set in, removing any hope he had of trying to see who the person was, or where they were. He thought he could hear the sound of swimming, but it was far off in the distance by now.

He watched for another few seconds, then heard footsteps above him. He walked back toward the stairs, ready to explain what he had seen to the rest of the group.

Before he reached them, a massive explosion threw him forward against the wall.

CHAPTER 33

The boat groaned beneath him as boards and supports buckled and collapsed, and the air was immediately filled with thick, acrid smoke.

He coughed, but the boat was still shifting dramatically, preventing him from even getting up to his knees. He turned his head just enough to see the rear section of the lower deck falling beneath the black waters.

Shit.

Reggie was at the top of the stairs, holding on with a white-knuckle grip.

"Ben! Is that you?"

Ben pulled himself up using a railing from the staircase. He knew the boat was taking on water, and fast. "Yeah, it's me. There was someone else down here, they planted explosives on the engine compartment."

Reggie uttered a muffled string of expletives, then turned again to Ben and took a few steps down the stairs. "Here, give me your hand," he said. "We need to get everyone to the top deck before we go under."

Ben reached up and allowed Reggie to help him up the stairs, which, at this angle, seemed more like the rungs of a ladder. He reached the next level and leaned against the wall as he caught his breath. Reggie was already rummaging through a closet a few paces away, tossing out whatever flotation devices he could find. There weren't enough for everyone, but Ben carried a few life preservers back to the stairs and prepared to climb up.

When he turned around to see about Reggie's progress, he was stunned to see that the closet was already taking on water, and Reggie was standing up to his ankles in the murky brown liquid.

"Take whatever you can up with you," Reggie said. "I need to try to get our packs from the room."

Ben knew the room would be mostly underwater at this point, but he did as he was instructed and carried up the flotation devices and coil of rope Reggie had tossed him.

The remainder of the group, aside from Reggie and Rhett, was waiting for him. He also noticed that Captain Garcia was absent.

"Where's Rhett?" He asked.

Amanda and Paulinho, holding his side, both shook their heads.

Archie Quinones stepped up to Ben and helped him with the life preservers. "He must still be down below," Archie said. "Where's Reggie?"

"Still down there," Ben said. "He's trying to find the backpacks. If anyone's still down there, Reggie will grab them." Ben said the words, but he wasn't sure he believed them. Someone had sabotaged their boat, and then swam to shore. Ben had seen them do it. If, by some strange twist of fate, it had been Rhett or the captain, Ben knew they wouldn't still be waiting around belowdecks.

The thought chilled him, and he forced it out of his mind for the moment. They would deal with the saboteur in time, but right now they had more pressing matters to concern themselves with.

Archie started passing out the life preservers, but Ben pulled him back. "Hold on," he said. "Let's use those to keep the backpacks afloat. I'm assuming we can all swim, right? These will just slow us down."

Archie nodded in agreement, and he and Ben began tying the flotation devices together using the rope. "It's crude, but it will do the job. One of us can tie it to our leg and pull it behind us."

"Where are we going?" Julie asked.

Ben looked up and into her eyes. Her anger had melted away into fear, and she seemed as though she had completely forgotten her and Ben's earlier feud. He knew her well, however. As soon as they were safely back on land, Julie would continue with her cold shoulder and silent treatment.

"We need to get to land, obviously," Ben said. "But there's no way will be able to break into the forest without cutting through the trees on both sides of us. We'll have to start swimming upstream and hope we find some sort of opening."

"Swim?"

Ben looked over at Paulinho and realized the man was still injured, and probably still in severe pain. "Will you be okay?"

"I should be," Paulinho said. "I'm not worried about my injuries, it's…" he looked at Archie, then back at Ben. Ben was confused, not understanding what was going on. He raised his eyebrows, waiting for an explanation.

Archie leaned in close to Ben, bringing his voice down so only he could hear it. "We are not on the main river anymore, where all the boat traffic is most of the time," Archie said. "Paulinho's right to be worried. There are almost as many predators in the water as there are on land."

Almost as many predators in the water? Ben tried to read the man's pained expression. *He's concerned now? After trying to convince me that the jungle was only dangerous if you were careless?*

"What other choice do we have?" Ben asked, matching the tone and level of Archie's voice. Julie and Amanda stepped closer to them and took over the lashing together of the floats as the Ben and Archie discussed the situation.

"None, really," Archie said. He looked at the group then back at Ben. "But we are not trained for this; none of us are divers or even very competent swimmers, I'm sure. If we get into trouble…"

"We're already in trouble," Ben said. "Look around. We're on a sinking boat in the middle of an offshoot of the Amazon River. No one is going to come save us; no one will even know how to find us." *Except the group of mercenaries who are already on our tail.* "We need to hurry, no matter what we do."

Archie nodded quickly, then turned and hurriedly helped the women finish lashing the floats together. Ben saw the top of Reggie's head appear on the stairs, and walked over to help him with two of the backpacks. One of them was soaking wet, one was dry, and one was missing altogether.

"I don't think there's anything that would've been damaged by the water," Reggie said. "But the river ate one of the packs, the one with the map and my rifle. We still have the hammocks and three tents, but keep close to that pistol, Ben, they're all we've got now. You guys ready to go?"

"Think so," Ben said. He slung the two packs over his shoulders and walked back toward the makeshift raft that had been built on the deck. The top level was now at the waterline, the back end rapidly sinking deeper into the river.

"Let's get on with it, then," Reggie said. "I would guess this section of river is deep enough to swallow two of these boats stacked on top of each other, so we are not going to get lucky waiting around up here."

Ben tossed the backpacks on the flotation materials, and he and the others hauled the floating island toward the edge of the boat and lifted it up and over the side. It made a gentle splash as it hit the water, and Ben held the rope to prevent it from drifting away.

Captain Garcia appeared on the stairs, his eyes wide and frantic. He ran up to Ben and Reggie and started babbling in Spanish. The only words Ben could pick out were *agua* and *depredadores. Water* and *predators.*

"Whoa, there, Cap'n," Reggie said. "Slow down, take a breather."

The captain shook his head, then walked up to Archie and continued rattling off Spanish Ben couldn't understand. Archie focused on the captain's words, the water creeping even closer to their feet.

Archie listened, then stopped for a moment, as if listening now to the sounds of the forest instead of Garcia's. He held a finger to his lips, quietly motioning for the others to join in.

"Quinones," Reggie said. "We don't have time for birdwatching. We need —"

"Shh," Archie said, silencing Reggie. "Just listen."

Given no other choice, Ben focused on the sounds of the rainforest around him. *What are we listening for?* All he could hear were the chirping of birds, buzzing of insects, and every now and then a holler from a monkey deep inside the safety of the trees. *The same sounds we've been hearing for days.* Aside from the odd stretch of silence just before the engine had exploded, the sound of the jungle had been almost deafening. To Ben, the sounds became a homogenized blur, unable to be separated out into its individual components.

And then, somewhere in the distance, he heard it.

A low, growling roar.

CHAPTER 34

The roar sounded like someone trying to pull-start a lawnmower, only the sound was choppier, spaced out.

The sound stopped and the jungle noises returned to fill the empty space. A moment later there was another noise, identical to the first, only from a different direction upriver.

"Anyone want to explain what that noise is?" Amanda said.

You had to ask, Ben thought.

"Melanosuchus niger," Archie whispered. Ben looked over at the man, seeing the older gentleman with his eyes closed, listening again for the sounds.

"Black Caiman," Reggie said, either interpreting the Latin explanation or jumping in with his own. "It's the apex predator around here, and the larger ones can take down anything in the basin."

"*Caiman?* Like a *crocodile?*" Julie said.

"One and the same, ma'am," Reggie said. "Closer in structure to an alligator, though."

Julie sighed and crossed her arms. "I don't really care what it's *like,*" she said. "I am not getting into the water with those things out there."

Reggie glanced back at Ben, who just shrugged. "Hate to break it to you, but we need to get to land. And the only way to get to land is by getting in the water."

"I'm with her," Amanda said. "Unless you can tell me you've got a way to keep them at bay."

Reggie pulled his pistol out of a pack and held it up. "I don't, but this is a start. It probably won't do much, but I'd rather have it along than not."

The water was up to Ben's ankles now, and the boat was sinking even more quickly. He felt the water creeping up to his calves and knew they didn't have much longer to decide their course of action. He walked forward, physically standing in-between Reggie and the girls.

"This sucks," he said. "I'll be the first to admit it. But we literally have no other choice. We're sinking, and in 10 minutes this boat is going to be at the bottom of the Amazon River. If we get started now, we can stick close to the shore and get to land the first time anyone spots an opening on that side. Jules, I'll be right next to you."

Julie was staring at Ben, but he felt like she was looking right through him. She wasn't crying, but her eyes were glistening with wetness, and he could see her breathing increase in speed as she took in all of the new information. If she felt anything like the way Ben felt at this moment, he knew she was terrified.

He also knew she agreed with him — they had no other choice.

"What about Rhett?" Paulinho asked. "Did anybody see him down there?"

Reggie shook his head. "No, but you're welcome to stay back and wait for him if you'd like."

Ben flashed Reggie a glance, but Reggie shook his head once more, this time making sure only Ben could see the motion.

He's suspicious of the kid, too, Ben thought.

"We can't just leave him down there," Archie said. "What if — "

"What if *what*?" Reggie said. "Listen up, everyone. There is not a 'no man left behind' policy here. There can't be, much as I wish there was. The lower two decks are completely underwater, so there's no way he's still down there, alive." Reggie paused, then looked around. "As hard as it is to admit it, you all know the truth: he's either not down there at all, or something happened to him when the boat blew up. Besides, I checked all of the rooms when I went down to grab the packs."

"What about the bridge?"

"If he was in the bridge, he would use the staircase to come up here," Reggie said.

Amanda stepped forward, getting right into Reggie's face. "What if he's hurt? Injured again? He —"

"He's not on the boat anymore," Ben said.

All eyes turned to Ben. Reggie seemed to be pleading with him silently, asking him not to reveal what he knew. Ben considered waiting, but they would all have to find out sooner or later.

"I think Rhett did it," he said. "We made a mistake bringing him along, but it wasn't anyone's fault. He tricked us."

Ben waited for the looks of shock and awe to register, wear off, then return to normal. As each person considered what he had said, he continued. "We can't worry about that now, even if I'm wrong. All I know is I saw someone jump off the boat and swim to shore, right before the engine exploded. We need to get to a safer place as soon as possible, then we can discuss what to do about Rhett."

And if it wasn't Rhett who'd sabotaged them, it will be too late for him. Ben pushed the thought out of his mind. There was nothing he could do for the kid now.

"Are you saying our boat was sabotaged?" Archie asked. He turned to the captain and relayed the message to him in broken Spanish and Portuguese.

"Without a doubt," Reggie said. "That engine was detonated by explosives. I don't know what kind, or how, exactly, but that's why we're here now. We'll figure out who it was later, but for now, we need to get off this boat."

"I'll take point," Reggie said. Without waiting for anyone to argue, Reggie dove off the angled deck railing and into the water. After three seconds, he surfaced into a perfect freestyle swim.

Carlo jumped in after Reggie, and though he was much more out of shape than the soldier, Ben had to admit he was an able-bodied swimmer.

Amanda grabbed Paulinho's arm as the captain shook his head, made a sign of the cross on his forehead, shoulders, and chest, and jumped into the water, feet-first. Ben could see Amanda's white-knuckled grip on Paulinho's arm, but the man and woman walked steadfastly to the edge, sat on the rail and swung their feet over, then plopped themselves into the river.

Ben knelt down to tie the rope to his ankle, and Archie made sure their makeshift raft was still floating, intact. Julie came down to Ben's level and leaned in close to his face.

"We're not really going to do this, are we?" Julie asked. Ben didn't answer. It was a rhetorical question, and besides — what could he have said?

She waited for Ben to finish, then followed him to the edge of the boat. "Ben, wait."

Ben turned and looked at her. He was struck by how beautiful she looked, the moonlight glancing off her face and hair perfectly, allowing shadows to fall and soften her appearance even more. She was scared, but all Ben saw right now was the woman he had fallen in love with months earlier.

"We're going to be okay, right?"

Ben wasn't sure what to say. He knew she was asking about their current situation, about jumping into the Amazon River in the middle of the night, but he couldn't help but think of their argument. He also didn't want to lie to her.

He nodded, then reached out and grabbed her hand.

She pressed into him and kissed him hard on the lips, and he pulled her close to him as he leaned forward and pulled them both off the railing and into the water.

CHAPTER 35

Hearing the sounds of the caimans far off in the distance didn't help Julie's terror.

Now, however, she was literally swimming toward them, in a river that was pitch-black and full of all kinds of things she didn't want to think about, trying to stay in front of a group of people who wanted to kill them all.

She focused on her breathing, and on Ben's large form swimming next to her in the river. She had never been a competitive swimmer, though she had taken classes as a kid and swam through high school regularly. It had been a while since she had been in a pool, and aside from a few excursions to a lake house with friends, she had never swum in a natural body of water before.

There was something downright unnerving about swimming in water you couldn't see through, a fact that would not leave Julie's mind. She wondered if she would feel any attack from below coming, or if it would sneak up on her completely. She wondered if a caiman was large enough to swallow her whole, so she wouldn't have to think about the alternative.

She also thought about their attackers — they had seemed so hell-bent on shooting them or blowing them up back in Manaus. Why were they allowing them to escape farther upriver? Were they working with Rhett? And if so, why hadn't they attacked them tonight, and instead decided to sabotage their boat and force their hand?

That was it.

She understood their maneuvering. She knew now what they were intending to do.

They still need us to lead them, she thought. *They need us to show them the way. The attacks back at Manaus and tonight were meant to keep us focused on finding the answer, to push us forward.*

She also knew that collateral damage would be perfectly acceptable out here. They needed Dr. Meron, not the rest of the group. Amanda was crucial, but she wouldn't travel alone, not out here. Amanda needed the rest of them, and their attackers needed Amanda.

But picking them off one by one was a terrific strategy — one that would keep them focused, running in the right direction, and scared enough to not deviate from the plan. Once they turned off of the main river channel, into a much smaller and narrower feeder river, their attackers could no longer follow them by boat without being seen. The mercenaries had sabotaged their boat in order to force the group to continue on land. Anyone injured or killed in the explosion would be considered icing on the cake.

But what was next? What happens after we reach land?

The water was warm, but Julie shuddered. She could feel the underwater currents and chop left by those swimming in front of her, and every tiny motion the river made gave her the feeling she was about to be attacked by some horrible, deadly monster.

But the attack never came. They swam in silence for fifteen minutes, even stopping to rest halfway through. They stayed together as a group, Reggie doing a great job keeping the pace slow enough for the others. When he stopped for the second time, Julie swam closer to the group, forming a tight circle of people in the water.

"There's a path between the trees right over there," Reggie said, pointing to the blackness of the forest. Julie had no idea what the man had seen, but she trusted his authority. "Let's get to the path, but keep moving once you're on land. We don't want to be in the way of a jaguar coming down for a late-night sip of water."

Why does he have to keep bringing up new creatures that want to kill us? The thought of a jaguar didn't scare Julie nearly as much, but the more she thought about it, the more she realized it was even more of a threat to them than some of the other animals that had been mentioned.

Nods all around, Reggie continued toward the bank. He lifted himself off the ground and out of the water, and allowed himself to drip off at the edge of the forest for a few seconds. He stomped forward into the jungle as the others followed closely behind, then turned to wait for them. Julie felt the soft riverbed beneath the water rising to meet her feet, so she rushed forward, all too excited to get out of the water. She struggled against an underwater branch that seemed intent on tripping her, then felt her other foot squish beneath the surface into a mud-filled hole.

Disgusting.

She had never considered the idea that she might one day be traveling on the Amazon River, so she especially hadn't considered how difficult it might be to actually walk *in* it. The mud, sticks, and debris that floated and settled below the waterline was like an invisible army, working hard to prevent her forward motion.

Holding me here, trying to trap me.

The thoughts rushed into her brain, causing her anxiety of being attacked by some unknown and unseen predator to only grow with every passing second. She looked up, trying to find someone to help her.

Where is Ben?

She realized how dark it was. The night had descended on the forest and seemed to grow thicker down here, closer to the water and surrounded by the thick, unforgiving jungle. She tried to control her breathing — she hadn't hyperventilated since she'd had asthma as a kid, but she thought she could feel the surge of constricting pressure beginning to seize her lungs.

Ben!

She wasn't sure if she yelled it or just thought it, but Ben was at her side, somehow arriving silently and suddenly.

"Jules, you okay?" he asked.

She nodded, looking up him. The moonlight found a perch between two branches far above them, graciously casting a deep, whitish glow over everything, providing their party with much-needed light. Ben grabbed her elbow and allowed her to lean on it as she freed her feet from the stick and mud hole.

As she stood up and lifted her torso out of the water, she watched Captain Garcia trudging forward through the water, about fifteen feet in front of her. He and Carlo had reached the tiny beach at about the same time, but Carlo was already joining Reggie on shore, their captain hanging back to help the others out of the water.

Captain Garcia turned now and helped Archie out of the river, then Amanda.

"Come on," Ben said, whispering. "We're almost at the edge. Let's get out and —"

Julie was focusing on the shoreline, staring straight ahead, so she missed the attack that happened just out of her peripheral vision.

It wasn't much of an attack, however. She heard a small splash, like the sound of a rock being dropped into a pond, then a larger thud, then Reggie yelling something incoherent. Her eyes involuntarily darted to the left, attracted by the noise. The moonlight made the scene difficult to interpret, so she simply stared for a moment.

Where Captain Garcia had been only moments before, a twisting, tumbling shadow danced halfway out of the water. She forced her eyes to focus, blinking twice. The shadow became two shadows, a man — Captain Garcia — and a...

A monster.

She saw the flicking of a massive tail, clawed feet scrambling for purchase on the man it was attacking, and an elongated, bumpy snout. The creature had wrestled Garcia to the water and was now rolling over and over again, slowly and methodically making its way back to deeper water.

"Ben! The packs!" she heard Reggie shout. "Grab my pistol!"

Ben was already behind her, grabbing the two backpacks floating behind him. He ripped open the top of the first pack and began rummaging through it.

Julie's voice returned, and she screamed. It wasn't any louder than Garcia's, but hers wasn't punctuated by alternating seconds of being underwater and above water. Out of the corner of her eye, she saw Reggie launch himself forward and into the water, but she had no idea what the man was planning to do.

Ben was at her side again, but he didn't stop moving. He ran forward, making slow progress in the water, and tossed the gun toward Reggie.

Ben, unbelievably, was still moving toward Reggie and the wrestling match taking place mere feet in front of her. *What is he planning to do?* Julie wondered.

She watched Reggie working with the pistol, but was shocked when she saw what *else* Ben had retrieved from the pack.

He lifted the machete over his head and waited for a moment to strike downward.

"Ben — don't!" Julie yelled. It was too late.

The water was unnervingly silent. Tiny ripples left on the surface were the only telltale signs of the onslaught, and the caiman didn't resurface.

Neither did the captain.

The group watched, no one daring to move, for almost an entire minute. Julie began sobbing, both from the adrenaline high as well as the emotional impact of what she had just seen, but she didn't care what anyone thought. Ben was next to her again, his arm around her, and he was gently pulling her along the rest of the distance to the shoreline, where the others now stood, waiting.

She felt a moment of relief as her feet fell on the soft, damp mud closest to the river, and she allowed Ben to lift her completely out of the water and onto dry land.

Her relief was only short-lived, however, as she realized that they would spend the remainder of their journey traveling through the forest on foot.

CHAPTER 36

Valère reached into his pocket and grabbed the cellphone. He hadn't even made it across the parking lot to his car before the phone began to vibrate. His appointment had gone well — nothing had changed, but nothing had grown worse, either. His doctor prescribed the same pills as always, and told him to rest and relax as often as possible.

The thought of taking time to rest or relax seemed like a joke to Valère.

He had a job to do, one that no one else in the world was fit to do. He had the skills, the contacts, and the resources needed to pull off the greatest feat of engineering anyone had ever heard of, and the Company was very close to achieving their goal, thanks to him.

Even if it kills me, it will all be worth it.

He held the cellphone up to his ear and accepted the call. "Yes?"

There was a two-second delay before the voice on the other end, crackling through a miserable connection and hard to understand, responded. "Valère. — Have been — so far. No update on — but will keep — posted."

Valère waited until the connection improved.

"— behind the girl and her group, moving forward as planned."

This is good news.

"Mission parameters remain unchanged, though the — has proven to be more resilient than initially assumed. — additional support?"

Valère frowned. "I was under the impression that you would require only a few men to accomplish this task. We have doubled your support already."

"Understood, except — faster with additional —"

Valère nearly cursed out loud at the horrible connection. "Negative, our resources are currently wearing thin for this project." It was a lie, but it was much quicker than explaining the truth. His 'resources' were more than enough to provide some additional support, but there would be no way to get the men in position this late in the game. Even if it was possible, Valère was already working on the next phase of this project.

The final phase of this project.

Valère could almost taste success. His plans in Antarctica had been going well, both the parts that the Company knew about and the parts that were known only to him. This small hiccup in Brazil was just that — a minor setback that, with or without Dr. Meron's research, would not interfere with his ultimate plan.

His phone crackled, and the connection died. He wasn't sure if his contact in Brazil had said anything else, but it sounded to him like their conversation had ended before it had even begun. No, there were no additional men he could send to Brazil, and no, there were no additional resources he would appropriate to their cause.

He replaced the phone to his pocket, and grabbed the bottle of pills out of his other pocket. Reading the label, he twisted off the cap. *Do not exceed one pill per every six hours.* He had just taken one before leaving the office, and he placed another one on his tongue now and swallowed.

Even if it kills me, it will all be worth it.

CHAPTER 37

The path that led out of the water and into the jungle was only a few strides long, a natural opening between two large bushes, likely made more prominent by the animals that used it as an access point to the river.

Ben tried to slow his breath down, hoping his heart rate would follow. It wouldn't be helpful to Julie — or anyone else — if he was still on edge and ready to snap. The caiman, a large adolescent, had come out of nowhere and taken Captain Garcia, kicking and screaming, to his watery grave. It was unreal, unnatural, and insanely terrifying to Ben, but he said nothing.

No one spoke, actually, until they'd been walking for five minutes into the densest forest Ben had ever seen. No pictures, movies, or books could do it justice. He was completely out of his element, surrounded by an alien world that hid both danger and beauty together behind every rock and tree.

"Okay, let's pause here," Reggie said. He turned around and addressed the group. "We have to keep moving, at least for now, but I wanted to take a quick breather. We'll take some time a little later to catch up on sleep, but we need to get away from the river as much as possible." Reggie fumbled around with one of the packs and pulled out a compass. He opened the clasp on the device and held it up, waiting for it to balance. He took a few seconds to check their direction and match it in his head with the destination they had decided upon.

Satisfied he was leading them in the right direction, he closed the device again and put it back into the pack.

No one spoke. Ben looked around at the rest of the group. Archie and Paulinho wore blank expressions, while Amanda looked upset, even angry. Julie looked as terrified as Ben felt, and Carlo seemed disinterested in the whole ordeal.

"Anyone want to say anything?" Reggie asked.

"What are we supposed to say?" Amanda shot back.

Reggie shrugged. "He was a good man, great things, stuff like that?"

"Are you kidding?" Julie was almost yelling. "He *died*, right in front of our eyes. You don't even *care*?"

Reggie paused, looked at the ground — a carpet of bright green mosses — then back up at Julie. He stepped closer to her and lowered his voice.

"Of course I care," he said. "He was one of us, just by virtue of being here with us. Now he's not here. I didn't know him, and neither did you. Doesn't mean we can't make something up, or ask Carlo."

This was an idea Ben hadn't considered, and Paulinho was already hobbling over to Carlo and whispering. Carlo nodded, slowly, then looked up at everyone.

"Good captain," he said in English. He said more in Portuguese, Paulinho translating aloud. "Good father, good husband, loved job."

It seemed like Carlo was finished, but Reggie waited another few seconds to be sure. "Well, I guess that does it. Anything else before we go?"

"Yeah," Paulinho said. "Where are we going?"

"The field hospital isn't more than a few miles away, I think," he answered. "Like I said before, it's off the river a bit, but considering we're no longer traveling by way of river, I'd say it just became a worthy destination for this next leg."

Ben nodded. "They'll have supplies there?"

"Not really, aside from a few tools to fix him up." Reggie motioned at Paulinho. "But it'll be a good enough place to rest, assuming they've got the space."

He turned around and began marching through the jungle, using the machete Ben had grabbed to hack his way through the denser vegetation. "Come on, let's see if we can get inland, farther away from the river. We don't want to be around here come breakfast time. We'll hike for a bit, then catch some shuteye for a couple hours. I'd like to get to the hospital and research station before daybreak."

Ben couldn't believe how detached the man seemed, especially at a time like this, but he was glad Reggie had the gall to step forward and admit it, all while keeping them focused on the next goal. Ben himself had been trying to figure out what their plan should be, but knew Reggie was right to choose the hospital as their next destination. They would need time to regroup, to plan out the next leg of their journey, and there was no sense focusing on any of that if they didn't have a safe place to do it.

He allowed Julie to walk in front of him, taking up the rear position as they followed Reggie's cutout path through the trees and brush.

I just hope it's a safe place, he thought.

CHAPTER 38

Julie was amazed by the level of humidity and heat that still plagued the jungle, even in the dead of night. Every large leaf she passed seemed to be a soaking wet towel, warmed by the day's sunlight and now releasing every drop of wetness it had collected back into the air. The humidity was trapped by the canopy far above their heads, the heavier air settling back down closer to earth and causing an effect not unlike that of a steam room.

They had been walking for two hours, drawn forward by the relentless forward progress of Reggie. He seemed to never tire, constantly hacking away at the thick strands of vines and brush that obstructed his target path. She wasn't sure how he knew where he was going, navigating only with a tiny compass he had attached to his pants. She hoped it wasn't an act of bravado and that he wasn't, in fact, just leading them farther from the river, their only hope of being rescued.

She picked up her pace and tried to walk alongside Reggie. It was difficult, as most of the time the path he was cutting was only wide enough for one person, that there were stretches of land between outcrops of trees that allowed them to walk side-by-side.

"So, what's your deal?" She hadn't meant the words to sound so harsh, but she knew there was nothing she could do to retract them now. She winced, waiting for Reggie's response.

Reggie simply smiled and looked at her. "I take it you're still pissed at me?" he asked.

"Why would I be pissed?"

"Your tone, for one," he answered, still grinning. "But you didn't seem to be too excited about our decision earlier, about not going to the hospital for Paulinho."

"It doesn't really matter anymore, I guess," she said. "That's where we're headed now, right?"

"It is, and it shouldn't be much longer."

Julie nodded, even though she knew Reggie couldn't see it. "Sorry — that's not what I meant though." She paused, trying to articulate her words. "I mean, you… what's your story?"

Reggie audibly laughed, scoffing as he chopped another section of thick vines away. "My *story*? Really?"

"Well, yeah. You're ex-Army, right?"

"Sniper, yeah. Did my time, but it seems like you never really leave it."

"You make it sound like a prison sentence."

"I didn't mind being deployed," he said. "Loved it most of the time, actually. I guess you could say it was the 'office politics' that finally changed my mind."

Reggie started struggling with a section of weeds and branches, and Ben suddenly appeared on his other side and grabbed the machete from his hands.

"Take a break," Ben said. "I'll take it for an hour or so."

Reggie didn't argue, falling back behind Ben next to Julie.

"Didn't really get along with people you worked with?" She asked.

"People I worked for, mostly."

Julie knew he was being purposefully vague, which only made her want more information. She had always been stubborn, but she wasn't gossipy. She was interested in the man's past, but she didn't feel an overwhelming need to pry, so she let it be. Reggie seemed like a man of few words, except when he was making a wisecrack. His silence about his past did not concern Julie; so far Reggie was trustworthy enough, and he seemed to be the kind of man who wasn't interested in sharing his own background with strangers.

Reggie didn't wait for her to ask another question. He walked up to Ben and waited at his side as he finished the machete work. Ben hacked away another handful of branches, revealing a small opening between the trees. Reggie held out his arm, stopping Ben before he could continue onward. Both men turned around and looked at the group behind them.

"Let's stop here for a few hours and try to get some sleep," Reggie said. "I'll check that we're still heading in the right direction, but either way I think we are far enough from the river now. Ben, want to help me with those packs?"

Ben swung the pack he was carrying over his shoulder and onto the ground. Reggie opened up his own pack and retrieved two large, zippered green bags. He unzipped one and dumped out the contents inside. He turned the large roll of nylon over in his hands a few times, looking for a corner. Satisfied, he grabbed a corner of the material in his fist and tossed the bundle outward in front of him.

Julie watched as the flattened shape of a triangular tent unfolded from the bundle. Ben and Archie attempted to roll out the tent from Ben's pack in a similarly practiced fashion, but lacked the flourish of Reggie's throw. Eventually, all three tents were laid out on the ground in the small clearing. The bags each had two small poles inside, and Julie helped assemble one of them for Ben. Reggie was busy tying a section of climbing rope to a tree he had found at the edge of their clearing.

"These are brand new," he said. "They are hanging tents, sort of a combination of hammocks and tents. They're a little heavier than I prefer, and a bit big, but they're pretty spacey inside, enough to cram four adults in each if you have to. They're expensive, too, so I expect that you will take good care of them."

Ben and Archie looked at Reggie incredulously. Julie herself was a little surprised by the statement, and she found herself eyeing the tents suspiciously. Carlo, who hadn't said a word since his captain had been eaten, didn't seem fazed by Reggie's statement, but then again, Julie wasn't even sure if he'd understood what he'd said.

"They're called Stingrays," Reggie said, completely oblivious to the stares he was getting from the group. "Tentsile makes them. Great company, and a fine product. I sell these back home — they're a huge hit."

"I've never slept in a hammock before," Ben said.

"Well, you're missing out," Reggie said. "And these aren't just hammocks, mind you — they're like a little piece of insulated utopia. Protection from bugs and insects, not to mention weather."

"And you think they'll hold all of us?"

"I know they will," Reggie answered. "Here, help me with this." He stretched out a corner of the three-cornered tent and carried it to a tree across the clearing, then tied the end to another section of rope. Ben grabbed the third corner and walked toward another tree on the other side. "Each one can hold plenty of human weight, plus gear. I've stacked five of these babies up, one on top of the other, before. Fifteen people sleeping in a little tent tower in the middle of the jungle."

Julie listened to Reggie and watched as he tied the knots to secure the corners of the tent to the tree. The man lit up as he talked about his equipment; he was clearly in his element. He wore the same characteristic smile as he tied and secured all three corners, showing Ben how to use the clasps. When all three corners were fastened, he tightened the tent's lines and the first tent lifted off the ground.

Julie was impressed. The apple-green floor of the tent was about four feet off the jungle floor, safely out of reach of any of the unwelcome visitors she imagined might want to visit them at night. It looked very secure, and the ratchet-tightened lines seemed more than strong enough to hold them all. She watched as Reggie jumped onto one of the lines, holding onto the trunk of the tree it was fastened around, and threw the line of a second tent around it, five or so feet higher. He continued this process for the other two corners, and the second tent rose, suspended in midair above the first tent.

"It's really cool and all," Julie said, "but how do we get in?"

Reggie tightrope-walked across one of the lines and dove into the top tent. He reappeared a moment later and threw down to the ground a ladder made of nylon. Satisfied, he stepped out of the tent feet-first and descended the ladder.

"Any other questions?" He asked.

Julie shook her head. She couldn't help but smile. *It was really lucky we found you,* she thought. She glanced over at Ben, who was leaning against one of the trees, looking at Julie. To anyone else, his face was unreadable. To Julie, it was judgment. She imagined what he was thinking right now.

You seem impressed with Reggie.

Do you like Reggie more than you like me?

I can keep us alive just as well as Reggie can.

She smiled at Ben, then turned and walked toward Amanda.

"How you holding up?" She asked.

Amanda frowned. "Everyone keeps asking me that," she said. "How do you think I'm doing?"

Julie tried to hide her surprise at the outburst, but failed. "I — I'm sorry."

She started to walk away, but then Amanda spoke from behind her. "No," Amanda said, "I'm sorry. This whole trip, this ridiculous journey, it all seems so…" she struggled to find the words.

"Unreal?"

"Yes, exactly. I mean, only a week ago we were finalizing the study that I was going to submit to a few university research programs, and then..."

Julie returned to Amanda and grabbed her wrist. She didn't realize until then how small and frail the woman seemed. "Listen, whatever happens out here, just know that we are with you on this. I know it's not much consolation, but Ben and I have been through something similar."

"No, that's actually helpful. None of this seems real to me, I think. The boat, that crocodile thing, and Reggie, acting like nothing happened. And I'm the reason we're all out here doing this."

"You can't think like that," Julie said. "As much as you think it's true, it's not. This company that's after us, if they're who we think they are, isn't going to stop until one of us figures out the solution to this puzzle. Even then..." Julie hesitated, not wanting to talk herself into a corner.

Amanda smiled. "It's okay," she said. "I get it. I might be naïve, but I see the writing on the wall. We are all out here chasing some weird anomaly, hoping to God it turns out to be something real so we don't waste our time and energy dying in the middle of the jungle. Even then — even if we find something — they're not going to just let us walk away from this."

Julie nodded. There was nothing else to say. Amanda was right — none of them had any idea how they were going to get out of this alive. She watched Amanda's eyes for another few seconds, noticing how much older they suddenly seemed. The woman was incredibly smart, but she knew how helpless and hopeless she felt.

"Just know that you're not alone in this," Julie said. "You're in good hands here, with Reggie I mean." She started to walk away, but Amanda stopped her.

"Hey," the woman said. Julie looked back at her. "We're all in good hands here with Ben, too. I mean, he's a great guy." Amanda's eyes flicked back and forth, and Julie could tell she was struggling to find the correct words. "Not that... I mean, back at the boat..."

"Don't worry about it," Julie said. "Not your fault." Julie said it, but she wasn't entirely sure she believed it. The woman standing in front of her, for as small and fragile as she seemed now, was stunningly beautiful. Her hair fell in all the right places, providing a perfect frame for a face that was a mixture of youthfully cute and respectably gorgeous. Julie felt a quick flare of jealousy, but forced it away.

"You ladies ready to get some sleep, or would you rather stand by that tree all night?"

The sound of Reggie's voice grated on Julie's ears. She felt embarrassed, but turned and looked at the man. "No, sorry, we're ready."

Reggie grinned. "Good deal. Let's roll. You two can share a tent, then Carlo and Paulinho, then Ben and Archie can have this bottom one." He motioned at each tent as he explained who would be occupying each.

"What about you?" Julie asked.

"I'm going to kick it in a hammock," he answered, pointing at a long, black hammock he'd tied just underneath the bottom tent. "Makes a better sleeping arrangement for me, personally."

Amanda was already climbing the ten or twelve feet straight up to the top tent, and Julie waited until she was completely inside before she started up the ladder. Once inside, she was again surprised at how spacious the interior of the small shelter was. The ceiling was a few feet above her head, not enough to stand up in, but providing enough height to make the dwelling feel larger than it was. Julie found a blanket on her side of the tent, and she wasted no time getting comfortable.

She hadn't even removed her shoes before she was drifting off into a deep sleep.

CHAPTER 39

"Ben, wake up."

Ben jolted upright in the tiny Stingray tent, causing the entire nylon structure to wiggle and writhe under his shifting weight. He rubbed his eyes and looked over at Archie. The older man snorted once, but seemed to still be fast asleep. Ben turned and looked at the small opening in the tent door that had been partially unzipped.

"Hurry up," Reggie said. "We need to keep moving. Get him up too, would you?"

Ben rubbed his eyes again, tapped Archie and pointed at Reggie, then began making his way to the tent door. He slid out feet first, searching for the rungs of the nylon ladder. Finding them, he descended the ladder and hit the ground. He could hear Archie working through the same groggy procedure, working out tired muscles and a fatigued body, no doubt struggling even more so due to his extra decades of wear and tear.

Reggie had already rolled and packed two of the Stingray tents, and he was waiting near Ben and Archie's to finish the third.

Ben stretched, attempting to force his body awake. "Reggie, come on," he said. "It's... what time is it?"

Reggie grinned. "Don't worry about the time. Out here, day is night and night is day."

"Seriously though," Ben said, I'm too tired for riddles. What does that even mean?"

"It means you've only been sleeping for a couple hours," Reggie said, still grinning. "Follow me."

Ben saw the others — Julie and Amanda, Paulinho and Carlo — already waiting for him and Archie, the last to wake. Ben shook his head in disbelief, still surprised by how tired he felt, but he knew from experience that once he was moving and warming up he'd feel much better.

Archie finally made his way out of their Stingray and to the waiting group. "Anyone make coffee?" he asked.

Paulinho and Amanda smiled, but Ben was still too tired to be amused. Julie seemed to be in a daze, and Ben didn't have the courage to see if she was still fuming at him for his interaction with Amanda back on the boat. He left her alone and waited to see what Reggie's plan was.

"Actually," Reggie said, digging for something from one of the backpacks, "Eat these. Helps with alertness, fatigue, hunger, pretty much everything. Be gentle — they tend to get me a little worked up if I get too big a handful." He tossed the small plastic bag to Archie, who grabbed a small green leaf from the bag and popped it into his mouth. When he was finished, he passed the bag around the group. Ben reached in and took two leaves, pocketing one.

"What are they?" Ben asked, chewing the plant.

"Coca leaf," Reggie said.

Ben stopped chewing.

Reggie laughed. "Perfectly safe, in small doses. 1% cocaine alkaloid per, typically. Which means it's enough for the US government to lose their mind when it comes to importing it, so it's damn near impossible to find… in the United States. But don't get addicted; it's an expensive habit."

Reggie had the last Stingray down and Ben and the others did what they could to help him roll it and pack it into one of the backpacks, still wet from the river. Ben swung the backpack over his shoulder and closed his eyes, silently willing the little leaf's drug to take effect.

He listened to the early morning jungle. It was still dark, but the animals around him were already beginning to get a head start on their day. He could pick out a few of the birds' individual calls to one another, but most of the more distant noises seemed to be just a surround sound mix of jungle life. It was peaceful, but there was an ominous undercurrent to the high-pitched symphony — he knew that some of the birdcalls, as beautiful as they might be, weren't the singsong melodies of courtship but instead the warning klaxons of imminent danger.

Ben knew part of this paranoia was based in his own fear of their situation, and his growing level of discomfort as they journeyed farther and farther from civilization. He chided himself for the feeling, knowing that most of his life he'd been consumed by nature, feeling more at home in the presence of tall trees and deep, silent woods, but he also understood that there was another reason for feeling unsettled: they were being hunted.

So far, the mercenary group behind them had stayed behind them, allowing them to pass through the first few legs of their journey undisturbed. But Ben knew it was only a strategy to wear them down; it was meant to terrify their group and keep them guessing at when — and from where — the next attack would come.

And it was working.

Ben couldn't help but feel the overwhelming pressure mounting. He felt as though his blood had been pushing through tighter and tighter veins, and the intensity of every moment here was growing to be too much to bear. He wondered how the others felt. Paulinho, a good guy, but nevertheless unaccustomed to being out in the elements like this. Amanda and Julie seemed only slightly more comfortable. Archie was doing his best to keep the rest of them — and probably himself, as well — in high spirits, but Ben saw through the veil, knowing that it was only a temporary tactic.

The only two members of the group that seemed to be at ease, or at least unshaken, by their situation were Reggie and Carlo, their boat crew's only surviving member. He knew Reggie was a basket case, trained by years of combat and specially-designed exercises to master his emotions, but he wasn't sure Carlo even understood what was going on. Archie had spent a few minutes discussing their situation with the man, but he genuinely seemed disinterested in the whole affair.

The group began walking, following Reggie through the side of the clearing and quickly reaching the thick, dense jungle once again. Reggie wasn't using the machete he had hanging at his side, instead pushing aside branches and bushes gently, as if he was trying to move quietly.

Ben picked up on the hint and tried to step softly. He was a large man, thick and muscular from many years living outdoors, but he had honed the skill of moving through forested areas silently. He'd developed the ability while learning to track bears, rabbits, and everything in-between. On one occasion he'd even had to find a human — a young boy who'd run off from his parents and gotten lost in the woods.

Here in the rainforest, however, he was way out of his element. This forest did not respect his attempts at stealth the same way the woods back home did. For every twig he accidentally snapped beneath a foot, the forest would echo the noise and reverberate it throughout the surrounding area. He could hear the cooing sounds of smaller monkeys, high above him, watching him through the darkness, and the clicking of millions of insects searching for a late-night snack. Every step he made through the jungle seemed to ignite a chorus of noises, all watching him, awaiting and calculating his next move.

It added to his paranoia. He wondered what other — larger — creatures were out here, and which ones were hungry enough to strike. He couldn't tell if Reggie would be any help in a situation like that, or if he'd even see it coming. He remembered the caiman's attack, and how... *helpless* he had been.

"What are we looking for?" Ben asked.

Reggie stopped, turned around, and looked Ben up and down.

"This," he said, pulling aside another branch, as if pulling back a curtain on a grandiose stage. He stepped forward and out onto a shelf situated slightly higher than the ground in front of them, providing a perch above the entire area.

Julie gasped.

The clearing in front of Ben was long and narrow, broken up by only a handful of shrubs and bushes, and stretched a half mile from their location to the other side, where the trees grew together once again and formed a tight, impenetrable wall.

The tallest of the Amazonian trees at the edges of the clearing connected back together in most places, far above their heads, creating a gigantic bubble of empty space surrounded by forest. It was an amazing sight, larger than any atrium he had ever seen. Even in early morning darkness, with nothing but moonlight poking through the slats between branches and casting long shadows over the entire space, it was a beautiful scene.

"It's wonderful," Amanda said. "Like a postcard."

It did, indeed, look like something out of a magazine, or a wall calendar. It was staged so perfectly, their view framed better naturally than any professional photographer could manage artificially.

But there was something still off about the scene, something Ben didn't realize for a few seconds.

"Is that smoke?" Amanda asked.

Ben squinted, trying to see what the darkness had done so well to hide.

"I think it is," Paulinho said. "Should we get down there?" he said.

Reggie was already moving forward, jumping down the slight grade that led to the floor of the amazing jungle atrium. Ben and the others followed once more, their pace quickened by the desire to learn what lay at the opposite edge of the great clearing.

"Any idea what it is?" Julie asked.

Ben struggled to make sense of the gently rising smoke, darker than the dark shadows of trees behind it, rising from the base of a larger rock outcropping.

No.

It wasn't a rock outcropping they were staring at. The base of the trail of smoke emanated from a structure, the remains of a building that had been scorched down to nothing. His senses immediately went on high alert, and he didn't need to hear Reggie's answer to know what lay ahead.

"It's the hospital," Reggie said.

CHAPTER 40

Both of the larger buildings — the main hospital and research station, as well as the smaller staff barracks — had been burnt to the ground, and there were square sections of smoldering rubble in two additional spots.

"Storage sheds, I'd guess," Reggie said, kicking blackened wood and charred debris out of the way. "Looks like napalm, or something similar. There's hardly anything left. They must have done it last night, around the time the boat sank. Very efficient, too. No explosions."

Ben walked slowly between the main hospital building and the smaller shack, taking it all in. He couldn't help but imagine what it was like for the doctor and researchers here, and whether or not they were able to get away. There was an empty pit at the bottom of his stomach, growing heavier with each passing minute. As if answering his own question, his eyes were drawn to a rectangular room inside the smaller building, now no more than a black outline, like a life-sized blueprint drawn on the ground. Inside the "room," he could see a metal file cabinet, most of the sides melted away, somehow still standing upright.

Next to it, a body. He recoiled, but didn't look away. The person inside the room had struggled, but hadn't left the room when the building went up. He wondered if they'd been locked inside, unable to escape.

He felt a flash of white-hot anger.

"But why do this?" Amanda asked from behind him. She was following Reggie around the perimeter of the razed structures. "Why would they burn it down? If they wanted to come for us, they would have."

"No," he said, "they wouldn't. They're playing with us, trying to force us into a trap."

"What kind of *trap?*" Paulinho asked. He, Archie, and Carlo stood nearby.

"They want us to give up Amanda. Make us think it's not worth it to continue."

It might not *be worth it to continue.* Ben couldn't help the inner monologue, but he pushed the thought aside.

Dr. Meron stepped closer to Reggie. "Is it? Should we just call it? They're not going to —"

"They're *not* going to stop," Reggie said, interrupting her to finish her sentence. "That's the point. They're after *you*, but they're really after what you *stand for*. What you know that they don't. You — *we* — are on to something here, and they know it. They sense it. They're trying to push us out, wear us down, give up the final prize. They're not going to stop if you get captured, they're just going to torture you until you give them everything they need. *Then* they'll kill you." He paused, then looked at the rest of the group gathered at the edge of the forest. "Goes without saying they'll kill the rest of us, too."

"Then how do we end this?" Paulinho asked.

"We finish the job," Reggie said. "We figure out what's hiding at the end of this journey."

"And then?"

Reggie didn't answer at first. "I'm still working on that part."

Amanda was visibly exasperated. "Still *working* on that? Reggie, what's the *plan*? Find this secret treasure, then hope there's a helicopter there too?"

"That would be convenient," he said.

"Why are you here?" she asked.

Ben looked at her. She'd finally asked the question to which they'd all wanted an answer, and she'd just asked it in a quick, no-nonsense way. Why had this man, unknown to just about all of them, stepped up and jumped onto their sinking ship?

He nodded once, then grinned, but his face quickly returned to an unreadable deadpan expression. "I get it," he said. "I really do. Why on Earth would I want to come out here? What's in it for me?"

The group nodded.

"Look," he continued. "I've been out for a while now, making a living by bringing tourists and a few hardcore survivalists just far enough into the jungle to give them an experience, and to get their money's worth. But I'm not a tour guide. I ain't interested in some half-ass jungle treks."

He paused, sighing. "When my wife left me, my life pretty much went on hold. She was the only person I ever knew who could keep up, and she just... lost interest one day. Went off to live in a city somewhere back in the States. I started dumbing down my training programs, taking on more corporate clients, and wasting away in my bunker. But then you — " he looked at Paulinho. "You called. You told me you needed help, and you said someone was after your friend. Call me insane, but I didn't need to know the details; I just wanted to jump in and *do* something for once."

Ben stared, unmoving, as the man told his story.

"But then I *did* hear the details, and the geek in me perked up. I was fascinated by what you think you're onto out here, and I thought to myself, 'hell, they're going to die out there. Might as well come along and offer some help.'"

"That's reassuring," Paulinho said.

Reggie flashed him a glance. "It's true, bud, and you know it. We all do. Shit, I do, and I'm the one who's trained to *be* out here."

Ben listened, trying to find the holes in the man's logic. He couldn't, but that didn't mean Ben believed the entire story. He couldn't figure out why someone would be interested in all of this just for the sheer *excitement* of it all. Ben himself wasn't one to feel excited about much, and when he did it was usually over something simple, like a perfectly cooked pot of chili or some other delicious foodstuff. "You just wanted one last adventure? A suicide mission?"

"I'm a realist, Ben," he said. "I try to see the world for what it is. This is a pretty long-shot play, but there's hope. We know where we're going, they don't. It's as simple as that. As long as we keep that one thing dangling just out of their reach, we'll be fine. I don't know how, so I don't have a plan to keep it that way, but I know it's true."

He looked at the rest of the group in turn, finally stopping again on Ben. Ben felt the weight of the man's gaze, and could almost hear his thoughts burning into his own mind. *And I've chosen you as the de facto leader if something happens to me, Ben.*

Ben considered this for a moment. It was true that Reggie seemed to have an unlikely affinity for him, and wondered what the man saw in him. Maybe he was just the best option out of the rest of the group, the only person who'd spent a real amount of time in a natural setting.

"Come on," Reggie said, "let's get out of the open and back into the safety of the trees. We need to —"

He stopped, mid-sentence.

Ben felt his blood run cold as he turned to see what Reggie was staring at.

CHAPTER 41

Past the far side of the smoldering remains of the hospital, Ben saw the trees move. He thought it was the smoke at first, until more of the trees began to shake and wobble gently. A large leafy bush, with sharp, spiny fronds of a bright green color was pressed sideways, and a man stepped into view and then out onto the open moss-covered floor of the atrium.

He was naked except for a strip of leather wrapped around his waist and between his legs, and his skin seemed to match the leather. Ragged and tough, it was bronzed and hairless, save for a crop of deep-black hair on his head and thick eyebrows. He was covered in jewelry, including bracelets on each wrist, beaded anklets, and piercings in just about every piece of cartilage available to him. The Indian's wrinkled and sun-beaten face was painted black, with a red stripe stretching from ear to ear, across his eyes.

Ben stared at the old man creeping slowly toward them, but it wasn't the detail of the native's dress and jewelry that he was focused on. The man held a long spear, stretching out equally in front of and behind him, that he carried without letting the tip drop. It pointed straight toward the group, unwavering as it crept forward in its owner's grasp.

"Ben," Julie whispered. She snuck up behind Ben and reached her arm around his. He nodded, silently acknowledging that he was seeing the same thing she was, but not wanting to respond aloud or turn his head away from the approaching stranger.

Reggie was standing just a few feet in front of them, and Ben saw him reaching down to grab the machete hanging from his belt. He wasn't sure if it was a good idea or a terrible one, but he didn't try to stop him. Reggie's hand fell around the machete's handle, and Ben watched him slowly lift it straight up, his torso still partially blocking it from the oncoming man's line of sight.

"I'm going to count to three," Reggie said, keeping his voice down but speaking loud enough for the group to hear him clearly. "Then we're going to run. Don't split up, but try to run a few feet away from each other."

Julie tightened her grip on Ben's hand.

"Don't worry about looking back," he said. "He's going to throw that thing, and it's going to hit its mark. You turn around, you better believe *you're* his mark."

Ben swallowed.

Reggie counted. "One."

The man crept forward, not increasing or decreasing his speed. His eyes seemed to be locked onto Ben's. His face was unreadable, indifferent to the outside world. He was intently focused on this singular moment in time, this place alone.

Focused on the hunt.

"Two."

The man continued, now only twenty feet away. Mere inches, it seemed. Ben watched the man's eyes, trying to see if he'd divert his gaze from the group, but he didn't. His eyes didn't give any indication that he was even alive, let alone moving toward them.

"Three!" Reggie yelled the last number, and Ben and Julie twirled around simultaneously.

And Ben found himself staring at the end of a long, sharpened spear blade.

Julie screamed, but Ben almost couldn't hear it. His body was on high alert, alarms ringing in his head, drawing his focus in to the object three inches from his face.

He could see the crude, yet careful work of the blade. The artisan had fashioned it from a rock, smoothing the sides and sharpening the tip to a perfect point. The dull pewter color of the stone reflected no light, but Ben could see through the thin, razor-sharp strip running alongside the extreme edge of the blade.

He flicked his eyes over to Julie, only now realizing that there were matching spearpoints in front of each of the other group members. Archie, Paulinho, Carlo, and Amanda were in front of Ben now, closer to the edge of the forest, and each of them had been stopped just short of their getaway by more spear-handling natives.

Ben turned his head again and looked behind him once more, hoping they would at least have a chance by getting around the first native. But the man had been joined now by even more tribesmen, some younger adolescent males and older, very capable-looking men. Each of the hunters wore the same face paint as their tribal leader, but only the first man they'd seen, the oldest of the group, was decorated with jewelry.

The old man broke his unwavering gaze, and barked some words in their direction. Ben looked around, but Reggie and the others seemed equally confused.

The man looked at Ben, then repeated the phrase. Ben shrugged, unsure of what else to do.

"We — we're not here to hurt you," he finally said.

Deep in the back of his mind, his inner critic laughed. *We're not here to hurt you?*

The man walked closer to Ben, now standing a few feet away. The spear leaned backwards, and Ben closed his eyes.

He waited.

He felt like the entire group was breathing in unison. He could hear breaths going in and out. *Is that me?* he thought.

A moment passed, and he opened his eyes again. The old man was staring at him, leaning on his spear handle, inches from Ben's face.

Ben's pulse quickened. He was afraid his heart might beat right of his chest, but he forced himself to stay still.

The old man made a chuffing sound, then he walked away, toward Reggie. He repeated the process, standing on his tiptoes to see into Reggie's eyes. He moved again a minute later, this time coming to a stop in front of Paulinho.

When he made the same noise after his inspection of Paulinho, he turned to the group of Indians encircling them, then spoke to his people. The hunters pressed inward, stepping closer to hear their leader's small shaky voice. Ben's group turned around slowly, all watching and listening to the older man speak to his people in a language none of them understood.

Ben watched the reactions of the men. They yelled single vowel sounds sporadically, some of them even clapping and stomping. The tribe leader's voice increased in volume and intensity, and the yelling and stomping ascended simultaneously.

Finally, when the man's speech seemed over, the leader reached for Paulinho's hand and held it up, screaming as loud as he was able one last order. Ben watched, horrified, as the hunters in front of him all lifted their spears shoulder-high and brought them back.

Ben caught the eyes of a young man, no more than twelve or thirteen years old, and the kid bared his teeth at him. His spear was shorter than the others, but even from this distance he could tell it was every bit as sharp.

And it was pointed directly at him.

Julie's hand was sweaty, but Ben held it, squeezing nearly as hard as he could.

This is it, he thought. He wanted to look at her, to tell her it was going to be okay, but he couldn't take his eyes off the kid that was about to kill him.

He longed to apologize to her, to tell her he was sorry for the way he'd been treating her, and that…

…And that he loved her.

Instead, he closed his eyes.

The old man yelled a final time and Ben opened his eyes again, unable to look away as the attack started.

Every one of the hunters dropped his spear to the ground.

He was nearly hyperventilating, unable to control his breathing. He glanced over at the old man, and frowned.

The leader was still holding Paulinho's arm, but he was now staring intently at it. He brought Paulinho's wrist closer to his face, studying it. Ben could see the small design, outlined in black, from here.

The tattoo.

The man started humming, slowly incorporating actual words into the melody. The rest of the hunters quietly watched, also unsure of what was happening.

The man pushed Paulinho's hand away, and Paulinho stumbled backwards, surprised at the rapid movement of the aging hunter. Amanda and Carlo caught him by the shoulders, steadying him.

Finally, the old man spoke. A single, consonant-laden word. A hush fell over the group, even deeper silence than before settling in. The natives seemed to suck in a breath simultaneously, stunned by the word.

Ben saw the professor in their group, over the old man's shoulder. Archie's eyes widened.

"I know that word," he whispered. "It's a Yanomami word."

Ben lifted his eyebrows as the native repeated the word to his group of hunters.

"Curse."

CHAPTER 42

Julie wasn't sure when she'd started holding her breath, but she gulped in a breath of hot, humid jungle air. She let go of Ben's hand and wiped her wet palm on the side of her pants. The native hunters stepped back, seemingly shocked and, somehow, terrified. A few pointed fingers at Paulinho and the rest of them, but looks of confusion were on everyone's face.

The leader of the group of hunters backstepped away from Paulinho, as if remaining on alert and readying himself for an attack. Paulinho, of course, stood still, his nostrils flaring in and out as he, too, tried to calm down. His eyes were wide, and his huge grin he'd worn when she'd first met him was long gone.

The group of hunters carefully made their way around Julie and the others until they were collected into a condensed group of natives. They stared directly at Paulinho, but none of them tried for any sort of attack.

"What just happened?" she asked, her voice shaky and still barely a whisper.

"I think Paulinho's tattoo just saved our behinds," Reggie said. For once, Julie noticed, Reggie seemed to be as scared as the rest of them.

"What is that tattoo?" Amanda asked.

"I — I'm not sure," Paulinho said. "It was on a necklace worn by my grandfather on my mother's side, as I said before. Just a neat design, I thought."

"Maybe it is," Archie said. "But I fear it is also much more than that."

Everyone turned to look at the professor.

"You *fear*?" Reggie asked. "That thing just prevented us from being native shish kabobs."

"Keep your voice down," Amanda said. "They're still here, and they don't look happy."

Ben saw that the woman was right. The hunters, fronted by the shorter older man, were still bunched together in the middle of the clearing, just past the hospital building's foundation. Smoke was still drifting into the air from the earlier fire, but it was hardly the situation Ben was worried about at the moment.

"What should we do? Anyone have any ideas?" Amanda asked.

"Go," Carlo said. The portly man was standing off to one side of their group, clearly disturbed and ready to leave the hunters behind.

"Yeah, I'm with him," Reggie said.

"Will they follow us?" Julie asked.

"Who knows? Maybe we'll just have to have Paulinho in the back, show off his tat once or twice if they get close."

Julie didn't think the plan was much of a plan, but he had to admit just about anything was better than sticking around to see if the hunters would eventually grow out of their fear.

"Right," she said, turning to Ben. "We're not getting anything from this hospital, obviously. And Paulinho's doing better anyway. The sooner we get back on track, the sooner we —"

Her voice was cut off by the sharp *crack* of a gunshot.

"Get down!" she heard Reggie yell.

Julie was already dropping, hitting the ground abruptly and nearly knocking the wind out of herself. She poked her head up, looking toward the group of tribesmen to find the source of the gunshot.

Another shot rang out, and she jumped.

The leader of the hunters fell forward, his eyes blazing into hers as his knees hit the ground. He wavered for a moment, sputtering a bit of blood from his mouth.

Julie wasn't sure what to think, but she didn't have time to formulate a coherent thought. The old man clattered to the ground face first, his jewelry tinkling on the hard forest floor. A bracelet pushed off from his wrist and rolled in her direction.

Two more shots smacked above her head, and the rest of the warriors began yelling battle cries and turning their spearpoints to the darkened forest. None of them had any idea where the gunshots were coming from, but they stood anyway, ready to fight.

Three more gunshots flared from three different directions, and only then did she realize they were surrounded.

"It's the mercenaries!" she yelled.

Ben replied, still at her side. "They're in the jungle, staying hidden! We need to get out from the middle of the atrium."

Julie nodded, but didn't move. She wasn't about to risk her life any more than it already was and call attention to herself. She hoped Ben would change his mind, and they could just lie here until it was over.

He's right, she thought. *You need to move.*

She felt a tugging on her arm, and she looked up to see Ben standing above her.

"Julie," he shouted. "Come on!"

She reluctantly pushed off from the moss-covered forest floor and broke into a run. The others were doing the same, Reggie nearing the edge of the trees with Archie and Amanda close behind him. Carlo and Paulinho had disappeared into the trees already, and she could see the plants moving and shifting in front of her, marking their location as they stumbled through them, fighting against the thick bundle of branches and leaves.

Spears were thrown, and two of them landed near Julie as they rushed into the relative protection of the jungle. She hoped they were aimed at the mercenaries instead of their group, but she wasn't about to stop and find out. Her heart was nearly beating out of her chest, the muscles in her legs and thighs working overtime to carry her forward and out of the attack.

The screams from the warriors, either in preparation for an attack or a reaction to one, almost drowned out the volume of the rainforest, but she could still hear the whooping sounds of monkeys, high above, watching the exchange between the three different groups of humans and shouting their appeal. Gunshots rang out from seemingly every direction, and Julie wondered how many mercenaries there were hiding in the forest, and, more importantly, if they were running directly toward any of them.

Just before Reggie stepped into the cover of the brush, it shook again, and Julie expected to see Carlo or Paulinho step out from behind it. Instead, a man appeared, dressed in the same garb as the rest of the group of natives.

Another tribesman. He snuck up behind us.

The man lifted a club-like length of wood and swung it out and across Reggie's face.

Julie gasped as Reggie went down.

She didn't have time to gawk, feeling Ben tugging at her sleeve. He pulled her to the left, sidestepping the scene in front of her. As they jumped over a fallen tree poking out at the edge of the clearing and entered the jungle, Julie tried to glance to her right to see if the man who had hit Reggie had seen them.

Someone else stood in front of them now.

Rhett.

Ben surged forward, and Julie watched as he focused all of his strength into the attack. Rhett seemed to barely register the two people running toward him before Ben hit him. The two toppled over, rolling over the jungle floor. They came to a stop with Rhett's back against a large rock, and Ben's knees pushing into his chest.

"Ben," Julie yelled. "What are you going to —"

Ben began punching the younger man. She had never seen him react with such violence, but she stood back and watched it happen. He alternated hands, each blow landing somewhere on Rhett's face. Julie could hear Ben's grunting and heavy breathing, as well as the small groaning sounds from the kid below him.

"I'm going to make you pay for everything you've done," Ben said between breaths. He did not allow himself longer than a moment for rest, quickly resuming his assault on the young man's head.

Rhett, trying to breathe through a blood-filled mouth, couldn't respond.

CHAPTER 43

"You tricked us," Ben said. "You made us believe you were —" Ben stopped, unable to continue without taking a breath. He wanted to kill the kid, to put a bullet in his head and end his life. It was a more difficult decision to refrain from that action than to carry it out, but Ben was unarmed.

He also wanted answers.

Ignoring the sounds of the battle between the natives and the mercenaries, he pulled Rhett up and toward him and spoke again, his voice shaking out from behind a tightly clenched jaw. "Why? What's in it for you?"

Rhett's upturned lip and flaring nostrils told Ben he wasn't going to get an answer easily.

"You're going to talk, you little sack of —"

"You already know the answer." Rhett's voice was strained, gurgling from a mouthful of blood and saliva. He spat to the side, wincing.

Ben cocked his head sideways. "What? What are you talking about?"

"I just told you," Rhett said. "You want to know who's after you, right?"

Ben still held Rhett's collar, but he loosened his grip slightly.

"I recognized you at the cabin. They told me to wait for you there, to make sure it was you."

Back at the cabin. He was waiting for us. For me. Ben wanted to start hitting him again, harder, until he was too exhausted to move, but he also needed to hear what the kid had to say. "How did you recognize me? Why do you know me?"

"The Company," Rhett said. He spat again, this time getting the mixture only partially out of his mouth. "They sent the picture of you and Julie. You're who they want eliminated, after they get the doctor lady." He paused. "They have no use for the others , but since they're with you…"

Ben didn't know what to say. There was no chance Rhett was lying, but Ben still didn't understand who he was. He had many questions for the kid, but he knew he wouldn't get the chance to ask them.

"You messed it up for them back at Yellowstone. It was a sideshow, really, so it didn't really matter. But they don't take too kindly to people trying to derail their plans."

"Yeah?" Ben said. "And what are those plans?"

Rhett struggled to laugh, but it came out as a strained cough. "Right. If you think I'd tell you even if I knew…"

"What's in it for you, then?"

"What's in it for *you*?" Rhett spat back.

Ben threw Rhett's head back, smacking it into the rock he was still hovering over, and the quick blow stunned the young man. He blinked a few times, spat again, and looked back up at Ben.

"You're not going to win," he said. "You've got stamina, I'll give you that. But you're not going to win."

Ben tried a new tactic. "What are we trying to win?"

"Again, if I knew, I wouldn't tell you. You have to know that, right?"

Ben looked around for some leverage, finding it in a fist-sized stone.

He snatched it off the ground and carried it back over to where Rhett lay, bleeding, on the moss-carpeted floor. Lifting it above his head, he aimed for the bridge of Rhett's nose.

"You're going to bash my head in with a rock?" Rhett asked.

"You got a better idea?" Ben said. "Give me a reason not to."

Again Rhett sneered back up at Ben.

"That's what I thought. I ain't going to make this hurt much — I'm not into that crap. But it'll be final. Got anything you want to tell me before —"

Ben felt someone pulling at his wrist, and he whirled around, bringing his free hand up to protect himself.

"Ben, Ben!" Archie said. "Stop — it's me."

Ben relaxed slightly, but jerked his wrist out of Archie's grip.

"Sorry," Archie said. "I did not mean to startle you." He motioned behind Ben at Rhett. "We need him. Alive."

Ben raised an eyebrow. "For what?"

Archie flicked his eyes to the left, then to the right. Paulinho was suddenly in view, standing just behind another tree. He was holding Reggie, only now coming to, struggling with the weight of the soldier and his own wound. Carlo was behind Archie, somewhat camouflaged in the shadows of the jungle. Ben realized he had been completely unaware of his surroundings for the past few minutes. The fighting and gunfire had ceased, replaced once again by the sounds of the jungle.

As he looked around him at his tattered and beaten group, panic set in.

"Wh — where are the girls?"

CHAPTER 44

Reggie opened his eyes, and all the pain came rushing back in.

In all his years, Reggie had never felt so out of his element. He had taken hundreds of survivalists, amateur explorers, and corporate executives out on wilderness expeditions, and he had brought every single one of them home, safe and sound. Before his life became serving a never-ending stream of hipster adventurers, he had spent his career in the Army, making a name for himself as a sniper. On deployments, he was surrounded and supported by a cast of well-trained soldiers, like himself, and on most missions he had nothing to fear but not making it back to base in time for a hot meal.

But out here, this particular time, things were different. Reggie was leading a ragtag group of people who were trying to find something that may not even exist. He'd talked them into it, and for that he felt partly responsible. But it had been their choice to come out here, to link up with this mission and take it on.

They were being chased by a group of trained killers who wanted to take Amanda Meron with them and exterminate the rest of his group, and now they were under attack from a group of tribal warriors as well.

Reggie rubbed his head as he tried to clear his vision once more. He was standing, but not on his own feet — at least he couldn't feel them currently. He blinked a few more times, and the memory of what had happened came rushing back.

He'd gone down after being struck by a club, from a native that was hiding behind a bush. He'd nearly tripped over a thick strangle of dry vines anyway, and hadn't been focusing on the man's location when he was ambushed.

He rubbed the spot where the man's club had landed, just above the temple on the left side of his head. *Could have been a lot worse.* Not feeling blood, he quickly assessed the area around the bruise and diagnosed it as a close call.

After the initial encounter, Reggie had assumed they'd made it out safely, somehow scaring the group away with Paulinho's odd tattoo. But then the guns started firing, and the all-out brawl began. He saw the leader of the group, a younger man close to Ben's age with dark, deep-set eyes, staring back at him from the cover of a tree on the other side of the clearing, and they'd locked eyes for a moment. Those eyes were familiar to him — the eyes of someone who was trained to kill. They were steady and unmoving, but they weren't simply *evil.* They had a sinister darkness to them, but they were framed by a slightly frowning expression, one Reggie recognized immediately as the expression of a man who was calculating the odds, choosing a course of action, and trying to accomplish his goal with the smallest loss to his team.

Reggie only saw the man for a moment, but it was enough. He'd even raised his pistol and aimed, but didn't have a clear enough shot. He didn't want to hit any of the natives, as he wasn't sure if they were being watched by any others that might be spying nearby. Even if there was another tribe — one in conflict with the one they'd come across — the tribes would likely communicate what they had found here.

And word traveled surprisingly fast in the jungle. The natives, to the outside observer, were generally considered quite primitive, but Reggie knew there was a fine balance of power between the jungle itself and its inhabitants, and many of the oldest tribes scattered throughout the immense land area were finely attuned to its whisperings. Societies that had existed for thousands of years may not have changed much technologically, but it was unwise to assume that they were also primitive when it came to communication.

Reggie had read about a tribe that sent out two runners whenever it needed to deliver messages to its constituents, in case one or the other got held up. They would travel opposite routes, ending up at the destination at generally the same time, then deliver the news and return.

If his group had somehow caused the native tribe that was about to kill them to feel uneasy, he wanted to keep that impression as long as possible, to prevent any other tribes or roaming bands of hunters from interfering with their plans. He didn't want to initiate a war with the indigenous peoples of the Amazon any more than he wanted to fight off the mercenaries.

So he chose the other option — run. He'd turned and run straight into the club of a native warrior, and blacked out. Likely scaring the man off, the native hadn't stayed around long enough to kill him, and for that he was thankful.

He pushed down with his feet, happy to find that they worked properly and he could now stand on his own. He patted Paulinho's shoulder, no doubt still feeling a bit of pain himself, and looked at Ben and Archie.

"What happened?" He saw the bloodied face of the kid, Rhett, and almost didn't recognize him.

"Found him in the woods," Ben said.

"Well, it's obvious you questioned him," Reggie said. "Hopefully you found something out?" He walked closer to Ben. "Christ, Ben, you look like you've had better days too."

Ben's jaw clenched and unclenched, and Reggie didn't need to look down to see that Ben's fists were making the same motion. Archie was looking at the ground.

"What's going on?"

"The girls," Ben said. "They took them."

CHAPTER 45

"Can we go on without them?" Archie asked.

Ben felt anger flash again, but he held back.

"I'm sorry," Archie said, noticing the fire in Ben's eyes. "I didn't mean it that way, I just thought that with fewer people, we could possibly get to the end of our line, then —"

"We're not moving forward without them," Ben said.

"I second that," Paulinho added.

Archie looked from Ben and Paulinho to Reggie. Reggie was leaning against the thin branch of a tree that poked out from the ground, seemingly not attached to any sort of trunk at all. It twisted around a few times, like a snake, then fell back to the ground about twenty feet away, where it ended in a mess of leaves and vines. The remaining members of the group were passing a water bottle around, each taking a quick sip before passing it along.

"They're right," Reggie said. "There's no point in getting there before them if they still have Amanda and Julie. That's the goal now — getting them back."

Ben nodded at Reggie.

"But," Reggie continued, "they know that we're going to be looking for them, and they know the longer we're out here running in circles, the better chance we have that we'll just die of natural causes."

"What are you saying?" Ben wasn't sure where Reggie was going with this line of reasoning.

"I'm saying that while our top priority is *of course* to get the girls, it still might be in our best interest to find whatever it is we're looking for."

"How do you figure that?" Archie asked.

Ben looked at Reggie to explain. Reggie nodded, took a breath and a sip of water, and stepped to the center of the group of men. "Easy," he said. "They have Amanda — and Julie — now they just need to find the ultimate prize they're after, then kill us. They're going to be following the same line we've been traveling, because by now they've figured out the general direction by following us. Amanda and Julie won't want to help them, but they eventually will if they're forced."

Ben clenched his fists. "Which is exactly why we need to find them *before* they're 'forced.'"

Reggie shook his head. "No. If we can get to the end of the line first, we can gain a bargaining chip."

"Something they want for something we want," Archie said.

"Right. And Ben, you're not out here to explore and dig for artifacts. You want to find the company that's behind all of this."

Ben nodded, slowly. *He's right, but I hate it.* He wanted to *act,* not continue forward and just hope they'd run into the other group eventually. *But it makes the most sense.*

"Ben," Reggie said. Ben looked up and saw that Reggie and the others were all staring at him. Reggie had the beginnings of a smirk on his face, but there was a softness behind it, in his eyes. "We're going to find them, Ben, but we have to push forward."

Ben took a deep breath of hot, humid jungle air. He could taste the rainforest in it, and he was quickly growing to hate it. "I know."

"Good deal," Reggie said. He turned to address the others. "We have to move quickly. Amanda was the only one of us they needed, since she's the one with the information to connect the dots between what she knows and what we were all looking for. They're going to have the same information we do, for the most part, so it's only a matter of time before they piece things together for themselves. Our best chance is to get there first, then figure out the next piece of the puzzle."

Reggie smiled, his full-on characteristic grin returning, and he stepped up to Rhett and pulled the young man to his feet. He reached for one of the packs and withdrew a section of rope and began binding the kid's hands behind his back. "Hope you're up for a walk, kid."

Ben wasn't able to outwardly match the man's seemingly lackadaisical attitude, but he now understood that the expression was worn not as a reflection of what was churning inside, but as a contradiction. It was a forced appearance, to put his team at ease, and to ensure he remained cool and collected in the face of mounting odds against them.

Ben had come to appreciate, respect, and even look up to the man. Reggie was like no one else he'd ever met, with the possible exception of his own father. Ben's father had always been good-natured, cordial, and yet always ready for action, tense with anticipation. He was the strongest man Ben had ever known, and the sudden memory of him brought on a feeling Ben hadn't experienced in a long time.

III

"…And, as his strength
Failed him at length,
He met a pilgrim shadow—
'Shadow,' said he,
'Where can it be—
This land of Eldorado?'…"

— Edgar Allan Poe

CHAPTER 46

The ropes binding Julie's wrists were starting to cut her. She'd struggled against them for an hour as they walked, but the thick cords of climbing rope didn't budge. Amanda walked by her side, her hands bound as well. She looked disheveled, her ponytail long since disbanded and her short, blond strands of sweat-soaked hair sticking to her forehead and around her ears. She was sobbing gently, only her slight sniffing giving her away.

Julie wanted to reach over and put her arm around her, but she knew she wouldn't be able to provide any consolation. She felt as bad as Amanda, and only out of sheer terror was she able to refrain from breaking down into tears as well.

The mercenaries had taken Amanda first, back in the clearing during the fight. Julie had followed Ben into the jungle and waited, shocked, as Ben took out his anger on Rhett. The kid had been a devious backstabber, but Julie was still surprised at Ben's reaction. She'd meant to stop him, to walk over and grab his outstretched hand before he could strike again, but the mercenary grabbed her and stuffed his large, sweaty hand over her mouth.

She couldn't scream. She couldn't even bite the man. He'd worked his other arm behind her elbows, effectively locking her in place in front of him as he quietly stepped backwards and into the thicker part of the jungle. Within seconds they were completely hidden from view.

Julie remembered the feeling well — it was an emotion of utter desperation, one she had never felt so strongly in her life. She watched as Ben disappeared, still beating Rhett. She could hardly breathe, either from the man's hand blocking her mouth and nose or from her own hyperventilating.

When the mercenary felt satisfied with their distance from Ben, he lifted her completely off the ground, swung her around, then set her down and pushed her through the remaining thicket and out into the open atrium. The ruins of the small hospital complex were still smoking to her left, but they didn't stop there. The man behind her pushed her all the way through the clearing, lifting her off the ground once more as he hustled to the opposite side of the atrium. When they reached the trees he pushed her another ten steps and into a smaller clearing.

She found herself in the middle of a group of men, all dressed in similar black shirts and pants, and all wielding assault rifles.

They bound her wrists, saying nothing to her, and blocked her mouth with a thick, moist bandana. She gagged, trying to breathe through the piece of fabric, but gave up and decided to force her breathing through her nose instead. After they'd finished with her, another rope was looped around her bound wrists and tied to a carabiner, which the man who'd taken her had clipped to his belt.

I'm on a leash, she thought.

Only then did she see Amanda, staring at her with huge, terrified eyes, also bound and gagged. She was clipped to another soldier, and without a word to either of them the soldiers started walking.

They had been walking for over an hour, the daylight of the morning trickling through the jungle canopy, when they finally stopped.

Julie was exhausted, but she didn't sit down. The man at the head of the line of soldiers turned and spoke to the two men directly behind them, and they broke off in a jog and ran ahead. The rest of the men spread out around the girls, forming a wall of mercenaries around Julie and Amanda. Julie counted ten men, not including the leader and the two that had run off.

Thirteen in all, she thought. *They* far *outnumber our group.*

Somewhere along the way Julie had accepted the reality that Ben would try, somehow, to come rescue her.

She knew he loved her, and she knew he'd do nearly anything for her, but she also knew that he wouldn't let these men walk away without answering for their crimes. Ben would stop at nothing to get her back, but he would also do it just out of principle.

It was why she loved him, and it was why she thought it was going to kill him one day.

Back at Yellowstone, mere months ago, Ben had displayed an uncanny amount of resolve that left her stunned and speechless. After it was over, she wasn't sure whether she should be praising his courage or berating his stupidity. He'd shrugged it off, and they never spoke of it again. Reporters and journalists lost interest when they realized they weren't going to find the next reality TV star in Ben.

The man in the front of the line, their leader, came and stood in front of Amanda.

"It's great to finally meet you," he said. His voice was calm, low, and held no outward emotion. Julie listened, trying to memorize every aspect of his speech. It seemed oddly familiar, though she knew she'd never met the man before.

Amanda was visibly shaking, and her eyes were welling up once again.

"It's okay, Dr. Meron," the man said. He smiled, his crisp features softening. Julie almost believed him.

He gently reached behind Amanda's head and untied the gag from her mouth. "If you feel like you need to scream, that's fine. We are far enough away that your group will not be able to hear you."

He waited, as if testing her. Amanda shook, then hung her head. She didn't respond.

"That's perfect. That attitude is going to keep you alive, Dr. Meron."

The man tossed the bandana to the ground, then walked over to Julie. She clenched her jaw, swallowing back the fear that had snuck up her throat, but she stared directly into the man's eyes. He was young, possibly the same age as her, and he seemed completely at ease in the jungle. His hair seemed to float, combed and resting perfectly on his head, and he was clean-shaven.

He didn't match the soldiers in appearance. The one who'd ripped her from behind Ben's back was bearded, covered in dirt and sweat stains, and had a wild look in his eye. The other men had common characteristics, but she could see that there was an Asian man, three black men, and others she couldn't exactly place. The man in front of her studied her.

"You and your boyfriend have caused my team a lot of grief," the man said. Julie continued to breathe out of her nose, waiting for the man to remove her gag. "My name is Joshua Jefferson. I am here on orders from my father and his company to retrieve Dr. Meron, acquire whatever it is you all are searching for, and neutralize any *extraneous variables*."

He waited, as if anticipating a response from her, but she was still gagged. Finally, after nearly a minute of his scrutiny, he reached behind her head and untied the bandana. Julie spat it out, and looked back up at him. His hand lingered, resting just above her neck, and she tried to push away.

Instead, he pulled her closer. She could feel his breath, somehow cooler than the surrounding rainforest air. "Juliette," he said, nearly whispering, "that means I am going to have to kill your friends. You know that, so there's no sense dancing around the subject."

She felt his grip tighten, his hand squeezing her just beneath her ears. She wanted to scream, but the air wouldn't escape her lungs.

"I am a very reasonable man," he continued. "But I am *thorough*. I have a commitment to my men, who are growing restless. We can expedite this little project quite a bit if you and Dr. Meron cooperate."

She wanted to respond, to yell and spit in his face, but she felt weak. He was mesmerizing, somehow removing from her all ability to move or react.

"Juliette, where is the location of the city?"

She breathed, gulping in a burst of air.

"The city of El Dorado. Where is it?"

He tightened his grip on her neck. "I — don't know," she said. "Honestly. We —"

"We know you don't know *exactly*," he said. "That much is abundantly clear. Let me clarify: what is your destination? The final point you are trying to reach?"

Julie was silent.

"Juliette," he said. "You understand what's about to happen if you don't answer my question, don't you?"

He waited for her to respond. She nodded.

"Good. Dr. Meron seems to be very interested in working with me and my team." He glanced over at Amanda, and Julie could see that Amanda's head was still bowed, unmoving. "Do yourself a favor and be the one who decides to contribute to this mission. You and I both know we need Dr. Meron, so she is safe for now."

Julie couldn't help but consider what he had said. *Why am I still alive?* She wondered. *What is he going to use me for?* He would need Amanda to help explain whatever they're going to find in the city, if they find it. But her? What good could Julie do?

"Juliette," the man said. She realized she was looking off into the distance, and her eyes snapped back toward Joshua. "I have another question for you; maybe you can answer this one first."

She waited, feeling the man's fingers play at the hair on the back of her neck. It made her shudder.

"Your boyfriend — Harvey? What is *he* looking for?"

Julie frowned, then saw Amanda whip her head around and stare at both of them.

Joshua Jefferson laughed. "You don't think I believe he is out here, in the middle of the rainforest, looking for an ancient city of gold, do you?"

Julie flicked her eyes back and forth, not sure where he was taking this line of questioning. She hesitated, waiting for him to speak again.

"It's a simple question, Juliette," he said. "What is he looking for?"

Julie tried to find a way out, a way to dodge the question. But she felt bound, like her wrists. Tied up with this man in the center of the jungle, coerced into giving him what he wanted.

Suddenly she realized the answer to the previous riddle. *Why am I still alive? Why didn't the team of mercenaries just kill me in the atrium?* As she fumbled around in her mind for a good answer to the man's last question, the answer to her previous questions fell out of some subconscious space deep within her.

He wants Ben. I'm his bargaining chip.

She knew immediately that this man would not kill her. At least not before he had Ben.

"Drache Global," she said, her voice wavering slightly. The words came out before she even realized she was going to tell him. But her moment of clarity provided her with another answer: this man already knew what Ben was looking for in the jungle, and he knew it was not a lost city. Ben was no more interested in ancient myths and mysteries then these men. They all wanted something else, something more. Joshua's team was trying to secure whatever Amanda's research was pointing them toward; the fact that it might exist inside an ancient, long-lost city, was just a bonus.

Ben didn't care what was in the city, or where it was located, or what they might find when they got there. He was interested only because Julie was interested, but the city was a simple stopping point along his larger journey: he wanted to find the company.

Joshua smirked. "I haven't heard it called that in quite some time," he said.

Julie frowned.

"Yes, that's one of its names," Joshua said. "Drache Global is a pharmaceutical company, and operates as the main research and development branch for the rest of the organization."

"Dragonstone? Or Drage Medisinsk?"

Joshua took a step back. He looked up at Julie, and she could see him studying her. Analyzing her. "Again, those are branches from the main trunk of the organization. But I can see you've done your research. How did you hear those names?"

Julie knew she should not underestimate the man, but she wanted to keep him talking as long as possible, to buy herself time. "Ben heard them, a few months ago, when your organization tried to poison the entire country."

Joshua cocked his head sideways a bit, but Julie couldn't tell if he was frowning or still studying her. He didn't react at first, and she wondered if he had even heard her.

"Why did they do it, Joshua? Why go through all that trouble? To teach us all a lesson?"

Finally, Joshua shook his head. "I advised them against that course of action," he said. "But they kept saying it wasn't about the virus, and it wasn't about the bombs. Everyone is always so singularly focused on what's directly in front of them that they can't see what's behind them. Or what's standing right next to them."

"What are you talking about?"

"I'm talking about misdirection, Juliette. When one hand is holding something that is captivating the attention of the entire nation, the other hand is doing something behind its back."

"I've heard that excuse before," Julie said. "Even if it made sense, it's not the truth. What is the truth?"

Something in the way Julie said the words set Joshua off. He rushed forward, his face again inches from hers. She thought she could see the gentle fading of red disappearing just beneath his skin. Whatever rage he had felt in that moment was gone a second later.

"The truth is exactly what I'm trying to understand," Joshua said. "They've been hiding things from me as well. My own father has been hiding things from me. It's how they operate; how they've always done business. Pay what you need to the people you need, but only give them enough information to get the job done. I've seen so many of my own men discarded and tossed aside by the Company."

He looked away, and Julie was suddenly struck with the realization that he had shared more than he had intended. His emotions must have been getting the best of him, and he poured out more information then he'd wanted to. He cleared his throat, then seemed to visibly loosen, shaking out his muscles and tense posture and replacing it with something that looked like a nervous bodybuilder trying to appear relaxed.

Julie looked around at the rest of the men standing near the trees, surrounding her and Amanda. They stood ramrod straight, each of them fully attuned to the forest and its noises, waiting for any sign of impending attack, from man or beast. They were all dressed the same way as Joshua, but he was the youngest of the group and the only one who had spoken to her so far. She didn't understand their hierarchy, or how Joshua had assumed command of this contingent, but it didn't matter. He was the one she needed to talk to; he was the one she needed to convince.

"Joshua, what do you want from me and Amanda?"

He thought about this a moment, then answered. "You already know what I want from you. It's what the company wants me to do with you. Find whatever it is you were looking for, ensure Dr. Meron's cooperation, and remove any possibilities that someone might talk."

Julie summoned whatever remaining courage she could find, and stared down the man standing in front of her. "Then what are you waiting for?"

Joshua's voice dropped to a whisper, and she had to strain to hear.

"I needed to know for myself, but I think what I've been suspecting is true." He paused, looking around to make sure his men were still at their posts, not focusing on his conversation. He was talking so quietly now there was no way any of them — or Amanda — could hear. "Juliette, Ben and I are looking for the same thing."

CHAPTER 47

"I'm going to ask you one more time," Reggie said. "What are you doing out here? Why not just kill us all when you had the chance?"

Reggie walked behind Rhett, pushing him along when the kid fell behind or veered off course. The kid hadn't spoken a word since Reggie returned, but Reggie knew he could outlast him. Rhett's hands were tied behind his back, the rope then tightened around his waist to form a sort of belt that further secured his hands. Ben walked in front with Archie and Paulinho, and the small Brazilian boat hand, Carlo, followed directly behind Reggie. They were traveling in the direction had Reggie pointed them, aided by a hand-drawn map. After losing the maps in the river, Archie Quinones and Reggie had taken a few minutes to recreate on some scraps of paper — to the best of their ability — the maps, as well as the intersecting lines they'd discovered. Between Archie's knowledge of the area and his own navigational skills, Reggie thought they could remain pointed toward their destination.

He hoped.

He'd never ventured this far into the Amazon before, and not many outsiders had. Those who had were typically on an exploratory mission, usually funded by a large organization or government, and they had the resources to support them. Still, large groups of people went missing every year in the Amazon Basin, due to high flooding, predators, or hostile natives. Others simply got lost.

Reggie wanted to make sure he and his group made it out of the jungle safely, but even with his skill set he knew it was a tall order. They'd soon be battling not just human and animal predators, but the elements as well. Dehydration could set in quicker without a constant supply of fresh, pure drinking water, and food would prove to be more and more difficult to obtain as the rations of MREs and coca leaves they carried in the packs wore thin.

On top of that, Julie and Amanda were gone, taken by the mercenaries. He'd wanted to scream when he found out, but he forced himself to push the emotion back and allow the logical side of his person to take over once more. He had decided they needed to move forward and accomplish their mission, allowing the mercenaries to meet up with them later. It was a difficult call to make, considering he now had no control over Amanda's and Julie's survival.

He was impressed with Ben's ability to see his point of view, as well. Ben, unlike Reggie, had skin in this game. He and Julie had arrived here together, and Ben would do whatever he could within his power to make sure they left that way. To agree with Reggie that their best possible course of action was to push forward and attempt to find the lost city would not have been an easy decision to make.

He stepped up closer to Rhett and pressed his fist between his shoulder blades. "You ignoring me now?"

"What do you want to know?" Rhett whirled around and faced Reggie, stopping short. "You're just trying to get me to talk, you don't actually need any information from me."

Reggie grinned. "Fine. You're right. But I think after the boat incident, you owe us at least one."

"Shoot."

"Same thing I asked a minute ago," Reggie said. "Why not just kill us all when you had the chance? Back at the cabin, or on the boat? Hell, why not just crash the plane? Definitely no survivors that way."

"That wasn't my mission," Rhett said.

Reggie let out a one syllable laugh. "Your *mission?* How old are you, boy? 25?"

Rhett's face reddened, but to his credit he did not let the anger affect him more than that. "I'm 27, just out of law school. And yes, this is my *mission.* The company sent me here, to make sure the others get the job done. You've already underestimated me three times on this trip; what exactly makes you think I am unqualified?"

Reggie chewed on an imaginary piece of tobacco as he looked the young man up and down. Then, with one fluid motion, he swung his right foot around behind Rhett's left knee. He carried through the movement, lifting Rhett completely off the ground for a second as his legs fell out from beneath him. Rhett hit the ground hard on his back, his hands and rear end taking the brunt of the blow. He yelped in pain, and rolled sideways, anticipating further attack.

Reggie put his right foot back down on the ground and continued fake-chewing. He laughed, then walked over, grabbed Rhett by the collar of his shirt and yanked him to his feet. There was a thick layer of dirt caked on the side of Rhett's face, and the young man wore a sneer that almost made Reggie pause.

"*That* is why I think you're unqualified. What kind of company are you working for, anyway? They sent *you?*"

Rhett breathed heavy gulps of air as he tried to calm himself down. The sneer never left his face.

Reggie cocked his head sideways, and he noticed Ben and Archie, Paulinho just behind, walking over to listen.

"Their leader's name is Joshua," Rhett said. "And he's not going to stop. None of it matters now. They're not going to let any of us go, including me. Even if — somehow — this doesn't work, they'll send another group. And another. They *won't* stop. You ought to just kill me now."

"You're resilient, kid," Reggie said. He nodded toward Ben. "I'm actually surprised Ben didn't already do that. Besides, what's the fun in that?"

Ben walked over and roughly pulled Rhett around so they were face-to-face. "You're lucky I don't just kill you right now."

Reggie held up a hand. "Easy, Ben. Let's make sure he's telling the truth first."

"Why would I lie to you about that? Don't you understand what's going on? There's *nothing left* for you here. They have the girl, they know where to go, they're not going to stop until it's finished."

"Then why send you?" Ben asked.

"They're thorough, the company. They don't stop until the job is done, and when it makes most sense, they'll opt for redundancy over saving resources."

"And their leader? Joshua?" Reggie asked. "Is he as… *qualified* as you?"

Rhett just smiled, his eyes remaining cold and locked on Ben.

Reggie pushed Rhett away, causing him to stumble for catching his balance and walking forward into the trees. Paulinho and Archie were still in front, but Ben held back next to Reggie. Carlo, ever the watchful sentinel, silently began walking at the back of the line when the group continued.

Keeping his voice low, Reggie turned to Ben. "What are you thinking?"

"I should have killed him when I had the chance," Ben said.

Reggie shook his head. "Push that aside for now, Ben. There's more at stake here. This 'company,' whoever they are, and whatever they're after, is obviously willing to spend a lot of money to accomplish their goal. And it seems like there may be some sort of distrust in the organization. Why else would they send two teams?"

"This isn't a *team*, Reggie," Ben said. "This is a *kid*."

"And this kid has gotten the jump on us quite a few times already. I don't intend for it to happen again, and I know you don't either. That's why we need to figure this out. Why send both of them?"

Reggie waited for a response, but Ben was silent.

"If these guys really are working for the same company," Reggie continued, "I wouldn't be surprised if he's telling the truth — this organization might send more. That means logistics are more difficult, communication is harder…"

"Can we use that to our advantage?"

"I really do like the way you think, Ben," Reggie said. "But no, not really. Not out here at least. We need to get to the end of the line, find the city, or whatever it is that's out there, and get the girls back. Then we tackle the problem of who's behind all of this."

Ben nodded. "Sounds like a plan."

They walked along in silence for a minute or two, neither man speaking as they followed directly behind Rhett. They crossed a few small streams and trudged through some low-lying swampland, eventually reaching a higher platform of trees and bushes.

Reggie wondered if Ben was still thinking about the exchange they'd had with Rhett a few minutes ago, but it was Ben who broke the silence first.

"And Reggie?" Ben asked.

Reggie looked over at Ben, waiting.

"You just say the word. Let me know when I can kill this little runt."

Reggie smiled a true, genuine smile, nodded once, then continued pushing through the rainforest, toward whatever lay ahead.

CHAPTER 48

"What do you mean, he's your brother?" Julie asked. She'd just told Joshua Jefferson about Rhett and his supposed sabotage.

"Keep your voice down," Joshua said. "That's not information I would like my men to overhear."

Julie sighed. "You've got us tied up, guns pointed at us, in the middle of the Amazon rainforest. The least you could do is explain what the hell is going on."

Joshua glanced around, making sure — for the hundredth time — none of the men walking around and in front of them could overhear them. "I told you already," he said. "The company has been lying to me. Something's going on, and it involves my father. There's *no way* he would send my brother out here, and certainly not on company business."

"But you? He would send you?"

"Look around, Julie," Joshua said, his whisper raised to an excited level. "I'm *trained* for this. I've led men into the darkest corners of the earth, and brought just about every one of them back alive. This is what I do."

"Steal innocent women and tie them up to use as bargaining chips later?"

Joshua looked away, then down at the ground as they walked. "Julie, come on. I told you the truth. I thought this was… I assumed something different."

"You assumed we were murderers and the only way to protect your company was to kill us?"

"Stop. Be reasonable for a second. I know it's hard to ask, but trust me. I was given orders, just like always. I always follow the orders, and then I get paid. I'm good at what I do, and I don't ask questions."

Julie just stared at him.

"I'm starting to ask questions, Julie." He looked over at Amanda. Julie followed his gaze, and her heart immediately fell. No one had touched her since they'd tied her wrists, but she looked beaten. No one had spoken a word to her, but she looked distraught. Julie wanted to call out, to say something to her that would lift her spirits, but it was hopeless. There was nothing she could say or do that would make Amanda feel any different about the situation. She almost wanted to ask Joshua to speak a little bit louder so that Amanda could overhear their conversation, for whatever good it might do.

Instead, she just waited for Joshua to continue.

"My father has worked for this company for as long as I can remember. After I quit my job with a private security detail, the company recruited me. It didn't take much — I was always intrigued by what my dad did, even though he rarely spoke about it at home.

"I was trained, given a brief overview of the expectations, then went through a barrage of psychological examinations. After that, I started running missions for them. I've been leading a group of men since then, all chosen by the company, and never the same group."

Julie was slightly taken aback by this statement. It seemed honest; genuine. At the same time, it didn't seem like any sort of military structure she'd ever heard of.

"They're secretive, all of them. I've only been contacted by three or four members of the organization since I've started working there, including my own father. But I haven't actually heard his voice in months."

"Why are you telling me all this," Julie asked?

Again, Joshua looked around. "They're working on something, and my father is a part of it. But I'm a pawn, someone they can send to do their dirty work for them. And that 'dirty work' has been getting a lot dirtier lately."

"Sounds like it's time to put in your letter of resignation," Julie said.

Joshua scoffed. "If only it was that easy," he said. "This isn't the type of company you just *leave*. Once you're in…"

"Okay, so what do you need from me?"

Joshua looked at her strangely. "Need? What you mean?"

"There's a reason you're telling me all this," Julie said. "And I think it has something to do with the fact that you don't trust your employer, and that I am out here because I want to *find* your employer."

Joshua still didn't speak.

"So how can I help?"

"That's the thing," Joshua said. "If you're asking how you can find my employer, I'm sorry. I don't think there's anything you can do to find them; they're good at staying under the radar. But if you're asking how you can help me get away from these guys and back to your group…"

Julie paused. She considered what he'd said. Bringing Joshua back to their group could be disastrous. She didn't want to ratchet up the tension by bringing the leader of their enemies directly into the hands of Ben and Reggie. On the other hand, it would mean she and Amanda might have a better chance at survival.

"How do I know this isn't just a trap? How do I know you're not using me to get back to my group?"

"Julie, listen to yourself. You and I both know that you are nothing more than a bargaining chip. Amanda is the reason we are out here, and once my team acquires whatever it is we're looking for, we won't need you, and possibly not even her. I'm offering you a chance."

The group of mercenaries, still surrounding Joshua, Amanda, and Julie, were walking through an area of the basin that had a lower elevation than where they had come from. The ground was starting to get mushy, and soon Julie found herself stepping into sections of forest floor that gave way to water. Within a few minutes, she was wading through a swamp. Her shoes, the same flats she had been wearing since they disembarked the plane, were starting to wear thin. Reggie had offered pairs of boots to the men only, as he didn't own any women's sizes. She knew it was only a matter of hours before she would be better off barefoot.

She wasn't prepared for this — none of them were. She took a long, hard look at the men surrounding her. Joshua was mostly at ease, save for a hardened look in his eyes that spoke volumes about his experiences. The rest of his men alternated swatting at insects and pointing their guns outward as they marched through the rainforest swamp. These were men who had seen combat, but they were not men fully prepared for an expedition into one of the most grueling climates on earth.

She wondered how her own group was holding up. Amanda, obviously, was struggling. Julie was no doctor, but she knew Amanda would be fine, so long as she had the strength to continue on. Paulinho seemed to be recovering well from his injury, and aside from any new injuries or an infestation, he would heal well. The professor, Archie, was stronger than he looked, and probably had more hours in the rainforest logged than any of them. She had no idea whether or not Carlo was most comfortable on a boat, back home — wherever that was — or in the jungle.

It was Reggie and Ben she worried about most. Reggie seemed to be the epitome of a leader; someone they could all trust with the challenge in front of them. He could carry them through just about anything, she thought, thanks to the way he carried himself and his obnoxious smirk. But every leader could crack; after a certain amount of pressure applied to them, and different scenarios thrown at them, every leader was capable of falling.

She never considered Ben a leader until this moment. He was, absolutely, a strong man. Capable of things she never thought possible for a mere mortal, but she admitted to herself a slight bias toward him. Still, he had proven himself worthy of her affection, and that wasn't worth nothing. She knew he would not stop until he was either dead or had accomplished his goal.

"Okay," she said suddenly, stopping Joshua in his tracks. "What are you thinking?"

CHAPTER 49

It had been a long time since Joshua had felt this confused. Usually, his orders were clear. Achieve this objective, accomplish this task, acquire this target.

The company was never arbitrary, never vague, and rarely unclear. Any instances he'd experienced the latter had been of his own failing, quickly remedied by a clarifying email or two.

Only in his thirties, Joshua was humble enough to know that he had a lot to learn. His father had drilled into him and his younger brother the power of a good work ethic and the necessary skills to succeed in social circles. Joshua was young, but he was already showing the signs of great leadership. All of the missions he had been assigned had gone successfully, with few casualties. His men, accustomed to high turnover and rapid replacement of their leaders, were pleasantly surprised at Joshua's longevity, even for his age. None of them had outwardly expressed any contention with the father-son relationship that existed in the company, if they even knew of it. They respected Joshua, and he respected them back, so long as they completed their objectives and proved to be a valuable asset to the team.

He adored — and even idolized — his father, a strong-willed, altruistic man. An officer in the Navy, he had retired and gone to work at the Company when Joshua was only a few years old. Rhett, his only sibling, was born shortly after. Growing up, he and Rhett were seen as equals by their father — a man who sought the best for his only sons.

Joshua, no doubt due to age, excelled sooner than Rhett in just about everything. Rhett was hot-tempered, and was constantly upset that his older brother seemed to earn the most praise from their father. As they grew up, Rhett began drifting apart from both his brother and his father, eventually choosing law, instead of military, as a career path.

It was a devastating blow to the family, a single-father household with no direct relatives. Joshua and his father were closer than ever when he reached adulthood, and Rhett quickly became the "other child." Neither purposefully treated him that way, but it was apparent at family dinners and gatherings that Rhett was the black swan of the group. He grew further apart from his family, and soon was nearly out of the picture entirely.

Shortly after the Company had hired Joshua, they'd asked about his brother. Was he a good fit for the Company? Did he have potential, like Joshua, to lead men into battle and achieve somewhat ambiguous goals?

Joshua remembered his answer well. *'No, he's not like me. I think he's a good kid, but he's still a kid. He's a hobbyist — someone who's interested in learning to fly one day, then learning how to manipulate the jury's emotions in a courtroom the next. He's a hotshot; he's not the type of guy who will focus on mastering something before moving on to the next.'*

Joshua knew his assessment was still true, even though he hadn't heard from his brother in over a year. Rhett had told him about a year and a half ago he was interested in getting his pilot's license, but couldn't exactly clarify what he was hoping to accomplish by doing so. Joshua had pressed him on it, but Rhett grew cold, flighty, and disengaged.

It wasn't a good memory, and Joshua wished it had been different. But family wasn't something you could change — what you were born with, you were stuck with. He'd even tried reaching out to their father, but didn't hear back. He wrote off the conversation as youth; Rhett was a young gun trying to live up to his brother's and his father's expectations. But deep inside, Joshua Jefferson knew the truth.

Rhett Jefferson was a loose cannon. He was unreliable, unfit for duty in any military, and not someone Joshua wanted to associate with professionally. It was a difficult decision, but he told the Company that Rhett was the type of man who would lead them to far more problems than solutions, and should only be used — if they still decided to employ him — in extenuating circumstances.

So when Julie asked him how she could help, and what their next move should be, he answered her the only way he knew how.

"We need to get control of the situation," he said.

They'd been walking side-by-side for an hour, and he wasn't sure if she even remembered that she'd asked him the question.

"And how do you suggest we do that?"

"Two of my men are loyal to me, and the rest are loyal to the company or just in it for the money," Joshua said. He motioned toward two men walking on their left side. "Riggs and Alan are good, but the others I can't vouch for yet. We're going to have to move quickly, so I'm going to need you to get Amanda and try to get ahead of us. I'll talk to those two and see about setting up a distraction."

Joshua looked at Julie to gauge her reaction. She was staring straight ahead as they marched through the forest, her expression steely and firm.

Good, he thought. *She's going to be just fine.*

"Also, I'm going to need you to hit me."

Julie snapped her head up and looked at Joshua. "I think I can manage that."

Joshua smiled, then slowed down slightly and walked behind Julie for a moment. He slid the edge of his knife against the ropes binding Julie's hands, and the cold steel cut easily through. Julie kept her hands held together behind her back, even as the ropes loosened and fell. Joshua continued onward, this time matching pace with the two men he had identified earlier.

"Change of plans," he said, his voice barely audible. The two men nodded once, quickly. "I need you two to buy us some time. Don't let the others follow us until we are safely out of range, got it?"

Again, nods.

With Riggs and Alan squared away, Joshua turned once more to Julie and caught her eye. He mouthed the word *"Ready?"* and waited for her response. She glanced over at Amanda, then gave her approval.

Satisfied, Joshua returned to her side and explained the rest of the plan. When he'd finished, they walked along in silence for a few more minutes. Just when Joshua was about to ask if Julie was comfortable with their plan, she struck.

The force of the blow was harder than Joshua expected. It landed perfectly, her fist crushing the side of his head and nearly knocking him unconscious. He had little left to fake, as he stumbled sideways and fell to his knees. She attacked again, this time finding the underside of his chin with her knee.

He groaned and fell on his face. Joshua heard two of the men at the back cry out and start running forward.

"Go," he whispered, barely able to speak.

The world around him was spinning, but he could see Julie grab Amanda's arm and pull her along, the two of them disappearing into the woods as the rest of his men tried to make sense of the attack.

Alan and Riggs were at his side. They lifted him up and waited for him to catch his balance. Three of the others had already broken off to go after the girls, and Joshua gave the order to Alan to have them called back. Alan ran off to accomplish the task, and Riggs looked down at Joshua, waiting. His gigantic body swayed slightly in front of his boss.

"Round them up," Joshua said. "Regroup, and have them continue forward. Our goal is to find the city. Let the women go."

Riggs didn't respond, but his eyes narrowed ever so slightly.

"Riggs, you hear me?"

"Boss, our mission —"

"*I* determine our mission, Riggs. Is that clear?"

Riggs stared, then finally answered, his voice low and menacing. "Yes, sir."

Without another word, Riggs turned and ran off into the jungle.

CHAPTER 50

Ben saw the gate between the trees just as Archie and Paulinho reached it. Both men stopped and stood in the light, waiting for the others to catch up.

The gate, nothing more than two huge trees twisted together and interconnected, was like the end of a tunnel they hadn't realized they were walking through. The bright sun, normally dampened by the thick covering of canopy trees high above their heads, had now found an entrance to the denseness of the forest. It bled in, enshrining everything in front of Ben in light.

The silhouettes of Paulinho and Archie were like beacons, and Ben found himself hustling to reach their location. It was already hot, multiplied by the humidity of the jungle. He had been sweating profusely since they'd stepped foot in the rainforest, but the directness of the sunlight still felt warm and life-giving as Ben stepped out onto the platform with Archie and Paulinho. Carlo and Reggie, pushing Rhett along in front of him, joined them soon after, and the six men stood silently for a moment as they stared downward into the valley.

Ben knew from Archie's descriptions of the area that the Amazon basin was mostly flat, by definition. Runoff and mountain rivers in the Andes joined together in a myriad of tributaries called the Amazon River. Over millennia of flooding, erosion, and the natural cycle of geological life, the entire basin had been flattened and pressed downward.

All except for the land directly in front of them. A huge, looming plateau stretched upward from the ground, raised high into the air and dwarfing the trees surrounding it. What was perhaps only a couple hundred feet of vertical height seemed massive compared to the elevation of the rest of the forest. The cliffs were solid rock walls, covered with luscious green blankets of mosses, small trees, and jungle shrubs. Weaving its way around the plateau, and forming the bottom — and base — of the valley they'd stumbled into, was a slow-moving, wide tributary river. Its water looked deep brown, with flecks of blue and green sparkling as the light hit it. Rocks and other landforms jutted out of it, giving it the appearance of being a relatively shallow body of water.

Archie explained that these sorts of "unknown" rivers were quite common in the Basin. The entire area was subjected to flooding for half the year during and immediately after the rainy season. Most of the larger tributaries, including the Amazon River itself, would swell up and cover a much larger area of land, but there were often low-lying sections of jungle that would become rivers for a few months of the year.

It was difficult to tell whether or not the river Ben was standing in front of now was unknown due to its nonexistence part of the year or because of its remoteness. There was a strong possibility it was a permanent fixture of the Amazon, just not one known to the outside world. They had reached an area of the world that was largely unexplored and undocumented, a completely remote section of the globe.

"I didn't know there were mountains in the jungle," Paulinho said.

"It's not a mountain, technically," Archie responded. "It's rock, but it's no more than a large formation. A plateau top, it appears, at least from this angle."

Ben idled over closer to the conversation to overhear.

"Because the land surrounding the cliffs is lower than the rest of the Basin, satellite mapping of the region wouldn't be able to accurately depict the shape of the raised area here. It is likely this small hill has gone completely unnoticed for the past few thousand years."

"If we're lucky," Ben said, "that's true." He shuddered at the thought of running into more natives.

Reggie broke up the geography lesson. "Let's get down into the valley, at least. We can decide whether or not to cross the river here or head upstream, but we need to get closer to it first."

"Cross the river?" Paulinho asked. Ben noticed that the man was holding his side. He hadn't spoken a word of complaint since they'd left the boat, but it had only been a couple days since he'd been injured. Ben hoped he was legitimately feeling better and not just acting courageous.

"Yes," Reggie said. "The lines intersect less than a mile from here, according to the printouts and the map I put together." He already had the map in his hands, and the others leaned in to examine it for themselves. Ben noticed that Reggie had scribbled in notes along the journey, in an attempt to keep track of their progress as they trekked forward. "Assuming the map is correct, and we've been diligent enough to be close," he continued, "the final destination of the city is actually straight ahead."

Ben frowned, looking from the map in Reggie's hands to the high cliffs on the other side of the river. He noticed that in front of the cliffs there were sections of water, separated from the larger river, that pooled around the bases of trees and rocks. The plants shot out of the murky depths, their roots sometimes poking from the surface as well.

A swamp.

They'd have to cross not only a river, but a swamp as well.

He told the others.

"Seems that way," Reggie said. "But once we're across, we can figure out how to get onto the plateau."

Ben wasn't sure what to make of Reggie's statement. "Wait, *on to* the plateau?"

Reggie and the others looked at Ben as though he was delusional. "Ben," Archie said, his voice calm, as if explaining the situation to a toddler. "We *must* get to the top of the plateau. You do understand that, no?"

Ben looked at each man, waiting for one of them to burst out in laughter. *This is a joke,* he thought. "You can't be serious," he said. "We can't *climb* the cliffs. There's got to be a way around, and —"

"Ben," Paulinho said. "We'll make it. I know we will."

"There's no other way, Ben," Reggie said. "The destination is on top of that plateau, and the only way to get there…"

Ben looked at Carlo. He hadn't spoken a word to the man, even when they were on the boat. He'd stayed with their party after the captain had been eaten, and he'd been helpful to the group whenever needed. As quiet as the man was, Ben hoped he'd still have a reasonable opinion about whether or not they should climb two hundred-foot cliffs.

Carlo shrugged.

Ben sighed. *Maybe that's Brazilian for 'you're right, Ben, and it's a bad idea.'*

"Looks like the verdict's been reached, then," Reggie said. "Down to the river, cross it and then the swamp, then figure out how to get up the cliffs."

Ben shook his head. *This started out impossible. I can't believe it's getting more impossible every minute.* He reached into his pocket and grabbed the second coca leaf he'd taken from Reggie, and popped it in his mouth. *Let's hope these things help with more than just hunger and fatigue.*

CHAPTER 51

Ben was sore and exhausted from the climb down the hill, and he was frustrated as well. They'd descended from the platform overlooking the expansive valley and raised plateau, and now the group was standing near the wide, shallow river. He wasn't excited about crossing another body of water, but as Reggie and the others had explained, there was no other choice.

He felt as though his shoes and socks had only just dried from their first river excursion. The humidity of the jungle air was stifling, and it made drying off from soaking wet a rare feat. He considered removing his shoes and holding them above his head, to have something dry to wear on the opposite bank, but quickly decided against it. Dry shoes were a luxury he couldn't afford at the expense of subjecting his feet to whatever tortures might lay underfoot on the river's bottom.

He shuddered as he considered his options. *Is there any chance I can wait here?* he wondered. The girls would be with the mercenaries, and if Reggie was correct, they'd be dumped out into the valley as well, shortly behind his group. He might be able to stay behind, hidden, and use the element of surprise to attack...

With what? He had nothing but Reggie's Sig Sauer handgun, and it was no match for the assault rifles he'd seen earlier. He might be able to get a few shots off before the enemy spotted him, but he was no deadeye. It was a long shot — literally.

Maybe they could all stay behind, save for one or two of them. It seemed Carlo was comfortable in the jungle, and he might not mind the trip. Archie, who obviously had a knack for the history of the tribes in the region, would be a good asset to send forward as well.

Ben shook his head, dismissing the absurd thoughts. They'd have to stay together — none of the others would agree to a plan that would split their group even further. They were already outnumbered, and with the girls missing as well, splitting into two smaller groups was a recipe for disaster.

The river, wide and a deep emerald color, loomed before him. He sighed. Reggie, still pulling Rhett along, and Paulinho all stepped in together, both men appearing undaunted by the task at hand. Their legs disappeared into the murky water, but only up to their knees. Ben watched on, waiting for one of them to fall off a shelf into deeper water.

The two men in the river continued forward, trudging onward unfazed, their knees barely covered. The current, if it existed, was weak and unfocused, and neither man had trouble navigating any underwater rocks or debris.

Carlo entered the water next, and Archie followed closely behind. Ben saw his opportunities for backing out of the endeavor drifting away with every passing second, and finally he made up his mind.

He stepped out and into the water. He stared down at his feet as the first, then the second, steps sank away into the mud. The water felt cool at first, but as his body acclimated to the temperature he reassessed, and determined the river here to feel about the same as an old, stale bath.

He cringed. *I'm walking through a section of the Amazon River, for the second time in days. What is wrong with me?*

He thought of Julie, and how he wished she was by his side instead of Carlo and Archibald Quinones. They were good men, and he appreciated both of them, both for their positive, optimistic attitudes, as well as their capabilities and experience. He wasn't able to share their enthusiasm for the trip, but Ben also knew that it was his own stubbornness that had brought them to Brazil in the first place.

With that memory came the reminder of what he was here for. The throbbing heat of a rage he'd long since pushed back inside of him came rushing back upward, and Ben clenched his teeth as he remembered.

All the people they killed. All the waste. Destruction.

He remembered the people he'd left behind at Yellowstone, his friends and fellow park staff. Julie had given everything to follow him, allowing him to dictate the course of their lives as they were intertwined together, tighter and tighter over the last few months.

She brought out the best in him, and he loved her for it, but it didn't change the fact that they were together now because they once shared a common enemy. That enemy was the reason their lives had been entangled with each other's, and that reason was now chasing him through the most remote jungle on Earth.

He plowed forward, quickly catching up with Archie, then to Carlo only steps ahead. A hot-tempered vigor pushed him onward, and he was surprised at the rapid change of heart he suddenly felt. He felt energized; he felt as though he'd been luxuriously rested and pampered for the past few days, not trekking through the rainforest. He charged toward the opposite side of the river, longing for dry land nearly as much as he longed for revenge. He'd find the killers, the company behind it all, and he'd start with the mercenaries behind them.

Ben had silently restated his mission to himself a few times, and the opposite bank was now closer than the one they'd started from, when he felt the bite.

It was quick, small, and subsided as rapidly as it arrived. He shook his leg, assuming his ankle had been caught by a sharp tree branch or stick.

The second bite stopped him in the middle of the river. He looked down at the river, his legs two feet beneath the surface. The rippling nearby was unnatural, not repetitive enough or rhythmic enough to be caused by the current flowing over some permanent obstruction.

The rippling became more intense, and he looked up to see Archie and Carlo nearby, both wide-eyed and breathing rapidly. He frowned, trying to understand the commotion. Paulinho and Reggie, dragging Rhett behind them, were already nearing the riverbank, but Ben had stopped and was waiting for someone to explain —

"Piranha!" Archie shouted. "Get out of the water!"

Ben felt a surge of sheer terror that launched him forward with a vigor that even his anger from before couldn't match. He half-swam, half-crawled toward Reggie, Rhett, and Paulinho, silently praying he was making progress, but feeling as though he was running in place. He felt stuck, mired by the soft muddy bottom of the river, waiting in horror for the inevitable strike of the carnivorous fish. It was like a dream he used to have as a child, in which he'd try as hard as possible to run forward, only finding that his legs and body were unresponsive and he struggled in place until he woke himself up.

This time, he didn't wake up to find it was only a bad dream. This nightmare was real, and he was very much alive and awake. He didn't feel any more bites, but he heard Carlo scream from somewhere behind him and to his right. He wanted to continue, to get to the edge of the river and escape the man-eating fish, but something inside him made him turn around. He reached out to Carlo instinctively, but Carlo wasn't paying attention.

In fact, Carlo wasn't even looking his direction. The man had fallen to his waist, and the dark color of the water around him was now stained an even deeper crimson. Carlo was batting at the surface of the water with his palms, trying to force the attacking predators away, but it was in vain. His mouth was open in a silent scream, and before Ben could react, he lunged forward and face-first into the water, and disappeared from view.

The whitewater frothed and churned from the thousand tiny splashes. The fish didn't let up, even as Carlo's body sank away. The fish continued their assault, pushing Carlo's body still deeper into the mud. Ben had walked nearly the same path as Carlo, so he knew the water where Carlo lay was the same depth — not deep enough to be fully submerged.

Ben knew what it meant. The only way to sink a body in shallow water was to make the body smaller, and that's exactly what he'd just witnessed. In less than a minute, the fish dispersed and Carlo was completely gone, the stain of an oil slick on the surface the only evidence remaining of the brutal attack.

CHAPTER 52

Joshua needed a plan, and quickly. Amanda and Julie had run off as he'd hoped, but he needed to find them before his men did. He knew there was a mutiny playing out, but he wasn't sure if all of his men were involved or just a few.

Riggs was a good soldier, someone Joshua could count on to get the job done no matter the cost. He had assumed this integrity was a sign of loyalty, but he had assumed wrong. Riggs was clearly planning to oust Joshua from his position leading these men. Whether he would take over that role or not was of no concern to Joshua. If Riggs had his way, Joshua would be dead by then.

He was running after Riggs now. The man had taken off in the direction they'd seen the women run, hoping to intercept them, subdue them, and likely make them pay for their insubordination. Joshua hoped Julie would be able to stay ahead of Riggs long enough.

Joshua was not an expert tracker, but Riggs — and the girls before him — had done a fantastic job leaving a trail behind them. He saw the broken sticks, crushed leaves and grasses, and footprints in the ground below his feet as he charged forward. As he ran he tried to listen for any sign of a skirmish, but the jungle around him was feverishly excited about the intruders chasing each other through it. He heard the hoots and howls of monkeys, the incessant buzz of millions of insects, and a thousand other unidentifiable noises that created the backdrop drone of the rainforest.

He turned left and nearly stumbled into Riggs. There was a river, wide and slow-moving, just in front of him. Riggs was standing on the bank just at the edge of it, preparing to cross.

"Riggs," Joshua said.

Riggs turned around, and in that instant Joshua knew the truth. *One of us will die here today.*

"Riggs, where are the girls? Did they already cross?"

"I was almost on them. The other side of the river slopes upward, so they'll be going slower. Since you're here now, though, I guess we can take care of our other business."

"It doesn't have to be this way, Riggs. The Company —"

"The *Company* has given you everything. They stuck you with us because your daddy told them to. You didn't earn this. You're just a rich kid who talked the talk and —"

Joshua dove forward and punched Riggs. He swung cleanly through, snapping Riggs' head to the side. Before Riggs could recover Joshua wrapped him up and pushed him back into the water. It was deeper than Joshua had expected, and both men disappeared beneath the surface for a moment.

When they came up, Riggs had the upper hand. Joshua felt the man's hands around his neck, trying to hold him underneath the water. The river was shallow enough to stand in, however, and when Joshua caught his feet on the bottom he lunged upward. Riggs' hold slipped and Joshua attempted to turn the balance of power back into his favor. He grappled for a moment with Riggs' arms, trying to subdue him, but Riggs was a far larger and stronger man.

Riggs got an elbow free and slammed it across Joshua's face. The pain exploded beneath Joshua's skin, but he ignored it for the moment. He found an opening and tried to knee Riggs, but they were still in the water and the action was slowed enough to be nullified.

Joshua ducked his head down just as Riggs came at him with a left hook, and he pushed Riggs backward back onto the shoreline. Riggs' body smacked against the soft, muddy ground and sank in just enough to hold him in place for a moment. Joshua took advantage of the small window of opportunity and landed a one-two punch on the man.

The punches were clean, solid and forceful, but Riggs hardly seemed to notice. He grunted and spat out a mouthful of blood, meanwhile bringing his foot and leg around Joshua's. The kick tripped Joshua, but he was able to fall with his knee downward, catching Riggs in the groin.

This attack garnered a reaction from Riggs, and his eyes rolled back for a second as he waited for the pain to subside. Joshua tried to wriggle free, but Riggs had placed him in a hold, locking him in place on top of himself.

For a moment both men lay still. Joshua's muscles ached with exertion, rock solid as they struggled to fight against the opposite force Riggs was providing. Joshua knew Riggs would win just about any hand-to-hand combat, but there was nothing he could use as a weapon. He tried to remember his training, searching in vain for something to use against his second-in-command.

He rolled onto his shoulder, attempting to focus all of his weight and strength in one direction. The move worked, and he somersaulted over Riggs and out of reach of the man's grasp. Joshua stood up and turned around.

Riggs was already on his feet, now brandishing a huge knife in his right hand. Riggs spat again, then smiled. "This ends here, *boss.*" He hissed the last word, enunciating his hatred for Joshua with a single syllable.

"Why, Riggs? What's in it for you?"

"It's not that hard to figure out, Jefferson. There's a lot of money involved, as always. The Company isn't loyal to you, or me, or anyone else for that matter. They just want results."

"We were going to get results. You know I wasn't going to stop until we —"

"That woman, the doctor, *is* the result. Whatever they think we're going to find out here can only be unlocked by her."

Joshua knew Riggs was right. He had been given the same orders. *Find Dr. Meron, find the lost city, and bring back whatever they could that might help their research.* Something the Company had found in Amanda's research linked to this area of the Amazon Rainforest, and they would do whatever it took to find it.

Riggs was also right about their loyalties. The Company would double-cross and betray anyone they employed to ensure they got what they wanted. It was a twisted, complex organization, willing to do anything and go to any lengths to accomplish their goals. Joshua grew suspicious of his own mission when he began talking to Julie. When she'd mentioned that his own brother had been with them — someone she would have no way of knowing otherwise — he'd tried to analyze all of the events leading up to his mission here.

Most of the interactions he'd had with the Company, as always, were through his father, Jeremiah Jefferson. The man was higher up in the organization, though Joshua had no idea how wide the web of hierarchy was spread. Usually, Joshua had regular phone calls with his father about upcoming missions and deployments. The Company chose to communicate with Joshua through Jeremiah, allowing both men somewhat autonomous decision-making when it came to the details of each mission.

That, too, was strange about this particular mission. Joshua hadn't spoken with his father in months. His communication lately had been via email. The emails, now that he thought about it, were short and written in a tone that didn't quite match his father's.

He suspected now that his father's email had been hacked, either by someone within the Company operating as a rogue, or by the Company itself, in one of the never-ending twists and turns that defined the organization's power structure.

The most obvious sign of his being played, however, was the fact that his brother, Rhett Jefferson, was out here as well. Their father would never send Rhett, and from the conversations they'd had months earlier and before, Joshua was convinced their father thought less of his younger son than even Joshua had expected.

He remembered one of the last conversations he'd had with his father. The subject of Joshua's kid brother came up, and Jeremiah Jefferson grew cold, his thick southern accent slowing down to enunciate his point. "Rhett is dangerous, not because of his experience and training but in spite of it. He doesn't know where his loyalties should lie, and his only authority is money and power."

Without overtly saying it, Jeremiah Jefferson had asked his eldest son to be wary of his younger brother.

"What's it going to be, Jefferson?" Riggs asked, snapping Joshua back to the present. "You want to fight this out to its inevitable conclusion, or can we do it the easy way?"

Joshua assumed the 'easy way' would end in his death, as Riggs would undoubtedly not want to allow Joshua to rejoin their group. The Company would write it off as an unexpected expense, but nothing more.

Joshua sighed. He glanced over to a large pile of sticks and branches that had floated into a corner of the river. Over time the mess had compressed itself together, forming a nearly impenetrable wall that domed upward above the water's surface. As he stared at the crop of broken sticks, he had an idea.

Riggs wasn't going to make this easy, regardless of Joshua's choice. He had no doubt he would lose in any sort of one-on-one combat, no matter how hard he fought. He couldn't use a distraction to any effect, and Riggs wouldn't fall for any type of gimmick. He was a hardened soldier, someone who had seen more combat than anyone on their team, a lifer who had killed more people than some of his men had ever even known.

Joshua sidestepped, inching closer to the water. Riggs matched his movements, stepping around to his right as well to keep Joshua directly in front of him. Soon, both men were standing at the edge of the water in inch-deep mud, eyeing each other in anticipation of the final battle.

Joshua waited until the larger man was standing opposite him, just in front of the mound of debris.

The nest.

He remembered reading about some of the more well-known predators they could expect to find in the jungle. The list of things that could kill them out here was nearly endless, but there were a few that topped the chart in Joshua's mind he called '*horrible ways to die in the rainforest.*'

He recalled one of these predators in particular, and their typical habitat. They preferred slow-moving rivers, almost swamp-like, murkier water that allowed them to sneak up on their prey, and nesting in the large mounds of sticks and debris that were common alongside Amazon tributaries and rivers.

It was a long shot, but it was all Joshua had. He jumped forward, hoping Riggs would take the bait.

He did, stepping backwards and onto the mound. It was a nearly involuntary reaction, a response to the sudden frontal assault.

Joshua stopped and waited. Riggs stood on the mound, warily eyeing his opponent.

Then it happened. Riggs was too heavy for the mound of sticks, and one of his feet broke through the ceiling of the dome. The interior of the mound was hollow, and Joshua saw and heard the splash of water as Riggs's foot hit the river's surface.

Riggs was surprised but unfazed. He cursed, trying to wriggle his foot free.

Come on, Joshua thought. *There'd better be someone home.*

Riggs pushed down with his free foot and pulled his leg out from the hole. Just as the sole of his boot lifted free from the top of the dome, the mound collapsed. Sticks, mud, water, and Riggs sloshed around in the river as Joshua looked on.

Riggs was just about to stand when something pulled him back. His upper body fell forward as his lower body was tugged backwards into the shallow water. He frowned as he lifted his head above the surface once more, and Joshua saw him make the effort to pull himself up and forward again.

His movement was betrayed yet again as the invisible force beneath the surface tugged on the man.

Riggs's eyes widened as he realized what he was fighting against now. Joshua stared, calmly looking into the broken nest and the man struggling against his fate.

The anaconda was obviously upset that its home had been ruined, and it made no difference to the large snake that it was a human intruder.

Riggs pulled himself to the shore, digging his fingers into the mud and forcing his torso up onto the bank. Only then did Joshua get a good look at the snake that had wound itself around Riggs's leg and lower body. The reptile was absolutely massive, over a foot wide at its thickest point.

The greenish-brown snake reacted to every motion Riggs made with an opposite one, using every ounce of the man's strength against him. Whenever Riggs exhaled, the snake wound its way up his body and tightened its grasp on its prey.

Joshua had read that the anaconda was a member of the boa constrictor family, aptly named for its ability to "constrict" its prey by wrapping itself around its food to suffocate it. Sometimes growing to a weight of 500 pounds, they typically only attacked small-to-medium-sized mammals, only rarely striking out at full-grown humans.

Joshua had hoped this particular snake would make an exception, and it had. Even if the snake had no intention of consuming Riggs, the man would be crushed beneath the weight of the monster in less than a minute.

Riggs struggled for a few more seconds, then looked over at Joshua. His eyes were bloodshot, his mouth agape yet eerily silent. He seemed to be calling out to Joshua, crying for help. Joshua ignored him, staring onward at the horrendous scene unfolding in front of him. A small part of him felt remorse, but he was able to look past those feelings and remind himself of the truth.

As the snake finished the job, Joshua heard the snap of a branch and the rustling of leaves to his left. One of the men from his group appeared in the jungle. The man looked at Joshua, then down at the snake-wrapped Riggs. When his eyes came back to meet Joshua's, Joshua was pointing his gun directly at him.

He fired two shots quickly, but the man was already moving. He ducked and fell to the ground, dodging the attack perfectly.

Joshua didn't wait any longer. There was no way he was going to stay and fight off the rest of his men, now turned against him. He dove headfirst into the river, briefly considering that the giant snake may have had friends lurking nearby. He swam freestyle across the water and to the other side, not slowing down until he had pulled himself from the river and into the trees. Joshua ran up the sloping hill in the same direction Riggs had said the girls were headed.

It wouldn't take long for the group to meet up, explain what had happened, and realize that Joshua was no longer on their side. From then on, he would be the enemy of not just Dr. Meron's and Julie's group but of his own as well.

A half hour later, he found Julie and Amanda. They were walking ahead of him, moving slowly, Julie half-carrying Amanda as they pressed onward through the jungle. He needed a plan, and fast. The girls were trying to meet up with their group, and Joshua needed to help them do just that, without getting himself killed in the process.

"Juliette," he shouted, running forward to intercept them.

CHAPTER 53

He hadn't realized his mouth was hanging open until Reggie called out to him. "Ben, you okay?"

Ben couldn't move his gaze from the water, but he nodded. "I'm okay. Carlo…"

"We saw, Ben. Nothing we can do."

Ben wanted to scream. He wanted to curse, to argue with Reggie. *We could have stopped it.*

But he knew the horrific truth. There was *nothing* they could have done. The attack was swift, stealthy, and there was no possible way to have prevented it. Even as it was happening, it would only have put more lives in danger if they'd tried to stop it.

Paulinho and Rhett were facing the other direction, looking onward into the thick stand of jungle that was now the only barrier between them and the cliff face. He felt a hand on his shoulder, pulling him gently away from the edge of the river. He turned to see Archie next to him, and Reggie walking over. "I'm sorry, Ben." Ben wasn't sure why the man should have been sorry. Carlo wasn't his employee, or friend, or even an acquaintance. Ben didn't know him any better than anyone else on the trip, and he should have been able to brush off the feeling with little concern.

But something nagged at him. The entire journey had been

reminding Ben of something, something he couldn't quite place. He hadn't tried to understand the feeling, and even actively refused it, but he knew it was there. It tugged at him, bringing him back to a time and a place he'd long since tried to forget.

His father was there, and his brother. A hunting trip. A bear cub had wandered into their camp, and Ben's brother had come between the cub and its mother. Ben's father died saving him. His mother never truly recovered.

That was almost fourteen years ago, and he'd become a park ranger shortly after that. He'd wanted a job that was solitary, something away from people and busyness. When he'd arrived at the park and started working, he realized immediately that he'd done it for the wrong reasons.

He loved the park job, and dedicated the next decade to it, but it was Juliette Richardson who'd finally forced him to realize the truth. He didn't hate people, he just hated the pain they caused. He wanted to help, and was stubbornly dedicated to the people he loved and worked with, and would do anything to protect them. He was reclusive because he was afraid, not because he was angry. She'd made him realize that.

Reggie soon joined Archie. "Ben, he knew the risks. We all do."

"He had nothing to do with —"

"None of us do, Ben. It's no one's fight, and that's exactly why you and I are fighting it."

Ben eyed Reggie suspiciously.

"I'm on to you, Bennett," Reggie said. "Julie filled me in on a bit of it, but I got the rest pretty quickly."

"What are you talking about?" Ben asked.

"You and I are the same this way, Ben. We care about people in a way that makes us stupid sometimes."

Ben frowned.

"It's not always a bad thing, man. You're here, and that's good.

No one else on the planet would throw themselves in the face of this willingly. You *flew* here. *On a plane. Two* planes, actually." Reggie grinned.

"She told you about that?"

"Yeah, sorry." Reggie rapped him on the back. "Everyone's got something, you know?"

Ben laughed.

"There aren't a lot of guys I've met like you. You're stubborn as hell, but you use it smartly. Under pressure."

Ben started walking away, trying to distance himself from the river and not think about the fact that when all this was over, when they'd finally found what they were looking for and somehow stayed alive, they'd have to cross it once more.

"Carlo was a good man, I'm sure," Reggie said. "We'll make sure to find his family. Right now, though, we need you. All of you. Understand?"

Ben nodded.

"Good. Julie's out there somewhere, and she needs you to get her back."

Ben tensed at the mention of her name, but he knew Reggie was right. The man wasn't pandering to him or manipulating his emotions. He spoke in truths, and laid out the facts. It was one of the things he liked about Reggie.

Archie had rejoined Paulinho and both men were checking the bruising that remained on Paulinho's torso. It was a terrible bluish-black color, but Paulinho seemed to be doing well. The bruise-covered area was already growing smaller too, it seemed. Archie poked and prodded it in a few places, and both men soon deemed it healthy enough to continue forward.

"You ready?" Reggie asked.

Ben thought for a moment, his subconscious still churning through scenarios that would allow him to not have to free-climb a rock wall. Not finding a suitable scenario, he nodded. "Ready as I'll ever be."

Reggie grinned. "You got this."

Reggie walked the few paces over to Archie, Rhett, and Paulinho and asked the same question, but before Ben could listen for their responses, he heard the unmistakable sound of gunfire cracking through the air. He squinted, trying to see across the river at the source of the commotion.

The gunfire continued, steady bursts of shots echoing over the river's surface and reaching Ben, then bouncing off the cliff face behind him and back over the water. It created a tin can effect, adding more confusion and threatening chaos to the mix of emotions Ben was feeling.

Julie suddenly stumbled out onto the same ledge they'd descended from less than an hour earlier, the gunshots continuing to rip through the jungle.

CHAPTER 54

"Julie!" he shouted. He waved his arms above his head, hoping to get her attention.

Julie didn't wave back. Instead, she jumped forward and down off the rock platform, her feet eventually finding the unstable jungle floor that sloped up below the ledge. She slid the rest of the way to the ground, barely stopping to catch her breath.

The same walk that had taken Ben's group about fifteen minutes had taken Julie less than thirty seconds.

Ben knew what that meant, too. *She's the one they're shooting at. She's running from* them.

His joy at her appearance was soon replaced, yet again, by fear, anger, and the slow, smoldering feeling of revenge. He shouted out to her again, but she was intently focused on getting across the river.

"Julie! Wait! There are —"

He knew she could hear him, but as he tried to shout his warning to her about the deadly predators lurking just below the surface of the water, he felt Reggie tugging on his shoulder.

"Ben, stop. Look."

Reggie pointed up at the ledge, and Ben's eyes followed him there. The ledge, he now realized, was probably the only entrance to the valley they were in. The natural form of the landscape, coupled with the density of the jungle they were in, did not allow any access to this place besides entering through the same tree pillars they'd found. The doorway into their little valley.

And that doorway was not empty.

Ben could see the younger mercenary — the one he recognized from the video at NARATech — looking down into the valley. His rifle was slung over his shoulder, but he held a pistol in his right hand. Ben could almost feel his eyes on him, staring. Ben clenched his jaw and started forward.

Again, Reggie held him back.

"Those shots were from assault rifles," Reggie said. "And he's not using one."

Ben listened for a moment and heard the popping sounds of gunfire still ringing out in the distance. The trees dampened the sound a bit, but the noise was crisp enough to carry easily into the valley.

"What are you saying?" Ben asked.

"He's not the one shooting at Julie, and I don't think he's trying to catch her. I think they're *all* running from the mercenaries."

Ben frowned when Reggie mentioned 'all' of them, but he continued to watch the platform and realized what Reggie meant. Behind the man standing on the ledge, he saw a splash of blond hair. *Amanda*.

"Dr. Meron's up there with him," Reggie said.

The man didn't wait for Amanda to catch her breath. He jumped forward just like Julie had, sliding down the ramp of twisted, rotting jungle flora and out onto the wide riverbank. Amanda followed. She botched the landing, but the man reached down and helped her to her feet.

"He's helping her," Ben said. He felt silly for not being able to do anything from their location, only offering commentary from afar.

When Amanda had recovered, the man stepped into the river and started across. Ben lifted his pistol and checked it, then held it out in front of him. He aimed toward the man, but knew it would be at least another minute before he was within range.

Julie neared the middle of the river, and Ben dropped the gun. He wanted to tell her to turn back, to wait on the other side of the river. But the man was following her, only a few paces behind, and there was still someone shooting at them on the other side of the river.

He forced himself to ignore the knowledge of what might be in the river, waiting for another victim, and he lifted the gun back up. He turned, expecting to see Reggie mirroring his action. Instead, Reggie was calmly staring off toward the river, as if nothing was wrong.

"What are you doing?" Ben asked.

"Something doesn't add up," he said. "I'm waiting."

"For what?"

At first Reggie didn't answer, but then he motioned with a quick flick of his neck at the ledge once more. Ben, again, looked up to see. He hadn't heard the gunshots in about a minute, and the reason why was standing in the doorway to the valley.

The mercenaries.

He could only fully see the two men standing next to one another out in front, but he could make out the shapes of at least six more men standing in lines behind them. The two men in front were staring down into the valley, just like Julie and the other man had done, assessing their options.

Ben tried to imagine their thoughts.

Shoot them from here, or move down to the river?

He strode forward, nearing the edge of the water. *Come down here,* he thought. *Let's make it a fair fight.*

Julie was across the river, and Ben was so focused on the mercenaries he almost didn't realize she was calling out to him.

"Ben!" she yelled again. He turned, surprised, and nearly fell backwards when she leapt into his arms, embracing him.

She was crying, but smiling. He pulled her in close and rested her head on his shoulder as he squeezed. "Are you okay?"

"Yes, you?"

"I'm alive, but I'm ready to be out of this jungle. That cruise sounds pretty good right about now."

Julie laughed, but Reggie was there to interrupt their rendezvous. "Time to go, lovebirds. We've got company."

Ben looked over to see that the man behind Julie had indeed made it across the river. Amanda was close behind him, and Archie and Paulinho were already preparing to wade out to help her. Reggie and Ben lifted their pistols and aimed at the man.

"Don't shoot, Ben," Julie said. "He's here to help."

Ben was visibly caught off guard but he didn't lower the gun.

"It's okay," the man said. "Julie's right.

Reggie took a few steps forward, still aiming at the man's chest. To his credit, the man in the river had his arms in the air, his rifle still slung over his shoulder and his pistol in a hip holster. Ben realized then what the man's strategy was. By wading through the river with Julie in front of him, Ben's group wouldn't shoot at him. With Amanda behind, the mercenaries wouldn't either. As long as it stayed that way, neither firing squad could harm the man.

It seemed as though the mercenaries had decided to take the safer way down, as they had disappeared from the platform back into the woods. Ben knew they were only a few minutes from emerging again on the other side of the river, and by then they'd be in shooting distance. He squinted in the sunlight, watching the three bodies progress across the river.

The leader of the mercenaries was about to walk into their camp, and Ben wasn't sure what they would do when he did.

CHAPTER 55

The men from Julie's and Amanda's group were waiting for him on the other side of the river. Julie had already reached Bennett, and Joshua saw them embrace for a moment on the shore. He felt a quick pang of regret, a feeling he wasn't entirely comfortable with, as he watched. He slowly raised his arms in the air to show his surrender.

"She's not lying," Joshua said again. "But we don't have a lot of time. They're coming down here, and they're not going to —"

"You *led* them down here," Ben said.

"Perhaps, but they would have found you anyway. I'm no tracker, but you leave a pretty obvious trail."

Joshua had made it almost to the edge of the river and he now felt the ground beneath him sloping upward. The slope continued past the waterline and into the dense jungle behind it, moving toward the bottom of a sharp cliff just beyond. He eyed the unique feature. A cliff was out of context here, in a generally flat basin like the Amazon. There were no mountains, no rocky outcrops, and certainly no cliffs.

Generally.

Like many other places he'd been in the world, surprises lurked everywhere. He should have expected he'd find something like this out here in the most remote section of the planet. The cliff wasn't particularly tall, either, which made it seem almost justifiable — it wouldn't be easily spotted by satellite reconnaissance, and the entire cliff structure was sunken into a larger, bowl-like valley that they were all now standing in.

The group was all staring at him as he made his way up the last few feet of the natural embankment. Two of the other men from the group had waded out to retrieve Dr. Meron, who was barely able to stand on her own. They'd hurried back with Amanda and all three were now exiting the river about ten feet upstream from him. He looked from one person to another, finally landing on the one standing a few steps behind the others, his head down.

Rhett.

Joshua felt all the rage he'd ever felt toward the back-stabbing, lying man he shamefully knew as his younger brother. He focused the feelings into his eyes, waiting for him to look up. When he didn't, Joshua charged forward.

"You lying piece of —"

Another man suddenly appeared in front of him, blocking his way. Joshua recognized the man who had joined the group back at the hotel, the one wearing the permanent grin on his face.

"Good to meet you," the man said, completely oblivious of Joshua's irate attitude. "Name's Reggie, and this —"

"Later, Reggie," Joshua said, trying to push his way past the man.

Reggie didn't budge. "Listen. We've got some questions for you, before you —"

"He's my brother."

All eyes, including Rhett's, snapped up to Joshua. Reggie took a step back, clearly confused. Ben was frowning. Joshua waited, trying to let the tension dissipate a bit from the situation, but the knowledge of the soldiers, *his* soldiers, somewhere directly behind them gave him a sense of urgency.

"We don't have time, like I said. We need to move, get to the city."

"Why are you here?" Reggie asked.

Joshua nodded. "Right, I apologize. I was — obviously — with the other group. We tracked you, trying to locate and acquire Dr. Meron and her research. Anything that might lead us to the city of El Dorado."

Reggie stared on, his face expressionless, while Joshua continued.

"I work for a company that is interested in acquiring whatever it is that's hidden in the city." He glanced over at Harvey Bennett, to make sure he was paying attention. "They think Dr. Meron's research and the city might be connected somehow, considering the speed and secrecy you all left with."

Ben stepped closer to Joshua. "What can you tell us about this company? And what made you change your mind and suddenly want to help us out?"

Joshua caught the sarcasm in the man's question, but he ignored it. "I'm telling you the truth, Ben. The company I work for will do *anything* to achieve their goals, including killing anyone — *anyone* — who gets in their way."

"We figured that out."

"Right. Well I think I became one of those people."

Reggie's face hadn't changed, but he finally spoke. "And this kid here's your brother?"

Joshua nodded. "My father works for the company, and he apparently sent me out here to find you all. I was just following his orders, but now I'm starting to doubt they even came from him."

"Why's that?"

"Because he never would have allowed *him* out here. He's untrained, untested, and you can't trust —"

Rhett, his hands still tied, suddenly ran forward and dove headfirst into Reggie. Reggie stumbled but didn't fall, but as he turned to fight off the attacker, Rhett pushed off of him and back onto higher ground.

Joshua reached for his own weapon, but Ben was advancing toward him. He considered his options, but his younger brother was already in motion.

Rhett looked as though he was in severe physical pain — and judging by the bruises and cuts on his face, Joshua assumed that was true. He had his arms outstretched, his hands the only part of his body not shaking.

Extending outward from one of his fists was Reggie's pistol, pointed directly at Reggie's head, only feet away from him.

"Okay," Rhett said. "It's time to get back to the others."

Joshua was furious, but he couldn't move. He knew Rhett would, without a doubt, shoot the man he was threatening. Any wrong movement or word would set him off.

"Rhett…" Joshua spoke calmly, hoping to ease his brother's anger and get him talking.

"Save it," Rhett said, blood and spittle flying out of his mouth. "You heard what I said. Now move!"

Ben was standing next to Joshua now, their shoulders nearly touching. Joshua kept his face straight forward but moved his eyes to better see the man standing next to him. He noticed that Ben didn't have his weapon up.

It would only be a half second, but it might be enough…

"I'm only going to ask this one more time," Rhett said, "and then your friend —"

Joshua, with a singular, fluid motion, pulled his own pistol upwards and toward Rhett. He had to carry his arm even higher than normal, as Rhett was standing on a section of ground a few feet higher than the rest of them, literally taking the higher ground as an advantage.

He felt, more than saw, Ben lifting his weapon up in reaction to his movement, but it was too late.

He fired twice, aiming for Rhett's chest.

CHAPTER 56

She'd started running as soon as she saw Joshua's gun raise. Aiming for Amanda, she realized that her trajectory would cross paths with another one — that of the bullets Joshua was now starting to fire.

Redirecting after the first two shots sounded, she found herself running toward Ben. He was standing safely out of the line of fire, but he too had his gun lifted, preparing to shoot.

"Ben! No!" she yelled, nearly tackling him as she collided with him near the water line.

Ben turned around as he was pushed sideways, a surprised look on his face. "Julie?"

"Don't shoot him," she said again, breathless. "He's on our side."

Ben looked from Joshua, to Julie, then toward Rhett. "H — how do you know?"

Rhett grunted, blood already pooling on his chest even as he stood, trembling, on the higher ground above them all. He tried to take a single step backwards but his foot never landed properly. He toppled, falling sideways and crumpling down to the ground. He coughed twice, blood spattering from his mouth and soiling the white, flat rocks that lay nearby.

Julie stared at the droplets of blood, her eyes transfixed. *What is happening?* She felt out of control, trying to rein in Ben while convincing him and the others of Joshua's innocence, but then — for some reason — he'd shot his own brother.

"Julie?"

She looked up. Ben was staring at her, but he wasn't alone. All of the group, besides the dying Rhett, were looking at her. *Waiting.* Ben and Reggie were both aiming pistols at Joshua's head. Joshua had dropped his own weapons, including his rifle, onto the beach and was now standing with his arms high above his head. He looked completely calm, even relieved, as if his own mission was finally over.

"No — I..." she wasn't sure what to say. "Don't kill him. I believe him."

No one spoke. Joshua's eyes fell on Julie, and he gave her a slight nod.

"Julie, what did he tell you?" Reggie asked.

"He already explained it. His men are loyal to the company they work for more than they're loyal to him. They're here for a paycheck, but he thinks the company double-crossed him."

"What company?" Ben asked.

"The company you've been searching for," she said. "Drache Global. Or Dragonstone, or Drage Medisinsk. They're all the same thing."

"Or Draconis Industries," Joshua said. They all looked at him. "It's the *actual* name of the company I work for. All the others are subsidiaries. Related, but not necessarily the same. Some are pharmaceuticals, some are research, some are computers and electronics. But my company has an interest in all of them, enough to have bought them out completely."

"They're all different languages for 'dragon,'" Archie said.

Joshua nodded. "It's a 'hidden in plain sight' thing," he said. "They think no one will suspect them, as most of their business is completely legitimate R&D."

"But they're a terrorist organization."

"No, far from it," he said. "They're just not afraid of destroying anything that gets in their way. They have unbelievable power, and just about an unlimited pool of resources. What keeps them out of scrutiny is that they keep things in one hand hidden from the other. And many of the countries they operate in are eating out of one of those hands anyway."

"What's in it for you?" Reggie asked. "Why tell us all this? A day ago you were shooting at us."

Joshua looked over at Amanda. She was leaning on Paulinho, who had his hand on his head, massaging his temples. "My team was ordered to bring Dr. Meron back, after finding the lost city of El Dorado and eliminating the rest of you. But I started to suspect that my father — the one I thought I was receiving communication from — was no longer in the picture, and that the Company had been using me. He never would have sent my brother out here."

Julie shook her head. "But that's what doesn't make sense to me," she said. "Why kill him? He's your *brother*."

Joshua clenched his teeth. "It had to be done. There was no way around it, and it was only a matter of time. He's been a thorn in our side for years, and there's no doubt he was the main reason the company was able to feed information to us about your location."

"Wait, what?" Ben asked. He still held the pistol in his hand, but his grip faltered a bit. Julie saw the gun dip slightly. "How did they know where we were? And for how long?"

Joshua stepped forward, and Ben brought the gun up, gripping it tighter once more. "How did he get that wound?" Joshua asked. He pointed to his brother's side.

"The knife wound?" Archie said. "He said you did that. Your team, at least. We found him in a house, and then he flew us to Manaus."

Joshua frowned. "No, we had no idea he was out here until Julie mentioned it. I was able to check in with the Company up until we entered the jungle outside of Manaus, and they just filled me in on your general location."

"Then how —"

"Give me a second," Joshua said, interrupting. He bent down to his dead younger brother, ripped open his shirt, and peered down at the knife wound. It had begun to heal, but there was still a purplish-black area surrounding the wound itself.

Joshua reached for his own combat knife, pulling it out of its sheath on his leg. He held it up over the wound, and Julie looked away, repulsed. She tried to ignore the sounds of flesh being cut.

"Here," he said, and Julie looked down again. Joshua's hand was covered in blood, but in his fingers he held up a small cylindrical device.

"Is that a tracking device?" Ben asked.

Joshua nodded.

"Sick," Reggie said. "Masochist."

"You don't know the half of it," Joshua said. "The good news is we're off the grid now." He used the blade of his knife to rip open the device, pulled out its electronic innards, and threw the lot of it down and stomped on it with the heel of his boot. "The Company can't find us out here," he said.

"Maybe not," Archie said, "but *they* can." Julie turned to see what he was pointing at.

The mercenaries were standing just on the other side of the river, preparing to cross. She wondered why they hadn't fired, then realized where they stood.

They have us pinned down. No need to waste ammunition. They can get closer, grab Dr. Meron, then pick us off one by one.

"Guys, we need to move," she said. "We're standing in front of a cliff. No way we're getting up and over it before they're here."

But Julie felt a sense of dread wash over her as she realized how wrong she'd been. The mercenaries opened fire, the first rounds hitting the water just feet from them. *They're not afraid to waste ammo,* she thought. *They want us all dead.*

As soon as possible.

CHAPTER 57

"Run!" Reggie yelled, but the command fell on deaf ears. All the others, including Amanda, were already diving into the trees at the edge of the river.

They were less than a hundred yards from the cliff face, and Reggie knew once they hit that, there were only three options for progressing forward: to the left, following alongside the cliff as it circled back through the valley, to the right, also following the cliff, or straight up.

The destination, according to their maps, had them scaling the cliff and continuing on in the same direction they had been traveling. But Reggie knew there was no possible way they could climb — without gear, of course — straight up the cliff and onto its top without the group of soldiers behind catching up and picking them off as they ascended.

That left two options: left or right. Neither got them closer to their target, but both were equally poor choices. In Reggie's mind, that meant they were both equally good choices. *As long as we stay together*, he thought.

The mercenaries were still firing at them, even though his group was well into the cover of the trees and into the swampy section of land surrounding them. He assumed their ammunition stores were far higher than he had originally anticipated, and that they were hoping for a lucky shot or two to zing through the forest and hit one of them.

Joshua ran directly in front of Reggie, giving Reggie a visible reminder of the other topic he was still mulling over. Joshua had shot his own brother, at almost point-blank range, without batting an eye. It was a heroic gesture, when Reggie considered that Joshua might have done it in the interest of saving the rest of them, but Reggie knew there were always at least two sides to every story. In this particular story, Joshua seemed to have always carried some grievances against his brother, and he knew Joshua was telling the truth when it came to his distrust for his younger sibling. Still, Joshua didn't even hesitate when Rhett sprang forward on the attack. He lifted his gun and fired — twice — into his own family member's chest.

Reggie considered that if Joshua was anyone else, he might have justified the action by assuming the reaction was involuntary, just a natural desire to protect oneself and survive. However, Joshua seemed to be as well-trained as Reggie himself, meaning that his ability to think on his feet and make split-second decisions was one of the characteristics that had kept him alive in his line of work so far.

Other than that, Reggie couldn't figure out any plausible explanation for Joshua to join up with their group under the guise of wanting to "help them out." His soldiers were stronger, better trained, and had far more experience than Reggie's own group, on average. Reggie was the only one of them with military experience, and certainly the only one with actual battlefield training. Joshua would be stupid to think that he needed to convince them he was better off fighting on their side than his own.

That left one final explanation for Joshua's actions back at the river. Reggie chewed on this, considering the different sides and motives involved, and finally landed on the truth. He considered Occam's Razor, a principle he used to define a situation by the number of assumptions that could be made about it. Whatever solution seemed simplest — in other words, had the fewest assumptions that could be made about it — was likely the correct solution.

The solution, according to this principle, was that Joshua was telling the truth. He had stumbled through the jungle with Amanda and Julie because he had helped free them after deciding his own company was no longer aligned with his interests. He needed the help of Reggie's group, and knew that his own chance of survival was greater fighting against the men he had led out here.

It wasn't an altruistic move, either. Reggie knew that the man was most interested in his own survival — just like everyone else in the world. It just so happened that he shared a common enemy with Reggie's group and had a common goal: figure out who was really pulling the strings in his organization. In order to do that, he would need to help Reggie and the others find the solution to their problem and get out of the rainforest alive.

Reggie realized they had made it to the cliff when he nearly bumped into Joshua. Paulinho, Archie, and Amanda were slightly behind the rest of them, but Ben and Julie were waiting already in front of a large, moss-covered rock. Directly behind that, the cliff rose up past the top of the tree canopy into the sky.

"Now what?" Ben asked.

Reggie waited for Paulinho, Archie, and Amanda to arrive and catch their breath. "I don't know, to tell you the truth," he said. "There's no way we're getting up that cliff with no gear, and especially not before the rest of your guys arrive." He directed the last sentence at Joshua, hoping that the man might have a suggestion. He smirked, and raised an eyebrow, waiting.

Joshua shook his head. "Unfortunately, I think I reached the same conclusion."

The gunfire had subsided for the moment, but Reggie calculated that they only had a minute, maybe two, before it started again. And unless they figured out how to disappear, it was going to be a bloodbath.

"Anyone have any bright ideas? Basically: left or right?"

Reggie looked around at his battered, broken group. Paulinho was still holding his head as if trying to force back a massive migraine. Amanda was holding her side, breathing heavy gasps of air. Archie, considering his age, was doing remarkably well but still struggling. Ben and Julie were holding hands, but he could almost feel the tension between them. It was a tension he felt as well; it was a tension he knew all too well.

His mind flashed back to another time, another place. He was running through the desert, trying to find the target he'd been ordered to bring in. His team was spread out over the dunes on either side of him, all running forward. The tension he felt then nearly matched the heat of the day, beating down on all of them as it blistered their bodies and gear. They ran for what seemed like an entire day, but he knew by the sun's refusal to move forward even an inch that they hadn't been traveling for more than a few minutes. He remembered wondering why his squad wasn't given any specific instruction beyond the few mission parameters they had. *Find target, acquire target, return to base.*

They never made it back to base. Reggie returned, alone, three days later.

"Reggie, you okay?" Reggie snapped up and saw that the others were staring at him. Ben stepped forward and grabbed his shoulder. "We're going left, unless —"

Reggie grinned. "Left sounds great. What are we waiting for?"

Ben smiled and returned to Julie's side.

Reggie turned the opposite direction and saw that Paulinho was still holding his head, only this time with both hands.

"I — I'm sorry, I cannot continue on much longer." Paulinho's words were stuttered, forced out through quick breaths of air.

"What's going on?" Reggie asked.

"My head," Paulina said. "I don't know what it is, but it's worse than I've ever felt."

"A headache?" Amanda asked. She reached up and put her hand on his temple, slowly massaging it. Paulinho seemed to appreciate the gesture, dropping one of his hands to his side, but he groaned in agony.

He nodded. "Yes, worse than any other migraine. It started on the boat, but I thought it was related to my injury." His eyes were closed, squeezed tightly shut in pain. "I didn't want to say anything, but —"

"Nonsense," Amanda said. "There might be internal bleeding. Something that snuck up on you; maybe you were hit harder than you —"

"No," Paulinho said, shaking his head. "It's not that. It isn't a physical pain. I'm not sure how to describe it, other than that."

Reggie walked over and examined Paulinho quickly. "There isn't much we can do out here, friend. But we have to move."

"No, that's — I understand," Paulinho said. "I just wanted to mention it, so that you know why I must stop…"

"You're going to be fine," Reggie said. He wasn't much for sentimental statements, and certainly not those he couldn't back up. He hated giving people false hope, but there was no other option. He refused to leave anyone behind. "Can you walk?"

Paulinho nodded slowly. "I will live. I will let you know if it gets worse."

Reggie knew they didn't have any more time to spare. Without another word he started walking to the front of the group and continued on into the forest, keeping the cliff to his right.

"They've crossed the river by now," he said to Joshua and Ben, knowing that both men were directly behind him. "Shouldn't be much longer before they're —"

"Get down!" Ben yelled from somewhere behind him. Without stopping to assess the situation for himself, Reggie fell onto his stomach into a prone position. Immediately the gunfire resumed, much closer than he had imagined it would be.

Each shot was doubled, the sound reverberating off of the cliff face and back to his ears a second time. He heard yelling as well, not from his own group but from the men tracking them through the jungle. They were signaling each other as to the whereabouts of their prey, which only meant they had found the location of Reggie's group.

He felt safe on the ground, lying down and keeping a low profile, but he knew it was only a relative safety. It was temporary. They needed to move forward, even at the risk one of the mercenaries' shots landing. They had only seconds before the mercenaries completely surrounded them. Only seconds before the mercenaries could aim at actual targets and not just voices bouncing off the cliff.

As difficult as it was, he pushed himself off the hard jungle ground and into a standing position, hoping the others would heed his example. He continued forward, checking that his pistol had a full magazine by reaching into the larger pocket of his cargo pants. He subconsciously recognized that there was only one clip remaining, and second-guessed whether or not he had packed more into the two bug-out bags they were still carrying.

Before he could determine whether or not they had enough ammunition to last one more firefight, Reggie remembered that they were — either way — completely outgunned and outmatched. They had two pistols to share between himself and Ben, and Joshua's rifle and pistol, and possibly enough ammo to last a few minutes of sustained fire. All of that would be against about ten assault rifles, wielded by professionals who had been well-trained on that particular weapon.

The odds were long, and they were running out of daylight. He ran through the plausible scenarios in his mind, trying to land on one and that did not end with their deaths.

Unsatisfied with the result, Reggie charged forward through the jungle after insuring that Ben, Joshua, and the others were following behind.

CHAPTER 58

Reggie was only a few feet in front of him, pacing himself at a speed that he must have assumed it was reasonable enough for the slower members of the group — Archie, Paulinho, and Amanda — could match. Joshua was running alongside Ben, and Julie was just behind him, keeping pace.

Ben wondered what the mercenaries were shooting at, since none of his group had yet been struck by a stray bullet. They kept up their three-round bursts, pushing Ben and his group forward with every trigger pull. Either they had an unlimited supply of ammunition they were using to scare their prey, or they were shooting at shadows.

Suddenly Ben considered that there may be a third option. *They might actually be shooting at people*, he thought. *Just not us.*

As soon as he felt the relief the realization implied, terror set in again. *If they are shooting at other people, who?*

The answer found him a few steps away. Ben's right boot hit the forest floor with a dampened *thud* as the moss and overgrown rocks consumed the sound. Before his left boot hit, his body was pulled sideways — hard — *into* the cliff.

He tensed, waiting to slam into the hard rock surface of the cliff. The moment never came, and instead he was pulled through a winding set of thick vines, their leafy sprouts completely obscuring the opening.

It was a hole in the cliff, like a cave, just a crack running from the ground upward. Wide enough for a man to fit through, but completely masked by the foliage hanging down. He nearly fell as he stumbled sideways, but the strong hands that held his arm and shoulder righted him as he regained his balance. The entire motion was too quick for him to even cry out, but he reached for his pistol.

Another hand was suddenly present, pressing his own hand to his side and preventing him from retrieving his weapon. He wanted to scream, pulled backwards into the darkness. He felt the humidity of the cave, somehow still greater than that of the forest outside, and the sweaty-palmed hands of his attackers increasing in number every second. Soon a hand was placed over his mouth and eyes, and he felt his legs being lifted into the air. The only connection to the outside world he had — the ground this place shared with it — was soon taken from him as well as he felt his body levitating in the air, supported by countless hands carrying him along.

Julie. The single word made him writhe and buck in denial, but it was no use. He was now completely at the whim of the thousand-hand attack that was dragging him deeper and deeper into the cave.

Deeper.

The cave seemed never-ending. Ben kept waiting to feel the hands constricting him, a human anaconda slowly squeezing him of life, but it never came. They simply carried him, steadily, stealthily, into the dark recesses of the cave. His mind drifted away, unable to fight against the soothing feeling of relaxation from so many hands and fingers applying pressure to his body as they held him in place. He again thought of Julie.

A light appeared, manifesting itself through a flickering of shadows above his head. He was on his back, the hands mostly beneath him and on his sides, and the shadows danced and played around the edges of his vision, some of the longer ones extending up and over his head. He called out to Julie, but heard no response. The entire ordeal was eerily silent, and the appearance of the shadows above and around him were the only indicator he wasn't dreaming.

The light became a tangle of grays on the rocks, then shades of dim color. The hands were real now, he could see them, each one a part of a pair that belonged to the people carrying him.

People. He felt their presence now, now that their silhouettes were bathed in light. They hadn't spoken, and he hadn't heard any of them making even the slightest noise, but now they were real to him. Ben could see their eyes, dark and hollow as they were washed in the far-off light from somewhere behind him. They walked into this light, and with each step became more and more human.

They were native Amazonian, similar in stature to the group of warriors they'd seen in the atrium, but he knew they were a completely different tribe. The men carrying him were covered in a gray coat of ash, each of them seeming to have grown out of the cave walls, living ghosts of the cliff. They wore headbands made of a woven rope, thin and wrapped once around their foreheads and tied at the back. On the tail of these headbands colored beads and stones were tied together, hanging at different lengths on each man's head. Many of the men were shorter than Ben, but all had the sinewy musculature of fit, lean warriors. None wore shirts, but he noticed a few of them wearing shorts or long pants.

One of the men nearest Ben's head leaned close to him and spoke something toward him. He couldn't discern any of the words, and the voice itself seemed alien. Gravelly, with a deep, mature tone, the sentence wasn't hostile or kind, but lay somewhere in-between. He looked up at the native, hoping he wasn't being asked a question.

The man repeated the words.

Ben tried to shrug but he was still being held in place by the mens' hands. They carried him a few more steps and he was out of the cave and back into the glaring sunlight.

He blinked the brightness away, then felt himself being set down, gently, on the grass. They took his weapons and pack away, the hands carrying them somewhere out of sight. Ben turned his head as he lay there, unsure of what they expected from him but still wanting to get a look at his new surroundings.

The sunlight was unimpeded, the canopy of trees he had grown accustomed to seeing overhead long gone. None of the thick foliage of the rest of the forest had found its way here, and Ben was shocked to discover that "here" was a circular, open area, surrounded on all sides by the cliff. There was no "top" to the plateau they'd seen — just a natural wall encircling a gorgeous, lush valley. Ben saw that there was even a stream winding through the center of the valley, fed by a tall, thin waterfall at the far end of the circle. It disappeared into a small lake, then continued past Ben and out a hidden crevice beneath one of the walls of the cliff.

Around the lake, dotting the gently sloped hill the entire area sat on, were buildings made of brush and trees. Some incorporated entire trunks or rocks into their frames or walls, but all appeared to be made from natural materials. A few larger structures rose up and dwarfed the smaller buildings, the largest of them closest to the lake. People wandered in and out of these buildings, each seeming to have a purpose and destination all to their own. Some of them were working, building more structures or cooking around large, smoky fires, and still others were sitting on the ground in groups, talking.

He then noticed a particularly interesting feature of the landscape as he examined it. There were only a handful of trees in the entire area, and all were of the same variety. He didn't recognize them, but that fact wasn't surprising to Ben, who'd felt out of his element since they'd arrived in the jungle. Each of the trees had large, yellow fruits blossoming on it and bowing its branches, some the larger ones nearly reaching the ground. Children ran between these branches and the trees themselves, knocking each fruit from its perch, picking them up and delivering them to women who hauled them away in baskets.

They were harvesting the plants, but something else struck Ben as odd as he watched the women deliver their baskets to their destination.

The men around him stepped back and allowed him to sit up, then stand. He rose to his feet warily, completely overwhelmed by the scene around him. He tried to search their faces for answers, but was met with a look of confusion from each of them that matched his own feelings.

He watched for nearly a full minute as the assembly line of fruit-pickers and deliverers continued their work in front of him. The women carrying baskets emptied their collection of fruit directly into the lake, walking onto a makeshift log pier that had been fastened to the shoreline. The baskets were turned over, emptied, then placed back on top of the woman's head, and the process continued. The fruits themselves sank completely into the tiny lake.

"Ben?"

He whirled around, searching for the source of the voice. His heart raced, realizing whom it belonged to.

Julie.

IV

"... 'Over the Mountains
Of the Moon,
Down the Valley of the Shadow,
Ride, boldly ride,'
The shade replied,—
'If you seek for Eldorado!'..."

— Edgar Allan Poe

CHAPTER 59

He saw her, standing on the opposite side of the stream, only twenty feet away. Next to her were Reggie and Archie, and coming out of another similar cave to their right was Paulinho, then Amanda Meron, each of them being carried on their own platter of hands and delivered to a spot surrounded by more natives.

"Are you okay?" she asked.

He wasn't sure what that question meant in this context, but he nodded anyway. *Am I okay? Is this even real?*

He started walking toward them and was surprised to find that the tribesmen didn't attempt to stop him. When he got close, Archie stepped forward and explained.

"I think they're watching us closely, but aren't worried we'll fight back." He nodded toward the center of the tiny village, and Ben saw immediately what Archie was focused on. He'd missed them the first time he'd scanned the village, but one of the groups was busy sharpening sticks.

Weapons.

"They're probably not worried about us because the only way in and out of here is through these little cave-tunnels."

"And I'm guessing they're a good shot with one of those spears,"

Reggie said. He stepped closer to the two men. "What is all of this?"

"It's a village," Archie replied. But I've never heard of or seen anything like it. Their homes and buildings are of a completely different technology. Ancient, even. Their clothing matches the rest of the contacted tribes of the Basin — piecemeal outfits from whatever articles of clothing they've been able to buy, steal, or trade for."

"But you don't think they're a 'contacted' tribe?" Julie asked.

"I can't imagine how they would have been. We are so far off the beaten path, and a place like this is not something I ever thought I would see in the middle of the Amazon."

"You mean this village?"

"No," Archie said. "This geologic structure. A raised plateau — even one as low as this — is strange enough. But this, obviously, is no plateau. It's called a *tepui*, and it's a landmass typically found far north of here. Sort of like a raised plateau, but instead of a flat top, the cliffs simply surround a sunken valley in the center."

"Well, it exists, and we're standing in it," Reggie said. "Unfortunately that won't help us very much. Any idea who they are?"

"Again, no," Archie said. "Their dialect doesn't sound anything like the other languages I'm familiar with."

"So they spoke to you, too?" Ben asked.

Archie nodded. "Couldn't decipher a word of it."

Behind him, Paulinho fell down. He hit the ground, hard, and Julie and Amanda rushed over to help. It took their group by surprise, and only then did Ben remember that the man had complained of a headache not long ago.

He looked around at the men who had carried them here, attempting to make eye contact with one of them and somehow ask them for help. Two of the men, one he recognized as the man who had spoken to him in the cave, were still conversing near the cliff wall. They had walked away from their fellow tribesmen to talk shortly after Ben arrived, and only now did Ben notice how lively their argument had become.

Before he could get their attention, one of the men stormed back to their group and began talking to the others, his voice more animated and excited than the first man's.

Within seconds, Ben felt the tribesmen converging on them and his hands ripped behind his back and bound. He was pushed to the ground, a spear suddenly poking its way through his shirt and held tightly against his upper back. He could only lift his head, and when he did he saw Julie once more. She was being shown similar treatment, her hands already tied tightly in front of her. Another man pressed down between her shoulder blades with his bare foot, keeping her on her side on the ground.

"Ben," she whispered, her eyes glistening. Her voice shook, even with the single syllable she'd uttered, and Ben felt the vulnerability of complete helplessness as he watched the men lift her roughly off the ground and carry her away.

Before he could say anything, the hands that had brought him here were pulling him upward again.

CHAPTER 60

Reggie fought against the strain of the hands that once again were carrying him. This time the hands were rougher, more concerned with moving him where they wanted him than with his comfort. He struggled, knowing that a single slip of some of the tribesmen's hands would be all he would need to wrestle free.

From there, he didn't know. He'd fight, surely, but to what end? They were outnumbered, and even if he could get Joshua free — also a trained soldier — how many of these men could they take? There were around 200 members of this remote tribe, at least in the village, but there could be many more still outside the cliff walls surrounding their little valley.

Still, he wasn't quick to admit defeat. As the men carried his group, each member lifted high into the air like an offering to an ancient god, he did his best to study his surroundings, shifting his head as much as the hands would allow to get a glimpse of any sort of edge he may have in breaking free.

He noticed a spear strapped to a man's back, poking out over his shoulder as he strode next to Reggie, holding his left side. *If I can just get my hands free…*

He pushed all his strength into his right hand, focusing on freeing himself from their grasp. They were nearing the center of the village and the small lake that dominated the landscape. Some of the children stopped their fruit-harvesting duties and watched as their fathers and brothers carried the strangers forward, but most of the villagers expressed no interest in the light-skinned intruders.

Reggie waited until he felt himself start to be pointed slightly downward, the men shifting the weight on their feet to compensate for the gentle sloping land that led to the low-lying lake. He twisted sideways and simultaneously ripped his arm upward, hoping the sudden movement would release their grasp.

It didn't. The natives increased their hold on his arm, and Reggie was stunned at the power of their grip. He'd failed, and he'd lost the opportunity to surprise them.

He wondered if Joshua or Ben had tried anything similar, and was almost positive they had. They wouldn't be content with being carried into the center of a tribal village, especially under the assumption the Amazonian tribe was hostile.

There had to be another way…

He racked his brain to come up with a solution, but he hadn't been trained for this. Being carried six feet off of the ground, hands pressed against his sides, weapons out of reach and completely unaware of his captives' motives was not a situation he'd ever expected he'd be in. Reggie was out of his element, literally and figuratively, and he could only hope the others would have more luck.

They didn't.

The indigenous tribesmen carried the group the last hundred yards to the lake. There, he was dropped to the ground and landed with a hard thud. Before he could squirm away, the men held his feet together while two of them tied them together with a thick, twisted rope made of grasses, then pulled him back up. They dragged him back a few feet and pressed him against a tall pole that had been pushed into the soft muddy bank of the lakeshore, then tied his hands behind it.

He watched the other members of his group get tied to their own poles, and waited for the job to be finished. The knots binding his wrists and ankles were solid, and he wasn't sure how long it would take to loosen them and break free. He knew it would be possible, eventually, to stretch the grass ropes enough to slip out, but it could be hours before that happened.

He was concerned with what might happen before then.

He glanced over at Ben. The larger man was staring directly at him, seemingly pleading with his eyes for Reggie to tell him the plan.

He shrugged. *Sorry, friend.*

Ben nodded. Reggie felt even more respect for him at that moment. Stuck to a pole in the middle of the Amazon, hundreds of miles away from any real civilization, and Ben had accepted the non-response from him without question.

He turned his head the other direction and saw Amanda trying to talk to Paulinho. Reggie could see that Paulinho's head was lolling sideways. His eyes were closed, but Reggie could hear him groaning, the soft sounds of painful moans drifting through the air.

"Paulinho, you okay?" Reggie asked.

Paulinho didn't answer.

"It's a headache," Amanda said. "He's not doing well." Her own hands and feet were already tied, but her voice seemed to carry an air of hopelessness. There was no desperation, no fight. Reggie just heard defeat.

The tribal men finished tying the group to their individual poles and immediately left the area. Reggie was about to call to the others, to attempt some sort of rallying speech, when they returned. They were carrying more poles, two men per pole. Each group of men began pushing the heavy poles into the ground, heaving as they forced the sharpened ends of the trunks deep into the mud. Reggie watched as they spaced out the poles in a curving line, starting near Paulinho's pole and working nearly halfway around the lake.

"What are they doing?" Amanda asked.

"They're getting ready to host more guests," Reggie said.

"What do you —"

Before she could finish, Reggie heard a chanting noise from more of the men from somewhere behind him. The chant grew in volume, and he waited until they walked near enough to the lake and looked over. There were at least ten more groups of warriors, each group holding another person above their head as they marched in lockstep toward the lake.

He knew their destination and was affirmed when the groups each stopped in front of one of the poles freshly stuck in the mud, the men were laid on the ground, and they were then bound to their own trunk.

He was shocked, however, when he saw who the men were.

"It's the mercenaries," he whispered, not intending for the words to carry farther than a few feet in front of him.

"They must have lost their fight with the tribe," Amanda said.

Reggie looked at Amanda, tied to the trunk just to his right, but she was looking at the mercenaries. She watched intently, the concerned look on her face not easing Reggie's fears.

The chanting continued, and even got louder. *There's something else going on here,* he thought. *They are waiting for something.*

Hordes of tribespeople descended on the lakeshore, all helping to secure the mercenaries to their trunks. The chanting rose to a chorus of deep, sinister growls and unintelligible words, and Reggie forced his mind to focus on the procession, not the droning sound.

Within minutes the job was done, and both groups — the mercenaries and Reggie's own people — were all fastened to their own poles around one side of the lake. The entire tribe was present around them, women and children included.

The chanting stopped.

All of the natives turned their heads and looked behind Reggie. He couldn't twist around enough to see what it was they'd reacted to, so he waited until whatever they were looking at came into view.

When he did see it, he nearly gasped.

CHAPTER 61

It's the golden man from the dream, he thought. He looked to his left and saw Paulinho, his head lolling while he groaned. When his neck rotated and Paulinho's face fell toward Reggie, he saw that the man's eyes were white, rolled up into his head.

"Paulinho, are you okay? Can you hear me?"

Paulinho didn't respond to Reggie's voice, but he noticed his face turning slowly. *He's watching the golden man.* Paulinho clearly couldn't see anything, but his face was somehow locked onto the steadily moving man nearing the lake.

The man was naked, but covered head to toe in a gold powder. It shimmered as it caught the last of the dying rays of sunlight, but Reggie couldn't tell if it was the powder itself that was reflecting or a layer of sweat on the man's skin. The powder seemed thick, almost syrupy, and it coated every inch of skin. When the man blinked, gold eyelids replaced white eyes. Two women and a younger girl followed the golden man, each holding half of one of the fruits Reggie had seen earlier. They kept pace with their leader, rubbing him down with the fleshy portion of the fruit as he neared the lake. When one of the women saw a spot that was unsatisfactorily covered, they'd reach out and smear the fruit on his skin.

Reggie was dumbfounded. The exact image Amanda had described in her subjects' dreams was walking directly toward them. Instead of actual gold, they were using the juice and pulp of a golden *fruit*, but the image was unmistakable. The man strolled as if taking in the scenery of a park, completely unaware of the captives tied to tree trunks yards away. He was heavyset but looked muscular, and he carried himself with an air of authority.

He's the chief, Reggie thought. There was something visceral in him, a feeling the man had evoked when he met eyes with Reggie. He knew, without a doubt, this man was in charge.

"That's him," Amanda whispered.

Reggie could see that her hands, bound at the wrists, were shaking. He nodded, then realized Amanda hadn't looked away from the golden man.

"I know," he said. "And I have a feeling we're about to be part of their special ceremony."

"It's the Muisca tradition," Archie said. Archie was mounted two poles over, between Amanda and Julie. Joshua was just on the other side of Julie, and Ben was tied to the pole at the far end. Reggie looked at Archie, waiting for him to explain. He almost grinned when Archie cleared his throat out of habit, looked at the others as if preparing a lecture, and continued.

"Remember, the Muisca are thought to be the originators of at least one of the El Dorado myths," he said. "No one knows exactly why, but during their initiation ritual, their chief would cover himself in gold dust and jump into the lake. The Spanish, and many others after them, drained the lake — Lake Guatavita — near the Muisca people's home, but the legends were never confirmed. Besides, this is nowhere near where they were thought to have lived."

"But you told us a few days ago that if El Dorado was not an actual city, but a *people*, they could move anywhere they needed to to stay out of the way."

Archie nodded, his head lowering. "It is true," he said. "But it is still hard to believe. I have wanted to believe in it since I heard the myth, but seeing this — actually watching this procession — it is still unbelievable."

Reggie looked at Amanda. "And you're sure this is the man from the dreams?"

She nodded. "Without a doubt." Her voice was shaking slightly, but her eyes seemed adamant.

"Okay," Reggie said. "Archie, what happens, in this 'legend,' *after* the chief jumps into the lake? Specifically, does the legend mention anything about the people tied up to poles around the lake?"

"No," Archie said. "But that was merely a legend. There is no boat here, either. In the stories, the chief would float out to the middle of the lake on a gold-covered boat."

The chief held his hands in the air, waiting for all eyes to turn to him. The only sound was the churning of the waterfall cascading down into the valley far on the other side of the lake. Satisfied, he lowered his hands and stepped into the lake.

His foot fell beneath the surface, but stopped after only a few inches. He strode forward, confidently, his other foot landing again just inches below the waterline.

"There must be a platform or something," Ben said.

"Boulders," Archie said. "You can barely see them, but only when the light catches them just right."

Reggie saw and confirmed this fact for himself. The slowly widening concentric circles left by the chief's steps revealed a line of huge rocks, perfectly placed, leading outward from the shore and rising to just below the water's height.

The leader of the tribe continued, never hesitating, until he reached the center of the lake. He stood up to his ankles and began to speak in a slow, deep voice. The words were unintelligible to Reggie, but they seemed to have a soothing effect on the gathered tribespeople. They sighed, and he heard some speaking the same syllables back to the chief, their voices lowered to a near-whisper.

They were witnessing an ancient ritual. The chief's arms were slowly rising again, this time until they were extended straight over his head. His words, the repetitive incantation, rose in volume and intensity to match his arms, and when he opened his palms directly above his head he was nearly shouting.

The villagers copied his enthusiasm, and he saw hundreds of hands raising simultaneously with the chief's. He noticed a few of the tribesmen to his left, near the last pole on the shore, walk toward the mercenary tied up and begin to untie the knots binding the man's wrists and ankles. They worked methodically, each member of the tribe performing their duty in ritualistic precision. Some of them untied, while others held him steady. Still others removed his clothes, one layer at a time, until he was nearly naked, standing only in his briefs.

"Now we know where they get their clothes," Reggie said to no one in particular.

In less than a minute the man, one of the men Reggie didn't recognize from the attack at the atrium, was standing with his arms held to his sides by a handful of indigenous people. They pressed in against him, preventing him from fighting back or lashing out, and they slowly gripped sections of his body until they had lifted him completely off the ground.

They half-dragged, half-carried the naked man around the edge of the lake and toward the hidden line of submerged boulders. Their trajectory brought the entire group directly in front of Reggie, and he tried to read the man's thoughts.

His eyes were dark, set deep into his head, and he wore a deep frown. Besides that he was completely motionless, allowing the tribal men to pull him along until he was in front of Joshua.

He quickly turned his head, staring down his former leader, and spat. The saliva reached Joshua's feet, landing on the side of his boot. Joshua clenched his teeth a few times but otherwise stared straight ahead, ignoring the obvious insult.

Reggie grinned — he couldn't help it — but the action from the mercenary was answered swiftly. Two of the warriors carrying him released their hold on him for a moment. In the second they'd dropped him, they lashed out with the weapons they were holding. One of the men reached for a club hanging in a belt on his waist and swung it up and onto the back of the mercenary's head, earning an angry howl from the man. The second tribesman pulled out a shortened spear he'd had slung over his shoulder and shoved it into his hip. This particular attack caused a much greater reaction, the mercenary falling limp, screaming in agony.

The group of indigenous men didn't falter, however. They pulled the man to his feet and out onto the first rock. Two of the natives poked at his back with spears, forcing him forward to the next boulder.

The mercenary obliged, holding his hip and working slowly to maintain his balance.

It was an excruciatingly long ordeal, but Reggie noticed that the chief hadn't so much as shifted his position on the rock in the center of the lake. Arms held high, he waited the ten minutes for the mercenary to join him.

When he did, the chief wasted no time. He lashed out with both hands, each of them holding a tiny dagger Reggie hadn't seen before, and plunged them into the man's neck. Reggie saw the mercenary reaching up to grab at his severed artery, but the two natives behind him immediately pushed forward with their spears and sent the tips through the man's back.

Amanda screamed.

Reggie couldn't help but look away. The entire sickening spectacle had lasted only a few seconds, but the massacre was the most gruesome he'd ever seen. When he looked back to the center of the lake, the mercenary was already falling sideways into the water. The two warriors held him still for a moment, then yanked their spears out of the man's flesh and allowed him to sink into the lake.

"Oh my God," Amanda whispered. "Oh, my God…" She was shaking uncontrollably, repeating the three words in a whimpering, defeated voice.

The two warriors with spears were making their way back to the shore, but the king was already beginning his chant again. When Reggie looked over at where the mercenary had been tied, he saw another group of warriors untying the second man in the line.

So this is what happens to the people tied to the poles, he thought. *But we're not even going to have to wait for the chief to jump in the lake.*

Reggie wished for a moment that the legend of El Dorado hadn't been passed down through the ages with only the good parts of the story intact.

CHAPTER 62

By the time the third mercenary had been slaughtered and sacrificed to the lake, the sun had completely disappeared and there was nothing but a crisp line of moonlight illuminating the village.

Ben had hoped that the tribe would pause their ceremony and continue it in the morning, but as of now it seemed as though they had every intention of finishing. He was beginning to lose control, a feeling he strongly disliked.

He was upset, not just at the tribe and village but at everyone he'd come here with. He wanted to blame them, to make it their fault he was here. But he knew it was foolish; he was the only one he could blame. He'd dragged Julie here, too, and now he had to watch her get murdered by a ruthless Amazonian tribe.

His only saving grace was that he likely wouldn't live long enough to have the weight of her death upon him.

Ben struggled against the bindings, but his wrists only ached more with every twist of his hands, the ropes never loosening. He looked over at Reggie, hoping the man would have found a way out by now.

Nothing. Reggie was staring straight ahead, directly at the chief standing in the middle of the lake with his hands above his head.

What is this supposed to be, anyway? he thought. *This isn't how sacrificial ceremonies are supposed to go.*

He had no idea if it was true or not, but he'd imagined there would be more fanfare, more excitement. *A purpose.*

To him, there was no purpose to all of this. The chief seemed hardly engaged in the ceremony, and even some of the younger children had lost interest.

"Ben."

Ben turned to his left and saw Joshua looking at him.

"That one on the end," he said, motioning with his head.

"Paulinho?" Ben asked.

"Yeah, him. What's up with him?"

Ben frowned. "What do you mean?"

"Back at the atrium, remember? You were surrounded by another tribe. A different tribe. But they backed off. Why?"

Ben had almost forgotten about their earlier encounter, but his mind was suddenly drawn back to the moment. He remembered beating Rhett and losing Julie and Amanda, but he did also remember the encounter.

"I — I think it was his tattoo."

"A tattoo?"

"Yeah, on his arm. Their leader grabbed his arm and looked at it, and got spooked."

"What was the tattoo?"

"No idea. He doesn't know, either. Just a design on something his granddad gave him."

Joshua nodded, thinking, and Ben tried to anticipate the man's thoughts.

"Why?" Ben asked. "You think it can help us here?"

"I don't know, but it's the only thing I can think of besides waiting in line to die."

The others had started listening, and Reggie spoke up. "I'm voting against waiting in line."

"What if it doesn't help us?" Amanda asked. She was still whispering, afraid to call undue attention to herself.

"What if it does?" Julie asked.

Ben cringed at her tone and tried to ease the hostility. "Amanda, it's our only hope. Look at him — he needs help either way."

"And that's why we need to figure out how to get *out* of here. Not ask them to kill us faster."

"I understand that, Dr. Meron," Reggie said. "But consider the options. We're stuck to poles, and without a *way* to get *un*stuck we're not helping anyone."

Amanda tried to wipe a tear from her eye by pressing her head to her shoulder, but couldn't reach. It rolled, slowly, down her face and fell to the ground in front of her. "At least try to wake him up," she finally said.

Ben watched as Reggie tried to urge the man to his left awake. Paulinho responded to the voice, but his eyes were still pulled up tight, revealing just bloodshot white spheres.

"Paulinho," Reggie tried again. Paulinho's eyes were still dead to the world, his face blank and expressionless. "Come on, man, wake up."

The fourth mercenary was dragged, naked, to the rock bridge where the chief waited.

"Hey!" Ben yelled. He wasn't sure what his plan was, but the one they had — the one where they just waited for their turn to be marched naked to their deaths — wasn't one he particularly liked. At the very least, he wanted to get their attention.

He yelled again and this time a small portion of the villagers looked his way.

"Yeah," he shouted. "Over here! Right here. I'm talking to you!"

Still more faces turned his direction.

"Ben," Julie said, "what do you think you're doing?"

He ignored her and started rolling his head around in circles. He didn't have access to his hands and feet currently, so his head was the only thing on his body that could move. *Hopefully it will be enough.*

A few of the tribespeople started walking toward him. He noticed a few of the warriors glancing over, so he continued yelling. Reggie and Joshua joined in, and finally Archie and Amanda. Julie was the last to jump on board with the plan, but she eventually gave in and began shouting at the people surrounding them.

Two of the warriors appeared in front of Ben, and he shouted as loud as he could, directly in their faces. To their credit, they seemed immune to his chaotic insanity, and more concerned that he was interrupting their sacred proceedings.

"Not me, you idiots," he shouted. "Go over there —" he motioned toward Paulinho. "He's the one you need to see."

Still more warriors appeared in front of them, and even some of the older men of the tribe milled around the poles Ben's group were tied to.

The fourth mercenary was marched outward from the lakeshore and onto the rock with the waiting chief. For an ostensibly ceremonious event, the chief quite unceremoniously jammed the blood-soaked daggers into the man's neck, and the man's two escorts followed up with their own stabbings.

Ben could hardly hear the man's screams as he died, struggling for breath as his lungs and throat were punctured. He was caught up in his own yelling, screaming for attention. *I just need one of you to understand me,* he thought. *Is that so much to ask?*

"Ben, look." Julie's voice somehow reached his ears over the cacophony, and he followed its instructions and looked back to Paulinho. Three of the warriors had gathered in front of the man, and more were heading toward him.

"I think it's working," Archie said. "I think they're —"

Six warriors surrounded Paulinho and began untying his hands and feet.

"No, no, *no*," Reggie said. "That's not what we —"

Paulinho still didn't resist as his shirt was ripped off of him. One of the warriors was working on his pants when the others started dragging him toward the lake.

"This is not good," Reggie said. "All we did was make them mad. They're turning their attention to our group now."

"No," Amanda said. "Please, we have to make them understand."

Paulinho had been stripped down to his underwear by now, and he was standing at the edge of the lake. The two men with spears pushed him forward, onto the first of the rocks. He took one precarious step forward, then another.

Whatever drug was affecting him had turned him into a calm, placated individual. He didn't struggle, he didn't fight back. He simply walked forward, walking toward his own death.

Does he even know what's happening right now? Ben thought.

Ben began to lose control. He forced his upper body to crouch down as low as he could, bending his elbows until the strain on his shoulders from his bound hands screamed in pain. He pulled the pole against his back, pressing it tightly to his torso, then he launched himself upward. He pushed with his feet, feeling them sink into the mud. The pole barely budged, but he knew it moved.

He repeated the process, again and again. He worked silently, all the while watching Paulinho and the chief out on the rock in the center of the lake. He didn't want to call attention to himself, yet he silently begged the others to notice him, so that they could begin freeing themselves as well.

The pole loosened with every thrust upward, but it was far too long for him to lift it out of the hole it sat in. *What next?* Ben wondered. He was just loosening the trunk, but he was still tied to it. Even if he could loosen it enough to lift it from the hole, his feet were still affixed to it.

Still, it gave him something to focus on, something besides watching his friend die at the hands of a religious nutcase.

The chief's arms were raised over his head, preparing for the sacrificial murder. Ben could almost feel the anxiousness of the villagers as they watched the proceedings. The two warriors behind Paulinho stood on the rock with their spears at the ready, awaiting their leader's next move.

Paulinho was in a daze, staring straight ahead. He was rail-thin, his lack of clothing only accentuating his lean physique.

Ben paused his attempts to loosen the pole from the dirt. He watched the back of Paulinho's head as it rolled around lifelessly. *Wake up*, he thought. *Please, for the love of God, wake up.*

Paulinho didn't wake up.

The chief's arms tensed in anticipation, and Ben saw his hands start to fall downward.

Ben wanted to close his eyes, but he couldn't. The chief's hands began the downward half-circles that would terminate on either side of Paulinho's neck, and Ben watched on in silent horror.

CHAPTER 63

Paulinho spoke, his voice resonating clearly over the water. Ben couldn't make out the word, but it was a guttural sound, heavy with consonants.

The chief paused, his arms now held out at his sides, elbows bent.

Paulinho repeated the word. The chief cocked his head sideways but didn't move his arms. The entire scene seemed to freeze in place, heavy with anticipation. Paulinho repeated the word a third time. Ben didn't understand it, but he turned and looked at Archie.

"I — I'm not sure what it means," Archie said.

"Have you heard it before?" Julie asked.

"Yes, I believe so. I always assumed it was just a curse, something said out of frustration toward another person."

"What language is it?"

"That's just it," Archie said. "I didn't think it actually meant anything in *any* language. Different tribes have used it, so I assumed that it was just a shared vernacular of the region."

The chief slowly lowered his hands and whispered a few words to the men standing behind Paulinho. They placed their spears over their shoulder once again and grabbed Paulinho's arms.

The chief stepped closer to Paulinho and stared at him. He was shorter, so he pulled Paulinho's head down to look into his eyes. The two warriors began poking and prodding Paulinho with their fingers, pinching his skin as they examined him.

One of the warriors stopped and dropped Paulinho's arm. He whispered something, a single word. Ben couldn't hear what it was from the shoreline, but the chief reacted swiftly.

He shouted, a long stream of consonant-laden words that seemed more like grunting than conversational speech. The remainder of the warriors jumped into action, and even a few of the women and children. The entire village sprang into life, an odd juxtaposition as Ben's group, the rest of the mercenaries, and Paulinho and the chief remained still.

One of the women stepped forward after a minute or two and offered two of the yellow fruits to one of the warriors who had returned to the shoreline. The indigenous warrior walked out to the lake center again and handed the fruits to the chief. The chief lifted one of the fruits to his mouth and bit a piece of its flesh. He held the other fruit toward Paulinho's mouth and waited.

There were a few people standing around, but most of the village had disappeared to perform some unknown task. Ben watched anxiously to see what Paulinho would do.

It took about ten seconds, but Paulinho slowly lowered his mouth down and bit off a chunk from the fruit. Ben could tell he was chewing, then he saw Paulinho's neck tense as he swallowed. He and the chief still stared at one another.

They began to sway, slowly at first then more rapidly as the fruit took its effect on them. Ben frowned, more surprised and confused than angry. *What in the world?* He watched Paulinho grow more and more unbalanced, finally convulsing into a heap on the large boulder at the center of the lake. The chief responded in kind, taking longer but eventually joining Paulinho on the boulder, both men's backs resting on the rock submerged beneath the surface.

The water lapped at Paulinho's face, but he didn't move.

"They killed him," Joshua said.

No one spoke. Ben and the others watched in silence for a few minutes, but neither man showed any signs of life.

Ben heard Julie whisper. "What's going on? Are they dead?"

"Better not be," Reggie said from Ben's left. "I have some words I need to exchange with that chief."

Another minute passed, Ben's group intently watching the center of the lake. Finally, Ben thought he saw Paulinho's arm twitch. He waited to make sure he wasn't going crazy. It moved again, and he saw the chief stir just behind Paulinho.

The chief gasped a breath of air, his eyes flying open in bewildered surprise. Paulinho's neck pulled his head upward while his hands shook and beat at the surface of the water. Both men convulsed a few times, as if experiencing the aftershock of a seizure. The chief stood up, blinked a few times, and fell backwards into the water.

Ben tensed, not expecting the chief to have disappeared so suddenly, but then remembered the legend.

The gold-covered chief jumps into the lake to rinse himself off and mark the close of the ceremony.

Finally, Paulinho sat up.

"Paulinho!" Reggie shouted. "What the hell was that about? You okay?"

Paulinho ignored him, shaking his head slowly. His hands rose to his forehead, and he began pushing inward on his skull.

"What's he doing?"

"He was complaining of a headache earlier," Amanda said. "I imagine whatever we just saw didn't help."

The chief was already back on the rock, dripping wet and no longer covered in gold, waiting for Paulinho. He didn't offer a hand, but when Paulinho began standing up the chief stepped close to him. Once more he pulled Paulinho's face close to his and spoke.

When he was done, the chief lowered his head and stepped back to the center of the rock. Paulinho turned and walked off the edge of the rock and onto the next. He stepped purposefully, not looking down to make sure his foot was hovering over the solid surface. His head was no longer rolling, his eyes no longer white.

Paulinho made it to the shoreline then turned to the group. Ben was intrigued, but still on edge. He felt the pole pressing against him, its full weight no longer secured by the thick mud and dirt. He leaned back against it, steadying himself. Paulinho marched to the edge of the lake and turned to address the group.

He cleared his throat, then began.

CHAPTER 64

"I have no idea what just happened," Paulinho said. Julie looked like she was in shock, watching a man she had grown close to visit the brink of death then come back full circle. He was very much alive, and yet he knew he was very much a different person.

Paulinho continued. "The fruit did something to me — to us," he said. "I feel… connected. I can understand what they are trying to do now, on a general level."

He realized only then that the tribespeople had begun cutting their bindings loose. He saw Julie's hands freed, then her feet. The two warriors who had previously marched Paulinho out to the center of the lake by spearpoint were now offering him his clothes. His shirt was torn beyond repair, so he was given a long, loose-fitting one by a child who had run up to him as he spoke.

"Why are they letting us go?" Julie asked.

"They know that we are safe. They understand that we are not here to upset their way of life."

"Yeah?" Reggie asked. "What do they think about *those* guys?" He motioned over to the remaining mercenaries, still tied to their tree trunks. He made the motion with the flick of his head, as he was still tied to his own pole.

Paulinho turned to address Reggie. "They do not know about

them," he said, simply. "I am the one who was drawn to them, and you are the ones who helped me return."

"Paulinho," Julie said. "What are you talking about? Are you sure you're okay?"

"I feel completely normal," Paulinho said. "There's just something… something *deeper* I feel as well. This tribe shares my blood. My family was descended from them."

Julie walked over and stood next to Paulinho. Slowly, as they were untied and freed, the others joined him. The moon had risen above the edge of the tepui, causing the lake and river to light up with a white glow. In light of everything happening, he found himself struck by the beauty of the place. He turned a full circle, capturing the essence of the beautiful scenery — he hadn't noticed most of it until now. The tall, thin waterfall fell from the top of the cliff far off in the distance, with only the sound of the gentle throb of running water to remind him that he wasn't looking at a postcard.

"How do you know?" Julie asked. "Are you sure you're not just hallucinating?"

Paulinho shook his head. "No, I'm sure. My grandfather used to wear this symbol on a necklace," he said as he revealed the tattoo on his wrist and stared down at it. "We never knew the name of the tribe we were from originally, as it was generations ago we left the rainforest and settled in the city."

Amanda was already checking Paulinho's head for any wounds or bruises. He continued explaining. "When I was unconscious, I dreamt again. But this time it was real; it was vivid like never before. I could see faces — the faces of these same people — but from a long time ago. I know their story now, and why they're here. They've always lived beneath these trees, but they've worshipped them as gods as well. The fruit gives them life and connects them, somehow. It opens up a channel to each of them, and they use it to communicate."

"Really?" Reggie asked. "ESP?" He could hear the skepticism in his voice. He felt it himself.

"No, not like that," Paulinho said. "Like shared memories, but stronger. I don't really know how to explain it."

"I think I do," Amanda said. The others turned to look at her, waiting for her to explain. "It's a chemical relationship between neurons, those associated with communication and ones that aid in memory storage. We're only beginning to unravel the mysteries of the brain, but it's long been assumed that humans have been suppressing some areas of our brains hidden in our evolution, including something resembling telepathy."

"'Resembling telepathy?'" Joshua asked, incredulously. "That's a pretty tall order."

"But — if it was true — wouldn't it be something your company would do almost anything to discover?" Ben asked. "If they even thought such a thing *might* exist…" Julie looked up at him as he asked the question. At some point, Paulinho realized, Ben had pulled Julie close to him, his arm over her shoulder.

"Yeah," Joshua said. "Yeah, it would. The potential…"

"It seems like I understand them now," Paulinho said. "I don't know how, but I know where each of them are, generally, and I can *feel* with them. I sense that they're feeling pain, or joy, or fear."

"It sounds like a hive mind," Reggie said.

"Yes, about as close to one as we can get," Amanda said. "This is absolutely fascinating. Our research was leading to this point, I believe. The 'golden man,' the chief of the tribe of El Dorado — it's a shared memory, strengthened in their minds for generations, and it lives deep within the subconscious memories of their descendants. As we saw in the lab, most of the subjects we tested didn't even know they had this memory. It's part of the reason why I've been interested in this type of research for so long. What sorts of memories do we have hidden away? What sorts of things are locked up inside our brains that we can't access ourselves? And the fruit — the "gold" of El Dorado, I guess — must contain a chemical that reacts with the brain and allows the ancient evolutionary traits to unlock."

"But why?" Paulinho asked. "Why are they sending a message?"

"I think we already know the answer to that question," Julie said. "It's why we were able to find them."

"It's a homing beacon," Joshua said.

"Right," Julie answered. "So their tribe — their people — will always know the way home."

"The science doesn't check out," Amanda said. "Shared memories, maybe. But the ability to send a *message* via those same channels? The ability to broadcast a location to anyone with the same blood? I don't know. The homing beacon idea —"

"But we *do* know it works," Julie said. "Paulinho is a testament to that."

Amanda nodded. "Of course, I know. I mean, it doesn't make sense, but that's only because we don't understand the mechanisms at work. It's not out of the question, anyway: at least the parts that we already know. The stronger the neuron connections in the brain, the more vivid the memory. Your ancestors are from this tribe, Paulinho, and as you got physically closer to them, you were able to recall vague 'memories' of theirs. When you ate the fruit, it jumpstarted the process. I'd imagine it wears off quickly, but until then — what else can you tell us?"

Before Paulinho could answer, three gunshots, in rapid succession, rang out.

"Gonna have to wait, friend," Reggie said, instinctively crouching lower to the ground. "Sounds like the party isn't over yet."

The rest of the group fell to the ground as well, following Reggie's lead. Joshua remained crouched, staring at the line of mercenaries tied to poles.

"Let me guess," Ben said, directing his words to Joshua. "Paulinho's tribe didn't capture all of your friends?"

CHAPTER 65

It had been an eventful day, even for Joshua. He'd seen things no man should ever experience, and he'd been in plenty of twisted situations. Still, the Amazon was new to him, and a situation like this was something he'd never thought — in his wildest dreams — he'd be a part of.

Paulinho — the man who'd not spoken a word since he'd met him, aside from his complaining about a headache — was now claiming to be part of some sort of hive mind. He thought he was able to 'tune in' to the frequencies of the tribe, understanding their emotional state as a whole.

It was quack science, but there was one reason he believed every word of it.

The Company believed it.

Draconis Industries, the company his own father had been a major part of growing, believed in it.

There was no other plausible explanation as to why they would spend an unbelievable amount of money trying to reach this destination. They had plenty of resources, but they weren't wasteful. Even their double-crossing and redundancies served a purpose for them, and Joshua understood their motivations for that.

Still, he had been surprised with his father's careless attitude about sending Rhett to follow and intercept him, and he had been surprised at the seemingly arbitrary mission parameters.

Now, however, it made sense.

The Company was, as always, acting in its best interests. It had done something with his father, pretending to *be* his father when they'd set up the mission, then asked his brother to keep an eye on him during the course of it all. They were after something, and it was something so important — so *powerful* — they were willing to risk one of their own to acquire it.

His father had paid the price for their greed, and his brother had lost his life as their pawn. Joshua felt no remorse at killing his own sibling, but he still wished he'd had time to reason with him; he wanted to explain to his brother how he had been fighting for the wrong side.

It didn't matter now. All that mattered was getting Dr. Meron and the others back safely, without allowing his men to intercept them and complete *their* mission. They were in it for a paycheck, and they wouldn't be receiving that paycheck without the prize. Joshua knew they'd fight tooth and nail to achieve their goal, and they'd kill anyone who got in their way.

He'd been one of those men, once.

It was usually easy to see the good in their duties as soldiers-for-hire, and if there wasn't any outwardly good qualities about their mission, Joshua made something up. He fought for good, and if he had to create that good, so be it. Now, however, there was no 'good' in what his men were fighting for. He saw it for what it was: they were fighting for an organization that wanted nothing more than power for themselves. There was no redemption in that.

When he'd finally realized that there were two men missing from the group it was too late. Alan — one of the men he'd thought was loyal to him — and another, older soldier named Hallord were not among the mercenaries the natives had brought into their village.

They must have followed us here, he thought. The shots had come from above, but it was still unclear what direction.

"Get down!" he yelled. He ran for the nearest 'building,' nothing more than a collection of branches and sticks that had been piled together around a hollow rectangle. It wasn't much for cover, but it was better than nothing.

Three more shots, this time louder and seemingly from another angle — whistled through the air and into the side of the building. The sticks and leaves exploded at impact, the bullet sizzling through the wall as if it were made out of paper.

Maybe this cover isn't *better than nothing.* He instinctively ducked, but forced his head up again to see if he could get a bead on the attacker.

He didn't see the man, but he saw the glimmer of something metallic on the man's vest. *There.* Just beneath the top of the cliffs, directly across the lake from where Joshua was hiding.

It was Alan and Hallord. *It had to be.* And if it wasn't for the darkness, Joshua thought they may have already taken some of them down.

The group was still encircling Paulinho at the edge of the lake. Reggie and Ben seemed to be trying to corral them all and get them running toward the tiny buildings, so Joshua took stock of the larger situation. The chief was gone, disappearing at some point after Paulinho had returned to shore and the group. The rest of the villagers, including the warriors, seemed to be focused on defending their home. There were shouts and yelling from every corner of the valley, and Joshua saw many of the men — and some of the women — gathering whatever weapons they could find.

Even with a limited supply of ammunition and only two shooters, Joshua knew the village didn't stand a chance. He wasn't one to back away from a fight, especially since he had a personal stake in it, but the odds weren't in his favor. He and the rest of his new group were unarmed, and that was the first problem he needed to solve.

Reggie was at his side. "What's the call? Think we can hold them off?"

Joshua looked at the unfolding chaos then back at Reggie. Ben and the others were close behind him, waiting for him.

"No," Joshua said. "I don't. They're going to free the mercenaries, then they'll look for the weapons. The tribe probably doesn't know what they are or they'd be using them already, but they wouldn't have just discarded them. They took them somewhere."

"Okay," Ben said. "So we get to the weapons first."

Joshua nodded, but kept his attention on the cliffs, trying to detect any movement. "Yes, that's good. But if we can't get to them first…"

He didn't have to finish the statement. The rest of the group knew the risk. He looked at Paulinho. "Anything you can add? Anything that might give us an edge?"

Paulinho's face scrunched up a bit, deep in thought. "I don't think so, unfortunately. I feel their fear, and their confusion, but I don't see what they see."

"Okay, fine. We'll make do. You and you — " he looked at Archie and Paulinho. "You two know the tribe better than any of us, so put your heads together and figure out how this plays out."

"You want us to stay here and…. Think?"

"No. I want you to stay here and *keep her alive*," this time he motioned to Dr. Amanda Meron. "And *also* think. Keep your eyes open, and shout if there's something we need to know about."

He turned to Reggie and Ben, awaiting their response.

Reggie grinned. "That's pretty much the plan I had," he said. Ben nodded.

"Great. Let's stick together, but watch your backs. Also, if you can, keep an eye on the lake. We need to know immediately when they start untying the rest of them."

CHAPTER 66

Joshua hadn't even finished the instructions before the shots rang out again. What they were aiming for, Ben didn't know. These three shots landed somewhere else in the valley, but he heard the screams of terrified villagers echoing back. *They're shooting at the villagers now.*

Ben clenched his teeth and rushed toward the next hut in the line. Joshua and Reggie were already checking two other huts, and so far they'd all come up empty-handed. He crouched down and glanced inside the hut he was standing in front of and saw a family — a woman and her three children — huddled together against the back wall. They tensed when they saw him, but he held up his hands as he backed away.

Come on, he thought. *They have to be around here somewhere.* He tried to remember what the warriors had done after they'd stripped him of his weapons and backpack. He racked his brain, but couldn't come up with anything useful.

We were at the edge of the valley just inside the cliffs when they tied us up. We would have seen —

He stopped. Taking a quick glance inside the next hut he came to and finding it empty, he realized something. They were checking the buildings at the center of the village, under the assumption that the villagers knew what modern weapons looked like. Following that line of logic meant that they would try to keep them safe, somewhere where they would be protected.

But if they had no idea what they were…

"Joshua! Reggie!"

Both men retreated from the buildings they were checking and looked at Ben.

"Back where we came in," he said. "Why wouldn't they have hidden them somewhere near the entrance?"

Joshua thought about this for a second. More gunfire — this time from both sides of them — erupted from a higher elevation and farther away. All three men ducked, but Ben realized they were still aiming at the indigenous tribespeople. He glanced over at the mercenaries and was satisfied to see them all strapped to their poles.

"Good point. Why don't you and Reggie head over there, and I'll take a look inside the last two buildings here."

Ben and Reggie nodded and immediately started running toward the cliffs. As soon as they left the relative cover of the cluster of mud and stick huts, Ben felt vulnerable. The valley was completely open, save for a few trees bearing golden fruit spaced out much farther apart than he would have liked. If the mercenaries on the cliffs decided to open fire on them, they were sitting ducks. He hoped they could run fast enough or their attackers were still too far away to get a good shot.

Still, he didn't waste time worrying about his precarious fate. Instead he tried to focus on the gunfire to see where it was coming from. He still only heard two distinct fighters, one on either side of the valley. One of them, however, seemed to be firing on the tribespeople from a much lower altitude than the other.

He swung his head to the left, trying to track the attacker as he ran. Reggie reached one of the trees and paused for a moment near its wide trunk. Ben caught up and stopped as well to catch his breath.

"Seems like there's one on either side of us," Ben said.

Reggie just nodded, his hands on his knees as he breathed deeply a few times. "Yeah, seems that way. Also seems like we're pretty lucky they've got other targets to focus on."

"You get a bead on any of them yet?"

"Nope, sorry. I've just been trying to not get shot."

Ben smiled. "Whatever you're doing, it's working. Let's keep pushing forward, and keep an eye out for the guy on our left — I think he's on the ground now. The other guy might be providing cover for him."

"Got it."

Reggie was off and running again much sooner than Ben had anticipated. Ben was in the middle of a deep inhalation, and begrudgingly started chasing after the much faster, much fitter man. They ran for another minute until they reached the edge of the valley and the cliff face. Stopping again, Reggie turned around this time and faced Ben.

"Your plan, boss," Reggie said. "Where to now?"

By now, Ben was gasping for air and he held up a finger for Reggie to give him a moment. Reggie smirked, nonchalant. Ben had no idea how the man kept up his cool, collected attitude in moments like this.

"Sorry," Ben said. "Anyway, I was thinking —"

The zinging of bullets whizzing by his head led Ben to drop to the ground, once again knocking the air out of him. They thudded into the rock wall beside them, and another burst flew in from the same direction, this one spreading wide.

"You hit?" He heard Reggie yell.

"No," Ben whispered in a wheezing, airless voice. "But it might have felt better if I had been."

"I can promise you that is not true," Reggie said. "Anyway, I think I saw him. About 2 o'clock, just northwest of where we are now."

"You've been keeping track of what direction we're facing?" Ben asked.

"Old habits die hard."

"Give me a break," Ben said in reply, still lying prone on the ground. He turned his head to see where Reggie was and was surprised to see the man crouching, partially hidden behind a large boulder. "Seriously? You've got cover and you didn't offer me any?"

Reggie was staring down the valley, toward the direction the gunshots had come from. "He's not shooting anymore. He started running and I lost sight of him after that." He shifted his focus and met Ben's gaze, then held out a hand.

Ben grabbed Reggie's hand and allowed him to help him up. Ducking behind the boulder, Ben noticed that the large rock was one of a collection of similar-sized boulders in the area. For the first time since they'd stopped there, he took in his surroundings in more scrutinized detail. The rock outcropping was one of two such formations situated on both sides of where they had entered the valley. Whether the rocks had fallen from the cliffs in this way or not was uncertain, as he realized they could have been rolled into position by the tribe.

When he started to consider this option, he had a revelation.

"Reggie, do you think these boulders are defensive stations?"

"Like a bunker?"

Ben nodded.

Reggie frowned as he looked at the boulder they were hiding behind, the rest of the boulders on the side of the entrance, and the similar arrangement of rocks on the other side.

"Could be," he said. "Make sense to me."

"In that case, let's get to the other one. There's nothing here, but
—"

Ben's last few words were cut off by the violent eruption of a grenade blast against the cliff wall. He felt his body being flung through the air like a rag doll, lucid only for the time he spent in the air.

When he hit the ground, he blacked out.

CHAPTER 67

When he came to, Ben had the sudden urge to remain in the peaceful sleep of unconsciousness. There was a war raging around him, and he had woken up in the middle of it. His vision was blurry, but he saw a dark shape leaning over his head.

"Ben! Ben, are you okay?"

The words sounded muffled to him, as if he was underwater. For a brief moment he thought about how, if he had made different decisions a week ago, he might actually have *been* underwater. He and Julie could have been on a cruise at this very moment, far away from the Amazon rainforest. Julie would be swishing some sort of fruity drink around in her hand while Ben nursed a beer with a lime in it.

"Ben, come back to Earth! Wake up!"

The words drifted into focus, as did his vision, and he saw that both the blur and the voice belonged to Reggie. Reggie was gently slapping his cheek.

Ben yanked his head sideways. "That technique really works?" Ben asked, groggy.

"I like your sense of humor," Reggie said. "But this is *really* not a good time."

As Ben's senses returned to him and the world came back into view, he realized Reggie was right. He thought he heard gunfire from all directions now, knowing that most of the effect was because they were right next to the hard surface of the cliff. The screams had grown in intensity, though they were still far off in the distance.

"All right, big guy," Reggie said, throwing Ben's arm over his shoulder. "Take it easy, but hurry. We were a little late to the party."

Ben looked over at the opposite set of boulders, about a football field away. At first, he saw nothing out of the ordinary. The rocks stared back at him blankly.

After a few seconds, however, he saw a head poke up from behind one of the boulders. As Ben tried to adjust his vision to focus on the new element in the scene, the head was joined by the barrel of a rifle.

"Get down!" Reggie yelled, pushing Ben back to the ground.

The assault rifle fire was far louder than it had been earlier, amplified by the natural reverberation chamber they were sitting in. They were pinned down, and Ben suddenly understood Reggie's frustration.

"How?" The single word was all Ben was able to form on his lips.

Reggie understood the question just fine. "One of them must have made it to the mercenaries already, and untied them. No idea how they found the weapons so quickly, but I'm sure having a vantage point above everything else didn't hurt."

Of course, Ben thought. *They can see the entire valley, and if the weapons weren't hidden in a building they would've been able to spot them from anywhere.*

"So what now?" Ben asked, even though he already knew the answer.

"I've got no idea," Reggie said. "I was hoping you had a way to call in an airstrike or something."

Both men waited for a moment as the gunfire aimed at them died out. It was the most harrowing situation Ben had ever been in —

completely locked down by enemies trying to shoot him on two fronts, completely unarmed and helpless. His mind raced, trying to come up with options and solutions, each coming up wanting. His body seemed restless, as if at any moment it would spring into action against his own authority and try to make a break for it. He willed himself to calm down, just as he had done so many times in the past.

His memory traveled back to a time many years ago. He saw a vivid depiction of his father, trying to rescue his younger brother from the mother bear that had taken issue with his proximity to her cub. Ben remembered the feelings surging through his body at that time, but he also remembered the feelings he had replaced them with. Through willpower and determination, and many years of practice, Ben had been able to extinguish the smoldering heat of pain and replace it with the burning embers of grit. His ability to home in on one goal — sometimes at the expense of people who cared for him — had been sharpened to a point. The vulnerability and complete helplessness he remembered feeling back then had almost fully been replaced by a numb, hollow recollection.

Almost.

Today, right now, in the middle of the Amazon rainforest far away from anyone who could help, Ben was experiencing the same feelings that plagued his younger self. He wanted to run away from it all, to hide, like he once did by becoming a park ranger, and escape the 'real world.' He wanted to ignore it, to let Reggie battle the demons trying to break into his protective shell.

He wanted to, but he wouldn't.

If there was anything Ben had learned in just over three decades of life, it was that he was not the type of person to shy away from danger. It didn't make sense, and the logical side of his brain screamed against the infuriating insanity of his stubbornness, but he knew that at this moment in time he would fight.

He looked at Reggie, trying to decipher what his new friend was thinking. Reggie had a way about him, a certain aspect of his character that consistently belied his true feelings, but Ben thought he knew.

Looking into his eyes, Ben thought he understood the turmoil that was going on inside him. *It was the same.* Reggie had a story, just like he had a story, and he wanted to know. He *deserved* to know, but even more importantly, Reggie *deserved* to tell it.

That would have to wait, but Ben felt a wave of assurance sweep over him as he made his choice.

He would fight to hear that story, just like he would fight for Julie. She was somewhere back in the village, waiting for his return. Reggie needed him. *She* needed him.

Something must have changed in his face, because something changed in Reggie's.

"So you're ready, I guess?"

Ben looked at Reggie and nodded, once. He gritted his teeth and spoke out of the thin line between them. "Ready as I'll ever be."

CHAPTER 68

Reggie knew that the next two minutes would be more important than the previous two days. If they weren't able to get to their weapons, there wasn't much hope they'd survive. And right now, it didn't seem as though there was any way to get to the guns.

At the very least he had a kindred spirit in Ben. If he was going to fight, he knew Ben would be at his side through the thick of it. He thought of Joshua, and how the man had really grown on him. He still didn't fully trust him, but there hadn't been any choice. He only hoped Joshua would honor his word and help them survive this.

"Reggie!" Ben yelled from his side. "Move!"

Reggie darted forward, heading for the cliff wall. He wasn't sure what Ben had intended, but he wasn't going to wait around for the men behind the rocks opposite theirs to start firing again. The cliffs were only a few feet away, but it was a specific section of the impenetrable wall he was aiming for.

Namely, it was the part of the cliff that was *not* impenetrable. They'd entered — albeit not on their own accord — less than a day earlier through a hidden passageway located somewhere along this wall. If he remembered correctly, it even seemed like there were multiple passageways through the stone, since he knew Ben had been carried through another entrance.

But it was impossible to tell exactly where these openings were by simply looking at the wall. Vines and thick vegetation covered the entirety of the wall, providing a carpet-like coating for the stone's surface. He knew there was a hole, he just couldn't see it.

And Reggie needed to find it, fast.

Ben was right behind him and reached the wall only a second after. Reggie jogged forward along the cliff, extending his left arm out and into the twisting vines. He pressed against the carpet, allowing his body to disappear halfway into the foot-thick wall of plants until his hand reached the cool stone. It was slow going, and the vines were heavy against his forward progress, but he continued until the wall gave way.

It happened almost exactly halfway between the rocks they were hiding behind and the opposite outcropping the enemy was currently occupying. He nearly fell sideways as the cliff swallowed him into it, but he caught his balance and continued into the tunnel. Within seconds the remaining light provided by the moon vanished completely, and he was thrust into utter darkness.

"Reggie?"

"In here," he replied, his voice echoing now deeper into the cliff. "Thought this might be a good place to regroup."

"This is a tunnel, remember? What if some more of the warriors return, and don't know we're the good guys? They'll come in this way. And besides, don't you think the mercenaries might be thinking the same thing?"

"Quite possibly," Reggie said. "But I'm not sure we have better —"

He felt the cold point of sharpened rock on his neck, and then felt the nagging sensation that he was being watched.

"Well," he whispered, "at least it's not the mercenaries."

Ben didn't respond. The spear point on Reggie's neck was joined by another, then another on his chest.

Someone from inside the deep black torrent of nothingness grunted a few words, which were answered by another man's voice, still deeper in the tunnel. From around a corner the orange trickle of a flame emerged and grew brighter as its carrier turned and drew near. Reggie saw for the first time the silhouettes of five tribal warriors, three of whom were holding spears out and toward his body.

Both groups stared each other down for a moment, neither speaking. Reggie forced himself to breathe, careful to not move more than was absolutely required. The men with the spears kept their points on him, pressing just enough to keep him alert but not hard enough to cause him pain.

The tribal warrior carrying the lit torch walked toward them. His face was a twisted, shaking mirage in the dancing shadows of firelight. Reggie stood his ground. In the background, Reggie could hear the thudding sounds of gunfire, deeply muted by the thick cords of vines and overgrowth covering the entrance to the tunnel. He thought of the others, hoping Joshua would keep his word and help protect the rest of the group.

Even if Joshua *did* keep his word, they would need all the luck they could get. Joshua's old team, the mercenaries, had already reached the stash of weapons and it was only a matter of time before they untied and freed the remainder of their crew.

The tribesman spoke, again a guttural, grunting sound, and Reggie raised his eyebrows. *No idea what you're talking about, man.* The man repeated the noises.

One of the other warriors spoke, then turned and sneered at Reggie. Reggie shrugged.

He heard the odd set of words spoken a third time. The man in front of Reggie raised his hands, pushing the spears up and out of the way. Reggie waited, unsure of what the man's intentions were. *Is this another sacrificial ritual?* He wasn't about to force the man's hand, but Reggie had never been the type of person to wait around for someone else to act.

Reggie took a slow, small step backward. The tribespeople tensed, but their leader didn't budge.

"What are you doing?" Ben whispered. He saw Ben out of the corner of his eye, frozen in place opposite him in the tunnel. He had only moved his mouth, clearly as terrified as Reggie.

"We have to make them understand..." Reggie muttered. "The guns."

Ben nodded. The leader of the indigenous warriors stepped forward, again closing the gap between himself and Reggie. Reggie thought about what he was going to say. *What do you say to a group of people who have no idea how to understand you?*

He decided not to say anything.

Reggie lifted his hands up, one in front of the other, in the shape of holding an invisible assault rifle. He curled the index finger of his right hand around a nonexistent trigger, and held his left hand in an upward-facing cupped palm. He pointed it to the side, toward the cave wall. *Don't want this guy to get the wrong idea.*

The man frowned, then brought the torch down to see Reggie's hands in greater detail. Reggie shook his hands gently, pretending to fire. He made the pattering sounds of gunshots with his mouth, keeping it quiet enough to — hopefully — not upset the warriors.

He repeated the process a few times, moving the positions of his hands to aim the "gun" in different directions, all the while continuing the noises. The warrior stared, still frowning, then brought his head back up and straightened.

His eyes widened and he turned to the others in his group. He pointed at Reggie, excitedly chattering with the two men closest to him. They discussed for a few seconds, and Reggie was relieved to see the spearmen place the butts of their weapons on the ground and stand at ease.

The lead warrior spoke again to Reggie, but his voice had changed. Where there was a slight gruffness before, the man was now using a different set of consonants, almost a singsong-like voice, and Reggie interpreted it as a question.

"See," he said under his breath, "that's the thing. I can't understand what you're saying." He enunciated the words out of frustration at the language barrier. Reggie pointed behind him, toward the covering of vines at the entrance to the tunnel, and performed the gun-holding action once again.

The warrior spoke again, this time to his team, and three of them peeled off from the group of five. They walked to the front of the tunnel and pushed aside the vines, exposing the tunnel to a surprising amount of moonlight. The gunfire grew louder, and Reggie noticed that there didn't seem to be as many screams emanating from the valley beyond.

We're running out of time.

The leader of the warriors pushed Reggie forward. Reggie heard Ben moving alongside him as well. The two men were marched to the tunnel's entrance, directed by the two warriors. When they'd reached the opening, the three warriors in the front suddenly broke into a run, aiming toward the group of boulders to the left.

They're going for the guns, Reggie realized. *Either they're going to help us or I've just taught them how to use the weapons against us.*

It didn't matter which it was — Reggie didn't have a choice. He was pushed out of the cave by the leader and into the vulnerable openness. He ran, hoping that Ben was behind him.

A head poked up from behind one of the boulders, just as it had before. They had only been in the cave for a couple minutes, so the men behind the circle of boulders were still guarding whatever weapons remained stashed there.

"Reggie, duck!" he heard Ben yell.

Before he could, he felt a cool swish of air just next to his head, then saw the head behind the boulder lance backward violently. Only then could he make out the outline of a spear, sticking up in the air above the soldier's head, affixed to his skull. The man didn't make a sound as he fell backwards.

Reggie was amazed. *What a shot,* he thought. The warrior who'd thrown the spear quickened his pace and reached the boulder at the same time as the first three men out of the cave. Reggie, Ben, and the leader of the small band of fighters were right behind them.

Unlike the other circle of rocks Reggie and Ben had hidden behind, this group of boulders had clearly been placed in a specific formation — a circle. In the center of the circle was a pile of weapons — the four assault rifles, sidearms, and combat knives from the four mercenaries who'd been sacrificed to the lake, as well as Reggie's own weapons and the two remaining backpacks they'd brought along. Ben didn't see the bag Joshua had been carrying, the smaller pack that the tribe had stripped from his back when they'd arrived.

While he was relieved to see a small stack of weapons piled there, it also meant that the *rest* of the mercenaries either already had their weapons back or were about to. He glanced to the lake but it was impossible to tell from this distance whether the soldiers were still tied to their posts. Once again he thought of Joshua, Archie, Paulinho, and the girls, and hoped they were safe or had somehow escaped.

There was also *another* problem. The guns weren't the only things waiting inside the circle of boulders. Two mercenaries, not including the one who had already been killed by the spear, were posted inside the circle, each facing outward a different direction, keeping watch. *I guess they're not tied up anymore.* One of the men was already swiveling around to see what the commotion behind him had been. He saw his dead comrade first, the spear protruding from the man's face, leaning backward at a steep angle. Then he noticed the native warriors, creeping over and around the wall of boulders. He lifted the gun and fired.

Reggie winced, ducking, as the first warrior went down. The second was able to launch a spear, but by then the second mercenary had turned around to help. Reggie retreated, grabbing Ben before he entered the ring.

"We're going around," he said. Ben nodded, but broke away from Reggie's grip. "What are you doing?"

"I'll go around the *other* way, then," Ben said. Before he could argue, Ben was gone.

Reggie ran around the rest of the rocks and aimed for the gap between two of the smaller boulders. This was where one of the soldiers had been posted up, and he gained speed as he entered the ring. He had no weapons, but he hoped he at least had the element of surprise. There were two more bursts of gunfire, and Reggie hoped the shots didn't land on target.

He breached the line of boulders and saw that Ben had made it to his entrance at the same instant. Both men ran toward the center of the circle, aiming for their chosen soldiers standing just next to the pile of weapons. In his peripheral vision he saw two of the natives, bleeding on the ground inside the ring. The leader of the group and the last warrior were nowhere in sight.

In the last split-second before impact, he focused again on his target — the soldiers both had their backs to him and Ben, holding their guns up and at the ready for a frontal assault. Reggie dove forward, aiming for the lowest part of the man's back. He hoped to not only tackle the man solidly but provide him with as much pain as humanly possible in the process. The connection was abrupt, and Reggie's vision lit up in a flash of white.

The pain quickly subsided and he had a brief moment of weightlessness as he felt himself soaring through the air with his prisoner beneath him. He wrapped his arms around the man, and both tumbled to the ground, hard.

He'd knocked the air of the soldier, but the man was recovering quickly, already starting to roll sideways to shake the attack. Reggie reacted faster, having the benefit of not being on the bottom of the pile, and he reached over and grabbed at whatever weapon lay nearby.

A pistol. *Good enough.*

The man was struggling beneath him now, but Reggie lifted the gun up and pressed it against the man's temple. "This ends *now*, buddy."

The soldier froze, recognizing defeat. Reggie felt him relax slightly but he continued to watch the man's hands. The pile of weapons was equally within reach for the soldier. "Don't even think about it," Reggie said. "Ben, you okay?"

Reggie didn't turn away, not daring to let the man he was sitting on catch him off guard. He still had the gun to his head, but Reggie wasn't taking any chances.

"Ben, you there?"

Reggie jumped at the sound of a gun firing directly behind him. He momentarily dropped the pistol from the man's head, startled.

The man took the opportunity to lurch forward a few inches and grab the knife on the ground in front of him. In a single, swift motion, he swiveled his upper body around and backhanded the knife point toward Reggie.

Reggie was in motion, but it was too slow. He saw the point of the knife falling closer and closer to his face, as if watching a slowed down instant replay from a separate camera angle. He forced his body to move faster, but he wasn't going to make it.

The knife curved through the air until it was an inch from his eye, then stopped. Only then did Reggie's mind register another gunshot. The soldier beneath him immediately sagged, his arm dropping back to the ground and releasing the knife. Reggie saw the open hole on the side of the man's head, the tiny circle of blood marking the entrance wound.

"What the hell, Ben?" Reggie yelled. "He surrendered. We could have used —"

"Well, we can't anymore. He's dead," Ben said. Reggie could hardly hear him. "And keep your voice down. You're screaming."

"*You* discharged a weapon next to my *ear*," Reggie yelled. "It's not funny."

"Didn't say it was," Ben said, shrugging. "Come on. Stop whining, you're supposed to be trained for this."

CHAPTER 69

"We need to get back to the lake and find the others," Ben said. Reggie was opening and closing his jaw, trying to regain his hearing.

"You go on," Reggie said, still talking far too loudly. "I'll hang back and cover you."

"You sure?" Ben asked. He hadn't expected the man to decline.

"I was a sniper back in the day, so I'm better off back here, anyway. Besides, someone needs to make sure the mercs don't get to the tunnels."

Ben hadn't considered that, but he knew Reggie was right. Whatever his decision, Ben was going to get back to Julie. "Okay, fine. Let me have some of those."

Reggie was already handing Ben the assault rifles. He ignored the knives, but kept his two pistols for himself.

"How many of them are left?" Ben asked.

"Bad guys? We took care of three here, the natives got four earlier, and I think they started with ten or eleven, right?"

"So a few more."

"Yes, but a few more *well-trained* soldiers, hunting us. And without weapons, we're fish in a barrel."

Ben nodded, then turned to leave.

"I got your back."

The four assault rifles were heavy. There was no possible way to carry any of them in a position he could actually fire one, and he was reminded once more at his complete reliance on Reggie's ability to 'get his back.' Ben was also not able to carry extra ammunition, so whatever was remaining in each gun's magazine was all they'd get.

He hoped it would be enough.

He increased his pace, fighting against the awkward weight of the rifles but plodding along without trouble. The lake was about 100 yards away, but it felt like a mile. His legs were straining, he was drenched in sweat, and the air was heavy with moisture. He was having a hard time breathing, as if in a steam room. Every inhalation was marked with stabs of pain as the exertion, stress, fatigue, and heat all acted against him.

The lake was growing larger and larger every second, and suddenly he was there. He'd reached the building closest to the small lake and used every bit of remaining strength he had to step over the dirt threshold and check the interior.

"Julie?" he shouted.

No answer.

He found them inside the second building, huddled together. Archie, Julie, Amanda, and Paulinho, who had somewhat of a dazed look in his eyes but was otherwise healthy. Ben assumed they were hiding, but when Julie didn't rush toward him when she saw who had entered, he took a closer look.

Joshua was lying on the ground in the center of the hut. Archie and Amanda were hard at work, treating a terribly bloody wound on his abdomen.

"It looks worse than it is," Archie said as he glanced over to Ben.

"Well, it looks pretty bad. What happened?"

"Shot, by his own man."

"It was Alan," Joshua said, straining his neck to peer up at Ben. "I thought he was loyal, but they were all working against me."

Amanda gently pushed his head back down and tried to force the man to rest, but Joshua continued.

"I think the Company's been planning this for some time," he said. "They got rid of my father somehow, and now they just need to get rid of me and my brother to tie up loose ends. I played right into their plan."

"You're being too hard on yourself," Julie said.

"Doesn't matter — it's too late now," he replied. "They're going to murder every single one of those villagers and then converge on these buildings. We're toast."

"No," Ben said. "We're not."

Finally, everyone turned to look at what Ben had dumped on the ground just inside the door of the hut. Without a word, Paulinho and Julie walked over and grabbed a weapon.

"You found the stash," Julie said. She smiled, then started to turn back to the others. Ben grabbed her arm before she could move away from him, spun her around, and kissed her.

He felt her tensed body relax after her surprise wore off, then she straightened up again and pushed herself closer to him. He pulled her lower back closer, still kissing.

"Okay guys, probably not a great time for that..." Amanda said. She grinned, but Ben felt his face flush from mild embarrassment.

Julie stood on her tiptoes and kissed him again, quickly, then finally pulled her hand from his and looked up at him. He knew she was uncomfortable to say the least, her clothes streaked with sweat, hair disheveled, and holding an assault rifle, but he thought she'd never looked better.

"Thanks, Ben," she whispered. The two words spoke volumes, and neither felt the need to fill the sudden silence with any more.

"Lucky man," Joshua said, grimacing from the pain of his gunshot wound. Ben snapped back to the real world, feeling his short-lived boost of confidence draining again as he remembered their predicament.

"So where's Reggie?" Paulinho asked.

"He's guarding the exits," Ben answered. "But they're going to easily outnumber him if they decide to regroup and head that direction. We need to get out there and give him some help."

"But Joshua —"

"I'm fine," Joshua said with his eyes closed. The word 'fine' was squeezed out through clenched teeth.

"You must rest," Archie said. "I believe this is only a flesh wound, but we'll need a doctor to look at it."

Joshua ignored Archie. "In my pack… I have a way to get a helicopter here. It's the emergency extraction protocol."

"And it'll work from way out here?" Paulinho asked.

Joshua nodded. "It should. Just enough juice to send a signal, assuming we can triangulate from here. There isn't any tree cover, so that should help."

Ben considered this plan. "But what about the pilot? Won't they be working for —"

"I'll discuss it with the pilot," Joshua said with an air of finality. He wasn't intending to discuss the plan with anyone, and if Ben was reading between the lines correctly, Joshua wouldn't actually be doing much 'discussing.'

"I can help out with the *discussions*, then," Ben said. "Where is this pack of yours?"

Joshua shook his head. "No idea. Alan's in charge now, chain-of-command. He's out there still, but they haven't been shooting at anything for a few minutes."

Ben noticed that as well. The gunfire, save for a few bursts every thirty seconds or so, had mostly ceased. *Probably not a good sign.*

"We're probably sitting ducks in here," Amanda said, voicing the concern Ben had just stumbled onto. "Shouldn't we —"

Her voice was cut off abruptly by another, coming from just outside the hut.

"On your feet, all of you. Outside, now."

CHAPTER 70

There was nothing he could do but comply. Without looking, Ben knew the voice would be accompanied by a man pointing a gun directly toward the back of his head.

Ben stepped backwards slowly, out into the moonlight. The area seemed brighter now, as if the moon had been afraid to fully rise earlier. He didn't turn around, but he continued backwards until he felt the heated circle of the gun barrel pressed against him.

"The rest of you," the voice shouted. "Outside!"

Ben saw Julie, then Paulinho, Amanda, and Archie come out of the doorway. Joshua did not appear. Ben looked at each of the members of the team he'd helped lead out here, met eyes with each, and attempted to convey the message of 'I'm sorry' with nothing more than a deep look. Each of the group wore a stubbornness on their faces, silently rejecting his apology and surrender. Paulinho's eyes weren't even open as he walked by Ben.

The man grabbed Ben's shoulder and yanked him backwards, where he was caught by two more mercenaries and held in place. The man, Alan, walked into the hut. Ben waited for the gunshot.

Instead, he heard a wrenching noise as one of the men holding him suddenly lost his grip. He turned around to see a wide-eyed man, his mouth full of blood, fall to the ground. The other man, stunned by the sudden attack, had momentarily forgotten his task and allowed Ben to wiggle out of his grip. Ben elbowed him in the nose and turned to face the last of the soldiers. This soldier was ready, and had already started aiming in the direction from which the spear had been thrown.

He opened fire, and Ben started running.

Julie was closer, and she gave the man a hard push. He lost his balance, and the gun dropped to his side as he tripped and fell to his knees. Ben was on him then, and he was about to grab for the gun, but another sickening, deep thud came from the man. Ben looked down to see a sharpened section of flat rock poking out from the man's back.

The handle of a six-foot spear stuck out the front of the man, and he instinctively dropped the gun and tried to pull out the spear. Ben, still watching the drama from behind, could hear the gasping strands of breath as the man struggled, in vain, to remove the weapon from his chest.

He could see them now, creeping forward in the shadows. They moved silently, knowing where to walk to avoid the direct light of the moon. They were wraiths, ghosts of an ancient civilization, enacting revenge on the intruders who'd threatened their way of life.

Ben felt completely helpless, and he was. His life was in their hands now. He could see only five of them, betrayed by the whites of their eyes, but he knew there were more. From all directions, watching them, moving slowly forward, there were more.

The warriors, but also the villagers. He saw a child, the streaks of dried tears still stuck to his cheeks. He held on to his mother, and both of them walked closer.

Ben whirled around, only then remembering the third soldier, the one whom he'd hit in the face. His worry was nullified, however, as he saw the man's arms lifted above his head, interlaced together. He was on his knees, waiting for the group to decide his fate.

Behind this man, waiting outside the hut, was the chief of the ancient tribe. The man who only an hour ago had been covered in gold and standing on a sacrificial dais at the center of the lake was now standing in the doorway, looking in.

What is he waiting for? Ben wondered. No one moved. Every party — Ben's group, the remaining mercenary, and the innumerable indigenous tribespeople watching on from the darkness — waited for the chief to act. Ben considered helping, but he was unarmed, and he had no idea what he could do anyway. The guns were still on the floor near the hut.

What is Joshua doing in there?

He knew they would be talking, the new leader explaining to the old the faults that led to this moment. The old leader, Joshua, would either ask for his life or ask for a quick death. They had been inside together for about a minute, so Ben wasn't sure where in the negotiating process they would be.

The skirmish started at that moment. He heard Alan yell something unintelligible, and Joshua shout a pained reply, then both men grunted with the unmistakable sound of the impact of two bodies. *He doesn't stand a chance,* Ben thought. Joshua's injury alone would be more than most men could bear, and he was now being attacked by a trained killer.

Ben had to force himself not to run forward and push the chief out of the way. Joshua was not on 'their team,' necessarily, but he trusted him. He'd already proven useful to their group, and they were all still alive, in no small part due to Joshua. Even still, it was Ben's hatred for the *other* group of men who'd chased them through the jungle that ignited his fury and urged him to help Joshua.

But the chief wasn't moving, and it was clear he wasn't going to. Ben tried to understand his motives.

Is he allowing the fight to happen, to find out which man was stronger? Is it one less person he has to sacrifice?

The end happened much quicker than Ben expected. He heard another grunt, this time louder and deeper, and he vaguely saw Alan stumble backwards toward the door. *He must have been kicked.* Alan was grabbing at his stomach, as if the air had been knocked out of him, and still moving backwards. He reached the opening in the tiny building and continued out, finally able to catch his balance.

The man heaved, pushed off his knees, and stood up. He had recovered well, and quickly. He took one final breath and lifted his foot to march forward again.

And the chief jammed the two miniature daggers into Alan's neck from behind. Ben saw, even in the darker moonlight, where they had appeared from. The chief wore bracelets on each wrist, and on each of these were fastened the two pointed strips of rock. He had a skill and control using them, and if Ben hadn't been standing directly behind the chief he might have missed it completely.

Alan coughed, choking as the daggers swirled around inside his neck. The chief left them there, then leaned in so his head was resting almost on Alan's shoulder, and spoke. The words were the same ancient-sounding language they'd all heard before, but the words were unrecognizable to Ben. The chief repeated the command, louder, then violently yanked the daggers from Alan's neck.

Alan sank to the ground, hard. There was no water here to catch his fall, and there were no spearman to quicken the transition from life to death. He gasped for air, all the while holding his neck with slick, blood-soaked hands.

Ben stared downward at the gruesome scene, but couldn't look away. He felt, in part, as if he *needed* to watch, *needed* the closure of it. He didn't cheer it on, silently or otherwise, but he watched. It was not cathartic or therapeutic but it needed to happen, and Ben knew that. He'd orchestrated some of this man's death, whether he chose to believe it or not, and the least he could do was watch it to the bitter end.

Another part of him realized the truth of their entire mission. He'd failed. He was no closer to understanding who the company or organization was that had been behind all of this, and Joshua didn't seem to be confident either of them would find anything. He wanted all of this to be different, but there was no going back.

He'd learned that before, many years ago. He couldn't 'go back.' There was no hiding, escaping, or withdrawing from his past. He'd withdrawn *himself,* but he'd never successfully escaped anything that he'd experienced, no matter how hard he'd tried. Today was no different, so he watched.

Alan gurgled once more, then died. The blood hadn't gotten the message that its owner had stopped living, so it continued pressing out of him, filling and staining the ground around his head and torso.

Joshua was at the doorway. "Anyone want to give me a hand?" he asked.

His face showed a sign of shock when it registered who was waiting for him at the door, but the chief seemed uninterested and turned away, walking back to his people.

Ben turned to Paulinho. "Anything you can tell us about all of *that?*"

Paulinho's eyes were wide. "I *felt* it," he said. "I felt *all* of it. It was weird, like I said before. I just knew what they were feeling, and how they were planning to act. I knew they were surrounding us, but I understand their motives weren't to harm us."

"What about the chief?" Julie said. "That was weird, right?"

Paulinho shook his head. "It was a fair duel, two men, both unarmed." Ben remembered seeing Alan drop his weapon just inside the door of the hut near the existing pile. "The chief would have had Alan sacrificed or killed anyway, I think. But he saw that the two men were already standing off, so he let it conclude first."

"Fascinating," Amanda said.

Archie nodded. "I could spend *weeks* out here, just studying them."

"Well, you may have your chance," Joshua said.

Everyone turned to him. He held up a shattered device from the pack Alan had been wearing, similar to an old cellular phone.

"Is that the way home?" Ben asked.

"It was," he said. "Alan destroyed it."

"Any chance he pressed the magic button before he did?"

"Doubt it."

"Okay," Amanda asked, her voice already rising. "What do we do?"

Ben looked at Paulinho. "You have to try to communicate with them," he said. "It's our only shot. Maybe they'll give us canoes or rafts or something."

"Yes," Archie said, "we can head downstream, and the current will be quite easy to navigate. It shouldn't take long at all to get back to Manaus."

Paulinho was shaking his head. "No, you don't understand. I can't *talk* to them. It's not like that. It is *feelings,* in a general sense."

"Paulinho," Amanda said. "We don't have any other options."

Crack! Ben fell to the ground as the gunshot rang through the air, unable to catch himself as he face-planted into the hard-packed dirt in front of the hut.

CHAPTER 71

Reggie saw Ben jump at the abrasive sound of the gun firing directly next to his ear. Ben had been standing off to the side of the group, deliberating with all of them, while Reggie had been sneaking up behind him. He'd waited for the right moment, then lifted the gun up so it was close enough to Ben's ear to cause him extreme alarm without too much hearing loss.

It was a nasty prank, but it had worked like a charm.

Reggie offered Ben a hand, grinning. Ben didn't return the expression.

"What the hell was that for?" Ben asked. His voice was louder than it needed to be, and Reggie couldn't control his laughter.

"Sorry, I owed you one."

"You could have made me go deaf!"

"Hardly, Ben. Besides, what were you going to do with this guy, anyway?"

Ben frowned, then turned to look at where Reggie was pointing. The last mercenary, the one Ben had elbowed, was lying on the ground, dead.

"Why'd you do that?"

"Like I said," Reggie explained, "I owed you one."

Reggie had already determined there was not a chance they'd be leaving anyone alive, and after the rest of the soldiers had been dispatched, he'd kept his sights on this one. They weren't going to extract any new information from him — and anything he did know would be information Joshua already had.

"Where'd you come from?" Julie asked.

Reggie just flipped his head back a bit, as if that was all the explanation needed. "Back there. Ben ran away and didn't invite me to the party."

He looked over to Ben to see if he got a rise out of him, but Ben was busy trying to shake the ringing sound out of his head.

"I didn't hear any gunfire, and I hadn't seen anyone in ten minutes, so I started walking over. The villagers came out of nowhere, but they didn't even stop me. They were all heading here, so I followed and stopped a little ways away, until the chief did, uh, that." He nodded toward the bloody mess of Alan on the ground. "Sorry I was late."

Reggie reached out his hand and offered it to Ben. Ben hesitated, but a moment later grabbed it and came closer.

"Thanks, man." Then he stopped the handshake, still gripping Reggie's hand, and added, "but you're still an asshole."

Reggie let out a verbal chuckle. "Don't mention it." He turned to the rest of the group, including Joshua at the doorway. "Now, how are we getting out of here?"

CHAPTER 72

Julie's heart was pounding, and she wasn't sure if it was from Ben's kiss, their terrifying experience in the Amazon, or the fear that remained surrounding how they would get home.

Maybe it was a little bit of everything.

They'd spent the night in the huts, after a round of silent hand-signal negotiations between the villagers and their group had determined that was what was intended. She'd slept well, a quick, dreamless sleep, even though the moment she woke up she felt the wave of insecurity envelop her once again as she realized they were, still, stuck in the middle of the world's most remote jungle.

She turned to Ben, who was snoring next to her, and watched him sleep for a minute. He stirred, somehow aware that he was being watched, and he sucked in a breath of air and saliva, then opened his eyes.

"You really are cute when you're asleep," she said, grinning down at him.

He squinted at her, deadpan.

She laughed. "You feeling okay?"

"I'm great, aside from a back that feels like it's been rolled over by a cement mixer and a headache that makes me think I'm being lobotomized. Not to mention my shoulder." He rolled over, wincing at a sore spot on his side as he massaged his shoulder.

"You're a baby."

Ben's mouth widened in mock surprise. "Are you being serious? I *shot* people! Give me a break."

Julie laughed again, then rolled on top of him before he could react.

"What are you —"

"How about a little *jungle fever?*" she asked.

"That's — what? That's not what that means," Ben said. "You're frisky this morning," he added.

"Sorry, just… there's been a lot, you know?"

Ben nodded. "I know."

"You guys really gonna do that here?" a voice said from deeper inside the hut. Reggie sounded groggy, his voice much deeper than normal. He coughed a few times, then stretched and stood up. They'd fallen asleep in two huts — Ben, Julie, and Reggie in one, Paulinho, Amanda, Archie, and Joshua in another. They didn't have any sort of bedding, and the floor of the hut was the same dirt and grass that existed in the rest of the valley, so they'd slept in their clothes. The trees out in the valley were too far apart to hang the Stingray tents, so they'd decided against trying to sleep outside. Reggie and Ben had used their packs as pillows, but Julie had been too exhausted to care.

Julie was already standing as Reggie walked toward the front of the hut, and she reached a hand down to Ben to help him up. She knew it was mostly just a kind gesture, as he had 100 pounds on her, but he grabbed her hand anyway and sat up.

She had aches and pains as well, and she worked to sate them. She pressed against the knots in her back and sides, massaging them with knuckles and the bottom of her wrists. Ben was still sitting, playing with his hair. It had gotten oily, and he was tousling it around as if it would make a difference.

"You take forever to get up," she said.

"Again, I *shot* people," he said.

"How long are you going to use that excuse?" she jibed.

"However long I can, and then a little more," he replied without hesitation.

"Hurry up. We need to see how Paulinho did."

Last night, after the chief had 'sacrificed' the leader of the mercenaries and their lodgings were negotiated, Paulinho had attempted to get an audience with the chief and some of the warriors and villagers to see about transportation out of the valley. It was clear the tribe no longer considered any of them a threat, but trying to break the language barrier to ask about boats or rafts proved to be an almost impossible task.

Reggie and Archie had urged Paulinho to draw stick figures in the mud, while Amanda still thought there might be a way to communicate with the tribe using nothing but Paulinho's mind. Julie and Ben thought it was hopeless, and had gone to bed.

The sun was cresting the top edge of the cliff at the far side of the valley, and the waterfall's mist was casting a long, thin rainbow over the entire scenic display. In short, it was breathtakingly beautiful. Julie hadn't been able to fully appreciate the geologic artistry that existed here, so she stood outside the hut and took it all in. Her phone was back at the hotel in Marabá, along with their luggage and rental car, so she had no way of capturing the moment digitally.

Ben was behind her, and he wrapped his arms around her waist and pulled her back to him. She smiled, still in awe at the beauty surrounding her.

The moment didn't last, however. She realized suddenly that there was a pall cast over the picturesque landscape — the nature was stunningly gorgeous in the morning light, but there was something her eyes had chosen to ignore about the scene.

The bodies.

There were villagers lying everywhere, dead. Facedown, women and children as well, cast around the valley as if they'd been grains of salt sprinkled haphazardly down by the hand of a giant. Some of the huts nearby were smoking, burning slowly and providing the area with a campfire-like smell. The lake was the only part of the area that appeared to be untouched, the gentle lapping waves hitting the shoreline the same way they had for millennia.

Julie looked around, trying to bring back the feeling of wonder she'd felt a moment ago, but it had passed. Now she saw the valley for what it really was: the smoking, charred husk of a once-fantastic civilization. At least half of the people who had, only hours ago, called this place home were lying lifeless on the ground.

Villagers were hard at work, some moving bodies to large piles at the sides of the valley. Others were using thick vines to pull down the few trees in the area, the ones that bore the golden fruit. She had to look harder to ensure her eyes were telling the truth, but it was true.

"Ben, they're cutting the trees down."

He didn't respond.

Paulinho arrived, a pained smile on his face. She'd admired his smile days ago, in Marabá, when it had the wide, lighthearted appeal of a man without worry. Now it was tainted, a smile that only offset a small amount the tired look in his eyes.

"Morning, Paulinho," she said, ignoring her mind's interpretation of the man's facial expression.

"I hope you slept well," he said. "We have boats." He turned and pointed to a path leading to the lake on the other side of the valley. There were four canoes sitting there, small but sturdy-looking.

She frowned. "Paulinho, that's fantastic. Why are you upset?"

He paused for a moment, collecting his thoughts. "I — I am not sure," he said. He dropped the smile. "It's this, I believe. All of this. These, at one time, were *my* people. But that isn't relevant now, compared to the devastation we've brought them."

Ben released Julie and stepped up to Paulinho. "Hey, Paulinho," he said. "*We* didn't bring this. *They* did. And they're not here anymore."

Paulinho nodded once, but his eyes fell. "Still…"

"We'll fix this," Archie said, who'd suddenly emerged from the hut next door. He was followed by Joshua and Amanda. "We'll make it right, somehow."

"I already have some ideas," Amanda added. "The research we can do now will help them strengthen their minds, giving them more of an advantage out here. We can —"

"No," Paulinho said. "No, they don't want that. They want — they've *always* wanted — nothing from us. They've tried for centuries to stay out of the way, living here and dying here, in the jungle."

Joshua looked around, and Julie watched his face. He was trying to make sense of the villagers, watching them work. "Why are they tearing the tress down?"

Paulinho spoke immediately, anticipating the question. "It's their tree, meaning that it's not only the basis for their city and entire way of life, but it *belongs* to them. To them it is a possession they all share. They've had to adapt and move to survive, like any other group, but their tree has always been a unique advantage. That's why they can't let the fruit or leaves — any of it — leave El Dorado. Where they go, the tree goes, to be replanted and grown somewhere new, and when they leave a place behind, they remove any remnant of the tree and its fruit."

"It's the only place on the planet with these specimens," Archie said. "Remarkable."

"And El Dorado is wherever *they* are," Julie added. "So they're leaving?"

Paulinho nodded. "Yes, they must. There is no other alternative."

"But we'll always have a way to get back," Amanda said, stepping closer to the Brazilian man who had acted as their unexpected liaison for the past day and touching his shoulder. "Paulinho, you have their blood, which means you have their memories. We'll be able to find them, no matter what."

He nodded, then took the final step forward between himself and Dr. Amanda Meron. She was shorter than he was, so her head naturally fell backward as she peered up at him. He didn't hesitate. He darted forward and pressed his lips to hers. She raised her hands to resist at first, then dropped them to her sides and leaned in to the kiss.

Julie smiled, the juxtaposition of the moment against the background of the villagers toiling away not enough to keep her from beaming.

"Come on," Reggie said. "*Way* too much kissing around here. Shouldn't we be testing those boats?"

Amanda pulled herself away from the taller man. "Give us just a minute. We have some catching up to do," she said.

CHAPTER 73

Ben's hand was sweating, but he didn't dare move it. Her fingers were wrapped tightly between his, clenched into a death grip. He wasn't sure he could move it, even if he'd wanted to. He'd originally grabbed her hand as their plane left the Manaus airport, ostensibly because 'he hated taking off.'

It was true he disliked flying, but he was starting to come around to the fact that he actually disliked not being in control. Ben was a man who wanted to control not only the situations that he — either purposefully or inadvertently — found himself in, but also control those situations that weren't even possible to control.

Love was a great example of that.

As Julie's head rolled sideways and found the perfect-sized nook between Ben's head and shoulder, he inched backward in the uncomfortable airline seat and tried to make the best of the situation.

It wasn't hard. Besides having zero control over the pilot's and copilot's decisions far up in the cockpit, the situation he currently found himself in was something he couldn't have designed for himself in a million years. He was more in love with the woman sleeping on his shoulder than he'd ever dreamed possible, and it didn't hurt that he was more attracted to her than anyone he'd ever met.

As if that wasn't enough, there was currently no one trying to kill him.

Dr. Amanda Meron and her new fling, Paulinho, returned to Manaus, then Marabá, along with a few of the 'golden fruits' they'd snuck out of the valley, to continue the research she'd started. She had some ideas about the fruit, and how it could help 'unlock' some of the powerful mechanisms she thought might still be hidden in the human brain. Paulinho had promised to use his connections in the government to provide her the legal protection she would need to start a new firm, away from the watchful gaze of Draconis Industries, or Drache Global, or Drage Medisinsk, or whatever it was called.

Reggie, a man seemingly as mysterious as Ben had always wanted to appear, provided him with a simple answer when Ben had asked him what was next.

He shrugged.

Ben laughed, then repeated the question.

Reggie just gave him the same goofy grin, too wide to be genuine, but with enough authenticity in his eyes that the smile couldn't have been completely fabricated, and turned around to catch a bus back to his home. His 'bunker' had been attacked by the Draconis soldiers, but as he'd explained on the canoe trip back to civilization, 'if it couldn't stand up to a few idiot radicals, what's the point of building a bunker?'

Dr. Archibald Quinones was a little more reserved on the trip back to Manaus, and when Julie had pressed him on it, he'd given a non-response. Ben had let it slide, but Dr. Meron had eventually backed him up against a wall and asked the same thing. He was still reserved, but he did vow to help Amanda in her research, and even mentioned an inheritance he'd been sitting on for some time that would be put to good use by investing in whatever she had in mind.

Finally, he thought about Joshua Jefferson, the son of a man intertwined in the dealings of an organization Ben had vowed to bring to justice. Joshua seemed to be a man of his word, albeit one who had been led astray by his own father, under the guise of doing good in the world. Joshua told Ben and the others that 'there would be more,' and left Ben to wonder what exactly that meant. Joshua had given Ben his word that he'd be in touch — he had to find his father first, but he did tell Ben he had plans to go after the company that had double-crossed his family and pitted them against one another. When he was ready, he said, Ben would hear from him.

Their ragtag group of unlikely adventurers had somehow morphed into a band of experienced explorers, and Ben was ever prouder to be named one of them. He needed a break, and he desperately wanted some 'downtime' with Julie, but he knew there was more to the Draconis story than he'd discovered in the jungle. They were working on something, and he wanted to know what it was.

The little he knew about the organization told him all he needed to know: they were not interested in altruistic applications for their advanced research. Draconis was cunning, without moral obligation, and interested in expending any amount of resources to achieve their goals. He didn't know what those goals were, but he knew they wouldn't lead to good. He had renewed his vow to bring them down, and he knew Joshua would help him see it through, somehow.

For now, though, he would try to enjoy the success they'd had: they had found the mythical lost city of El Dorado, and though its 'gold' was not what anyone in history had expected, they had finally uncovered its secret.

As the flight attendant passed by and delivered his rum and Coke, he smiled, closed his eyes while sipping the drink, and tried to talk his mind into believing that the plane wasn't going to go down in a fiery blaze.

THE
ICE CHASM

NICK THACKER
TURTLESHELL PRESS

CHAPTER 1

Roald Montgomery fumbled with the zipper on his Canada Goose expedition parka, trying to force it the remaining two inches to the bottom of his chin. Even with the five-fingered ski gloves that allowed enhanced maneuverability, it was nearly impossible to grip the small zipper.

He stopped, his boots packing the soft layer of snow down into a compressed block beneath his feet. Roald inhaled, careful to breath in the frigid air slowly through the layers of protection offered by the balaclava and neck gaiter that he wore over his face.

He checked the thermometer on his watch.

-68. Fahrenheit.

His body didn't need a reminder of how cold it was outside, but seeing the number seemed to give him an extra boost of energy, and Roald finally pulled the zipper up to its topmost position. Satisfied, he started moving forward again.

Trudging was a better word. He'd only walked about 200 yards, and he was already feeling the strain of exertion. Part of the problem was the wind. *The damn wind,* as the others back at the station said. He'd never thought walking in a straight line could be so complicated, but then again he'd never been to Antarctica.

Until now.

Roald had joined his older brother, Scott, only a month ago at the research station, taking a 6-month assignment that he'd fought tooth and nail to earn. It was difficult to get a job at the bottom of the planet, and it was even more unlikely there would be two siblings stationed there at the same time. It didn't mean anything, except that Roald felt even more scrutinized because of it — he couldn't mess up. They'd expect him to do his job exceptionally well.

And he intended to. He'd left the Mars-1 Humvee running, as per protocol, but left it at the center of his 100-yard-radius circular route. His mission was simple: walk around and take notes on anything he saw.

It was, admittedly, one of the more mundane tasks the scientists were required to check off their daily to-do lists, but he'd drawn the short straw today. Choose a location, drive the Humvee to it, then park and walk around the vehicle in a pre-defined radius. Then observe the surroundings — weather, snow drifts, anything that catches the eye — and record the verbal data by talking it into a recording device in his jacket pocket.

He'd already taken measurements on barometric pressure, temperature, wind speed, and snowfall since the prior day, and none of that would change by the time he finished his circle and headed back to the monstrous vehicle. He was already looking forward to the heat of the Humvee's cabin and his sleeping bunk within. His return trip would be tomorrow, first thing in the morning, as he would need to perform the same circuitous route around the vehicle once again twelve hours from now.

Roald picked up his pace. There was no benefit to dragging this out, and the sooner he returned to the Mars-1 the sooner he could strip down to his under layers and jump into the computer strategy game he'd been consumed with lately.

He focused on the crunching sound of the snow. It was a beautiful day — the sun was out, no clouds in sight, and the wind was relatively stable. Not light, but stable. He found himself walking to the tempo of the game's soundtrack, all the while listening for the *crunch, crunch* of each boot as it landed —

Thud.

The sound was different this time. His left boot had landed with a crunch, but there was a deeper sound that came with it. A *hollow* sound. Roald frowned.

He looked down at his feet, one in front of the other, and lifted his left boot once more. He stepped down, faster this time, and the *thud* was there, even more noticeable.

"What the —"

The data recording log would have to parse out the speech that wasn't specific to Antarctic atmospheric conditions, but he didn't care. How else was he supposed to respond to that type of sound?

He stomped twice more, just to be sure, then bent down and started brushing away the top layer of snow. Within a few seconds he reached the hard-packed snow beneath, and knelt down further to start breaking it away.

He worked silently, his breath and the scraping sounds the only noises in earshot. He'd dug a hold nearly a foot deep when he saw it.

Something dark.

In the ice, just beneath the snow.

Roald stood up again and reached around in his pockets for the knife he was carrying. It was a small blade, but it would have to do. He jammed the point into the ice and continued breaking away the layers. He fell to his knees, fully engaged in the task.

The log will wait.

He would have plenty of time to debrief and record an analysis of what he was doing here, but right now he needed to focus on freeing whatever object lay beneath the ice.

Fifteen minutes passed, then thirty, and Roald found himself staring down at a large, square metal plate. He still hadn't reached the edge of it, so he continued working for another hour until the sun began to sink further down on the horizon.

He only had an hour left, and it didn't seem as though he was making any progress. He dug, pried, and broke off chunks of ice and lifted mounds of snow up and off of the plate, and still it felt like the metal scrap was a never-ending section of the ground itself.

He labored in the dwindling light, checking every few minutes to make sure that his Humvee hadn't inexplicably wandered off on its own. It was a nervous reaction to the isolation and cold, he knew, but he couldn't help it. Antarctica often brought out the hidden habits and quirks of her inhabitants, for better or worse.

Finally he reached the edge of the square of metal. His knife lifted off a large sheet of ice and revealed a straight, man-made edge, and he stopped for a moment to revel in his work. His fingers were sweating inside the ski gloves, but he thought they could still feel the extreme cold just beyond the fabric as he brushed the metal surface clean. He changed directions, opting to follow the edge of the metal square up and away from him.

A few more minutes passed and he reached a corner. A few more after that, another corner.

He stood and looked down at his work.

It's a...

He didn't want to think it, because it made absolutely no sense, but he couldn't help it.

It's a door.

CHAPTER 2

There, lying in front of Roald Montgomery, at the edge of the Antarctic continent at the bottom of the planet, was a *metal door.*

He saw a massive hinge mechanism strapped to the side of the door, poking out from beneath an area of snow and ice he hadn't yet uncovered, but it was easy work to free the hinge — and the two others like it — from the frozen ground.

The door was now fully exposed, a full three-by-six foot slab of metal. A small door, compared to a 'typical' doorframe, but a door nonetheless. Besides the hinges on one side and edge of the door, there was nothing on the surface of the metal. No markings, descriptions, or anything else that might identify why there was a door here.

He stood at the foot of the door for another two minutes before a strange thought occurred to him:

Doors lead somewhere. This is a door.

He briefly wondered why he hadn't thought of it before, but this was, without a doubt, a door, and that meant there was something on the *other side* of it.

He knelt down again and started prying at the sides of the door, knowing that it would, at best, be frozen shut. *I spent all this time, might as well at least see if it opens.*

He checked the Mars-1 Humvee again with a quick glance behind him. The vehicle was idling nicely, the white trail of steam floating upwards in the dusk light. Turning back to the door, he continued working his fingers around the sides of the heavy slab.

He heard a *click*. It was louder than the sounds he had making, and — most disturbingly of all — he knew he hadn't made that sound. Roald stopped working for a few seconds and waited.

The click was replaced by a gentle, soft *hissing* sound, and he felt the door move.

He *knew* it moved, but he began second-guessing himself as soon as the thought crossed his mind. *The door didn't move. You must have moved. Maybe you're —*

The internal monologue was cut short by a definite shaking feeling beneath his hands and knees. The hissing increased in volume, then stopped with a loud *pop*. He held his breath.

Then, against all reason and beyond every logical explanation he could muster, the door opened.

It swung outward and he had to move his hands and lean back to allow the metal sheet to pass by him. The door was automated, a giant gear he could now see just beneath the door's surface providing the leverage needed to move the huge object. It reached at ninety-degree angle to the ground and stopped.

Roald blinked, not sure what reaction he was supposed to have.

He was looking down into a dark, square shaft. Alone, that fact would have had him retreating back to the Humvee and dutifully recording his findings for the station's analysis.

But the square shaft wasn't what had Roald's attention at the moment.

Instead, his eyes were locked on the barrel of a gun, pointed directly at him, held by a man wearing an all-white parka and pants, his face completely masked by a snow-white balaclava and ski goggles.

"Do not talk," the man said. The voice was synthesized, as if being run through a processor and out a small speaker. "If you talk, I shoot."

Roald swallowed, then nodded.

"Now, come with me."

ABOUT THE AUTHOR

Nick Thacker is an author from Texas who lives in a cabin on a mountain in Colorado, because Colorado has mountains, microbreweries, and fantastic weather. In his free time, he enjoys reading, brewing beer (and whisky), skiing, golfing, and hanging out with his beautiful wife, tortoise, and three dogs.

In addition to his fiction work, Nick is the author of several nonfiction books on marketing, publishing, writing, and building online platforms.

If you are interested in learning more about the fiction writing process and time-management for writers, be sure to check out The Fiction Writer's Guide to Writing Fiction (www.writehacked.com/course), a completely FREE 20-week e-course!

Visit Nick's website at www.nickthacker.com to find updates about upcoming releases!

ALSO BY NICK THACKER...

Fiction:

The Golden Crystal

The Depths

The Enigma Strain

The Atlantis Deception (A.G. Riddle's The Origins Mystery series)

The Lucid: Episode One (written with Kevin Tumlinson)

The Lucid: Episode Two (written with Kevin Tumlinson)

Relics: The Dawn (Book 1)

Relics: Reckoning (Book 2)

Killer Thrillers (3-Book Box Set)

I, Sergeant (Short Story)

The Gray Picture of Dorian (Short Story)

Uncanny Divide (Short Story Anthology)

Nonfiction:

Welcome Home: The Author's Guide to Building A Marketing Home Base

Expert Blogging: Building A Blog for Readers

The Dead-Simple Guide to Guest Posts

The Dead-Simple Guide to Amazing Headlines

The Dead-Simple Guide to Pillar Content

DO ME A FAVOR?

If you liked this book (or even if you hated it…) write a review or rate it. You might not think it makes a difference, but it does.

Besides *actual* currency (money), the currency of today's writing world is *reviews*. Reviews, good or bad, tell other people that an author is worth reading.

As an "indie" author, I need all the help I can get. I'm hoping that since you made it this far into my book, you have some sort of opinion on it.

Would you mind sharing that opinion? It only takes a second.

Thanks,
Nick Thacker

P.S. You should connect with me on Twitter: @NickThacker or on my website: www.NickThacker.com.